HENRI BARBUSSE

Under Fire

Translated by Robin Buss
With an Introduction by Jay Winter

PENGUIN BOOKS

PENGUIN CLASSICS

Published by the Penguin Group
Penguin Books Ltd, 80 Strand, London WC2R ORL, England
Penguin Group (USA) Inc., 375 Hudson Street, New York, New York 10014, USA
Penguin Group (Canada), 90 Eglinton Avenue East, Suite 700, Toronto, Ontario, Canada M4P 2Y3
(a division of Pearson Penguin Canada Inc.)
Penguin Ireland, 25 St Stephen's Green, Dublin 2, Ireland (a division of Penguin Books Ltd)
Penguin Group (Australia), 707 Collins Street, Melbourne, Victoria 3008, Australia
(a division of Pearson Australia Group Pty Ltd)
Penguin Books India Pvt Ltd, 11 Community Centre, Panchsheel Park, New Delhi – 110 017, India
Penguin Group (NZ), 67 Apollo Drive, Rosedale, Auckland 0632, New Zealand
(a division of Pearson New Zealand Ltd)
Penguin Books (South Africa) (Pty) Ltd, Block D, Rosebank Office Park, 181 Jan Smuts Avenue,
Parktown North, Gauteng 2193, South Africa

Penguin Books Ltd, Registered Offices: 80 Strand, London WC2R ORL, England

www.penguin.com

First published in French as *Le Feu* in 1916
This translation first published in Penguin Books 2003
Published in Penguin Classics 2014
002

Translation copyright © Robin Buss, 2003
Introduction copyright © Jay Winter, 2003

The moral right of the author has been asserted

Printed in Great Britain by Clays Ltd, St Ives plc

A CIP catalogue record for this book is available from the British Library

ISBN: 978-0-141-39343-8

www.greenpenguin.co.uk

C90 2227995

Under Fire

HENRI BARBUSSE was born in 1873 in Asnières-sur-Seine, France. He fought as a volunteer in the First World War, which inspired his masterpiece *Under Fire* (1916). The book was criticized for its harsh naturalism and hatred for militarism, but won the Prix Goncourt. A noted pacifist and later a communist, Barbusse's socialist novel *Clarté* (1920) lent its name to a short-lived internationalist movement. His other works include *The Knife Between the Teeth* (1921) and *Le Judas de Jésus* (1927). Henri Barbusse died in the Soviet Union in 1935, of pneumonia. He was writing a second biography of Stalin at the time.

ROBIN BUSS translated several works for Penguin, including a selection of writings by Sartre, and Camus' *The Plague*. He also wrote books on French and Italian cinema. He died in 2006.

JAY WINTER is Professor of History at Yale University. Between 1979 and 2001 he was Reader in Modern History at the University of Cambridge and Fellow of Pembroke College. He is the author of *Sites of Memory, Sites of Mourning: The Great War in European Cultural History* (1995) and, with Jean-Louis Robert, *Capital Cities at War: Paris, London, Berlin 1914–1919* (1997). With Emmanuel Sivan he edited *War and Remembrance in the Twentieth Century* (1999). He is founder of the Historial de la grand guerre, Peronne, Somme, France, and was the writer and co-producer of the Emmy-award-winning television series *The Great War and the Shaping of the Twentieth Century*.

Contents

Introduction: Henri Barbusse and the Birth of the Moral Witness

THE MORAL WITNESS

In the aftermath of war there has always been a tendency for those who create representations of the conflict to take on the mantle of consolation. Tolerable or sanitized images of combat or of violence against civilians are easily marketed and politically useful, since they present observers with elements of hope. They make war thinkable, even in the aftermath of terrible carnage. At times these positive narratives become intolerable to some of those who lived through these events. Such men and women then decide to take a stand. They speak with what Joan Scott has termed 'the authority of direct experience',[1] and aim to strip away from the conventional story romantic or heroic readings of the past.

This rejection of anodyne or bowdlerized approaches to war and violence, or of romantic accounts of resistance to violence, is evident in the testimony given by many people during and after the two world wars. Such individuals form a general category of observers, the significance of which has grown over time. Witnesses have proliferated in part because war-crimes trials have taken place all over the world. But not everyone who gives evidence in a courtroom shares the same outlook or perspective.

Some of these observers have been termed 'moral witnesses'. Such people are witnesses not in the religious sense of someone prepared to affirm her faith by dying for it nor in the legal sense, indicating simply someone who testifies at the bar. They are rather storytellers of a special kind. They are individuals with a terrible tale to tell, whose very lives are defined by those stories. What sets apart the narrative a moral witness has to tell is that it is based on the individual's direct and personal experience of what Kant called 'radical evil'.[2] Avishai Margalit has investigated the philosophical claims of 'moral witnesses' and argues that such people are carriers of what he terms our collective memory of radical evil and of those destroyed or disfigured by it.[3] Witnesses have special standing as spokesmen for the injured and the dead, and in particular for those who suffer through war, political repression and racial persecution.

Moral witnesses testify at trials, and, to be sure, trials are theatres of memory, places where memory is performed. But moral witnesses speak out in many other ways. They write memoirs; they give interviews; they present evidence to the reading or viewing public. Some become public figures. Rigoberta Menchú Tum and Elie Wiesel, both Nobel-Prize-winners, come to mind in this context.

Moral witnesses carry a special kind of memory and make special claims to our attention. They have a particular story to tell but it is frequently one that is constructed against the grain of conventional wisdom. In the aftermath of the two world wars narratives of heroism and romantic notions of armed struggle spread widely. Some survivors went along with these tales; others were revolted by them and decided to expose the lies and distortions imbedded in the generally accepted story. In doing so they stood up as moral witnesses.

Such people told their stories out of anger. They framed their words and thoughts in the context of representations that troubled them, and which they could not abide. When they reached this conclusion they tried to set the record straight. At times this happened in a courtroom, but not always. Moral witnesses live amongst us long after the termination of the wars which disfigured their lives and long after judicial proceedings are closed. They are truth-tellers, with a story to tell and re-tell. But they are also determined to stop others from lying about the past or from sanitizing it.

BARBUSSE AND SOLDIERS' PACIFISM: WITNESSING FROM WITHIN THE WAR

The first in the line of such moral witnesses in the twentieth century were the soldier-poets and novelists of the Great War. And the first among them was Henri Barbusse. Born in 1873, he was already an established writer when he joined the 231st Infantry Regiment, at the age of forty-one. In the early days of the war he had no doubt that the French cause was the cause of humanity. By early 1915 he had lost such idealized notions of warfare. He served as a common soldier, a stretcher-bearer in an infantry division on the Western Front. Between 9 and 13 January about half of the men in Barbusse's unit were killed on the front near Soissons, to the north-east of Paris. He then served in Artois, and participated in attacks in September and October 1915. He lived in mud, in filth, among the body parts of the dead, and with the constant terror of artillery bombardment. 'Only on a battlefield like this', he wrote to his wife, 'can one have a precise idea of the horror of these great massacres.'⁴ Cited twice for bravery, he saw combat over a period of seventeen months. He contracted a lung condition, dysentery and exhaustion. The combination resulted in his being invalided out of the front lines, and reassigned to a desk job. There he had the time to reflect on what he had seen, and to draw up the outlines of a story which became *Under Fire*.

His intention was to tell the story of a single squad, men from all over France, men of little learning but much generosity of spirit. These were men of flesh and bones, filled with fear and anguish and occasionally beset with a kind of black depression the French termed *le cafard*, the cockroach, crawling up their backs. They were not self-conscious heroes, men who cheered the slaughter on or who made little of the hardships they suffered. In sum, they were ordinary soldiers.

Writing of this kind was almost unknown in wartime. There was military censorship to deal with, and a kind of self-censorship of the press, which by ennobling the men in uniform stripped them of their humanity. Consequently a gap opened between the language soldiers used to describe their world and the representations civilians were offered about it.[5] To close the gap, to return the French infantryman to the ranks of identifiably human beings, warts and all, rather than to perpetuate a set of noble lies about war, Barbusse wrote his novel.

He first published it in serial form, in the monthly literary review *L'Oeuvre*. This exposure was a normal facet of contemporary literary life; serializing novels never hurt their subsequent reception or sales. Instead, choosing this kind of publication for his story enabled Barbusse to bypass the censor, whose gaze was fixed more firmly on printed books. When the time came for it to be vetted for publication as a book Barbusse could point to its existence as a serialized novel already in print. His moral standing as a decorated and wounded soldier also helped ensure that his book, despite its pacifist message, did see the light of day.

Under Fire was a phenomenal success. It was published in January 1917, and won the highest literary honour in France, the Prix Goncourt. In fact, this award was given to *Le Feu* even before it had been published.[6] Its critical reception was exceptionally warm; reviewers called it 'immortal' and celebrated its publication as a landmark in truth-telling about the war. The rapturous welcome of the book's apocalyptic vision suited the third year of the war. One month after *Le Feu* appeared the Tsar was overthrown; by the spring mutinies had broken out in the French army following the disastrous Chemin des Dames offensive. The old shibboleths of war to the bitter end, to victory whatever the cost, were gone. War-weariness was the order of the day, and Barbusse was its chronicler.

In its first year the book sold 200,000 copies, and was translated into English, in which version it was also widely acclaimed.[7] It was read by soldiers in the trenches, who wrote to Barbusse praising the book, and asking for the author to send more copies to the men in the ranks.[8] One soldier saluted the author for having produced a book 'for [the dead], for the unfortunate ones who are still to fall, for women and the aged who do not love the carnage, for those who do not go over the top with a "smile on their lips", as the bluffers say, those masters of eyewash'.[9] Jacques Bertillon, of the medical statistics service of the army, wrote to Barbuisse on 28 March 1917 praising his courage and his honesty: 'I have read *Le Feu*. It is a masterpiece. It is perfectly observed. It is better than literature. It is a document which will remain as a witness [*témoin*] to this war, a war unique in the history of humanity (let us hope it remains unique).'[10]

At times the elegiac tone of Barbusse's admirers reached absurd levels. One editor of a literary journal sent Barbusse a three-page romantic poem about the book, filled with verses like these:

> When men will no longer kill each other
> When women will tremble no more
> We must remember
> That you shone in the midst of the storm.
> You the true king. The true flag. The true God.
> Pouring out your illumination on the beastly quarry,
> O, what a touch of the future in the thrust of the poet
> O, Fire![11]

There were detractors too, but Barbusse was protected by his status as a disabled veteran, a man who had seen the war at its worst and had returned to tell the tale.

Under Fire is a novel in the form of a memoir written by a soldier, a moral witness in uniform. The book offered a moral condemnation of war as radical evil, a conclusion which only people who had earned the right to say it – the soldiers – could affirm in wartime. Barbusse spoke for this new kind of witness. Their aims were twofold. First they spoke out against civilian lies and obfuscations, whatever the risks. And secondly they constructed organizations to perpetuate the memory of their comrades, to secure decent pensions for the veterans and to act as defenders of the truth they had learned so bitterly – that war itself is a crime.

Proceeds from the sales of *Under Fire* went directly into the creation of a veterans' organization, ARAC (Association Républicaine des Anciens Combattants). It was among the earliest elements at the core of the French veterans' movement, a remarkable array of organizations, most of which adopted a pacifist outlook. This is what made *Under Fire* so important in the immediate aftermath of the war. It both expressed and signalled a growing consensus among French veterans that war was not a source of nobility or honour; it was, they affirmed, a monstrous crime, a slaughterhouse.

Barbusse became a communist after the war, and took ARAC with him into the international communist movement. But his war novel *Under Fire* was written before his communist period. It speaks from a populist rather than a communist perspective. Barbusse wrote in the tradition of Émile Zola, the author of *Germinal*, the great novel about working-class life and struggles in the mines. Like Zola, who had courted ignominy by defending Captain Dreyfus when everyone believed him to be guilty, Barbusse wrote his own accusation, his own condemnation of war at a time when many civilians saw war as either an adventure or a noble crusade. Barbusse was a man who could not bear such ignorant lies and who therefore had to stand up, whatever the risks, to set the record straight. In this way he set an example which moral witnesses of later wars and cruelties continue to follow to this day.

THE TRUTH AND NOTHING BUT THE TRUTH

The life history of this novel did not end there. Its echoes were heard throughout the inter-war years and beyond. In many ways it was the first in a long line of war novels which told the world about the war from the inside. Barbusse's stature as the man who had exposed the lie that war was noble adventure prepared the ground for that other great bestseller about the war, *All Quiet on the Western Front* by Erich Maria Remarque, published in 1929. Remarque's account of a German squad follows the path laid down in Barbusse's novel though *All Quiet* lacks the white-hot anger which the French writer had brought to his task a dozen years before. Within the corpus of war literature Barbusse pointed the way and a host of other war writers – Remarque among them – followed his lead.

To be sure, there were those who refused to do so. Some writers drew non-pacifist messages from their war service. The German writer Ernst Jünger, author of *Storm of Steel*, published in 1920 and reissued five times in the subsequent decade, was one of them. But others objected to Barbusse's novel not because it was pacifist but because it was fiction. Jean Norton Cru was a French citizen, and a professor of French literature in the United States, who returned to France to serve on the outbreak of war even though he had no obligation to do so. Like Barbusse, his sense that the war was a noble cause did not survive the first few days of combat. And like Barbusse, he became determined to expose the lies of those who talked of war without knowing the first thing about the subject.

Norton Cru was commissioned by the Carnegie Endowment for International Peace to write a volume on French soldiers' writing about the war, a kind of archive of contemporary sources produced by men in uniform. To this end he constructed an elaborate catalogue of 300 war books, which he analysed one by one in terms of their veracity and dedication to the truth. When he was done the ferocity of his judgements convinced the Carnegie Endowment that they could not publish the book; it was filled with vicious criticism, some of which bordered on the libellous. They rejected Cru's book but helped him find a publisher. The outcome was a volume entitled *Witnesses: An Analytical and Critical Essay on War Memoirs Published in French from 1915 to 1928.*[12]

Norton Cru reserved some of his most withering criticisms for *Under Fire*. In Norton Cru's view, Barbusse, the truth-teller, had created a concoction of truth, half-truth and total falsehood. Many of the incidents he describes could not have taken place in the way Barbusse says they did. He gets uniforms wrong; he reverses chronologies; he describes facets of daily life or military dispositions as they never could have been. He writes about an attack in a way that suggests that he never took part in one. His errors are either deformations of events he saw or simple repetitions of legends. The soldiers he describes in the book are puppets, not real human beings. We do not see their terror; we do not really hear their language, which, Norton Cru asserts, is cleaned up in Barbusse's prose. In sum, Barbusse had concocted a phony war, one filled with morbid images remote from the minds of the soldiers.[13]

THE SOCIAL CONTRACT OF THE MORAL WITNESS

The root and branch condemnation of Barbusse's novel by Norton Cru brings out one of its most important features. It offers fictional not documentary truth. In *Under Fire* Barbusse constructed a narrative about a class of events which disclosed the enormity of war. Some of these events occurred; others did not, but the cumulative effect of the stories is the same. They all show that war is an abomination.

To make his case, Barbusse offers many different kinds of stories. The book starts and ends with a vision; there are fantasies in it as well. But throughout we are brought into the daily lives of soldiers in such a way as to lead us to believe that what we are being told is a plausible story about ordinary men in an extraordinary war. Here is the terrain of war literature: it mixes the documentary and the melodramatic, the factual and the fictional, and refuses to distinguish between the two.

To a man like Norton Cru, a professor of literature, this *mélange* was lethal. From his perspective Barbusse was a hypocrite. He had stood up to tell the truth but managed only to tell lies. But Cru's form of literary positivism reveals much about the power of Barbusse's novel, and the example it set in subsequent years. What Norton Cru missed was the exemplary character of the stories moral witnesses tell. What Barbusse offered was the statement 'something like this happened in the trenches of the Western Front'. He never said 'precisely this happened in the trenches', only that what he described resembled the war in which he had fought. Even if it can be shown – as Norton Cru demonstrated – that a particular event could not have occurred in the way the novel proposes to the reader, it is still the case that the novel stands as a representation of a new kind of war, one which stretched ordinary men beyond the limits of human endurance.

And yet Norton Cru's objections cannot be summarily dismissed. The reader of *Under Fire* may come to believe that particular events in the novel actually took place, and Barbusse offers no caveat about the issue of fact versus fiction. Most war novelists do exactly the same.

It is impossible to tell which parts of Robert Graves's memoir *Goodbye to All That* are accurate and which are entirely made up. The mix is the message. These writers lead us to believe that many similar events did occur, and when we discover that some elements are fabricated we may well ponder the borderland between truth and fiction in accounts of war. For the landscape of battle is so confusing and so full of the uncanny and the bizarre that only fools fail to wonder about our capacity to reproduce it accurately. All soldier-writers can do is to sketch out some of the features of the strange world of killing, and leave the rest to our imaginations. This is precisely what Barbusse achieved in *Under Fire*; this is the central reason it still merits our attention almost a century after it first appeared in print.

THE LANGUAGE OF THE SOLDIERS

This new translation of Barbusse's war novel offers us a new rendering of his prose. Barbusse's achievement, recognized by serving soldiers while the war was still going on, was to recapture some of the vernacular of the men who served in the trenches and to locate their words in the harsh material conditions in which they had to serve. The first English translation of the book, published in 1917, realized this aim only in part. When *Le Feu* appeared in English during the war the translator chose lofty language, and he did so in part because Barbusse's reveries moved in that direction. But when we meet the French peasants of the squad Barbusse describes we hear their voices through a kind of Edwardian high diction chosen by the translator. It made sense at the time, but now it appears odd and misleading.

For this reason alone we are grateful to Robin Buss for completing the task of bringing into ordinary English Barbusse's rendering of the language of the *poilus*. Whenever possible the translator adopts a low-key or a direct cadence, thereby escaping from some of the high-flown rhetoric which the first translator, W. Fitzwater Wray, offered in abundance in 1917. Throughout the translation Buss brings the language of Barbusse down to earth, and it is the earthiness of the novel and the way it presented the gestures and words of ordinary soldiers which has earned it its place in the first rank of twentieth-century war literature.

Herewith a few instances of the way this translation transformed what Robert Graves called 'big words' into smaller words, the words of men of little education but great feeling and terrible suffering. The novel starts with a vision, reminiscent of the end of Thomas Mann's *Magic Mountain*, published a few years after *Under Fire* appeared. A number of convalescent people look out from their sanatorium, beyond Mont Blanc, and see in the distance a mass of men below them. First Wray's 1917 translation, then Buss's one of 2003:

Wray:
And there amid the baleful glimmers of the storm, below the dark disorder of the clouds that extend and unfurl over the earth like evil spirits, they seem to see a great livid plain unrolled, which to their seeing is made of mud and water, while figures appear and fast fix themselves to the surface of it, all blinded and borne down with filth, like the dreadful castaways of shipwreck.

Buss:
Now, in the sinister light of the storm beneath black dishevelled clouds, dragged and spread across the earth like wicked angels, they seem to see a great livid white plain extend before them. In their vision, figures rise up out of the plain, which is composed of mud and water, and clutch at the surface of the ground, blinded and crushed with mire, like survivors from some monstrous shipwreck.

Two sentences, not one; a 'sinister light' in place of 'baleful glimmers'; soldiers clutch at the ground rather than 'fast fix themselves' to the surface of it – we have left behind the late-Victorian prose of the Wray translation and entered another literary register entirely.

The same escape from elevated romance into quieter prose marks the Buss translation of conversations among the soldiers themselves. In fact the chapter on soldiers' gross vernacular expressions – 'Les Gros mots' – in Wray's 1917 translation is actually entitled 'The Big Words'; there is no connection here with Graves's use of the term,

Wray just used it as a euphemism for cussing. Buss calls the chapter 'Swearwords', and rightly so. Here is an exchange between one member of the squad, Barque, and the narrator:

Wray:

Narrator: 'I shall put the big words in their place, dadda, for they're the truth.'

Barque: 'But tell me, if you put 'em in, won't the people of your sort say you're a swine, without worrying about the truth?'

Narrator: 'Very likely, but I shall do it all the same, without worrying about those people.'

Barque: 'Do you want my opinion? Although I know nothing about books, it's brave to do that, because it isn't usually done, and it'll be spicy if you dare do it – but you'll find it hard when it comes to it, you're too polite . . .'

Buss:

Narrator: 'I'll put the swearwords in, because it's the truth.'

Barque: 'But tell me, if you do put them in, won't people like you, but who don't care about truth, say that you're a foul-mouthed pig?'

Narrator: 'Probably, but I'll do it even so and not bother about those fellows.'

Barque: D'you want my opinion? Though I don't know much about books, that's brave, that, because it's not done, and it would be great if you did dare, but at the last moment you'll find it hard, 'cos you're too polite . . .'

The title of Chapter 14, 'Of Burdens' in Wray's translation, is rendered in Buss's more directly and simply as 'Kit'. And then consider this moment, when the narrator and his mate Paradis discover the body of a man and see that it is the brother of another man in the squad, Joseph:

Wray:

'So now,' says Paradis, 'Joseph's left alone, out of six brothers. And I'll tell you what – I don't think he'll stop long. The lad won't take care of himself – he'll get himself done in. A lucky wound's got to drop on him from the sky, otherwise he's corpsed . . .'

Buss:

'That way,' Paradis says, 'Joseph is the only one of six brothers to survive. And I'll tell you something else, I don't think he'll be the only one for long. That kid won't look after himself, he'll get himself bumped off. What he needs is for God to send him a lucky wound, or else he's buggered . . .'

The laconic style offered by Buss enriches the text; it makes it more accessible to our own generation. But it also offers small changes which add up to big differences. Here is one instance. In an outburst of anger Corporal Bertrand, soon to become yet another casualty of war, shakes his fist at war itself. Here is the tirade in French: 'Honte à la gloire militarie, honte aux armées, honte au métier de soldat, qui change les hommes tour à tour en stupides victimes ou ignoble bourreaux.'[14] The 1917 translation renders this as: 'Shame on military glory, shame on armies, shame on the soldier's calling, that changes men by turns into stupid victims or ignoble brutes.'[15] In the current translation there is a small change. The end of the phrase has it that war changes men by turns 'into stupid victims, others into base executioners'. Executioners, not brutes. The difference is slight, and yet it is huge. Buss has found the core of Barbusse's message: he too was a murderer, he too had blood on his hands, he too had to find some way to escape from the moral quicksand of war. Telling the story was his way. Reading it may be ours.

Jay Winter

NOTES AND REFERENCES

1. Joan Scott, 'The evidence of experience', *Critical Inquiry*, xvii (Summer 1991), pp. 780ff.
2. Immanuel Kant, *Religion within the Limits of Reason Alone*, trans. Theodore M. Greene and Hoyt H. Hudson (New York: Harper & Row, 1960), pp. 28ff.

3. Avishai Margalit, *The Ethics of Memory* (Cambridge, Mass.: Harvard University Press, 2002), pp. 147ff.

4. Quoted in Jay Winter, *Sites of Memory, Sites of Mourning: The Great War in European Cultural History* (Cambridge: Cambridge University Press, 1995), p. 180.

5 Antoine Prost, *Republican Identities in War and Peace: Representation of France in the Nineteenth and Twentieth Centuries* (Oxford: Berg, 2002); Stéphane Audoin-Rouzeau, *Men at War* (Oxford: Berg, 1992).

6. Bibliothèque nationale (BN), Paris, NFA 16484, letter of Etienne Bourget and Leon Daudet, 15 December 1916, inviting Barbusse to receive the Prix Goncourt.

7. BN 16484, review in the *Manchester Guardian*, November 1917.

8. BN 16484, letter of Francois Bazire, telephonist, to Barbusse, 10 January 1918: 'All my comrades who read a lot during the long nights of waiting say that it is the only true book that an author has written on the war. Could you send a copy?'

9. BN 16484, letter of A. R. Lefebvre to Barbusse, 23 November 1917.

10. BN 16484, letter of Jacques Bertillon, Ministry of War, medico-surgical statistics section, to Barbusse, 28 March 1917.

11. BN 16485, letter of Leo Poldes, editor of *Le Grimace*, to Barbusse, 15 May 1917.

12. Jean Norton Cru, *Témoins. Essai d'analyse et de critique des souvenirs de combattants édites en français de 1915 à 1928* (Paris: Les Etincelles, 1929). On Cru see Jay Winter, *The Great War and After* (New Haven: Yale University Press, 2003), ch. 13, and Frédéric Rousseau, *Le procès des témoins de la grande guerre: L'affaire Norton Cru* (Paris: Seuil, 2003).

13. Norton Cru, *Témoins*, pp. 555–65.

14. Henri Barbusse, *Le Feu: Journal d'une Escouade* (Paris: Flammarion, 1917), p. 214.

15. Barbusse, *Under Fire*, trans. F. Wray (London: Dent, 1917), p. 257.

Translator's Note

Much of Henri Barbusse's novel is written in dialogue, using the language of the *poilus*, the French soldiers in the trenches during the First World War. There is even a chapter in the book (Chapter 13, 'Swearwords') in which a soldier asks the author whether he is going to reproduce the speech of his fellow soldiers accurately, because 'you won't ever hear two *poilus* chat for a minute without them saying something or repeating something that the printers won't much like to print'. Barbusse assures the man, Barque, that he will tell it as it is.

A few miles along the line, to the west, British soldiers were enduring conditions very similar to those described in Barbusse's novel, and using equally colourful language. At first glance, it might seem easy to 'translate' one slang into the other; yet, as soon as you consider doing this, you come up against a problem that is inherent in the nature of slang. Standard speech may be designed to communicate across a whole language community but slang is the language of a specific social group at a particular time, and trying to translate it into the specific language of another group raises more problems than it solves. To take one example: in Chapter 4, Volpatte is delighted to get a relatively light wound which means that he will be evacuated to the rear. British soldiers had a word for this: it was 'blighty' (because it meant going back to Blighty [England]) – but the term is clearly inappropriate with reference to Volpatte. And these French soldiers have a life that is significantly different from that of British infantry-men on the Western Front in 1916, with their rations of wine and coffee, their relations with the surrounding population, their experiences at home . . . to make them speak like cockneys or Lancastrians would simply underline the anomalies – quite apart from the fact that what they say might be hard for readers outside London or Lancashire to understand.

What I have tried to do, therefore, is to adopt a language that conveys the feel of the slang that Barbusse uses without making it too specific or too obscure. This has meant compromises. But, at least, the language of this translation should seem more immediate and less musty than that of the only previous English version, by Fitzwater Wray (Dent, 1917); and English printers are certainly less easily offended now than they were in his day by the swearwords that Barque was worried about, so some of Wray's omissions can be restored. No translation is perfect, but I hope that this version, despite its unavoidable shortcomings, will bring new readers to Barbusse's extraordinary book.

I am grateful to my friend Dr Jean-Pierre Navailles for his help in clarifying several points in the text. I should also like to thank Simon Winder, editor at Penguin, and Emma Horton for her meticulous work in copy-editing the manuscript.

Robin Buss

Under Fire

*To the memory of the comrades who fell beside me
at Crouy and on Hill 119.
HB*

I

The Vision

The Dent du Midi, the Aiguille Verte and Mont Blanc stare down at the bloodless faces emerging from under the blankets lined up along the gallery of the sanatorium.

On the first floor of the palatial hospital, this terrace with its balcony of carved wood supported by a veranda is isolated in space and overhangs the world.

The fine wool blankets – red, green, havana brown or white – with emaciated faces emerging from under them, and radiant eyes, are still. Silence reigns over the chaises longues. Someone coughs. Then nothing more is heard but the turning of the pages of a book at long, regular intervals; or a murmured request and hushed reply from a bed to the one beside it; or sometimes on the balustrade, the flapping like a fan of a venturesome crow, a fugitive from the flocks that make rosaries of black pearls in the transparent void.

Silence reigns. In any case, those people, rich and independent, who have come here from all parts of the earth, struck down by the same misfortune, have lost the habit of speech. They have turned in on themselves and think about their lives and deaths.

A maid appears in the gallery. She walks softly; she is dressed in white. She is bringing newspapers which she hands around.

'That's it,' says the first one to unfold his paper. 'War has been declared.'

Expected though it was, the news causes a kind of astonishment because those who hear it sense its extreme importance.

These men are cultured and intelligent, their minds deepened by suffering and reflection, detached from things and almost from life, as distant from the rest of the human species as if they already belonged to posterity, looking far ahead towards the incomprehensible land of the living and the mad.

'Austria is committing a crime,' the Austrian says.

'France must win,' says the Englishman.

'I hope that Germany will be defeated,' says the German.

They settle back under the blankets, on their pillows, facing the mountain peaks and the sky. But despite the purity of space, the silence is filled with the news that they have just received.

'War!'

A few of those lying there break the silence, repeating the word under their breath and considering that this is perhaps the greatest event of modern times, perhaps of all time. And the annunciation even casts a kind of confused and murky veil over the clear landscape before their eyes.

The calm expanses of the valley dotted with villages pink as roses and soft pastures, the splendid outlines of the mountains, the black lace of the pine trees and the white lace of the eternal snows, are filled with the bustling of mankind.

Multitudes teem in clearly defined masses. On the fields attacks sweep forward, wave after wave, then come to a standstill; houses are gutted like men and towns like houses; villages appear in crumpled white as though they had fallen on to the earth from the sky; frightful loads of dead and wounded men alter the shape of the plains.

You can see every country where the borders are eaten away with massacres constantly tearing new soldiers from its heart, full of strength, full of blood; your gaze follows these living tributaries for the river of the dead.

North, south and west, battles rage, on all sides, in the distance. You can turn this way or that; there is not a single horizon on which there is no war.

One of the pale men watching rises on his elbow, counting and reckoning the present and future combatants: thirty million soldiers. Another man stammers, his eyes full of slaughter:

'Two armies engaged in battle are one great army committing suicide.'

'They shouldn't have done it,' says the deep, hollow voice of the first man in the row.

But another man says:

'It's the French Revolution all over again.'

'Crowned heads beware!' murmurs another.

And a third man adds:

'Perhaps it is the war to end wars.'

There is a pause, then a few brows shake, still pale from the wan tragedy of a night of perspiring insomnia.

'An end to war! Can that be? An end to war! The world's affliction is incurable.'

Someone coughs. Then the immense calm of meadows under the sun where bright cattle softly shine and black woods and green fields and blue horizons submerge the vision, quelling the glow of the fire that is consuming and breaking the old world. An infinite silence covers the murmur of the hatred and suffering of the dark teeming of the world. The speakers slip back, one by one, into themselves, preoccupied with the mystery of their lungs and the health of their bodies.

But when evening is about to fall across the valley, a storm breaks over the massif of Mont Blanc.

No one is allowed out on this dangerous evening when one can feel the last waves of wind break under the vast veranda, right beneath this port where they have taken refuge.

These men, severely smitten, eaten away by an inner wound, stare at the confusion of the elements. They watch the thunder break over the mountain, lifting up the clouds on the horizon like a sea, each clap of the storm throwing out at once into the dusk a column of fire and a column of cloud. They turn their ashen, hollow-cheeked faces to follow the eagles circling in the sky that watch the earth from on high through rings of mist.

'Stop the war!' they are saying. 'Stop the storms!'

But the watchers on the threshold of the world, free of partisan passion, free of prejudices, blindness and the shackles of tradition, also have a vague sense of the simplicity of things and of gaping possibilities . . .

The one at the end of the row exclaims:

'You can see things, down there, things rearing up!'

'Yes . . . They're like living things.'

'Sort of plants . . .'

'Sort of men.'

Now, in the sinister light of the storm beneath black dishevelled clouds, dragged and spread across the earth like wicked angels, they seem to see a great livid white plain extend before them. In their vision, figures rise up out of the plain, which is composed of mud and water, and clutch at the surface of the ground, blinded and crushed with mire, like survivors from some monstrous shipwreck. These men seem to them to be soldiers. The plain is vast, riven by long parallel canals and pitted with waterholes, and the shipwrecked men trying to extract themselves from it are a great multitude . . . But the thirty million slaves who have been thrown on top of one another by crime and error into this war of mud raise human faces in which the glimmer of an idea is forming. The future is in the hands of these slaves and one can see that the old world will be changed by the alliance that will one day be formed between those whose number and whose suffering is without end.

2

In the Ground

The great pale sky is filled with claps of thunder. Each explosion reveals at once, falling out of a reddish flash, a column of fire in what is left of the night and a column of smoke in the already dawning day.

Up there, on high, far away, a flight of fearsome birds, panting powerfully and with broken breath, which can be heard but not seen, spirals upwards to look down upon the earth.

The earth! The desert has started to appear, vast and full of water, beneath the long and desolate light of dawn. Ponds and craters, their waters pinched and shivering under the sharp blast of early morning; tracks left by last night's troops and convoys in these fields of sterility, streaked with ruts which shine like steel rails in the weak light; and piles of mud with here and there broken stakes emerging from them, broken trestles in the shape of a cross, packages of rusted wire, twisted, like bushes. With its puddles and its banks of slime it looks like an oversized grey canvas sheet floating on the sea, submerged in places. It is not raining, but everything is wet, oozing, sodden, drenched. The pale light seems to be pouring across it.

You can see a maze of long ditches in which the last remnants of night linger. This is the trench. The bottom of it is carpeted with a viscous layer that clings noisily to the foot at every step and smells foul around each dugout because of the night's urine. The holes themselves, if you lean over them as you pass, smell like a whiff of bad breath.

I can see shadows emerging from these side holes, moving shadows, huge and shapeless masses, like bears stumbling around and muttering. That is us.

★

We are wrapped up like inhabitants of the Arctic. Sweaters, blankets and sacking loom over us and package us in odd, round shapes. A few people stretch and vomit up a yawn. You can see faces, reddened or livid white, streaked with dirty scars and pierced with eyes like night lights, hazy and gluey around the edges, bristling with untrimmed beards or sooty with unshaven bristles.

Crack! Crack! Boom! Rifle shots, cannon fire. Everywhere above us it crackles and thunders, in long bursts or single rounds. The dark, flaming storm never ceases. Never. For more than fifteen months, for five hundred days, in this corner of the world where we are, the bombing and the firing have not stopped from dawn to dusk and dusk to dawn. We are buried in the depths of an eternal battlefield; but, like the ticking of the clocks in our houses, in the olden days, in that almost mythical past, this is something that you only hear when you listen for it.

A baby face, with puffy eyelids and cheeks as rosy as if they had little squares of red paper stuck to them, emerges from the ground, opening one eye, then the other. This is Paradis. The skin on his chubby cheeks is lined from the folds in the tent canvas that he wrapped round his head before going to sleep.

He looks round him through his narrow eyes, notices me, waves and says:

'Well, that's another night over, old chap.'

'Yes, my son. And how many more do we have to go?'

He lifts his two fat arms towards heaven. He has managed, with much shoving, to climb the steps out of the dugout and is now standing beside me. After stumbling over the vague mass of some character sitting on the ground in the half-darkness, who is scratching himself vigorously with hoarse sighs, Paradis hobbles off, splashing and swaying like a penguin through the diluvian scene.

Bit by bit the men are defined against the depths. You can see a dense shadow form in the corners, then these human clouds move and break apart. You recognize them, one by one.

Here is one appearing, using his blanket as a hood. He looks like a savage, or, rather, a savage's tent, swaying from right to left and walking along. Close up, in the middle of a thick border of knitted wool, you notice a square face, iodine yellow, as though painted with blackish blotches, a broken nose, slanting Chinese eyes, pink-rimmed, and a little moustache, damp and bristly like a grease-brush.

'Here's Volpatte. How's it going, Firmin?'

'It's goin', s'goin' and s'cummin',' says Volpatte.

He has a thick, drawling accent, made worse by a cold. He coughs.

'I've caught me death, this time out. By the way, did you hear it, last night, that attack? Talk about a hammering, old man. A choice dose of physic!'

He sniffs and wipes his concave nose on his sleeve. Then he sticks his hand into his coat and tunic, looking for the skin, and scratches it.

'I've killed thirty of them with the candle,' he mutters. 'In the big dugout, next to the tunnel, me old mate, it's like a pile of moving breadcrumbs! You can see them running around in the straw, as plain as the nose on your face.'

'Who was it attacking? The Boche?'

'Them and us too. It was up by Vimy Ridge. A counter-attack. Didn't you hear it?'

'No,' fat Lamuse, the human bull, answers for me. 'I was snoring. Mind you, I was on night fatigue the night before.'

'I heard it,' says the little Breton, Biquet. 'I slept badly; or, so to speak, I didn't sleep at all. I've got a dugout of me own. There, that's it, the bugger.'

He points to a ditch at ground level where there is just room for a body on a thin layer of muck.

'How's that for a nutshell?' he says, shaking his rough, rocky little head, with its unfinished look. 'I hardly slept a wink. I did doze off but I was woken up by the relief of the 129th as it went past. Not by the noise – by the smell. Ugh! All those lads with their feet right next to my face. It gave me such a pain in the nose, it woke me up.'

I've known the same myself. I've often been woken up in the trenches by the thick smell that a troop of soldiers on the march drags behind it.

'If only it would kill the bugs,' says Tirette.

'Quite the opposite: it stirs 'em up,' says Lamuse. 'The more disgusting you are, the more you stink, the more they like you!'

'And it's just as well they did wake me up with their pong,' Biquet went on. 'Because, as I was saying to that great paperweight, I opened my peepers just in time to grab the groundsheet in front of my hole before one of those shit-heaps swiped it from me.'

'They're a lousy bunch, those 129ers.'

Down at our feet we could see a human form untouched by the light of dawn which was wriggling around, hunched over, grasping the carapace of its clothing in both hands. It was Old Blaire.

His little eyes glittered in a face liberally sprinkled with dust. His moustache was a large yellowish mass above the hole of his toothless mouth. His hands were horribly black, the upper part so caked with dirt that it seemed to have a coat of down and the palm covered in a hard grey lacquer. His person, bent double and powdered with earth, smelled like an old saucepan.

While busy scratching himself he kept on talking to Big Barque who lent towards him, at a slight distance.

'I'm not as dirty as this in civvy street,' he said.

'Why, you poor old chap, it must be a hell of a change for you,' said Barque.

'Just as well,' Tirette added. ''Cos otherwise you'd be giving your missus little niggers for kids!'

Blaire got angry. His brow furrowed and the filth on it turned deeper black.

'No need for you to have a go at me. And what about it? There's a war on. Look at yerself, bean-head, don't you think the war's changed your mug and your manners? Yeah, take a look at yerself, monkey-face, arse-skin! How daft d'you have to be to talk like you do?'

He wiped a hand over the dusky layer decorating his face, only to find that after the recent rain it was truly indelible. He went on:

'And then, if I am as I am, it's 'cos that's how I want it! First of all, I've got no teeth. For ages now, the major's been telling me: "You haven't got a tooth to your name. It's not good enough. Next time you're relieved, go and take a look in the stomachological trailer."'

'The tomatological trailer,' Barque corrected him.

'Stomatological,' said Bertrand.

'It's 'cos I want to that I haven't been,' Blaire went on. ' 'Cos it's for free.'

'So why then?'

'No reason, just for a change,' he replied.

'You're like a cookie,' said Barque. 'That's what you should have been.'

'I quite agree,' Blaire answered, not seeing the joke.

We laughed. The blackened man was offended and got up.

'You give me a pain in the gut,' he said, contemptuously. 'I'm off to the latrines.'

When his too dark silhouette had vanished the others hammered away at the truism that down here cooks are always the filthiest of men.

'If you see a bloke all mucky, with his skin and his clothes spattered with dirt so that you wouldn't want to touch him with a bargepole, you can tell yourself he's prob'ly a cookie! And the dirtier he is, the more of a cook he is.'

'That's the honest truth,' said Marthereau.

'Well, well! Here's Tirloir! Hey, Tirloir!'

He comes up busily, sniffing right and left, while his narrow head, pale as chlorine, bobs up and down in the cushion of his greatcoat collar, which is far too thick and wide. He has a pointed chin and his lower teeth jut out. A crease beside his mouth, full of dirt, looks like a muzzle. As usual he is furious and as usual he is raging aloud.

'They nicked my kitbag last night!'

'That was the relief of the 129th. Where did you leave it?'

He pointed to a bayonet stuck in the wall of the trench near the entrance to a dugout:

'There, hanging from that toothpick by there.'

'You blockhead!' they all cried together. 'Within reach of any passing squaddie. Are you crazy or what?'

'It's a crying shame for all that,' Tirloir mutters.

Then suddenly he is overwhelmed with fury. His face creases with rage and his little fists tighten, tighten, like knots of string. He brandishes them in the air.

'Oh, I tell you . . . If I could get hold of the swine who did it! Take my word, I'd break his neck for him, I'd smash his guts, I'd . . . There was a whole Camembert, untouched, in there. I'm going to take another look for it.'

He rubs his belly with his fist, in small, tight movements like someone playing a guitar, and drifts off into the grey of the morning, dignified yet grimacing, his figure hunched like a patient in a dressing gown. You can hear him muttering away until he vanishes.

'What an idiot,' says Pépin.

The others snigger.

'He's mad and crazy,' says Marthereau, who is in the habit of bolstering his ideas through the simultaneous use of two synonyms.

'Hey there, laddie,' said Tulacque, coming up. 'Look at this, will you?'

Tulacque is splendid. He is wearing a lemon-yellow cloak made out of an oilskin sleeping bag. He has cut a hole in the middle for his head and over this carapace he has fastened his shoulder straps and his army belt. He is tall and bony. As he walks he stretches his face forward – an energetic face with squinting eyes. He is holding something.

'I found this when I was digging last night, at the end of the New Tunnel, when we were changing the rotten duckboards. I took a liking to it straight off, this contraption. It's an old-fashioned axe.'

It really was old-fashioned at that: a pointed stick fastened in a bone handle brown with age. It looked to me just like some prehistoric tool.

'It feels good to hold,' said Tulacque, waving the object. 'Yeah, indeed, it's not such a bad bit of design. Better balanced than the regulation-issue axe. In a word, it's damned good. Go on, try it . . . No? Give it back, though, I'm keeping it. You see, it will do me well . . .'

He brandished his prehistoric axe, like some Neanderthal decked in tatters, lurking in the bowels of the earth.

One by one we had gathered, we of Bertrand's squad and the half-section, at a bend in the trench. At this point it is a little wider than on the straight where, if you want to pass, you have to flatten yourself against the wall, rubbing your back against the earth and your belly on that of your mate.

In the reserve, our company occupies a second-line parallel trench. Here there is no night watch. After dark we are liable for digging work on the forward line, but as long as it is daytime we have nothing to do. Piled up on top of each other and pressed elbow to elbow we have to get through to evening as best we can.

Daylight has finally managed to seep into the endless crevasses that pit and pock this region of the earth. It reaches right up to the entrances to our holes, a sad, northern light, a narrow, muddy sky, which also looks as though it is heavy with the smoke and smell of a factory. Under this feeble glow the variegated dress of the inhabitants of these depths appears plainly, in the immense, desperate poverty that produced it. But this is like the monotonous rattle of rifles and the roar of the guns: the great drama, in which we are the actors, has lasted too long, and we have ceased to be surprised by the appearance we have taken on or the clothing we have invented to protect ourselves from the rain that falls from above, the mud that comes from below and the cold, that sort of ubiquitous infinity.

Animal skins, rolls of blankets, balaclavas, woollen hats, fur hats, scarves, spread out or wound into turbans, paddings of knitwear and darnings, surfacings and roofings, glued, rubber, black or in every (faded) colour of the rainbow, cover the men, disguising their uniforms almost as much as their skin, and expanding them. One has fixed a square of oilcloth at his back with a big red-and-white chequered pattern on it, which he found in the dining room of some overnight stopping-place: this is Pépin, who can be spotted from a distance more easily by this harlequin board than by his pale street urchin's face. Over there you can see the swelling of Barque's shirtfront, cut out of a stolen eiderdown, which was once pink but is now discoloured and stained by dust and darkness. Here, big Lamuse looks like a ruined tower with the remains of posters clinging to it. Moleskin, stuck on him like a suit of armour, gives little Eudore a beetle's shiny back. And Tulacque stands out among them all with his orange breastplate of an Indian chief.

The helmets give a degree of uniformity to the upper part of these creatures – but, even then, the habit that some have of putting the helmet over their kepis, like Biquet, or on their balaclavas, like

Cadilhac, or on their cotton caps, like Barque, makes for diversity and complicates appearances.

And as for our legs! Just now I went down, bent double, into our dugout, a little low cellar, smelling of damp and mould, where you trip over empty tin cans and dirty rags, and where two long bundles were lying asleep, while in one corner the shape of a kneeling man was rummaging through a kitbag . . . As I climbed out again, through the rectangular opening, I noticed the legs. Horizontal, vertical or sideways, stretched out, bent up or crossed, blocking the way and cursed by passers-by, they were a multicoloured and many-shaded collection: gaiters, black and yellow, high and low, of leather, khaki cloth or some kind of waterproof material; puttees in dark blue, light blue, black, green, khaki and beige . . . Alone of all his kind, Volpatte has preserved the little gaiters he got when he was first called up. For the past fortnight Mesnil André has been wearing a pair of coarse, green, ribbed woollen stockings; and we've never known Tirette to have anything except some strips of grey linen taken off a pair of civilian trousers hanging goodness knows where at the outbreak of the war . . . As for Marthereau's leggings, he has some that don't match, because all he could find to hack up were two bits of worn coat, each as filthy as the other. And there are legs wrapped in cloths and even newspapers, held on by spiralling lengths of string or, more effectively, telephone wire. Pépin amazes his pals and anyone else who sees them with a pair of fawn gaiters, taken off a corpse. Barque, who reckons he's pretty good at making do and full of clever schemes – and doesn't let you forget it, I have to say – has white calves, having wound bandages around his leggings to make them last longer, the white at one end of him echoing his cotton cap which shows under his helmet, with his red clown's hair showing under it in turn . . . For the past month Poterloo has been walking around in some German private's boots, lovely ones, almost new, reinforced with iron at the heels. Caron gave them to him when he was evacuated because of his arm. Caron himself got them off a Bavarian machine-gunner who was shot near the Pylônes road. I can still hear him telling us about it:

'There he was, old chap, this Hun, his bum in a hole, bent in two: he was eyeing up the air and showing me his boots as if to say that they were worth having. They'll fit, I told myself. But you can't imagine what a job it was getting the gear off him! I worked on it, pulling them, turning them and shaking them, for half an hour and still I couldn't manage it. With his feet stiff like that the bloke wasn't doing much to help. Then, finally, after I'd pulled them this way and that, the funny fellow's legs came off at the knees, his trousers tore and the whole bang shoot came away, crack! There I was, all of a sudden, with a full boot in each hand. I had to empty the legs and feet out of them.'

'You're laying it on a bit thick!'

'Ask the cyclist Euterpe if it ain't true. I tell you, he done it with me: we stuck our paws in the boots and pulled out some bone, bits of sock and lumps of foot. But just look! Wasn't it worth the trouble?'

While waiting for Caron to come back, Poterloo is getting some wear out of the boots that the Bavarian machine-gunner never wore out.

This is how one contrives to ward off the dreadful discomforts of trench life, according to one's native wit, energy, abilities and nerve. Each of us seems to be visible proof of it: 'Here's what I've managed, been able or dared to do, in the great misery that has befallen me!'

Mesnil Joseph is snoozing, Blaire yawning, Marthereau smoking, staring straight ahead. Lamuse scratches himself like a gorilla and Eudore like a marmoset. Volpatte gives a cough and says: 'I'm dying.' Mesnil André has got out his mirror and comb, to cultivate his fine nut-brown beard like a rare plant. The monotonous calm is interrupted from time to time by outbreaks of frantic agitation provoked by the endemic, chronic and contagious presence of parasites.

Barque, an observant fellow, looks around, takes his pipe out, spits, winks and says:

'We don't look much alike, I must say!'

'Why should we?' says Lamuse. 'It would be a bleeding miracle if we did.'

How old are we? All ages. Ours is a reserve regiment which has been successively reinforced, partly with front-line units and partly with territorials. In our half-section there are territorials, green recruits and veterans. Fouillade is forty. Blaire could be Biquet's father, Biquet being a chicken from the class of '13. The corporal calls Marthereau 'grandad' or 'old wreck' according to whether he is joking or being serious. Mesnil Joseph would be in barracks if there was no war. It's an odd feeling when we're being led by our sergeant, Vigile, a sweet little lad with the shadow of a moustache who was skipping with a rope alongside some kids the other day when we were at our billets. In this mixed bunch of ours, this orphaned family in its heartless home, there are three generations side by side, living, waiting, standing like shapeless statues, like posts.

What race are we? All races. We've come from everywhere. Take the two men next to me: Poterloo, the miner from the Calonne pit, is pink; his eyebrows are straw yellow, his eyes flaxen blue, and as for his great golden head, it took a long hunt through the shops to find the huge blue tureen that he's wearing. Then there's Fouillade, the boatman from Cette, rolling his devil's eyes in his long, gaunt, mus-keteer's face with sunken cheeks, the same colour as a violin. In fact, my two neighbours are as different as day and night.

No more alike are Cocon, the thin, dry character with the glasses, his complexion chemically corroded by the miasma of the slums, in contrast to Biquet, the rough-hewn Breton, with his grey skin and granite jaw – just as André Mesnil, the comfortable pharmacist from some small Norman town, with his pretty, fine-haired beard, who talks so much and so well, has little in common with Lamuse, the lump of a peasant from Poitou, whose cheeks and neck are like roast beef. The working-class accents of Barque, whose great legs have tramped the streets of Paris from one end to another, jar with the sing-song, almost Belgian tones of those of 't'North' who come from the 8th Territorials, with the sonorous speech of those from the 144th, rolling their syllables as they roll over the cobbles, or with the patois that is exhaled from the groups that the Auvergnats of the 124th insist on forming among themselves, like ants attracted to one another . . . I remember the first sentence to emerge from that funny fellow Tirette, when he arrived: 'Here, lads, I'm from Clichy-la-Garonne! Can any-one beat that?' – and the first complaint that brought Paradis to me: 'They don't give a toss for me, 'cos of how I'm from Morvan . . .'

What jobs did we do? A bit of everything, lumped together. What were we in former times, when people had a station in life, before all our destinies were buried in molehills lashed by rain and shrapnel, which we must constantly rebuild? Farm workers and factory workers, most of us. Lamuse was a farmhand, Paradis a carter and Cadilhac, whose undersized helmet sits unsteadily on his pointed skull – like a dome on a belfry, Tirette says – owns his own land. Old Blaire was a tenant farmer in the Brie. Barque, a delivery boy, used to weave in and out of the Parisian traffic, trams and taxis, on his delivery bike, heaping lordly abuse on the pedestrians as they scattered like hens along the avenues and across the squares. Corporal Bertrand, who always keeps to himself a little, silent and dignified with his fine masculine features, upright, eyes front, was a foreman in a casing works. Tirloir used to splash paint on carriages, apparently without a murmur. Tulacque was a barman at the Barrière du Trône and Eudore, with his soft palish face, used to keep a tavern on a main road not far from the present front; the place got a bad shelling – of course, because Eudore is famously unlucky. Mesnil André, the one who is still vaguely distinguished and well-groomed, used to sell bicarbonate of soda and infallible remedies on some market square, his brother Joseph sold newspapers and penny dreadfuls in one of the state railway stations, while far away in Lyon Cocon, the giglamps, the statistician, wore a black gown and busied himself behind the counter of an ironmonger's shop, the graphite glistening on his hands, and Bécuwe Adolphe and Poterloo would be up at dawn, swinging the dim stars of their lamps and trailing around the coal pits of the North.

There are others whose jobs one never remembers, mixing them all up, and the country jacks of all trades who carried a dozen jobs around in their knapsacks – not to mention that dubious character Pépin who presumably had none at all (all we know is that three months ago, at the depot, while convalescing, he got married . . . so that he could apply for the soldier's wife's grant).

There is no one from the liberal professions among those around me. There are some schoolteachers who are NCOs in the company or medical orderlies. In the regiment there is a Marist brother who is a sergeant in the Red Cross, a tenor who is a dispatch rider for the major, a lawyer who is secretary to the colonel, and a man of independent means who is mess corporal in the Compagnie Hors Rang.* Here we've got nothing of that sort. We are front-line troops and in this war there are practically no intellectuals, artists or rich men who have risked their heads above the parapet, unless they were just passing by or wearing lots of gold braid on their kepis.

Yes, it's true, we're very different. But at the same time, very alike.

Despite all the variations in age, origin, education and status, and everything that used to be, despite the gulfs that used once to divide us, broadly speaking we're the same. Behind the same crude shape we conceal and exhibit the same manners, the same habits, the same simplified character of men who have reverted to their primal state.

The same language, composed of workshop and barrack-room slang and dialect, spiced with a few neologisms, blends us, as in a sauce, into the multitude of men who, for some time already now, have been emptying the land of France and gathering in the North-East.

And here, bound by an inescapable fate, borne forward in spite of ourselves in a single rank by this great adventure, we are obliged like the weeks and nights to resemble one another. The frightful narrowness of communal life compresses us, adapts us and blends us into each other. It is like some kind of fatal contagion, with the result that one soldier looks like another, even if you do not observe us from such a distance that we are only a few grains of dust rolling across the plain.

We are waiting. We get tired of sitting down, so we get up. Our joints stretch with creaking sounds, like warped wood or old hinges: damp rusts a man as it does a rifle, more slowly, but more profoundly. And we start to wait again, differently.

You are always waiting, in wartime. We have become machines for waiting.

For the moment what we are waiting for is grub. Then it will be letters. But everything in its own time: we'll think about the letters when we've finished the meal. Then we'll start to wait for something else . . .

* HQ Support Company. [trans.]

Hunger and thirst are gnawing instincts that have a powerful effect on the minds of my comrades. When the rations are late they start to complain and get impatient. The need for food and drink grumbles out of their lips:

'Eight o'clock! I mean, what's wrong with this grub? Why doesn't it show up?'

'Yeah, and I've been waiting for it since midday yesterday,' Lamuse says, moodily, his eyes wet with longing and his cheeks daubed with spots of what looks like burgundy-coloured paint.

The dissatisfaction grows minute by minute:

'Plumet must have poured my wine ration down his throat that he was meant to bring us, and others along with it, and he'll be lying pissed over there someplace.'

'That's certain sure,' Marthereau agrees.

'What a load of scoundrels and vermin they are, those blokes on fatigue!' Tirloir bellows. 'What a disgusting breed! Drunken, lazy devils, the lot of them! They twiddle their thumbs all day long in the rear and can't be buggered to come round on time. Now if I was in charge, I'd get them into the trenches in our place and make sure they did some work. First off, I'd say everyone in the section can be greasy joe and soup boy in turn. Those who want, of course. And then . . .'

'I'm quite sure,' Cocon says, 'that it's that pig Pépère who's making the others late. First of all, he does it on purpose, and then he can't show a leg in the morning, poor little kid. He must have his ten hours' shut-eye, like the sissy he is! Otherwise, His Highness is in a bad mood all day.'

'I'd show him what for!' Lamuse mutters. 'You see if I'd get his arse out of the sack, if I was there. I'd kick him up the backside, I'd drag him through the brambles . . .'

'I counted, the other day,' Cocon went on. 'He took seven hours, forty-seven minutes to get here from No. 31 shelter. You need five hours at the most, no more.'

Cocon is the calculator. He loves, he thirsts for exact figures. He rummages around in everything to find statistics which he hoards with the patience of an insect and dishes out for anyone ready to listen. At this moment, as he wields his figures like weapons, his meagre face, made up of dry, bony ridges, triangles and angles with the twin circles of his glasses perched on them, is contorted with bitterness.

He climbs on to the firing step, cut out at the time when this was the front line, and raises his head furiously above the parapet. In the slanting light of a cold little ray of sunlight still clinging to the earth, we can see his glasses shining and also the drop on the end of his nose, like a diamond.

'And that Pépère – he's no better than a sieve! You wouldn't believe how much stuff he can drop in the mud in a single day.'

Old Blaire is fuming in his corner. You can see his big moustache trembling like an ivory comb, whitish and drooping.

'Shall I tell you what I think? Those catering corps types, they're dirty devils. They do bugger all, and with them it's: "I don't give a bugger." Buggery-muggery, that's them!'

'They're a stinking lot altogether,' Eudore sighed, emphatically. He is lounging on the ground, his mouth half open, with a martyred look, his dull eyes watching Pépin as he walks backwards and forwards like a hyena.

The bitter sense of irritation with the latecomers grows and grows. Tirloir the Grumbler bustles and multiplies. He is in his element. He sharpens the anger around him with little pointed gestures:

'If we could tell ourselves: "It'll be good" – but it will just be some more muck you have to stuff down your throat.'

'Yes, lads, what about the gristle they sent us yesterday; did you see such a grinding stone? Was that beef steak, I ask you? More like bicycle steak. I told the boys, look out you, don't chew it too quick, you might break your choppers, if the cobbler forgot to take all the nails out!'

This witticism from Tirette (a former manager of a travelling cinema, so they say) would have made us laugh on any other occasion, but hackles are up and his words are received with a growl from all sides.

'And other times, to stop you complaining that it's tough, they give you some grub that's all soft, some tasteless spongy muck, some poultice. When you eat it, it's like drinking a pint of water, no more, no less.'

'There's no consistency in it,' says Lamuse. 'All that stuff, it doesn't fill you up at all. You think you've had a meal, but deep down in your gut, you're empty. That way, bit by bit, you keel over, poisoned by lack of grub.'

'Next time,' Biquet says in exasperation, 'I'll ask to talk to the old man. I'll tell him: "Captain . . ."'

'And I'll report sick,' says Barque. 'I'll say: "Major . . ."'

'Whether you kick the bucket or not, it's all the same to them. They're all in league to take it out on the poor private.'

'I'm telling you, they want our guts.'

'It's the same with the firewater. We have the right to get it in the trenches – seeing as how it was voted somewhere, I don't know when or where, but I know it was – and in the three days we've been here they've been dishing out our brandy ration on the end of a fork.'

'Bleeding hell!'

'Grub's up!' declares a *poilu** watching at the corner.

'About time!'

And the storm of violent recriminations abruptly abates, as though by magic. Suddenly you can see their fury change to satisfaction.

Three men on mess fatigue, breathless, their faces pouring with sweat, put some large dixie cans on the ground, with a petrol can, two canvas buckets and some loaves held together with a skewer. With their backs against the wall of the trench they wipe their faces on their handkerchiefs or their sleeves. And I see Cocon go across to Pépère, smiling, and forgetting the insults that he has just been heaping on the man's reputation, cordially hold out his hand towards one of the cans which are wrapped around Pépère, swelling him out like a lifebelt.

'What's to eat?'

'It's there,' the second orderly replies, evasively. Experience has taught him that describing the menu always leads to acrimonious disillusionment.

---

* Lit. 'hairy', the name respectfully given to the regular front-line infantrymen of the French Army. [trans.]

Still panting, he launches into a rant about the length and difficulty of the journey that he has just made: 'There are people everywhere! It's a proper misery trying to get through. Sometimes, you have to be as thin as a cigarette paper . . . Oh, I know, some people say we have it cushy in the kitchens!' Well, he would a hundred thousand times rather be with the company in the trenches on guard duty and digging, than have a job like this, twice a day, at night-time, too!

Paradis has lifted the lids of the dixies and inspected the containers in them:

'Beans in oil, hard tack, mush and coffee. That's the lot.'

'Heavens above!' Tulacque brays. 'What about wine?'

Some thirsty men hurry over, scowling.

'Oh, shit!' these men exclaim, disillusioned to the depth of their being.

'So what's that in the bucket?' says the orderly, still red and sweating, designating the object with his foot.

'Yeah,' says Paradis. 'I got it wrong. There's some wine.'

'What a jerk!' says the orderly, shrugging his shoulders and giving Paradis a look of inexpressible contempt. 'Put your giglamps on, if you can't see straight.'

Then he adds:

'A quarter of a litre per man. Perhaps a little less, because some idiot bumped into me as I was going through the Boyau de Bois and a drop got spilled . . . Mind you,' he hastens to add, raising his voice, 'if I hadn't been so weighted down, you'd see what a kick he'd have got up his arse! But he set off at full speed, the brute.'

And, despite this confident statement, he makes good his escape, followed by a shower of curses – full of unflattering allusions to his sincerity and sobriety – inspired by this confession of the diminished rations.

Meanwhile they throw themselves on the food and eat, standing, crouching, kneeling or sitting on a dixie, a kitbag dragged out of the pit in which we sleep, or flat out on the ground, their backs against the earth, disturbed by anyone going by, cursing and cursed. Apart from these few swearwords or taunts, delivered on the hop, they say nothing, first and foremost concerned with swallowing, their mouths and the area around them as greasy as the breech of a gun.

They are happy.

When the jaws first stop moving, they serve up dirty jokes. They all push and shove and clamour to get their word in edgeways. You can see Farfadet smile, that delicate employee from the town hall who in the early days would hold himself so upright and proper that he seemed like a foreigner or a convalescent. Lamuse's mouth, like a tomato, spreads and breaks open under his nose, his delight oozing in tears. You see Poterloo's pink peony open and reopen, Old Blaire's wrinkles jiggle with jolliment as he gets up, points his head forward and gesticulates with the short, slender body that serves as a handle to his huge, drooping moustache. You may even catch the lined and lean face of Cocon light up.

'Aren't we gonna reheat this juice?' asks Bécuwe.

'How? By blowing on it?'

Bécuwe, who likes his coffee hot, says:

'Lemme look after it. 'Sno great prob. Jus' make a little fireplace 'ere and a grill wiv some sheaths from your bayonets. I know where there's some nice wood. I can get 'nuff chips wiv me knife to heat the pot. See ya . . .'

Off he goes looking for wood.

While waiting for our coffee, we roll cigarettes or fill our pipes. Everyone gets out his tobacco pouch. Some people have leather or rubber pouches which come from a shop, but they are in a minority. Biquet gets his tobacco out of a sock with a string round the upper end. Most of the others use the wrapper for anti-gas pads which is made of some waterproof material and excellent for keeping baccy or shag. And there are some who just rummage around in their overcoat pockets.

The smokers sit round in a circle, just at the entrance to the dugout where most of the half-section lives, and spit their nicotine-stained saliva on the very place where people put their hands or knees when bending down to get in or out. But who cares about such details?

Now they're talking commodities, in connection with a letter from Marthereau's wife.

'Mother writes,' says Marthereau, 'that fat pig we've got, the fine fellow, d'you know what he's worth now?'

The state of the economy has suddenly degenerated into a violent argument between Pépin and Tulacque. Some unambiguous remarks have been exchanged, then:

'I don't give a toss for what you say or what you don't. Shut it!'

'I'll shut it when I'm ready, you piece of trash!'

'A six-pounder will shut it for you.'

'Who's going to give me that?'

'Come and see, just come and see!'

They foam and grind and square up to one another. Tulacque is grasping his prehistoric axe and his squinting eyes are flashing. The other man, white as a sheet, with a greenish eye and hooligan's face, is clearly considering his knife.

Lamuse extends his hand of peace, large as a baby's head, and his bloodshot face between the two men who are lashing each other with their looks and ripping each other with words.

'Come now, you don't want to do yourselves an injury. That would be a pity.'

The rest pitch in as well and the two opponents are separated. They continue to cast savage glances at each other across the wall of their comrades.

Pépin is chewing over some remaining insults in a voice trembling with malice:

'The ruffian, the hooligan, the rat! Just wait, he'll pay for it!'

On his side, Tulacque tells the soldier beside him:

'That louse! Did you see him? You know, it's a fact, in this place you have to mix with a load of dubious types. You know them and yet you don't. But that one, if he wants to monkey around, he's picked the wrong fellow. Just wait, I'll show him what for one of these days, you see if I don't.'

While the conversations resume and drown the last double echoes of the argument, Paradis says to me: 'It's like this every day. Yesterday, it was Plaisance who was determined he'd clout Fumex around the mouth over some nonsense or other – some opium pills, I think. First it's one, then it's the other who talks about doing someone in. Do we really have to get like animals, even though we look like them?'

'They're not serious, those blokes,' remarks Lamuse. 'They're kids.'

'Of course they are, because they're men.'

The day comes on. A little more light has filtered through the mists that cover the earth. But the sky is overcast and now it dissolves in rain. The water vapour thins out and falls. It drizzles down. The wind brings its great damp void back on us, with depressing slowness. The fog and raindrops dampen and tarnish everything, even the roast-beef cheeks of Lamuse and the orange peel covering Tulacque; the water seeps into our very depths, reaching the core of joy that the meal has brought us. Space has shrunk and the field of sadness of the sky has clamped down on the earth, that field of death.

We are stuck here, idle. It will be hard to reach the end of today, to shake off the afternoon. We shiver uncomfortably, shifting on our feet, like cattle waiting at a gate.

Cocon is explaining to his neighbour how our trenches are laid out and linked together. He has seen a master plan and made some calculations. In the regiment's sector there are fifteen lines of French trenches, some abandoned to the grass and almost filled in, others kept up and bristling with men. These parallel trenches are joined by countless linking ones that twist and turn like old passageways. The network is even more compact than we think, those of us who live in it. Across the twenty-five kilometres that form the front of our army, there must be a thousand kilometres of trenchwork: trenches themselves, linking trenches and dugouts. And the French Army has ten armies. This means that there are around ten thousand kilometres of trenchwork on the French side and as much on the German . . . And the French front is only about one-eighth of the war front across the surface of the world.

That's what Cocon says, turning to his neighbour in conclusion and saying:

'And you see what we are in all that.'

Poor Barque, with his anaemic slum-kid's face outlined by a red goatee and marked with a lock of hair like an apostrophe . . . He lowers his head:

'True, when you think about it. A soldier, or even lots of them, are nothing, or less than nothing in the mass and so we're quite lost, drowned, like the few drops of blood we are in this deluge of men and things.'

Barque sighs and falls silent. And, in the pause in this lecture, you can hear a fragment of a story, told in an undertone:

'He only came with two horses. Wheee . . . A shell! He's only got one horse left.'

'It's a bore,' says Volpatte.

'But we hang on,' Barque grumbles.

'You've got to,' says Paradis.

'And why?' Marthereau asks, without real feeling.

'For no reason, since we've got to.'

'There isn't any reason,' Lamuse agrees.

'Yes, there is,' says Cocon. 'It's that . . . Well, there's lots, in fact.'

'Belt up! It's better to have no reason, since we've got to hang on.'

'*Even so*,' says Blaire, in a hollow voice, never missing an opportunity to slip that phrase in. 'Even so, they wanna kill us.'

'To begin with,' says Tirette, 'I thought about loads of stuff, turning it over, working it out. Now, I don't think any more.'

'Nor me.'

'Nor me.'

'I've never tried.'

'You're not as daft as you look, flea-face,' says Mesnil André in his high-pitched, jeering voice.

Vaguely flattered, the other man expands the idea for him: 'Firstly, you can't know anything about anything.'

'You only need to know one thing and that one thing is that the Boche are over here, that they're dug in, and that they mustn't get through and that one day they're even going to have to bugger off – the sooner the better,' says Corporal Bertrand.

'Yes, yes, they'll have to get their skates on, no mistake, otherwise, what? There's no sense in racking your brains over anything else. The only thing is, it's taking a long time.'

'It is that, by buggery,' Fouillade exclaims. 'I'll say.'

'Oh, I'm not complaining,' says Barque. 'At the start, I moaned about everyone: those in the rear, civilians, locals, shirkers . . . Oh, yes, did I moan! But that was at the start of the war and I was young. Now, I put up with things.'

'There's only one way to take things and that's as they come.'

'You bet, otherwise you go nuts. We're crazy enough as it is, don't you think, Firmin?'

Volpatte nods with deep conviction. Then he spits and examines his spittle attentively.

'I'll say,' Barque agrees.

'You mustn't look too far ahead. You've got to live from day to day, or even hour by hour, if you can.'

'That's right, walnut-face. We've got to do what we're told to do, while we wait until they tell us to go home.'

'There you have it,' Mesnil Joseph yawns.

With their baked, tanned faces, encrusted with dust, they make their views known, then fall silent. Clearly these men who, a year and a half ago, descended on this frontier from every part of the country, now have the same thoughts in their heads: giving up understanding, giving up being themselves, the hope of not dying and the struggle to live as best they can.

'You've got to,' says Tulacque, emphatically. 'If you don't get out of the shit yourself, no one's going to do it for you, don't worry!'

'They've not designed him yet, the chap who'll look after someone else.'

'It's every man for himself, in war.'

' 'Course it is, 'course it is!'

Silence. Then from the depths of their deprivation, these men conjure images of delight.

'All that,' Barque goes on, 'isn't a patch on the good life we had, that time, in Soissons.'

'Oh, by God!'

A glint of paradise lost lights up their eyes and even seems to warm their mugs, already reddened by the cold.

'Now that was a party,' sighs Tirloir, thoughtfully, as he stops scratching himself and stares into the distance, across the land of trenches.

'Good Lord! That whole town, almost entirely evacuated, which more or less belonged to us! The houses, with their beds . . .'

'Their cupboards!'

'Their cellars!'

Tears have risen to Lamuse's eyes, his face has lit up and his heart is bursting.

'Were you there long?' Cadilhac asks. He came later with the reinforcements from Auvergne.

'Bloody months!'

The conversation, which had almost died out, flares up brightly again as they recall the time of plenty.

'You used to see old timers,' said Paradis, as though in a dream, 'coming in a stream along the houses and behind them, on their way back to the camp, with chickens hanging at their belts and under each arm a rabbit that they'd borrowed from some bloke or his missus who they'd never seen before and wouldn't see again, either.'

They consider the distant tastes of chicken and rabbit.

'There were some things we paid for. There was loads of cash around, too. We had it all going for us in those days.'

'There was a hundred thousand pouring into the shops.'

'Millions! You can't imagine it, draining away all day long. It was a sort of carnival, out of this world.'

'Believe it or not,' Blaire told Cadilhac, 'in the midst of all that, just like here and wherever you go, what we had least of was firewood. You had to hunt for it, find it, earn it, huh? Oh, boy! How we hunted for a fire!'

'We were in the CHR camp. The cookie there was the great Martin César. He could do it, he could find any wood there was to find.'

'Oh, yes! He was the tops. No two ways about it, he knew what he was about!'

'There was always a fire in his kitchen – but *always*, old chap. You'd run into cookies dashing this way and that around the streets, snivelling because they hadn't any wood or coal, but he'd have a fire going. When there wasn't nothing at all, he'd say: "Don't you worry, I'll manage." And in no time, there it was.'

'He'd overdo it, sometimes, you could say. The first time I was in his kitchen, d'you know what he'd got to heat the pan? A violin what he'd found in some house.'

'Now that's a bit naughty, even so,' said Mesnil André. 'Well, I know there's not much use in a violin, but even so . . .'

'Other times he used billiard cues. Zizi just managed to pinch one for a cane, but the rest went in the fire. After that, the chairs from the drawing room, which were mahogany, they went. He snitched them and cut them up at night, 'cos some NCO might have objected.'

'He used it up quick,' said Pépin. 'We made do with some old piece of furniture that lasted us a fortnight.'

'And why shouldn't we have a bit of it? The soup's got to be made, but they don't give you wood or coal. After it's all been doled out, you're there, empty-handed, in front of a pile of raw meat, surrounded by the lads making fun of you, until they start slagging you off. So what then?'

'It's not our fault, it's the job.'

'Didn't the officers have anything to say when you pinched stuff?'

'They were up to their necks in it themselves, believe me! D'you remember, Desmaisons, the time when Lieutenant Virvin was smashing a cellar door in with an axe? A *poilu* saw him and he gave him the door for firewood, just so the bloke wouldn't spread it around.'

'What about poor Saladin, the catering corps officer? The lad was caught one evening coming out of a basement with two bottles of white in each hand. As he'd been nicked, he was forced to go back into the bottle mine and dig some out for everyone. Even though Corporal Bertrand, who's a man of principle, didn't want to drink it. Ah, d'you remember that, old sausage?'

'And where is he now, that cook who always found the firewood?' asked Cadilhac.

'Dead. A whizzbang fell in his bangers. He wasn't hurt, but he died even so, of a stroke when he saw his macaroni all shot to pieces – a heart seizure, so the quack said. He had a weak heart; his only strong point was finding wood. We gave him a good burial. We made him a coffin out of some parquet flooring, we fixed the planks together with nails from the pictures in the house and used bricks to knock them in. While we were carrying him, I thought to myself: "Just as well he's dead, 'cos if he could see this, he'd never get over not having thought of the parquet flooring for his fire." Oh, he was a right one, that son of a gun.'

'A squaddie gets by with the help of his friends. When you get out of a fatigue or take the best piece or the best place, someone else has to carry the can,' Volpatte muses, philosophically.

'I've often swung it so that I don't have to go up into the trenches, I don't know how many times I've got out of it, I have to admit. But when my pals are in danger, I'm no shirker and dodger. I forget my uniform, I forget everything. I see some blokes and I march. But otherwise, mate, I think of number one.'

This is not idle chatter. Lamuse is certainly an expert at swinging the lead, but he has saved the lives of wounded men by going to fetch them back under fire.

He tells you about it without any boasting:

'We were all lying in the grass. It was hotting up. Crack, crack! Ping, ping! When I saw they'd been hit, I got up – even though someone was shouting at me: "Keep down!" I couldn't leave them like that. There's no great merit in it, 'cos I couldn't do anything else.'

Almost all the boys in the squad have some feat of military valour to their credit and the Croix de Guerre have been lined up, one by one, on their chests.

'Now me,' says Biquet, 'I've not saved any Frenchmen, but I've bagged a few Boche.'

In the May attack he dashed forward; we saw him vanish to a point, then come back with four lads in coal scuttle helmets.

'And I've killed a few,' says Tulacque.

Two months ago he lined up nine of them in front of the trench he had taken, just to show off.

'But,' he added, 'it's those Boche officers I'm mainly after.'

'Oh, the pigs!'

They shouted it several times, with real feeling.

'Ah now, old fellow,' said Tirloir. 'They do talk about the dirty Hun. When it comes to the private soldiers I'm not sure if it's true or if they're having us on and if, underneath, they're not really men a bit like us.'

'They probably are,' says Eudore.

'You think!' says Cocon.

'In any case, we're not sure about the men,' Tirloir continues. 'But the German officers, oh, no, no, no, they're not men, they're monsters. They really are a special, nasty breed of vermin, old man. You could call them the microbes of war. You've got to have seen them close to, those horrible great stiff things, thin as nails, but with calves' heads on them.'

'Or there are plenty who've got snakes' faces on them.'

Tirloir goes on:

'I saw one, a prisoner, once, coming back from delivering a dispatch. The filthy swine! A Prussian colonel with a prince's crown, they told me, and a gold crest of arms on his leathers. He was in a right paddy because people had brushed against him as they were taking him along the trench! And he was looking down on everyone over his stiff collar. I said to myself: "Just wait, old girl, I'll give you something to complain about!" I took my time and squared up behind him and kicked him up the arse as hard as I could. Over he went, half strangled . . .'

'Strangled?'

'Yes, with fury, when he realized what was up and that he'd just had his high-ranking posterior clouted by the hob-nailed boot of a simple *poilu*. He started to scream like a woman and wave his arms like an epileptic . . .'

'Now, I'm not mean,' said Blaire. 'I've got kids and it churns me up at home when I kill a pig that I know; but one of those, I'd happily spear him right in the bread basket . . .'

'Me too!'

'Quite apart from which,' Pépin says, 'they've got silver helmets and pistols you can resell for a hundred francs whenever you like and prismatic binoculars that are priceless. Oh, dearie me, what a lot of chances I let slip by in the first part of the campaign! I was such a greenhorn then – worse luck! But don't you worry, I'll get a silver helmet, you listen here, I swear I will. I don't just want the hide, but the togs of one of Willie's brass hats. Don't you worry, I'll have my hands on one before the war ends.'

'You believe the war will end, do you?' someone asks.

'Don't you worry,' says the other.

Meanwhile there is a bit of a commotion to our right and suddenly you can see and hear a group in which dark shapes mingle with coloured ones, moving towards us.

'What's that then?'

Biquet has gone over to get a closer look. He comes back and, pointing with his thumb over his shoulder, indicates the multicoloured mass:

'Hey, fellows, come and have a look at this. People.'

'People?'

'Yeah, gents, you know . . . Civilians with some staff officers.'

'Civilians! Let's hope they hold out!'

It's the hallowed phrase: as long as the home front holds out. There is laughter, even though we've heard it a hundred times and, rightly or wrongly, a soldier will twist the meaning and consider it an ironic assault on his life of privations and dangers.

Two men are approaching, two men in overcoats, with walking sticks, and another in hunting gear with a plush hat and a pair of binoculars.

Behind, steering the way, are some pale blue tunics, with fawn-coloured or patent leather shining on them.

With his arm, on which glitters a gold-embroidered silk armband, picked out with gold flashes, a captain points to the firing position in front of an old slit, and invites the visitors to step up and try it out. The gentleman in travelling costume mounts the step with the help of his umbrella.

Barque says:

'Have you seen the station master in his Sunday best at the Gare du Nord showing a rich sportsman into his first-class carriage on the first day of the season? "This way, sir." You know, when the toffs are all togged out in new gear, leather and ironmongery, and prance around in the get-up they have for killing small animals.'

Three or four *poilus* who are not properly turned out disappear underground. The others do not move, rooted to the spot. Even their pipes go out and all that can be heard is the murmur of conversation between the officers and their guests.

'It's the tourists of the trenches,' whispers Barque.

Then, louder: 'This way, ladies and gentlemen – as the guides say.'

'Knock it off!' Farfadet mutters, fearing that Barque's loud mouth will attract the notice of the bigwigs.

Some heads in the group turn towards us. A gentleman walks in our direction; soft hat, loose tie. He has a white goatee and looks like an artist. Another comes behind, this one wearing a black overcoat, with black bowler, black beard, white tie and pince-nez.

'Oh! Oh!' says the first gent. 'Here are some *poilus* . . . And real ones, too.'

He comes a little closer to our group, rather cautiously, as in the zoo at the Jardin d'Acclimatation, and holds out his hand to the one nearest to him, with a certain awkwardness, like offering a bit of bread to the elephant.

'Aha! They're drinking coffee,' he observes.

'They call it "juice",' says the magpie-man.

'Is it good, my friends?'

The soldier, who is also intimidated by this strange and exotic encounter, grunts, smiles and blushes, and the gentleman says: 'Huh, huh!'

Then he gives a little nod and retreats, walking backwards.

'Very well, very well, my friends. You're fine chaps.'

The group, with its dull tones of civilian clothes interspersed with bright military colours – like geraniums and hortensias against the dark earth of a flowerbed – wavers, then goes by and vanishes in the opposite direction to the one from which it came. We hear an officer saying: 'We've still got lots to see, *messieurs les journalistes.*'

When the radiant group has disappeared we exchange looks. Those who had vanished down their holes gradually exhume themselves, head first. The men gather their wits and shrug their shoulders.

'They're journalists,' says Tirette.

'Journalists?'

'Yeah, those fellas what write the papers. You don't seem to have grasped it, dunderhead. If you've got papers, there must be chaps who write them.'

'So they're the ones stuffing nonsense in our skulls?' says Marthereau.

Barque puts on a falsetto voice and pretends to be reciting from a newspaper in front of his face:

' "The Kronprinz is mad, after being killed at the start of the campaign and, meanwhile, he has every illness you can think of. Kaiser Wilhelm will die this evening and again tomorrow. The Germans have no munitions left and are eating wood. According to the most authoritative estimates, they can't last more than a week. We can take them when we like, with our rifles shouldered. The only reason we're waiting a few days longer is because we don't want to leave life in the trenches, we're so well-off here, with water, gas and showers on all floors. The only drawback is that it's a bit too warm in winter . . . As for the Austrians, they gave up long ago, they're only pretending . . ." It's been like that for fifteen months and the editor is telling his hacks: "Hi, boys! Take a look at this and try to tickle it up again for me in five secs and spread it over these five confounded white sheets we've got to blacken." '

'Yes, yes,' says Fouillade.

'Well, Corporal, you laugh, but isn't there some truth in what I'm saying?'

'A bit, but you're too hard on them and you'd be the first to make a row if you had to do without the papers . . . Huh? When the newspaperboy goes past, why do you all shout: "Me, me!"?'

'And then, what harm can it do you?' says Old Blaire. 'You're making a big fuss about the papers, so just do what I do: don't worry about them.'

'Yeah, yeah, that's enough of it! Turn the page, donkey-face.'

The conversation is breaking down, people's attention is wandering. Four blokes get together for a game of manille that will last until night makes it impossible to see the cards. Volpatte is trying his best to catch a cigarette paper that has slipped from his fingers and is hopping and zigzagging in the wind against the wall of the trench like a wayward butterfly.

Cocon and Tirette are remembering barrack days. The years of military service have left an indelible impression on their minds, providing a rich fund of memories, bathed in light and always ready for use, so that for the past ten, fifteen or twenty years they have drawn on them for something to talk about. And on it goes, even after a year and a half of war in every shape and form.

I can hear part of the discussion and guess the rest. In any case, it is always and infallibly the same kind of stories that old troopers tell about their army days: the narrator managed to shut some evil-minded NCO up with a few audacious and well-chosen words. He dared to do it, he spoke out loud and clear. Huh! A few snatches reach my ears:

'So, d'you think I flinched when Nenoeil laid that lot on me? Not a bit of it, old chap. All the rest of 'em kept their mouths well shut, but I said to him, plain as you like: "*Mon adjutant*," I goes, "that may be so, but . . ."' (I didn't catch the rest of the sentence.) 'Oh, yeah, I gave it to him straight. He didn't bat an eyelid. "Very well, very well," he says and off he goes; and after that he was sweet as pie with me.'

'I had just the same with Dodore, the warrant officer of the 13th, when I was on leave. A right bastard. Now he's in the Pantheon, as warder. He really had it in for me, so . . .'

And each of them brings out his personal collection of historical sayings.

Every one of them is just like the rest – each saying: 'I'm different from the rest.'

'The post orderly!'

He is a tall, broad man with fat calves, as neatly and comfortably done up as a gendarme.

He's in a bad mood. He has received new orders and now has to go every day and bring the mail to the colonel's command post. He is ranting about this new requirement as though it had been exclusively designed against him.

Meanwhile, right in the midst of his rant, he is talking to one then another, as he usually does, as he passes by, calling the corporals to fetch the letters. And despite his resentment, he does not keep all his news to himself. Even as he is undoing the string on the packets of letters he hands round the supply of verbal information with which he has come provided.

First of all he tells us that the report carries an explicit ban on the wearing of hoods.

'Hear that?' Tirette says to Tirloir. 'Now you've got to throw your fine hood away.'

'Not likely! I don't agree. This is nothing to do with me,' says the hood-wearer whose pride as well as his comfort is at stake.

'It's an order from the General Commander of the Army.'

'Then the General Commander will have to command the rain not to fall. I don't want to know about it.'

Most orders, even less extraordinary ones than this, are always greeted in this way, before being carried out.

'The report also states that beards must be cut,' says the letter-man. 'And your thatch, cropped, with clippers.'

'Keep mum, boss!' said Barque, whose nut is directly threatened by this regulation. 'You didn't see me. You can keep quiet about it.'

'Tell me! Do what you like, I don't give a damn.'

As well as definite, written news there is other information, which is fuller but also less reliable and more fantastic: the division is supposed to be relieved to go either on leave – but real leave, lasting six weeks – or else to Morocco or Egypt.

'Eh! Oh! Ah!'

They listen. They are seduced by the appeal of something new and wonderful. Even so, someone asks the post orderly:

'Where did you get that from?'

He describes his sources:

'The adjutant in command of the detachment of territorials who do the fatigues for the AC HQ.'

'The what?'

'The Army Corps Headquarters. And he's not the only one who's saying it. There is, you know, that customer whose name I've forgotten, the one that looks like Galle, but isn't Galle. There's someone, I'm not sure who, in his family who's something or other. Anyway, he's in the know.'

'So what?'

They have all gathered round the storyteller with hungry looks.

'You say we're going to Egypt? I don't know it. I know they had pharaohs there when I was a kid at school, but I don't know about since then . . .'

'To Egypt . . .'

The idea sinks gradually into their brains.

'Oh, no,' says Blaire. 'I get seasick. But then seasickness doesn't last for ever. Yeah, but what would the old lady say?'

'What d'you think? She'll get used to it. You'll see Negroes and streets full of big birds like we see sparrers here.'

'But I thought we were meant to be going to Alsace?'

'Yes,' says the post orderly. 'Some people in the pay office think that too.'

'I wouldn't half mind that . . .'

. . . But good sense and experience triumph and dispel the dream. We have been told so often that we were going to leave for distant parts, we have so often believed it and so often been disappointed . . . It's as though at a particular moment one wakes up from a dream.

'All that's a load of codswallop! They've tried it on too many times. Just wait and see – and don't put your shirt on it!'

They go back to their corners, with here and there some carrying the light but important burden of a letter.

'Ah,' says Tirloir, 'I've got to write. I can't go a week without writing. There's nothing for it.'

'Me too,' says Eudore. 'I have to write to the little woman.'

'Mariette? Is she well?'

'Yeah, yeah, don't worry about Mariette.'

Some people have already settled down to their letters. Barque, standing up with his paper lying flat on a notebook in a crevice in the trench wall, seems to be seized by a wave of inspiration. He is writing away, bent over the paper, with the fixed look and concentrated air of a galloping rider.

Lamuse, who has no imagination, sits down, puts his folder of writing paper on the padded summit of his knees and moistens his ink pencil, then spends his time rereading the last letters he has received, not knowing what to say except what he has said already and obstinately trying to say something else.

An aura of sentimental sweetness seems to have enveloped little Eudore who is crouching in a kind of niche of earth. He is meditating, his pencil between his fingers, gazing at the paper: he looks at it dreamily, staring . . . he sees and you see that other sky shining down on him. His gaze goes all the way there: he has reached out for home.

Letter-writing time is the moment when we are most and best what we were. Several of the men abandon themselves to the past and the first thing they speak about is food.

Others, beneath a covering bark of coarseness, let their hearts obscurely release a memory, recalling long-lost days of light: a summer morning when the fresh green of the garden is reflected on the white walls of a country room, or when the wind blowing across the open fields shakes the corn with slow, strong billows and rustles the smaller patch of oats nearby with quick little feminine shudders. Or else a winter evening and the table, with the women and their softness around it, on which stands the lamp, caressing you with the gentle glow of its life and the dress of its shade.

Meanwhile Old Blaire has gone back to the ring that he started. He has twisted the still formless circle of aluminium on a round piece of wood and is rubbing it with a file. He is absorbed in this task, concentrating with all his might, two lines etched into his forehead. At times he stops, sits back and contemplates the little object tenderly, as though it were looking back at him.

'You see,' he once told me, talking about another ring, 'it's not a question of well or not well. The main thing is that I've made it for my wife, you understand? When I had nothing to do and was just lazing about, I used to look at this photo' (and he showed me the picture of a plump, chubby-cheeked woman) 'and then I had no trouble getting started on this confounded ring. You might say we made it together. D'you see? The proof is that it kept me company and I said goodbye to it when I sent it to the missus.'

Now he's making another with some copper in it. He is working eagerly. It's his heart that wants to express itself as best it can and does so doggedly in this sort of calligraphy.

In these bare holes in the earth, these men bent respectfully over their trinkets – light, elementary trinkets, so small that the large, calloused hands find it hard to hold them and let them drop – seem still more savage, more primitive and more human than at any other time.

You think of the first inventor, the father of all artists, who tried to impress on hard metals the shape of what he saw and the soul of what he felt.

'Someone's coming by,' Biquet announces, moving along; he's the one who acts as concierge in our sector of the trench. 'There's a whole load of them.'

At that moment an adjutant appears, with straps round his belly and his chin, waving the sheath of his sabre.

'Out of the way, you lot! Come on now: I said mind out! You're loafing around there . . . Come on, shoo, beat it! I don't want to see you in the way again – huh!'

We reluctantly move out of the way. A few, on the sides, slowly dig themselves into the ground.

There's a company of territorials whose job in this sector is to do trenching on the second line and the upkeep of rear trenches. They appear, carrying their tools, dragging their feet and miserably attired.

We watch them as they approach, one by one, pass by and vanish. They are stunted little old men who have their cheeks dusted with ash, or else great broken-winded ones tightly bound up in their worn-out, stained coats which flap open toothlessly where their buttons are missing.

Those two jokers Tirette and Barque at first stare at them in silence, their backs pressed to the trench wall. Then they start to smile.

'The street-cleaners' procession,' Tirette proclaims.

'Let's have a bit of a laugh,' says Barque.

Some of the old workers are funny. Here's one, coming along in the line, with shoulders that droop like a bottle. He's very narrow in the chest and thin-legged, but despite this has a pot belly.

Barque can't resist it:

'Hey, there, Belly Boy!'

'Threadbare,' Tirette remarks as one greatcoat walks past, endlessly patched, in every shade of blue.

He calls out to the veteran:

'Hey, there, Samples! Yes, over there! You!'

The man turns round and stares at him, open-mouthed.

'Tell me, dad, would you be really kind and let me have the address of your London tailor?'

Antiquated and scribbled over with lines, the face chuckles, then the fellow, who has paused for a moment when Barque called out to him, is jostled and carried away by the crowd behind him.

After a few, less outstanding bit players, a new victim appears to be taunted. Some kind of dirty sheep's wool is vegetating on his rough red neck. With knees bent, body forward and back arched, the territorial can hardly keep upright.

'Look here!' says Tirette, pointing at him. 'It's the famous accordion man! You'd have to pay to see him at the fair. Here you can see him for free!'

The object of these taunts stammers back some insults, while here and there a few people laugh. But this is enough to excite the two comedians: the urge to put in a word that will get a laugh from this undemanding audience leads them to ridicule their old comrades-in-arms who are labouring night and day, on the outskirts of the great war, to prepare and repair the battlefields. And the other spectators follow suit, in their misery, taunting those more miserable than they are.

'Just take a look at that one! And what about that one!'

'No, give me a photo of that little short-arse! Huh? Flat on the earth!'

'And that one, who goes on and on – talk about a skyscraper! He takes the biscuit! Really, old chap, you do!'

The man in question is taking short steps, carrying his pickaxe in front of him like a candle, his face contorted and his body bent under the effects of lumbago.

'Hey, grandad. Do you want two sous?' Barque asks him, tapping him on the shoulder as he goes by.

The *poilu*, who is going bald, grunts irritably: 'You lousy good-for-nothing.'

So Barque calls out shrilly: 'Now then, show some manners, you fart-faced old shit-mill!'

The veteran swings round and mutters something, in fury.

'No, what!' Barque shouts, laughing. 'He's got some spirit, the old relic! Look at that, he's in fighting mood. He could be dangerous if he was sixty years younger.'

'And if he wasn't drunk,' says Pépin – a gratuitous insult – as he searches for other victims in the stream of men.

The hollow chest of the last straggler appears, then his bent back vanishes.

The procession of these worn veterans, filthy with the dirt of the trenches, peters out amid the sarcastic, almost malevolent faces of the sinister troglodytes half emerging from their caverns of mud.

Meanwhile the day wears on and evening starts to turn the sky grey and to blacken everything. It blends with blind fate, as well as with the dark, ignorant soul of the multitude buried there.

In the half-light, a sound of footsteps, a rumbling and another troop of men is coming past.

'Moroccans.'

They march past with their terracotta, yellow or dark brown faces, their beards, which are scanty, or dense and curly, their yellow-green coats and their muddy helmets which have a crescent in place of the grenade on ours. The eyes, shining like coins, look like ivory or onyx marbles in their faces, which are either flat or else, on the contrary, sharp and angular. From time to time in the line the coal-black mask of a Senegalese marksman sways above the rest. At the back is a red banner with a green hand in the middle.

We watch them and say nothing. These ones you don't shout at. They are imposing and even a little frightening.

Despite that, the Africans seem quite merry and in good spirits.

Naturally they are going up to the front line. This is their place and the fact that they are coming past indicates that there will very soon be an attack. They are designed for going over the top.

'You have to admit, we don't half owe them a lot – them and the 75 gun. The Moroccan Division's been sent everywhere at the vital moment.'

'They can't adjust to us. They go too fast. And then you can't stop them . . .'

Some of these devils in yellow wood, bronze and ebony are serious-looking; their faces are disturbing, silent, like snares that you can see. The others are laughing, showing their teeth, and their laughter tinkles like the sound of strange instruments playing exotic music.

People talk about the character of these darkies, how ferocious they are in attack, how they love to put in the bayonet, how they don't like to give quarter. We repeat the stories that they themselves freely tell, and all more or less in the same terms with the same gestures: they raise their arms: 'Kam'rad, kam'rad!' – 'No, not kam'rad!', and they mimic the movement of the bayonet driven forward at belly height, then dragged back, from above, with the help of the foot.

As he goes past one of the snipers hears what we are saying. He looks at us, gives a broad laugh in his turbaned helmet and repeats, shaking his head: 'Not kam'rad, no, not kam'rad, never! Cut off head!'

'They really are a different race, with their skin like canvas,' Biquet admits (though he's no coward himself). 'You know, they hate resting. They're just waiting for the moment when the officer puts his watch back in his pocket and says: "Off you go!" '

'They're real soldiers, in a word.'

'We're not soldiers, we're men,' says fat Lamuse.

It's darker now, but this true, clear observation seems to cast a light over those who are here waiting, since this morning, and for months.

They are men, ordinary men who have suddenly been snatched away from life. Like ordinary men as a whole, they are ignorant, not too keen, narrow-minded, and full of good old common sense, which sometimes goes astray; they are liable to let themselves be led and to do what they are told, inured to hardship, able to suffer long.

They are simple men who have been still further simplified, their only primordial instincts accentuated by force of circumstance: the instinct of self-preservation, egotism, an obstinate hope that they will survive forever, the joy of eating, drinking and sleep.

Intermittently cries of humanity, deep shudders, emerge from the darkness and silence of their great human souls.

When it is so dark that one can no longer see well, we hear, first as a murmur, then getting closer, louder, ringing, the order: 'Second half-section! Muster!'

We fall in. Our names are called.

'Gee up!' says the corporal.

We start moving. In front of the tool store there is standing and tramping of feet. Everyone gets a shovel or a pickaxe. An NCO holds out the handles in the half-dark:

'You, a shovel. Nah, get along. You, another shovel. You a pickaxe. Come along, hurry up and move on.'

We leave by the trench at right angles to our own, straight ahead, towards the moving, living and awful frontier of now.

Against the grey of the sky the powerful, broken pant of an invisible aircraft coming down in great descending circles fills the space. In front, on the right, on the left, everywhere, claps of thunder spread large, but short-lived lights across the dark blue of the sky.

3
The Descent

The greyish dawn barely tints the formless, still-black landscape. There is a field between the sloping road that comes down on our right out of the darkness and the sombre cloud of the Bois des Alleux – where, without seeing them, you can hear the carriages of the combat train getting ready and starting up. We of the 6th Battalion reached here as night was ending. We stacked our weapons and now, in the midst of the circle of vague light, our feet in mist and mud, in dark groups faintly tinged with blue or as solitary spectres, we have halted, all heads turned towards the path leading over there. We are waiting for the rest of the regiment, for the 5th Battalion, which was in the front line and left the trenches after us.

There is a noise . . .

'There they are!'

A long vague mass appears in the west and spreads like night across the half-light of the road.

At last! This accursed relief operation started yesterday at six in the evening and has been going on all night. Now the last man has set foot outside the last trench.

This stay in the trenches has been frightful. The 18th Company was in the vanguard: eighteen killed and some fifty wounded – at least one man out of three in four days. And that was without any attack, just from shelling.

We know this and as the mutilated battalion comes towards us and our paths cross, trampling the mud of the field, we recognize familiar faces, leaning towards each other: 'Hey, what about the 18th?'

As we say it we think: 'If things go on like this, what will become of us all? What will become of me?'

The 17th, 19th and 20th arrive in turn and stack their arms.

'Here's the 18th!'

It comes last of all: since it was holding the first trench, it was the last to be relieved.

Daylight has cleared a little and is casting a white light on things. We can make out the captain of the company coming down the path, alone, ahead of his men. He is walking with difficulty, with the help of a stick, because of his old wound from the Marne, revived by rheumatism – and another pain. His head is bent under its hood; he looks like someone following a funeral; and one can see what he is thinking – that he is indeed following one.

That's the company. It emerges, very much in disorder. At once our hearts ache. It is visibly shorter than the other three in the line-up of the battalion.

I reach the road and cross in front of the men of the 18th as they come down. The uniforms of these survivors are uniformly yellowed with soil; you would think they were dressed in khaki. The cloth is quite stiff with the ochre mud that has dried on it and the skirts of the greatcoats are like planks flapping over the yellow bark covering the knees. Their heads are haggard and sooty, their eyes large and feverish. Dust and dirt line their faces.

Arising from among these soldiers returning from the frightfulness of the lower depths, is a deafening din. They are all speaking at once, very loudly, waving their hands, laughing and singing.

To see them, you would think that a festive crowd was pouring down the road!

Here is the second section, with its tall sub-lieutenant whose greatcoat is wrapped and strapped around his body like a rolled umbrella. I elbow my way along as I follow the march until I reach Marchal's squad, the hardest hit: out of eleven friends who had been together for a year and a half, only three men are left, plus Corporal Marchal.

He sees me. He gives a cry of joy and a smile fills his face. Leaving go of his rifle strap, he holds his hands out to me, with his baton hanging from one arm.

'Hello, old man. Is all well with you? What have you been up to?'

I turn away and almost in a whisper:

'So, my poor friend, things have been hard.'

The smile fades and his face takes on a serious look.

'Yes indeed, old chap. It can't be helped. It was awful this time. Barbier was killed.'

'So they said – Barbier!'

'On Saturday, at eleven in the evening. He had the top of his back taken off by a shell,' Marchal says, 'as if it had been cut with a razor. Besse had a piece of shrapnel through his belly and his stomach. Barthélemy and Baubex were hit in the head and neck. We spent the night racing backwards and forwards along the trench, avoiding the gunfire. You remember little Godefroy? The middle of his body was blown right away. He was emptied of blood on the spot, in an instant, like turning over a pail. Small as he was, it's incredible the amount of blood he had: it made a stream of at least fifty metres along the trench. Gougnard had his legs blown off by shrapnel. He was not quite dead when we picked him up. That was at the listening post. I'd been on guard with them, but when the shell fell, I'd gone back to the trench to ask the time. I found my rifle, which I'd left behind, bent in two as though someone had done it with his bare hands, the barrel like a corkscrew and half the stock shredded to sawdust. There was a smell of blood that made you want to throw up.'

'And Mondain, too, I hear?'

'He got it the next morning – that's to say, yesterday – in the dugout that was caved in by a shell. He was lying down and his chest was crushed. Did they tell you about Franco, who was next to Mondain? The roof falling in broke his spine. He talked after they dug him out and sat him down on the ground. He put his head on one side and said: "I'm dying." Then he died. Vigile was with them, too. His body was untouched, but his head was completely flattened, like a pancake, and huge, as wide as this. Seeing him lying on the ground, black and changed in shape, you could have taken him for his shadow, the sort of shadow you sometimes get when you're walking along at night with a lantern.'

'Vigile, the class of '13, a mere child! And Mondain and Franco, such great fellows in spite of their stripes. So many fine friends less, my dear old Marchal.'

'Yes,' says Marchal.

But he is swept away by a horde of his comrades, shouting at him and ragging him. He answers them back, replying to their sarcastic remarks and they all laugh and jostle one another.

I look from one face to the next. They are merry and, through the weary lines and stains of earth, they seem triumphant.

What does it mean? If they had been allowed to drink wine when they were in the front line, I would say that they were all drunk.

I pick out one of the survivors who is humming a tune and marching along to it with a lightsome air, like the hussar in the song;* this is Vanderborn, the drummer.

'Well, Vanderborn, you look pretty pleased with yourself!'

Vanderborn, usually a quiet fellow, shouts to me:

'It wasn't me this time, see? Here I am!'

And with a sweeping gesture like a madman he claps me on the shoulder.

Now I understand . . .

These men are happy, despite everything, as they emerge from hell – for the very reason that they are emerging. They are coming back, they are saved. Once again death was there, but spared them. The duty roster means that every company is in the forward line every six weeks. Six weeks! For everything, great and small, front-line troops have a child's philosophy: they never look too far around them or in front of them. They think more or less from day to day. Today, each of these men is sure that he will live a little while longer.

This is why, though they are crushed by weariness and still spattered with the recent slaughter, and their brothers have been snatched away from around them, in spite of everything, in spite of themselves, they rejoice at having survived and enjoy the infinite glory of being on their feet.

* *'Le Rêve passe'*, a popular song at the time, in which a *poilu* dreams of a better life. [trans.]

4
Volpatte and Fouillade

When we got to our quarters, someone asked:

'Where's Volpatte?'

'And what about Fouillade, where's he?'

They had been requisitioned and taken up to the front line by the 5th Battalion. We were to meet up with them at the quarters. Nothing. Two men of the squad were lost.

'Bloody hell! That's what happens when you lend your men,' the sergeant bellowed.

When the captain was told, he swore, blasphemed and said:

'I must have them. Find them at once. Now!'

Farfadet and I were called by Corporal Bertrand from the barn where we had already settled down, flat on our backs, and were falling asleep.

'Must find Volpatte and Fouillade.'

We got up quickly and left with a shudder of anxiety. Our two pals, requisitioned by the 5th, have been carried off when it was stood down. Who knows where they are and what's happened to them.

We climb back up the hill. We are starting to go over the long road that we have been following from early morning, but in reverse. Even though we are without our packs, just our rifles and equipment, we feel weary, sleepy, paralysed, in this sad landscape beneath the sky powdered with mist. Farfadet is soon panting. He talked a bit at the start, then tiredness shut him up whether he liked it or not. He is brave but frail, and in all his earlier life he never learned to use his legs, in the mayor's office where, from the time he made his first Communion, he scribbled away between a stove and some old cardboard files going grey with dust.

Just as we are coming out of the wood, slipping and sliding towards the area of communication trenches, two slender silhouettes appear ahead of us. Two soldiers coming: we can see the lump of their backpacks and the outline of their rifles. The swaying double shape becomes clearer.

'It's them!'

One of the shadows has a large white bandage around his head.

'One of them's wounded! It's Volpatte!'

We run towards the ghosts. The soles of our boots make a sound of gluey sticking and unsticking and our cartridges rattle in the cartridge belts as we shake them.

The two men stop and wait until we are within hailing distance.

'About time!' yells Volpatte.

'You wounded, old chap?'

'What?' he asks.

He has become deaf with the thick roll of bandages around his head. You have to shout for him to hear you. We walk towards him, shouting. Now he does answer:

'It's nothing . . . We've been in the hole where the 5th Battalion put us on Thursday.'

'You've been there ever since?' Farfadet shouts, his sharp, almost feminine voice easily penetrating the wrapping around Volpatte's ears.

'We stayed there, of course we did,' says Fouillade. 'Bugger it all, for Christ's sake! You don't think we'd fly away do you, and still less that we'd take to our heels, without orders?'

Both of them sink down on the ground. Volpatte's head, wrapped in bandages with a large knot on top and the yellowish-blackish shape of his face, looks like a parcel of dirty washing.

'We forgot you, you poor things!'

'I'll say you did!' Fouillade shouts. 'I'll say you bloody forgot us! Four days and four nights in a shell hole with bullets flying all round us and, to top it all, the place smelt of shit.'

'You bet,' says Volpatte. 'It wasn't no ordinary listening post where people come and go regular. It were some shell hole just like any other shell hole, no more, no less. On Thursday, they told us: "Take up position there and keep firing" – that's what they said. Next day there was some bloke from liaison in the 5th Battalion who stuck his nose

49

over and said: "What're you doing there?" "Why, we're firing, 'cos we were told to fire," says we. "Since that's what we was told, there must be some reason for it. We're waiting for someone to tell us to stop firing and do something else." The bloke took off. He didn't seem too sure about it and didn't look up to another shelling. "Watch yerselves," he said.'

'All we had,' says Fouillade, 'for the two of us, old chap, was a bran loaf and a pitcher of wine that the 18th gave us when they put us there, plus a whole box of cartridges. We fired off the cartridges and drank the plonk – though we sensibly kept a few cartridges and a crust of the fruitcake, but we didn't keep any wine.'

'Bad move,' said Volpatte, 'seeing how thirsty we've got. I don't suppose you blokes have something to wet the whistle?'

'I've got a little drop of wine,' said Farfadet.

'Give it to him,' said Fouillade, nodding towards Volpatte. 'Since he's lost some blood. I'm just thirsty.'

Volpatte was shivering and his little slanting eyes were burning with fever in the huge layer of bandages resting on his shoulders.

'That's good!' he said, drinking.

'And what's more,' he added, while tossing away the drop of wine at the bottom of Farfadet's mug, as a gesture of politeness, 'we bagged a couple of Huns. They were crawling about the field and fell into our hole without seeing it, like moles into a snare, the idiots. We tied them up. And that's it. After firing for thirty-six hours, we had no ammo left. So we filled the magazines of our pistols with the last of the cartridges and waited, with these parcelled up Boche in front of us. The liaison chappie forgot to tell anyone that we were there and you in the 6th forgot to ask after us and the 18th forgot us as well and since we weren't in a busy listening post where they relieve you regular, like they do at HQ, I could see us staying there until the regiment came back. In the end it was some lazy buggers from the 204th who'd come to rummage around for fuses who reported that we were there. So we were given the order to fall back at once. We got our kit on, having a good laugh about that "at once". We untied the legs of the Boche and took them along, handed them over to the 204th, and here we are.

'On the way we even picked up a sergeant who was crouched in a hole and didn't dare come out, seeing he was shell-shocked and that. We gave him a good telling off, which stirred him up a bit. He thanked us for it. His name was Sergeant Sacerdoce.'

'But what about your wound, mate?'

'It's my ears. A small shell, and a whopper, which blew up right beside me. My head managed to get caught between the blasts, so to speak, but only just. It was a close call and the lugholes got it.'

'You should see it,' said Fouillade. 'It's disgusting: the two ears are hanging off. We had our two packets of bandages and the stretcher-bearers gave us another. That means he's got three bandages round his nut.'

'Give us your things, we're going back.'

Farfadet and I share out Volpatte's load. Fouillade, sullen and thirsty, with the dryness burning his throat, grumbles and insists on keeping his weapons and pack.

Off we go, slowly. It's always fun not to be marching in ranks – and so rare that we feel surprised and better for it. Very soon all four of us are cheered by a breath of freedom. We're walking through the countryside, as if out on a ramble.

'We're hikers!' says Volpatte, proudly.

When we get to the bend at the top of the hill he starts indulging in pleasant thoughts.

'It's a great wound, old man. It means I'll be evacuated, no doubt about it.'

His eyes are shining and glinting inside the huge white ball swaying above his shoulders, reddish on either side where the ears are.

We hear ten o'clock strike from the village in the valley.

'I don't give a sod for the time,' Volpatte says. 'Time doesn't matter to me any longer.'

He is getting talkative. A little fever drives his talk forwards at the rhythm of his slow walk, which is already an amble.

'They'll stick a red label on my coat and send me back, make no mistake. There'll be some really polite bloke to lead me along this time, saying: "This way, then turn here . . . Ah, you poor old chap!" Then the ambulance and the hospital train with the ladies of the Red

Cross pampering you all the way as they did Crapelet Jules, then hospital at the base. There'll be beds with white sheets, a stove in the middle of us roaring away and blokes whose job is to look after you while you just sit and watch. Then there'll be regulation slippers, my old mate, and a bedside table – furniture! And in those big hospitals, you wouldn't believe how well you eat. I'll have these fantastic meals and take baths; I'll enjoy everything there is. And little treats without having to fight for them tooth and nail. I'll have my two hands on the sheets doing nothing, like luxury items – like toys, huh? – and under the sheets my legs will be warm as toast from top to bottom and my tootsies blossoming like violets . . .'

Volpatte stops, feels in his pockets and takes out his famous pair of Soissons scissors, together with something that he shows me.

'Have you seen this?'

It's a photograph of his wife and two boys. He's shown it to me a dozen times already. I look and nod approvingly.

'I'll go on convalescence,' Volpatte is saying, 'and while my ears are sticking back on, my old lady and the kids will watch me and I'll watch them. And all the while they'll be sprouting up like lettuces and the war will be going on . . . The Russians . . . Well, no one knows, do they?'

He mumbles on, consoling himself with his happy thoughts, thinking aloud, already apart from us, enjoying his private celebration.

'You bandit!' Fouillade shouts at him. 'You're too bloody lucky, you bastard!'

How can we avoid envying him? He's off for one, two or three months, and all that time, instead of being cold and miserable, he will be transformed into a gentleman of leisure!

'At the beginning,' Farfadet says, 'I thought it odd when I heard people say they wanted a "good wound". But all the same, whatever you say, I understand now that after all it's the only thing a poor soldier can hope for that isn't totally mad.'

We were approaching the village, just rounding the wood.

Suddenly, at the corner of the wood, a woman's silhouette appeared, the sun's rays surrounding her with light. She was standing at the edge of the trees which made a background of violet-coloured hatching, slim, her head lit up with its blonde hair. And, in her pale face, you could see the dark shapes of her huge eyes. This shining image stared at us, her legs trembling, then suddenly plunged into the undergrowth like a burning torch.

Volpatte was impressed both by the apparition and its disappearance. He lost the thread of what he was saying:

'That woman was a doe!'

'No,' Fouillade said, not quite catching this. 'She's called Eudoxie. I know her 'cos I've seen her before. She's a refugee. Don't know where she's from, but she lives in Gamblin, with a family.'

'She's slender and beautiful,' Volpatte remarked. 'You'd like a nibble at that one. Good enough to eat, a real chick. And what about those eyes!'

'She's odd,' says Fouillade. 'Never in one place. You see her here, with that blonde hair on her, then, shoo! There's no one there! And she doesn't understand danger, you know. Sometimes she wanders around almost in the front line. She's even been seen in no man's land. She's a rum one.'

'Look, there she is again! A real apparition! She keeps looking at us. D'you think she's interested?'

This time the shape, brightly outlined, was lighting up the other end of the copse.

'Women? They don't bother me,' said Volpatte, entirely taken up with the idea of evacuation.

'There's one person in the squad who's really got the hots for her anyway. Look: talk about a wolf . . .'

'You can see the tail . . .'

'Not yet, but almost . . . Look!'

We saw Lamuse, like a red boar, his muzzle pointing as he emerged from a clump of bushes to our right . . . He was stalking the woman. He spotted her, crouched and then, scenting his prey, pounced. But as he headed towards her he came upon us.

When he recognized Volpatte and Fouillade, big Lamuse shouted for joy. For the time being, all that concerned him was to take the packs, rifles and haversacks.

'Give me that lot! I'm rested. Come on, let me take it.'

He wanted to carry everything. Farfadet and I were happy to get rid of Volpatte's gear and Fouillade, who had no strength left, agreed to let go of his packs and his rifle.

Lamuse became a walking heap. He vanished beneath the vast, awkward bundle and, bent double, could only take small forward steps.

But you could feel that he was still prey to his *idée fixe*. He kept looking to the side. He was looking for the woman he had been following.

Every time that he stopped to adjust his burden, catch his breath or wipe away the greasy sweat from his brow, he would take a sly look around and stare towards the edge of the wood. But he did not see her again.

I did. And this time I had the impression that she was after one of us.

She half emerged over on our left from the green shade of the undergrowth. Steadying herself with one hand against a branch, she was leaning forward and showing her dark eyes and her pale face which, brightly lit on one side, seemed to be carrying a crescent moon. I saw, too, that she was smiling.

And following her eyes, which were directed, I noticed, a little to the rear of us, I saw Farfadet, also smiling.

This is how I learned of the understanding between this lithe, delicate gypsy, who was not like anyone else, and Farfadet who stood out among all of us, slender, pliant and sensitive as a lilac . . . Of course!

Lamuse saw nothing, blinded as he was and squashed beneath the things that he had taken off Farfadet and me, carefully trying to balance his load and watching where he put his dreadfully over-weighted feet.

However, he seems unhappy. He is moaning and groaning under the pressure of some heavy burden on his mind. It is as though I can hear his heart beating and thumping in the hoarse sounds of breathing from his chest. When I think of Volpatte helmeted with bandages, next to the powerful, sinewy man, in the depths of whose being is this eternal yearning, its pain so sharp that only he can know it . . . then I ask myself which is the more seriously wounded of the two . . .

At last we reach the village.

'We'll get a drink,' says Fouillade.

'I'm going to be evacuated,' says Volpatte.

And Lamuse goes: 'Ugh! Ugh!'

Our comrades cry out and run across, gathering on the little square which has a church with two towers so badly mutilated by a shell that you can no longer look it in the face.

5
Sanctuary

The pallid road that rises through the middle of the wood at night is strangely cluttered, and obstructed by shadows. It is as though, through some enchantment, the forest has broken away and is rolling along in the depths of the night. This is the regiment, on the march, looking for a new billet.

The heavy ranks of shadows, laden upwards and across, are jostling against one another, blindly. Each wave, driven forward by the one behind, comes up against the one in front. To the side, detached from the rest, the slender ghosts of the NCOs advance. A dull noise, composed of a mixture of exclamations, fragments of conversations, orders, coughs and songs, rises from this dense throng, held in between the embankments. The tumult of voices is accompanied by the drumming of feet, the clinking of bayonet cases, metal cans and cups, and by the rumbling and groaning of sixty vehicles in the fighting convoy and the regimental convoy that are following the two battalions. And this is the mass trudging along and spreading across the rising road where, despite the infinite dome of night, we are drenched in the odour of a lion's den.

From the ranks you can see nothing; sometimes, when your nose goes up because of a stir going through the throng, you are obliged to note the white of a mess tin, the blue steel of a helmet or the black steel of a rifle. At other times, in the dazzling stream of sparks from a tinderbox or the red flame bursting from the lilliputian stem of a match, you notice the outline of the irregular ranks of shoulders and helmets swaying like waves against the massiveness of the dark, beyond the nearer, brighter relief of hands and faces. Then all the lights go out and, while his legs take one step after another, each marching man's eyes are endlessly fixed on the spot which he assumes is the back of the man in front.

After several halts when we let ourselves drop on to our packs, next to the stacks of rifles – which we set up, at the sound of a whistle, with feverish haste and agonizing slowness, because of our blindness in this inky dark – there is a hint of dawn, which then spreads and captures the sky. The walls of darkness crumble, in confusion. Once again we take in the grandiose spectacle of day breaking over the eternally wandering horde that we are.

We are finally emerging from this night march, apparently passing through concentric cycles of less intense blackness, then half-light and finally a dreary haze. Our legs have a wooden stiffness, our backs are numb, our shoulders bruised. Our faces remain grey and black, as though barely emerging from the night from which we can never entirely free ourselves nowadays.

The great ordered flock is going to new quarters, this time to rest. What is this place where we will stay for a week? It is called – so they say (but no one is sure of anything) – Gauchin-l'Abbé. Great things are told about it:

'They say it's tops!'

In the ranks of these men, whose shapes and features are becoming distinguishable, their heads and yawning mouths starting to stand out against the background of the dawning day, some voices can be heard in even higher praise:

'There's never been a billet like it. There's the Brigade there and the Court Martial. You can find everything in the shops.'

'If the Brigade is there, it must be good!'

'D'you think we'll find a table for the squad to eat at?'

'Whatever you want, I tell you.'

A prophet of doom shakes his head:

'I don't know what these quarters will be like,' he says, ' 'cos we've never been there. What I do know is that it'll be just like all the rest.'

No one believes him, though, and as we emerge from the tumultuous fever of the night we all feel that we are heading for some kind of promised land, as we march eastwards through the icy air towards this new village with its promise of light.

At daybreak at the bottom of a hill we reach some houses which are still sleeping, wrapped in thick grey mist.

'It's here!'

Phew! We've done twenty-eight kilometres in a night. But what's this? We're not stopping. We carry on past the houses which sink back gradually into their shapeless fog, enshrouding their mystery.

'It seems we've got to carry on for a long way yet. It's way ahead – over there, always over there!'

We march mechanically, our limbs prey to a sort of petrified torpor, our joints crying out – and making us cry out.

Daylight is late arriving. A coat of fog lies across the earth. It is so cold that when we halt, even though they're weighed down with tiredness, the men don't dare sit down but wander backwards and forwards like ghosts in the thick damp. A bitter winter wind lashes us, sweeping away our words and our sighs, dispersing them.

At last the sun breaks through the dank mist around us, moist to the touch. It is as though some magic circle has opened up among the terrestrial clouds.

The regiment stretches, wakes up properly and gently raises its face to greet the gilded silver of the first rays.

Then, quite quickly, the sun starts to blaze and it is too hot. In the ranks we are panting, sweating and grumbling more than we did a while ago, when our teeth were chattering and the mist was wiping its wet sponge over our faces and hands.

The land through which we are marching on this torrid morning is chalk country: 'They make the roads with lime, the bastards!'

The whiteness of the road is blinding, a long dried cloud of chalk and dust rising above the line of marching men and grating on us as we go past.

Faces grow red, shiny and bright, blood-shot faces that seem to be smeared with Vaseline, cheeks and foreheads are covered with a rust-coloured layer that hardens and cracks. Feet lose the vague shape of feet and seem to have been trampling in a builder's cement trough.

Packs and rifles are dusted with white and to right and left our stretched-out crowd is leaving a milky trail along the grass verges.

To cap it all: 'Keep right! A convoy!'

We move to the right, hurriedly, with some pushing and shoving.

A convoy of lorries, a long chain of huge, square vehicles, wrapped in a deafening din, pounds along the road. Curses! As each one goes by it raises the thick carpet of white powder covering the ground and tosses it across our shoulders. Now we are dressed in a transparent grey veil, with white masks on our faces, thicker around the eyebrows, the moustache, the beard and in the furrows. We seem to be at one and the same time ourselves and some peculiar old men.

'When we're old geezers, that's how ugly we'll be,' says Tirette.

'You're spitting chalk,' Biquet remarks.

When we halt we look like a line of statues with some unkempt remnants of humanity showing through the plaster.

We resume our march. No one speaks. We are suffering. Every step becomes hard to take. Faces are contorted in grimaces that become fixed beneath the pale leprosy of dust. The interminable effort cramps us and fills us with dismal weariness and disgust.

At last we can see the oasis towards which we have been marching for so long. Beyond a hill, on another hill, even higher, are slate roofs in clusters of greenery that have the colour of fresh lettuce.

There is the village. We stare at it eagerly. But we are not there yet. For a long time it seems to be retreating as fast as we plod towards it.

At long last, just as midday is striking, we reach this billet which was starting to seem improbable and mythical.

The regiment, at the double with arms shouldered, floods across the street in Gauchin-l'Abbé. Most villages in the Pas-de-Calais have only a single street – but what a street! It is often several kilometres in length. Here, the single main street divides around the town hall and forms two other streets, so that the whole place has the shape of a large Y, with an irregular border of low houses.

Cyclists, officers and orderlies split off from the long, moving mass. Then, in batches, as we move forward, some men disappear through the doors of barns, any proper houses still available being reserved for officers and administration. At first they take our platoon to the end of the village, then – because there's been some mix-up among the quartermasters – back to the other end, the one where we came in.

This coming and going takes time and, in a squadron that has dragged itself in this way from north to south and from south to north, in addition to enormous tiredness and the irritation of walking unnecessarily, we show signs of feverish impatience. It is vital to get settled and dismissed as soon as possible if we are to carry out the plan that we have cherished for a long time: to find a local inhabitant with a place to rent and a table in it where the squad can sit down for its meals. We have talked at length about this matter and its charms. We have agreed, taken a collection and finally decided to take on this additional expense.

But will it be possible? Many places have already been bagged. We are not the only ones to arrive here with this dream of comfort and there will be a dash for the tables . . . Three companies are arriving after ours, but four have come before us and there are the nurses, clerks, drivers, orderlies and so on who have to have their unofficial messes, as well as the official messes for NCOs, the Section and who knows what else. All these folk carry more weight than soldiers of the line, they can move about more easily, they have more money and they can make plans in advance. Already, as we are marching in columns of four towards the barn that has been assigned to the squad, we can see some of these characters on the thresholds of conquered premises, engaged in domestic tasks.

Tirette moos and bleats.

'Here's the stable!'

It's quite a large barn. The chopped straw sends up clouds of dust as we walk on it and smells of piss. But the place is more or less enclosed. We take our places and get out of our equipment.

Those who had dreamed once more of some paradise are once more disillusioned.

'Well, well! It looks no better than anywhere else to me.'

'It's six of one and half a dozen of the other.'

'God knows it is.'

'Of course . . .'

But we mustn't waste time talking. We must make do and get ahead of the others, using our wits, as much and as fast as we can. No time to lose. Though our backs ache and our feet hurt, we are determined on this last effort; our comfort for the week depends on it.

The squad divides into two patrols who set off at the double, one to the right, the other to the left, along the street which is already full of busy *poilus* on the scrounge – and every group keeps an eye on the others, watching . . . and hurrying. In some places, groups clash and jostle one another, with an exchange of invective.

'Let's start at once over there, otherwise we're sunk!'

It seems to me like a kind of desperate battle between all the men in the streets of this village that we have just occupied.

'For us,' Marthereau remarks, 'war is a constant struggle – a battle, on and on!'

We knock on door after door, introducing ourselves shyly, offering ourselves like some piece of goods that no one wants. One of us speaks up:

'You wouldn't have a little space, would you, madame, for some soldiers? We'd pay.'

'No, because I've got some officers . . .' or 'some NCOs . . .' or else 'because this is the mess for the band' – or the clerks, or the mail orderlies, or those gentlemen from the Ambulance Corps . . .

One disappointment after another. Every door in turn is closed on us, after having been half opened and, back outside, we look at one another with a diminishing amount of hope in our eyes.

'God Almighty! We're not going to find anything, you'll see,' says Barque. 'Too many lousy bastards have been here before us. What a load of crap they are!'

The level of the crowd is rising on all sides. The three roads are all filling up, like communicating vessels. We meet some of the locals, old people or disabled men, with club feet or ill-shaped faces, or else young ones concealing the mystery of some hidden disease or friends in high places. Among the women, old ones and a lot of young girls, fat, with plump cheeks and the whiteness of geese.

Suddenly, in a narrow alley between two houses, I have a fleeting vision: a woman crossing between shadows ... It's Eudoxie – Eudoxie, the hind that Lamuse pursued across the countryside, like a faun, the one who appeared on the morning when we were bringing back Volpatte wounded and Fouillade, on the edge of the wood, exchanging a smile with Farfadet.

She is the one I've just seen, in this alleyway, like a ray of sunlight. Then she vanished behind the wall and the place slipped back into the shadows. Is she here already? Has she followed us on our long, painful trek? Something must have attracted her . . .

In fact, she looked as though she was enchanted by something: even though I had only a brief glimpse of her face in its light frame of hair, I saw that it was serious, thoughtful and preoccupied.

Lamuse, just behind me, didn't see her. I said nothing. He will soon be enough aware of this pretty flame that draws his whole being towards it, while avoiding him, like a will-o'-the-wisp. In any case, for the time being we are busy. We absolutely must find the place that we need. We return to the hunt with the energy of despair. Barque is dragging us onward: he has taken it to heart. He is shaking so much that you can see his tuft of hair quiver, powdered with dust. He leads us on, pointing like a dog, suggesting that we make a try at that yellow door across the road. Quick march!

Near the yellow door we meet a figure bent over. It is Blaire, with his foot on the doorstep, hacking away with a knife at the sole of his shoe and knocking lumps off it. He looks like a sculptor.

'You've never had such white feet,' Barque quips.

'No joking,' says Blaire. 'Don't you have any idea where it is, that bloody van?'

He explains: 'I've got to find the dentist's van, for him to fit my dentures and take out the old choppers I've got left. They do say it stops around here, the tooth-puller's van.'

He folds up his penknife, puts it in his pocket and moves off, hugging the wall and haunted by the idea of resurrecting his jaws.

Once again, we deliver our beggar's plea: 'Good morning, madame, I don't suppose you have a little place where we could eat. We'd pay for it, of course, we'd pay . . .'

'No.'

An old bloke raises his curiously flat face in the aquarium light of the low window; it is crisscrossed with parallel lines and looks like an old page of writing . . .

'You've got the little shed over there.'

'There's no room in the shed and anyway, as we do the washing there . . .'

Barque grabs at the opportunity: 'That'll do, probably. Could we see it?'

'We do the washing there,' the woman mutters, as she carries on sweeping the floor.

'You know,' Barque says, with a winning smile, 'we're not the sort of bad-mannered chaps who get drunk and make a mess. Can we have a look, eh?'

The woman has put down her broom. She is scrawny and shapeless. Her dress drops from her shoulders like something on a coat hanger. Her face is unexpressive, fixed, like cardboard. She looks at us, hesitates, then reluctantly shows us to a dingy spot with earth walls, full of dirty linen.

'Magnificent!' Lamuse exclaims, quite sincerely.

'What a sweet little poppet!' Barque says, tapping the round cheek – like painted rubber – of a small girl who is staring at us and showing her dirty little nose out of the shadows. 'Is she yours, madame?'

'And this one?' Marthereau suggests tentatively, noticing an over-ripe baby, its cheek inflated like a bladder with shiny remnants of jam on it attracting the dust. And Marthereau blows an uncertain kiss in the direction of this moist, highly coloured countenance.

The woman does not deign to reply.

We are there, shifting from one foot to the other and giggling, like beggars expecting an answer.

'Let's hope she agrees, the old bitch!' Lamuse whispers to me, flushed with anxiety and desire. 'It's great here and, as you know, everything else has been bagged.'

'There's no table,' the woman says at last.

'Oh, don't worry about the table!' Barque says. 'Look, over there, leaning against the wall there's an old door. That'll do.'

'I hope you're not going to move all my things around and mess it

63

all up,' the cardboard woman answers defensively, clearly regretting that she didn't send us packing straightaway.

'Don't you bother yourself. Look, I'll show you. Come on, Lamuse, old man, give us a hand.'

They put the old door on two barrels while the virago watches with displeasure.

'With a bit of a clean-up,' I say, 'it'll be perfect.'

'Yes ma. We'll brush it down and we won't need a tablecloth.'

Not knowing what to say next she looks at us with hatred.

'We've only got two stools; how many of you are there?'

'Roughly a dozen.'

'A dozen! Christ Jesus!'

'What does it matter – it'll be fine with that plank over there. It's a ready-made bench, isn't it, Lamuse?'

''Course it is,' says Lamuse.

'Now that plank,' the woman goes, 'I need that. Some soldiers who were here before you already tried to take it off me.'

'Ah, but we're not thieves,' Lamuse says, in a moderate tone, so as not to upset this creature who has our comfort in her hands.

'I'm not saying you are; but you know soldiers – they destroy everything. Oh, what a trial this war is!'

'So, then, how much will it be to rent the table and to heat a few things up on the stove?'

'It'll be twenty sous a day,' the hostess declares reluctantly, as though the amount was being extorted from her.

'It's expensive,' says Lamuse.

'That's what the others gave me when they were here, and they were a nice lot, real gentlemen, and they made it worth my while to cook for them. I know it's not hard for soldiers. If you think it's too dear, I'll have no trouble finding others to take the room and the table and the oven – and there won't be twelve of them. They'll be coming all the time and they'll pay even more if I ask them. Twelve!'

'When I said it was expensive I didn't mean we didn't want it,' Lamuse hastens to add. 'It'll do, won't it?'

We give our assent in answer to this purely formal question.

'Why not have a little drink?' says Lamuse. 'Do you sell wine?'

'No, I don't,' the woman answers – adding, with a little tremor of anger: 'You see, the military authorities oblige those who have wine to sell it at fifteen sous. Fifteen! What a trial this accursed war is! We're losing money at fifteen sous, monsieur. So I don't sell wine. I've got wine for us, of course. And I'm not saying that sometimes, to be obliging, I don't part with some of it to people I know, people who understand how things are; but as you may well imagine, gentlemen – not for fifteen sous.'

Lamuse is one of those who understand how things are. He presents the can that always hangs at his belt.

'Give me a litre. How much?'

'It will be twenty-two sous, which is what it cost me. But you see, I'll do it to oblige you because you're soldiers.'

Barque, at the end of his tether, mutters something to himself. The woman gives him a sullen, sidelong glance and makes to give the can back to Lamuse. But he, seeing the opportunity to drink some wine at last and reddening, as though the liquid were already spreading gently across his cheeks, hastens to intervene:

'Don't worry, ma, this is strictly between ourselves. We won't inform on you.'

Not making a move, embittered, she raves on about the price of wine. Overcome by desire, Lamuse takes his abject abandonment of all conscience as far as to say:

'What do you expect, madame – it's the Army! You mustn't try to understand.'

She takes us down to the cellar. Three fat barrels fill the place with their impressive rotundity.

'Your little personal supply, I assume?'

'She knows what's what, the old cow,' Barque grouses.

The shrew swings round angrily:

'You don't expect us to ruin ourselves in this damned war, do you? We lose enough money already on this and that.'

'On what?' Barque asks, probing.

'Anyone can see your money's not at risk.'

'No, we're just risking our lives.'

We step in, disturbed by this discussion taking a turn that might threaten our immediate interests. Meanwhile the door of the cellar starts to shake and a man's voice comes through it, shouting: 'Hey! Palmyre!'

The woman hobbles off, careful to leave the door open.

'That's it!' says Lamuse. 'We've got it.'

'What bastards these people are,' Barque mutters, unable to stomach this behaviour.

'Disgusting and shameful,' says Marthereau.

'Anyone would think this was the first time you'd seen something like that!'

'And you, smileychops,' Barque says, accusingly. 'Sweet as pie while she's pinching our wine: "It's the Army!" Well, you rotter, you don't scare easy.'

'What else could I do or say? Otherwise we'd have had to do without the table and the plonk. Even if she was asking forty sous for her wine, we'd take it, wouldn't we? So we should consider ourselves lucky. I admit, I wasn't sure we were home and dry, so I laid it on a bit thick.'

'I know it's the same everywhere and always, but even so . . .'

'The locals do what they can, no? Some of them have got to make a fortune. We can't all get ourselves killed.'

'Oh, the brave people of the East!'

'Yes, and the brave people of the North!'

'Who welcome us with open arms . . .'

'And open palms . . .'

'I tell you,' Marthereau repeats, 'it's shameful and disgusting.'

'Shut it! The old cow's coming back!'

We went back to the billet to announce our success, then off to the shops. When we got back to our new dining room we were crowded out by preparations for lunch. Barque had gone to supplies and had managed to take direct delivery of the meat and potatoes representing the share of fifteen men of the squad, thanks to his personal relations with the cook – who did not, in principle, favour this division of rations.

He had bought some lard, a little chunk for fourteen sous, so we could make chips. He had also got some peas, four tins of them. Mesnil André's tin of jellied veal would be our hors d'oeuvre.

'Nothing to complain of in that!' said Lamuse in delight.

*

We inspected the kitchen. Barque was happily moving around the cast-iron stove which furnished one side of the room with its hot, steaming mass.

'I've added a saucepan for the soup without telling anyone,' he whispered to me, lifting the lid off it. 'The fire's not very hot. I chucked the meat in there half an hour ago and the water's still clean.'

A moment later we heard him arguing with our hostess. It was all over this additional pot: she didn't have enough room on her stove; we'd told her we'd only need one pan; she believed us; and if she'd known we were going to cause trouble she would never have rented us the room. Barque replied, joking, and being a good-humoured sort managed to calm the monster.

The others came in, one by one. They blinked and rubbed their hands, full of delicious dreams, like the guests at a wedding feast. As they passed from the bright light outside into this dark cube their sight failed, and they stayed for a minute or two, lost, like owls.

'There's not a lot of light,' said Mesnil Joseph.

'Huh! What do you expect, old man?'

The others exclaimed, all together:

'It's bloody brilliant in here.'

You could see their heads nodding in the inky blackness.

One incident: Farfadet accidentally brushed against the soft, dirty wall and it left a large mark on his shoulder, a mark so black that it was visible even in here. Farfadet, who cares about his appearance, grumbled and, trying to avoid any further contact with the wall, bumped into the table and knocked his spoon on the floor. He bent down and felt around on the uneven flooring onto which for years dust and cobwebs had been falling in silence. When he found the spoon, it was sooty black and had cobweb threads dangling from it. Clearly it's a disaster if you let anything drop here. We'll have to take care.

Lamuse puts his hand, greasy as a sausage, down on the table between two places.

'Right! Grub up!'

We eat. The meal is plentiful and of good quality. The murmur of conversation mingles with the sound of emptying bottles and filling jaws. While we are savouring the pleasure of enjoying it sitting down, a shaft of light filters through a small window and brings a dusty dawn to a slice of the air and a corner of the table, reflected on to a knife, the peak of a cap, an eye. Secretly, I am watching a mournful party that is overflowing with merriment.

Biquet is describing how he had to go round begging until he could find a washerwoman ready to do him the favour of washing some linen – but: 'It was dear, damn it!' Tulacque is describing the queue in front of the grocer's: they're not allowed in, so they're stuck outside like sheep.

'And even though you're outside, if you're not happy about it and complain too much, they throw you out of there.'

What else is new? Severe penalties are decreed for any damage caused to local civilians; the report already contains a list of punishments. Volpatte has been evacuated. The boys from the class of '93 are being sent to the rear; this applies to Pépère.

Barque, bringing the chips, announces that our hostess has some soldiers at her table: the machine-gunners' ambulance men.

'They thought they'd got the best, but we're the better off,' says Fouillade confidently as he settles back in this narrow, evil-smelling hole where we are just as cramped in the dark as in a dugout (though no one would dream of making the comparison).

'D'you know,' Pépin says, 'the lads of the 9th are cushy! Some old girl has taken them in for free, on account of how her old man, who died fifty years ago, used to be in the light infantry in his day. It seems she's even given them, for nothing, a bunny rabbit which they're scoffing right now in a stew!'

'There are decent folks everywhere, but the lads of the 9th were bloody lucky to find the very house in the whole village where the decent folks are!'

Palmyre brings the coffee which she has agreed to supply. She softens a little, listens to us and even asks some questions in a haughty manner:

'Why do you call the warrant officer *le juteux*?'

Barque replies sententiously: 'So it always was.'

When she's gone we assess her coffee:

'Look how weak that is! You can see the sugar swimming around at the bottom.'

'She's charging ten sous for it.'

'It's filtered water.'

The door half opens and a beam of light comes in, with the face of a little boy in it. We coax him in like a little cat and give him a piece of chocolate.

'My name's Charlie,' the kid chirrups. 'We live next door. We've got soldiers too. We always have them. We sell them what they want. Only thing is, sometimes they're drunk.'

'I say, kid, come here,' Cocon says, taking the boy between his knees. 'Listen. I expect your dad says: "Hope the war lasts," doesn't he?'

'Sure he does,' says the boy, nodding. ''Cos we're getting rich. He says that by the end of May we'll have earned fifty thousand francs.'

'Fifty thousand francs! It's not true!'

'Yes, it is, it is,' the child says, stamping his foot. 'He says that to Mum. Dad wants it to be like this always. Mum isn't so sure, sometimes, 'cos my brother, Adolphe, is at the front. But we're going to have him sent to the rear and, in that way, the war can go on.'

High-pitched cries from our hosts' apartments interrupt these confidences. Biquet, always on the move, goes to investigate.

'Nothing,' he says when he returns. 'The old man's ticking off the woman because she doesn't know what's what, according to him, because she's put the mustard in a glass and no one ever does that, or so he says.'

We get up and leave the powerful smell of pipe tobacco, wine and stagnant coffee in our cellar. As soon as we emerge a heavy breath of heat wafts across our faces, carrying the scent of frying that inhabits the kitchen and drifts out whenever the door is opened.

We walk through the clouds of flies that gather in black layers on the walls and rise up in black clouds whenever anyone passes.

'It's going to be like last year! Flies outside, lice in.'

'And even more microbes inside.'

Something moves beside the chairs and tables, pots and pans, in one corner of this dirty little house, cluttered with old junk and the dusty relics of past years, full of the cinders of so many extinguished suns: it is an old man with a long bare neck, pink and knotted, which reminds you of the neck of a chicken plucked of its feathers by disease. From the side, he has the face of a chicken, too: no chin, but a long nose. His sunken cheek has a grey tuft of beard and you can see his eyelids, rounded and horny, rising and falling like lids across the smooth beads of his eyes.

Barque has already had a look at him:

'Just watch: he's looking for a treasure. He says there's one somewhere in this hovel – he's father-in-law here. You'll suddenly see him go down on all fours and stick his big snout in every corner. There, just watch.'

The old man proceeded to make a methodical search with the help of his stick, tapping on the bottom of the wall and on the stone floor. He was pushed aside by the other inhabitants of the house as they came and went, as well as by visitors and Palmyre's broom, though she let him get on with what he was doing without saying anything, no doubt thinking to herself that exploiting the national disaster is a treasure that outweighs any imaginary treasure chests.

Two gossiping women are having a confidential chat in low voices, standing in a recess beside an old map of Russia peopled by flies.

'Yes,' one is murmuring, 'but where you have to be careful is with the Picon. If you're too heavy-handed, you won't get your sixteen measures out of a bottle and, in that case, you'll lose out. I'm not saying you'll be out of pocket, no, of course not, but you won't be making what you should. To avoid it, the retailers ought to agree among themselves, but it's so hard to agree, even when it's in everyone's interest.'

Outside, blazing heat, riddled with flies. The creatures, hardly to be seen a few days ago, are multiplying and spreading the buzz of their tiny, innumerable motors. I leave with Lamuse. We're going for a walk. Today, we can relax: it's total rest, after last night's march. We could sleep, of course, but it's much better to take advantage of the rest time to walk around freely. Tomorrow we'll be back on drill and fatigues.

A few people are less lucky than we are and already caught up in the tedious round of fatigues. When Lamuse asks him to come and stroll with us, Corvisart replies with a tap on his little round nose, stuck horizontally like a cork on his long face:

'Can't. I'm on crap duty.'

He shows us the shovel and brush he has to use, bending over in the foul air, alongside the walls, as he carries out his task as crossing-sweeper and lavatory man.

We walk along idly. The afternoon weighs down on the dozing countryside, crushing stomachs richly supplied and dressed with food. Occasionally one of us makes some remark or other.

Someone is shouting in the distance: Barque has fallen victim to a nest of cackling women . . . And the scene is being spied on by a pale-faced little girl, with her hair tied behind her head in a knot of hemp and her mouth dotted with fever spots, as well as a group of women who have settled in a patch of shade by their front doors to engage in some dull laundry work.

Six men go by, with a quartermaster corporal at their head. They are carrying stacks of new greatcoats and bundles of shoes.

Lamuse looks down at his rough and swollen feet:

'I need some boots and no mistake. In no time, you'll be seeing my trotters through these ones. I can't go marching on my bare tootsies, can I?'

An aircraft rumbles. We watch it manoeuvre, heads in the air, necks stretching and eyes watering from the glare of the sky. When our heads come down again, Lamuse says:

'Those contraptions won't ever have any practical use.'

'How can you say that! They've made so much progress, so fast.'

'Yeah, but that's where it'll stop. They won't ever go any further, never.'

I don't argue, for once, against this stubborn denial that ignorance raises, whenever it can, against the promise of progress; I leave my fat comrade in his blinkered illusion that the astonishing efforts of science and industry have suddenly come to a halt with him.

Now that he has started to reveal his inmost thoughts to me, he comes closer and bends down to say:

'You know she's here: Eudoxie?'

'Oh!' I say.

'Yes, old man. You never notice anything, so I've seen' (and he smiles indulgently at me). 'Anyway, you understand; she must've come here because she's interested, no? She followed us because of one of us, that's for sure.'

He carries on: 'Do I have to spell it out, old man? She's come for me.'

'Are you sure of that, old chap?'

'Yes,' the ox says, in a hollow voice. 'Firstly, I want her . . . Then, two times she's crossed my path, you understand, just on my path. You may say that she ran away and I agree, she's shy . . .'

He stopped in the middle of the street and looked at me. His thick face, cheeks and nose moist with fat, was grave. He raised a chubby fist to his carefully trimmed, dark yellow moustache, and stroked it tenderly. Then he continued to pour his heart out to me.

'I want her, but you know I'd gladly marry her too. Her name's Eudoxie Dumail. Before I didn't worry about marrying her, but since I learned her family name it's as though something's changed and I'd gladly do it. Oh, God's truth, how pretty the woman is! And it's not just that she's pretty . . . Oh!'

The big lad was overflowing with sentimentality and a feeling that he wanted to put into words.

'Old man, there are times when I have to hold myself back with a hook,' he insisted, in a gloomy voice, while the blood flooded to his fleshy cheeks and neck. 'She's beautiful, she's . . . And I'm . . . She's so different – I'm sure you've noticed, 'cos you notice things. She's a peasant, yes, but, I don't know, there's something about her which is no worse than a Parisienne, even a smart one in her best clothes, you know? She . . . And I . . .'

He puckered his red brow. He was trying to explain the magnificence of his ideas, but he did not know how to express himself, so he fell silent, alone with his inexpressible feelings, always alone in spite of himself.

We were walking along, next to one another, beside the houses. In front of the doors there were carts laden with casks. The windows overlooking the street were ablaze with many-coloured stacks of tins and bundles of tinder – everything that a soldier has to buy. Almost all these peasants were growing groceries. It had taken some time for trade to get going around here, but now it had taken off and everyone was involved, infected with a passion for numbers and dazzled by multiplying figures.

The bells tolled. A cortège emerged: a military funeral. The coffin draped with a flag was on a cart, led by a *tringlot** from the Supply Corps. Following it was a squad of men, an adjutant, a padre and a civilian.

'A poor little half-arsed burial!' Lamuse said. 'The ambulance is not far off,' he murmured. 'It's emptying, what do you expect? Oh, the dead are happy, but only sometimes, not always. That's it!'

We have walked beyond the last of the houses. In the open country, at the end of the street, the regimental convoy and the fighting convoy have set up camp, with the mobile canteens and jingling carriages that follow them with their jumble of equipment; the Red Cross cars, lorries, forage vans and the post orderly's cab.

The drivers' and guards' tents cluster around the carriages. In between, horses, with their hooves on the empty ground, stare up at the hole of the sky with their metallic eyes. Four *poilus* are setting up a table. The open-air forge is smoking. This diverse, teeming city, planted on the ruined field, its parallel or winding ruts petrifying in the heat, already has a wide fringe of rubbish and dirt.

At the edge of the camp a large white-painted vehicle stands out from the rest by its cleanliness and neatness. It looks like the luxury trailer in the midst of a fairground where you pay more than in the rest.

This is the famous dentist's van that Blaire was looking for.

And there is he, standing in front of it and looking at it. No doubt he has been walking around it for a long time, staring. The divisional hospital orderly, Sambremeuse, is coming back from his shopping and going up the painted wooden stairway that leads to the van door. In his hands he has a tin of biscuits, large size, a loaf of quality bread and a bottle of champagne.

* Member of the army service corps. [trans.]

Blaire calls out to him:

'Hey, there, fat-arse, is this the dentist's van?'

'That's what it's got written on it,' Sambremeuse replies; he's a chubby little man, well-scrubbed and starchy, with a clean-shaven white chin. 'If you can't see that, it's not the dentist you need, but the vet – to improve your eyesight.'

Blaire goes over and examines it.

'It's a rum place,' he says.

He goes nearer still, then further back, uncertain whether to risk his jaw in this van. Finally he makes up his mind, puts his foot on the steps and vanishes into the caravan.

We continue our walk, turning down a path between high hedges sprinkled with dust. The noises fade. The sunlight is blazing everywhere, warming and cooking the sunken path, casting blinding and burning whiteness here and there, and shimmering in the perfect blue sky.

At the first turn we have no sooner heard a light crunch of footsteps than we find ourselves face to face with Eudoxie!

Lamuse gives a dull cry. Perhaps he is once more under the illusion that she has been looking for him, and he believes in some gift of fate. He stumbles heavily towards her.

She looks at him and stops, framed in honeysuckle. Her strangely thin pale face grows anxious and her eyelids flicker over her magnificent eyes. She is bare-headed, her linen blouse cut low at the neck, to the dawning of her flesh. From so close she is really tempting in the sunlight, this woman crowned in gold. The lunar whiteness of her skin attracts and astonishes the eye. Her own eyes sparkle and her teeth are shining in the raw wound of her half-open mouth, red as a heart.

'I say . . . I must tell you,' Lamuse pants. 'I want you so much.'

He puts an arm out towards the precious wayfarer, who stands there, without moving.

Then she shrugs and answers: 'Leave me alone. You disgust me!'

The man's hand grabs one of her little hands. She tries to pull it away and shakes him to let her go. Her bright blonde hair comes loose and ripples like flame. He pulls her towards him. His neck stretches out towards her, his lips too. He is trying to kiss her. He urges to with all his strength, with all his life. He would die to touch her with his mouth.

But she struggles, with a stifled cry. You can see the veins in her neck beat and her pretty face grow ugly with hatred.

I go across and put a hand on my friend's shoulder, but there is no need for me to intervene. Defeated, he steps back and growls.

'Are you mad, by any chance?' Eudoxie shouts.

'No,' the poor man groans, stricken, bemused, bewildered.

'Don't try it again, that's all!' she says.

She sets off, breathless. He doesn't even watch her go, but stays there, beside the place where she was, his arms hanging at his side, cut to the quick with nothing left to beg for.

I lead him off. He follows me, silent but in turmoil, sniffling and breathless as though he had been running for a long time.

He bows his massive head. In the pitiless brilliance of this eternal spring, he is like a poor Cyclops wandering along the antique shores of Sicily, derided and tamed by the luminous force of a child, like some monstrous toy, at the dawn of time.

The itinerant wine-seller, pushing his humpbacked barrel on a wheelbarrow, has sold a few litres to the men on guard. He vanishes round a bend in the road, with his face flat and yellow as a Camembert, his sparse light hair spun into flakes of dust, so thin in his loose trousers that his feet seem to be held on to his body by strings.

Under the swaying, creaking signboard at the far end of the village that serves to announce the name of the place, the bored *poilus* of the guard strike up a conversation about this wandering puppet.

'He's got a right ugly mug,' says Bigornot. 'And, apart from that – don't you agree – they shouldn't let so many of these civilians amble around at the front, willy-nilly, pertic'ly blokes what no one knows the origins of.'

'You're way off there, you louse,' replies Cornet.

'Shut it, flat-face,' Bigornot says, emphatically. 'We're too trusting. I know what I'm saying when I say it.'

'No, you don't,' says Canard. 'Pépère's going to the rear.'

'The women round here,' La Mollette mutters, 'they're ugly enough to put you right off.'

The other men on guard, their gaze roaming intently across the sky, are watching two enemy aircraft and the tangled skein that they are tracing. Around these stiff mechanical birds which, according to the light, look either as black as crows or as white as gulls up in the air, a host of shrapnel bursts are scattered across the heavens like a long train of snowflakes in the fine weather.

We're on our way back when two people walk towards us: Carassus and Cheyssier. They announce that the cook, Pépère, is going to the rear, picked up by the Dalbiez Act,* to join a territorial regiment.

'There's a good idea for Blaire,' Carassus said. He has a large, odd kind of nose in the middle of his face which doesn't suit him.

In the village *poilus* are going past in groups or couples, linked by crisscrossing lines of talk. You see lone figures meet, then separate, then rejoin each other, still full of conversation, attracted to one another like magnets.

An excited crowd. In its midst, the fluttering of white sheets of paper: for two sous the newsvendor is selling the one-sou paper. Fouillade has stopped in the middle of the road, thin as a hare's paw. At the corner of a house Paradis is offering his face, pink as ham, to the sun.

Biquet comes over to us, in undress – jacket and police-cap – licking his chops.

'I met some pals. We had a drink. You see, tomorrow we'll have to get down to it again, first of all cleaning our rags and our catapult. It's going to be hard enough just getting my coat decent. It's not a coat any longer, it's some kind of breastplate lining.'

Montreuil, office clerk, appears suddenly and hails Biquet:

'Hey, kid! You've got a letter. I've been hunting for you for an hour. You're never there, numbskull!'

---

* The Act, passed in August 1914, called for 50,000 specialized metal-workers to be recalled from the front and sent to work in factories. [trans.]

'I can't be in two places at once, fathead. Hand it over.'

He looks at it, weighs it in his hand and announces, tearing open the envelope:

'It's from my old mum.'

We slow down. He reads, tracing the lines with his finger, shaking his head with an air of conviction and moving his lips like an old woman at prayer.

As we get closer to the centre of the village the crowd grows. We salute the commandant and the chaplain who marches beside him, in black, like a nursemaid. Pigeon, Guenon, young Escutenaire and the *chasseur** Clodore greet us. Lamuse appears blind and deaf, as though he had forgotten everything except how to walk.

Bizourne, Chanrion and Roquette dash over, with an important piece of news:

'Do you know? Pépère is going to the rear.'

'Funny how people get things wrong,' Biquet says, looking up from his letter. 'The old girl's worried about me.'

He shows me the passage in his mother's letter: 'When you get this letter,' he reads, spelling out the words, 'no doubt you will be in the mud and the cold, with nothing, wanting for everything, my poor Eugène . . .'

He laughs.

'Ten days ago she wrote that. She couldn't be more wrong. We're not cold, seeing as it's been fine since this morning. We're not miserable, 'cos we've got a room to have our grub in. We have seen some trouble, but we're fine now.'

We get back to the kennel that we've rented, thinking about what he said. The touching simplicity of the remark moves me, because it reveals a soul – a multitude of souls. Because the sun has come out, because we've felt its rays and a kind of comfort, past sufferings no longer exist, nor do the terrible things that the future has in store. 'We're fine now.' That's all there is to say.

Biquet sits down at the table, like a gentleman, to answer the letter. Carefully he sets out and checks the paper, ink and pen, then with

---

* A soldier prepared to be deployed rapidly. [trans.]

a smile extends his large handwriting in regular lines across the little page.

'You'd laugh,' he tells me, 'if you knew what I'm writing here, to the old girl.'

He rereads his letter, savouring it, and smiles.

6
Habits

We are enthroned in the yard.

The fat hen, white as cream cheese, is sitting on her eggs in a basket, near the hut whose proprietor is rummaging around, shut up inside. But the black hen can walk about. She raises her elastic neck, then pulls it back in jerks, and moves forwards with large, mannered steps; you can see her profile, with a bit of straw glinting in it, and her voice seems to be coming out of some metal spring. Shimmering with a black and lustrous sheen, she advances like a gypsy's bonnet and, as she goes, she scatters here and there across the ground her uneven line of chicks.

Instinct breathes on these light little yellow balls, making them all ebb backwards and forwards as they dart beneath her legs with short swift dashes and peck the ground. The line comes to a halt; two chicks in the heap are motionless and thoughtful, ignoring their mother's voice.

'That's a bad sign,' says Paradis. 'A thinking chicken is a sick chicken.'

And he crosses and uncrosses his legs.

Beside him on the bench Volpatte stretches his own legs out, gives a great yawn that he calmly allows to take its time and carries on looking; because of all the men he is the one who most loves to watch poultry, as they hasten to pack as much eating as they can into their short lives.

We observe them together, as well as the bald old cock, worn to a thread, through whose patchy down one can see the rubbery thigh, naked and dark as a grilled cutlet. He goes over to the white broody hen who turns her head away in a curt 'no', giving a few dull, rasping sounds, then observes him with the little blue enamelled watch dials of her eyes.

'We're well off here,' says Barque.

'Look at the little ducks,' Volpatte answers. 'They're killingly funny.'

We see a line of ducklings going past – still little more than eggs on legs – their big heads pulling the scrawny hobbling bodies forward, very fast, by their stringy necks. From his side, the big dog is also watching them with his deep, black, honest eye, across which the sun, lying on him like a scarf, has drawn a tawny ring.

Beyond the farmyard, past the indentations of the low wall, lies the orchard where the rich earth is covered by a thick, damp, green carpet and above it a screen of foliage with a garnish of flowers, some white as statues, the others satiny and many-coloured like bow ties. Further on is the meadow where the shadows of the poplars fall in greenish black and greenish gold; and further still, a square field of standing hops and a square field of cabbages seated in rows. In the sunshine of the air and that of the earth you can hear the bees at their musical work – as the poets say – and the cricket which, despite the fable, sings without humility, his voice alone filling the whole of space.

Over there, whirling out of the peak of a poplar tree is a magpie, half white, half black, like a partly burnt sheet of newspaper.

The soldiers stretch themselves in delight on a stone bench, their eyes nearly shut, enjoying the rays of the sun, which in the bowl of this huge farmyard heats the air up like a bath.

'Seventeen days we've been here! And we thought we'd be leaving from one day to the next!'

'You never do know,' says Paradis, shaking his head and clicking his tongue.

Through the yard gate where it opens on to the road we can see a group of *poilus* strolling along with their noses in the air, taking in the sun, and then, all alone, Tellurure. He is in the middle of the street swinging that expansive belly of his and proceeding on his bandy legs, like two basket handles, spitting at all around him richly and generously.

'To think that we thought we'd be as badly off here as in our other billets. But this time, it's a real rest, both because of how long it lasts and because of what it is.'

'You don't have too much drill or too many fatigues . . .'

'And in the meantime you can come here to put your feet up.'

The old man slumped at the far end of the bench, who was none other than the grandfather of the treasure whom we saw on the day we arrived, came over and wagged a finger.

'When I was young I saw a lot of women,' he said, shaking his head. 'I've been the undoing of a lot of young ladies, I have.'

'Really?' we said, absent-mindedly, our attention distracted from his senile mutterings by the promising sound of a wagon, struggling along fully laden as it went by.

'Nowadays,' the old man was saying, 'I only think about money.'

'Oh, yes . . . that treasure you're looking for, grandad.'

'Of course,' the aged peasant said.

He sensed the incredulity around him and tapped his skull with his forefinger, before pointing at the house.

'Now look at that creature,' he said, indicating vaguely some creepy-crawly running across the plaster. 'What's she saying? She's saying: "I'm the spider what makes Our Lady's thread."'

And the old relic added:

'You mustn't ever judge what you do, 'cos you can't ever judge what happens.'

'Very true,' Paradis agreed, politely.

'He's funny,' Mesnil André muttered, searching for a mirror in his pocket so that he could admire his looks in the flattering sunlight.

'He's nuts,' murmured Barque, ecstatically.

'I'll be going,' said the old man, so anguished by his obsession that he was unable to sit still.

And he got up to carry on searching for his treasure.

He went into the house behind us. As he left the door open we could see into the room where, next to the huge fireplace, a little girl was playing with her doll so intently that Volpatte thought a bit, then said: 'She's right.'

Children's games are serious business. Only grown-ups play.

After watching the animals and strollers go past we watch time passing, we watch everything.

We can see the life of objects, we take part in nature, mixed in with the weather, mixed in with the sky, coloured by the seasons. We have grown attached to this bit of country where, in the midst of our wanderings, fate has kept us longer and more peacefully than anywhere else: this relationship makes us sensitive to all its shades of difference. Already the month of September, August's tomorrow and October's yesterday – and, because of where it stands, the most touching of months – is scattering a few warnings across its sunny days. Already one starts to understand the meaning of those dead leaves that flutter across the flat paving stones like a flock of sparrows.

The truth is that we've grown accustomed to being together, this place and us. We, who have been so many times transplanted, are implanting ourselves here and don't really consider leaving, even when we are talking about it.

'The 11th Division got a whole month and a half's rest,' says Volpatte.

'And what about the 375th? Nine weeks!' Barque adds, irrefutably.

'It's my view that we'll stay here at least as long, at the very least,' I say.

'We could well finish the war here . . .'

Barque gets carried away, almost to the point of believing it.

'After all, it's got to finish some day, hasn't it?'

'It has,' the others agree.

'Of course, you never know,' Paradis adds.

He says it weakly, without much conviction. And yet it is a statement that defies an answer. We repeat it softly, like the chorus of an old lullaby.

Farfadet joined us a little while ago. He has taken up a position near us, but a little apart, sitting on an upturned barrel, with his chin on his hands.

Now, there's a man whose happiness is more solid than ours. We know it, he knows it too; looking up, he cast the same distant gaze over the old man as he set off on his treasure hunt and our group as we talked about not leaving here! A kind of selfish glory shines about our sensitive and sentimental friend which makes him a being apart, gilding him and isolating him from us, despite himself, as though an officer's tabs had descended on him from heaven.

His idyll with Eudoxie has been continuing here; we have proof of that, and he even spoke about it once himself.

She is not far off and they are very close to one another. Didn't I see her going by the other evening, beside the presbytery wall, her hair loosely held in a mantilla, clearly on her way to an assignation – didn't I see her, hurrying, leaning forward, already starting to smile? Even though there is nothing between them yet but promises and assurances, she is his and he is the man that will hold her in his arms.

Apart from which, he is leaving us. He's going to be ordered to the rear, to Brigade Headquarters, where they need a puny specimen who can use a typewriter. It's official, in writing. He is saved – and that dark future, which others dare not contemplate, is clear and definite for him.

He is staring at an open window, one that looks in on the dark hole of some room, over there: he is dazzled by this shadowy room, he is hoping, he sees double. And he is happy, because future happiness, which does not yet exist, is the only kind on this earth that is real.

So a meagre spirit of envy starts to develop around him.

'You never know,' Paradis mutters once again, but with no deeper conviction than on the previous occasions when, in the narrow circumstances of our present life, he has proffered this boundless statement.

7
Embarkation

The next day Barque addressed us:

'I'll tell you how things are. There are some people in ch –'

A savage whistle cut his explanation short on that syllable. We were in a station, on a platform. The previous night we had been dragged from sleep and from the village by an alarm and marched here. Our rest period was over, we were going to a new sector, to be thrown into battle somewhere else. We left Gauchin under cover of night without seeing anything or anybody, without a goodbye glance, without a last impression to take away.

A locomotive was shunting right next to us and screaming with all its might. I saw Barque's mouth, silenced by the roar of this enormous creature, shaping an oath, and I saw the other faces wince, deafened and powerless under their chin-strapped helmets – because we were the sentries in this station.

'After you!' Barque yelled furiously at the whistle with its plume of steam. But the frightful contraption continued imperiously to thrust our words back into our throats, if anything louder than before. When it shut up, leaving its echo ringing in our ears, the thread of what he had been saying was forever broken and Barque simply concluded with a brief: 'Yes.'

So we looked around us.

We were stranded in a sort of town.

Endless lines of coaches, trains of between forty and sixty carriages, looked like rows of houses with identical dark, low façades, separated by side streets. In front of us, running beside the mass of moving houses, was the main line, the street without limits at both ends of which the white rails vanished, swallowed up in the distance. Lengths of train and whole trains were clattering along, displaced and replaced in great horizontal columns. From every direction you could hear the regular hammering of engines on the steel-lined ground, strident whistles, the clang of the warning bell and the loud metallic clash of these cubic monsters adjusting their steel stumps, with a shuddering of chains and a rattling that spread through the long articulated carcass of the train. On the ground floor of the building in the centre of the station, like a town hall, you could hear the rapid tinkle of the telegraph and the telephone, punctuated by bursts of speech. On all sides on the coke-strewn ground were goods sheds, low stores through the doors of which you could see their cluttered interiors, signalmen's cabins, bristling points, water spouts, and pylons in iron lattice work with wires that crossed the sky like music paper. Here and there were signals and, rising into the sky above this dark, flat city, two steam cranes like church steeples.

Further away, in the waste ground and vacant areas around the maze of platforms and sheds, military carts and lorries stood idle and horses were lined up as far as the eye could see.

'What a business it's going to be!'

'The whole army corps starts to entrain this evening.'

'Look, they're beginning to arrive.'

A cloud approached, wrapped around a noisy shuddering of wheels and the clatter of horses' hooves, growing larger in the avenue leading to the station, formed by lines of buildings.

'Some guns have already been loaded up.'

Over there, on flat wagons, between two long pyramids of packing cases, you could indeed make out the silhouette of wheels and the slender beaks of artillery pieces. The cases, guns and wheels were striped and blotched with yellow, brown and green.

'They're camouflaged. In some places even the horses are painted. Look, get a load of that one, yes, the one with the big hooves and what look like trousers? Well, it used to be white, but they changed its colour.'

The horse in question was standing apart from the rest, who seemed to be suspicious of it. It was done out in a greyish yellowish hue, clearly artificial.

'Poor bastard!' Tulacque said.

'See?' said Paradis. 'Not only do they get the old nags killed, they make their lives a misery, too.'

'It's for their own good, isn't it?'

'Yeah? Just like it's for our good, as well!'

With the evening the soldiers started to arrive, coming towards the station from all directions. Deep-voiced NCOs could be seen running along at the head of the lines. Almost everywhere the streams of men were confined and channelled along barriers or inside fenced squares. The men stacked their arms, put down their kitbags and waited, pressed close to one another in the half-light, not allowed to leave their places.

As dusk fell so one incoming throng followed another at an accelerated pace. Along with the troops came motor cars. Soon there was an endless rumbling of limousines, amid a vast tide of small, medium and large lorries. All of them lined up, slotted in and settled down in their designated places. From this ocean of beings, as it broke against the outside of the station and began to seep through in places, arose a vast murmur of voices and various other sounds.

'This here's nothin',' said Cocon, the statistics man. 'Just for the Headquarters Staff there are thirty officers' cars; and you can't imagine,' he added, 'how many trains of fifty carriages each they'll need to fit in the whole army corps – the men and their baggage – not counting the lorries, of course, which will be moving to the new sector under their own steam. Don't even guess, mate. They'll need ninety of them.'

'Shit! And there are thirty-three army corps!'

'Thirty-nine, don't you mean, arsehole?'

The turmoil increases. The station fills and overfills. As far as the eye can see any shape or ghost of a shape, there is hustle and bustle, toing and froing as lively as panic. The whole hierarchy of NCOs is deployed, passing and repassing like meteors, waving arms bedecked with stripes, shouting commands and counter-commands carried by orderlies and cyclists weaving among the throng, the first slow, the latter moving rapidly in and out like fish through water.

Evening has now definitely come. The blobs formed by the uniforms of *poilus* clustered around the stacks of rifles are becoming indistinct and blending into the earth; then the groups are perceptible only by the lights of their pipes and cigarettes. In some places on the edge of the clusters, the uninterrupted succession of little bright dots shines through the darkness like the streamers of lights in a festive street.

Across this confused and stormy expanse voices mingle like the sound of waves breaking on the shore; and, rising above the limitless murmur, are more orders, shouts, cries, all the commotion of loading and unloading, the din of the steam-hammers working away in the shadows and the roar of the locomotive boilers.

In the great dusk, full of men and things, lights start to go on.

There are the flashlights of officers and detachment leaders and the acetylene lamps of cyclists which zigzig backwards and forwards, intensely bright dots with pale areas of resurrected light around them.

An acetylene searchlight comes on, blinding, spreading a cone of daylight around it. Others follow, breaking into the greyness of the world. Now the station assumes a fantastic appearance. Incomprehensible forms rise up and are pasted against the dark blue of the sky. Heaps take shape, huge as the ruins of a city, and one glimpses the end of great lines of things stretching away into the night. You can guess at the vast bulk of sunken masses, the topmost peaks of which rise out of some nameless gulf.

On our left detachments of cavalry and infantry are constantly advancing like a heavy flood. We can hear a confused murmur of voices; some lines stand out in a flash of phosphorescent or red light, and we listen for drawn-out trails of sound.

There are wagons into which artillerymen are leading horses up gangways; you can see their grey shapes and black openings in the flickering smoky flames of torches. There are calls, cries, a frenzied trampling battle and a furious clanking of hooves as some reluctant animal – to the sound of his handler's oaths – kicks against the walls of the van where they have shut him.

Next to that cars are being transported onto flat trucks. People are

milling around some bales of fodder. A scattered crowd tackles huge
piles of bales.

'Three hours we've been on our feet,' Paradis says, with a sigh.

'And who's that?'

In some brief spots of light we can see a band of gnomes surrounded
by fireflies appear and vanish carrying some bizarre implements.

'That's the searchlight section,' says Cocon.

'You're very thoughtful, comrade; what's on your mind?'

'There are four divisions at the moment in the army corps,' Cocon
answers. 'It varies, sometimes there are three, sometimes five. But
just now it's four. And each of our divisions,' the walking statistic,
the glory of our squad, continues, 'consists of three IRs (infantry
regiments), two BCPs (battalions of *chasseurs à pied*) and one TIR
(territorial infantry regiment) not counting the specialist regiments:
artillery, engineers, transport, etc., and without counting the ID (infantry division) Headquarters and the services not attached to a
brigade but directly to the ID. A regiment of the line of three battalions
takes up four trains: one for the HQ, the machine-gunners' company
and the support company, and one for each battalion. Not all the
troops are going to entrain here; they'll board the train at intervals
along the line according to where they are stationed and the dates
they are due to be recalled.'

'I'm tired,' says Tulacque. 'We don't eat enough solid grub, we
don't. We stay on our feet because it's in fashion, but we don't have
strength nor spirit left.'

'I've been making enquiries,' Cocon continued. 'The troops, the
real troops, will only start entraining in the middle of the night. They
are still at their assembly points scattered all over in villages ten
kilometres around. The first to leave will be all the services of the
army corps and the ENE (the *éléments non endivisionnés*, which means
directly attached to the AC),' Cocon obligingly explained.

'You won't find the balloonists or the squadron among the ENEs:
they are too large, so they travel under their own steam with their
staff, their offices and their hospitals. The regiment of *chasseurs* is
another of these ENEs.'

'But there isn't any regiment of *chasseurs*,' Barque said, without thinking. 'They come in battalions. That's why they talk about this or that battalion of *chasseurs*.'

In the darkness, we see Cocon shrug his shoulders, with a contemptuous flash from his spectacles.

'Is that a fact, blockhead? Well, if you had any brains you'd know that there are foot *chasseurs* and horse *chasseurs* – and they're quite different.'

'Damn!' said Barque. 'I forgot the horse ones.'

'You think that's all you forgot?' Cocon goes on. 'The ENEs in the army corps include the corps artillery, which is the central artillery which is additional to the divisional artillery. It includes the HA (heavy artillery), the TA (trench artillery) and the AD (artillery depot), as well as the mobile guns, anti-aircraft batteries and heaven knows what! There are the engineers, the military police – namely, the rozzers on foot and mounted – the sanitary service, the veterinary service, a squadron for the equipment train, a territorial regiment for guards and fatigues at HQ, the army service corps (together with the administrative convoy which is called the ADCO, not AC, so as not to be confused with the army corps).

'You've also got the cattle herd, the repair depot, and so on; the automobile service – now there's a gravy train I could talk to you about for an hour or more if I wanted; the paymaster, who looks after the pay office and the post, the war council, the telegraphists and all the electricity boys. Each of these has its managers, its commandants, its branches and sub-branches, plus a whole tribe of pen-pushers and orderlies and all the rest. You can see all the things the CO of an army corps has round him!'

At this moment we were surrounded by a group of soldiers who, as well as their usual equipment, were carrying boxes and parcels wrapped in paper, struggling along with them and planting them down on the ground with a *phew!*

'These are the staff secretaries, attached to the HQ, that is to say, something like the general's personal staff. When they move, they take with them their files, their tables, their registers and all the nasty little things they need for their scribbles. Look over there: that's a typewriter that those two – the grandad and the little fella – are trundling around with a rifle through the handle of the parcel. They are in three offices and you'll also find the postal section, the chancery, the ACMS (army corps mapmaking section), which distributes maps to the divisions and makes maps and plans on the basis of information from air observers, ground observers and POWs. The staff of the army corps is made up of the officers of all the departments, under a chief and his aide – both colonels. But the HQ proper, which also includes orderlies, cooks, storemen, workers, electricians, gendarmes and escort riders, is commanded by a commandant.'

At that moment we received a terrible collective shove.

'Hey, watch it! Move over!' shouted a man, by way of apology, as with the help of several others he was pushing a trolley towards the railway carriages.

It was hard work. The ground sloped upwards and as soon as they stopped leaning against it and clinging to the wheels, the trolley started to roll back. The dark shapes of the men pressed against it, grinding and groaning, as though on some monster in the heart of the dark.

Barque, rubbing his back, calls out to one of the frenzied toilers: 'Think you can manage, old man?'

'God in heaven!' the soldier grunts, concentrating on what he is doing. 'Watch that paving stone! You'll wreck my cart!'

With a sudden movement he pushes Barque again, and this time starts to insult him: 'What are you doing there, you shit-heap?'

'Hang on! Have you been drinking?' Barque snaps back. 'Why am I here? That's a good one! I won't forget that, you lousy bastards!'

'Out of the way!' cries a new voice, at the head of some men bent beneath variegated but equally crushing burdens.

There's nowhere for us to go: we're in the way wherever we are. We move forwards, split up, go backwards in all this crowd and confusion.

'And as well as that,' Cocon continues, impassive as a professor, 'there are the divisions, each of which is organized more or less like an army corps.'

'Yes, we know. Give it a miss!'

'It's making a hell of a fuss, that four-legged brute in his stable on wheels,' says Paradis. 'It must be a right pain in the arse.'

'I'll bet that's the major's brat of a horse, the one the vet said was a calf in process of becoming a cow.'

'It's well organized, whatever you say, you can't deny that,' Lamuse remarks admiringly, thrust aside by a flood of artillerymen carrying boxes.

'True,' Marthereau admits. 'It takes more than a load of blockheads or even a load of dimwits to get all this lot under way ... God Almighty! Look where you're putting your damned boots, you rotten bastard, you blackguard!'

'Talk about chaos! When I moved to Marcoussis with my family we made less fuss about moving. Though I have to say I'm not a fusspot, myself.'

'To transport the whole French front-line army – and I'm not talking about the army in the rear, which is twice as large again, or services like the ambulance corps which costs nine million and takes out seven thousand patients a day ... If you were to transport it in trains of sixty carriages each, setting off continuously every quarter of an hour, it would take forty days and forty nights.'

'Oh!' they say.

It's too much for their imagination; they've lost interest, sickened by the size of the figures. They yawn and, with watery eyes, amid the chaos of galloping, shouts and smoke, neighing, lights and flashes, they follow the awful line of the armoured train in the distance as it crosses the fiery glow on the horizon.

8
Leave

Eudore sat there for a moment, by the well next to the road, before taking the path that led across the fields to the trenches. With one knee in his folded arms, raising his pale face – with no moustache under the nose, only a little flat mark brushed in at each corner of his mouth – he whistled, then yawned in the face of the morning until the tears came.

A *tringlot* – a chap from the army service corps – billeted on the edge of the wood (you could see a line of carts and horses, like a gypsy encampment), attracted by the well, came up with two canvas buckets swinging around at the end of each arm and stopped in front of this unarmed soldier with his bulging bag and his longing for sleep.

'You on leave?'

'Yes,' said Eudore. 'Just going back.'

'Well, old man,' said the *tringlot* as he walked away. 'You've got nothing to complain about, with six days' leave like that under your belt.'

Just as he said it four men were coming down the road, heavy-footed, taking their time, with shoes that were enormous because of the mud, like caricatures of shoes. They stopped like a single man when they saw Eudore.

'There's Eudore! Hey, Eudore! Hey, you old chump, so you're back, are you?' they shouted all at once, hurrying over to him, holding out hands as large as though they had been wearing red woollen gloves.

'Hello there, kids,' said Eudore.

'All well? How's tricks then, old man?'

'Yeah,' said Eudore, 'not so bad.'

'We've been on wine fatigue. We've done our bit. Let's go back together, shall we?'

They carried on down the road along the verge in single file, then set off arm in arm over the field with its grey clay, which made a noise like dough being kneaded as they walked.

'So, you've seen your wife, your little Mariette, since that was the only thing you lived for and you couldn't open your mouth without telling us about her.'

Eudore's pale face winced.

'Yes, I saw my wife all right, but just one short time. There's no way we could do any better. It was bad luck, I must say, but that's how it is.'

'How's that?'

'Well, you know that we live in Villers-l'Abbé, a hamlet of just four houses, on each side of a road. One of the houses is our café and she's managing it – or rather re-managing it, since they stopped chucking shells at the village.

'Well, seeing as I had leave, she asked for a pass to go to Mont-Saint-Eloi where my folks are, and my leave pass was for Mont-Saint-Eloi. See what's coming?

'As she's a clever little girl, like, she asked for her pass well before the date we thought would be the time of my leave. Even so, my time came, so to speak, before she got her pass. Well, I left in spite of that: as you know, you can't risk losing your turn in the company. So I stayed there with the old folks, waiting. I'm very fond of them, but I was sulking even so. They were pleased to see me, and fed up because I was fed up at being with them. What could I do? At the end of the sixth day, at the end of my leave, the day before I left, a young man on a bike – Florence's son – brought me a letter from Mariette, saying that she hadn't yet got her pass.'

'Oh no! Shit!' the others exclaimed.

'So,' Eudore went on, 'there was only one thing to do, which was for me to ask the mayor of Mont-Saint-Eloi so that he could ask the military authorities for me to go myself, at the double, to see her in Villers.'

'That's what you should have done on the first day, not the sixth!'

' 'Course, but I was afraid that our paths wouldn't cross and I'd miss her, given as how, since I got there, I'd been waiting for her and expected to see her at any moment in the doorway. I did what she told me to.'

'So, in the end, did you see her?'

'Just for one day – or, rather, one night,' Eudore replied.

'That's enough!' Lamuse exclaimed, merrily.

'I'll say!' Paradis said, picking up on the idea. 'In a night a bloke like you can get a lot of work done – and even pave the way for more!'

'Yes: you see how tired he looks! You can tell he's been having a rare old time, the good-for-nothing! You wicked old bugger, you!'

Eudore shook his pale serious head under the shower of suggestive remarks.

'Come on, fellows, button it for a minute, would you.'

'Tell us about it, lad.'

'There's nothing to tell,' said Eudore.

'So, you said things weren't so good between you and your folks?'

'I'll say! Even though they tried to make up to me for Mariette with some fine slices of our own ham, and plum brandy, darning my clothes and spoiling me in other little ways . . . I even noticed that they made an effort not to shout at one another as they usually do. But what difference did it make? And I still kept on looking at the door to see if it wouldn't open and change into a woman. So I went to see the mayor and set out yesterday, around half-past two – or fourteen hundred hours, rather, since I'd been counting the time since the day before. And I had just one night's leave to go!

'As we approached, that evening, through the door of the little railway carriage that still runs there on some branch lines I recognized half the countryside, and half I didn't. Here and there I could feel it remake itself and melt inside me as though it was talking to me. Then it shut up. In the end, we got out and the worst of it was that we had to walk to the last station.

'I tell you, old man, I've never known anything like it. For six days it had been raining, six days in which the sky washed the earth and then washed it all over again. The ground was soft, moving under your feet, going into holes and making new ones.'

'Here too. The rain only stopped this morning.'

'Just my luck. There were flooding streams and new ones, wiping out the edges of the fields like lines on paper, and hills that were running with water from top to bottom. There were gusts of wind that suddenly brought rain clouds dashing overhead, lashing our hands, faces and necks.

'One thing I will say: when we did get to the station, on foot, it would have taken a lot of urging to get me to turn round and go back!

'Anyway, when we did get to the village, there was a whole gang of us: other chaps on leave who weren't going to Villers, but had to go through it to get somewhere else. In that way, we joined up: five old comrades who didn't know one another. I couldn't make anything out. They've been hammered worse by the shells over there than here, then there was the rain, and then it was dark.

'I told you there are only four houses in the village. Trouble is, they're some distance from each other. You arrive at the bottom of the hill. I didn't know precisely where I was, and no more did the others – even though they did have some idea of how the land lay, since they came from thereabouts – and all the less, with the rain coming down in bucketloads.

'It was getting impossible to go any faster. We started to run. We went past the Alleux's farm – a sort of stone ghost! That's the first house. Bits of walls like broken columns rising out of the water: the house was shipwrecked, see? The next one, a little further on, was completely drowned.

'Ours is the third. It is by the side of the road at the very top of the slope. We climbed up into the rain which beat against us and was starting to blind us in the darkness – you could feel the cold wetness in your eyes – and to break up our ranks like machine-gun fire.

'The house! I ran towards it like a flash of lightning, like a Moroccan going over the top! Mariette! I saw her in the doorway raising her arms, behind that net curtain of dusk and rain – rain so hard that it was driving her back and keeping her leaning forward between the doorposts like a virgin in a niche. I ran forward as fast as I could, but still thought to make a sign to my comrades to follow. We went inside. Mariette was laughing a little and had tears in her eyes at the sight of me, but was waiting for us to be alone together before she started laughing and crying properly. I told the lads to make themselves at home and sit down, some on the chairs, some on the table.

' "Where are these gentlemen going?" Mariette asked. "We're going to Vauvelles." "Jesus!" she said. "You won't make it. You can't go those miles at night with the roads all broken up and flooding everywhere. Don't even try." "Right then, we'll go tomorrow; it's just a question of where we can spend tonight." "I'll come with you," I said. "To the Ferme du Pendu. They've got plenty of room there. You can have a good snore, then start off at daybreak." "Okay, let's get going."

'Out we go again. What a downpour! We were soaked right through until we couldn't hold any more. The water came in through the soles of your shoes and down your trouser legs, which were sodden and filled right up to the knees. Before we got to Le Pendu, we met a shadow in a great black coat with a lantern. He raised the lantern and you could see some gold braid on his sleeve, then an angry face.

' "What d'you think you're doing here?" the shadow said, stepping back and putting a fist on his hip, while the rain clattered against his hood like hail.

' "These are men on leave going to Vauvelles. They can't be going there tonight, so they want to sleep at the Ferme du Pendu."

' "What are you on about? Sleep here? Are you crazy? This is the police station. I'm the NCO on guard and there are Jerry prisoners in the building. And I'll tell you," he even added: "You'd better make yourselves scarce around here in less than two ticks. Goodnight."

'So we about-turned and started back, staggering around as if we were tipsy, sliding, panting, slithering and splattering each other. One of the boys shouted to me through the rain and the wind: "We'll just come with you as far as your place: since we've nowhere to go, we have the time."

' "Where will you sleep?" "Don't worry, we'll find somewhere for the few hours we've got to spend here." "We'll find somewhere, there's no doubt," I said. "Meanwhile come inside for a moment." "Oh, just a little moment, we won't say no." So Mariette sees all five of us marching back indoors, soaked to the skin. And there we are turning round and round in the little room which is all there is to the house, which is no palace.

' "Excuse me, madame," one of the lads asks. "There isn't by any chance a cellar here?"

' "It's got water in it," goes Mariette. "You can't see the bottom step of the staircase, and it's only got two."

' "Damn," he said, " 'cos I can see there's no attic."

'After a little while longer he gets up and says: " 'Night, old man. We'll be on our way."

' "What, lads, are you going out on a night like this?"

' "Do you think," this bloke says, "that we'd stop you from being with your wife?"

' "But, old chap . . ."

' "There's no but. It's nine o'clock in the evening and you've got to leave before dawn. So, 'night, 'night. You coming, the rest of you?"

' "You bet!" they say. "Goodnight, ladies and gents."

'They go over to the door and open it. Mariette and I looked at each other. We didn't move. Then we looked at each other again and made a dash for them. I caught hold of a bit of coat and she a belt, everything so wet you could wring it out.

' "Never on your life! We're not letting you go. It can't be done."

' "But . . ."

' "No buts," I say, while she locks the door.'

'So what then?' asks Lamuse.

'So, nothing,' replies Eudore. 'We stayed like that, behaving ourselves, all night. Sitting propped up in the corners, yawning, like people watching over a corpse. At first we chatted a little. From time to time someone would say: "Is it still raining?" Then he'd go and look and say: "It's raining." In any case, you could hear it. One fat bloke, with a moustache like a Bulgarian, tried his damnedest not to fall asleep. There were moments when one or two among them were sleeping, but there was always another one yawning and opening an eye, politely, or stretching and half sitting up to make himself more comfortable.

'Mariette and I didn't sleep. We looked at each other, but we were also looking at the rest, who were looking at us. And that's it.

'Then morning came and washed the window's face. I got up to have a look at the weather. The rain hadn't eased off a bit. In the room I could see brown shapes moving and breathing deeply. Mariette's eyes were red from looking at me all night. Between her and me a *poilu* was shivering and filling his pipe.

'There was a knocking on the window. I half opened it. A shape appeared, with a helmet streaming with water, as if carried and driven there by the frightful wind blowing outside that came in with him. He asked: "Eh, there in the café, any chance of getting a cup of coffee?"

' "Coming, sir, coming!" says Mariette.

'She got up out of her chair, still quite numb. She said nothing, took a look at herself in our bit of a mirror, gave her hair a little brush and then the good lass says quite simply: "I'm going to make coffee for everyone."

'When we'd drunk it we all had to go. In any case, there were customers arriving every minute.

' "Hey, lass!" they'd shout, shoving their heads through the half-open window. "Give us a cuppa. No, make that three! Four!" "And two more with them," says another voice.

'We went over to Mariette to say goodbye. They knew that they had got in the bloody way that night, but I could see that they didn't know if it was polite to mention the fact or not to say anything about it.

'The big Macedonian decided he would: "We were a bit of a nuisance for you, weren't we, my girl?"

'He said that to show he knew how to behave.

'Mariette thanked him and held out her hand: "It's nothing, sir. Have a good leave."

'And I hugged her in my arms and kissed her for as long as I could, for a whole half minute. I wasn't happy – damnation, I had some cause – but I was still glad that Mariette didn't want to put the lads outside like dogs in the rain. And I could feel that she thought it was right of me not to do it, either.

' "But that's not all," said one of the men, opening his coat and hunting around in his inside pocket. "That's not all. How much do we owe you for the coffee?"

' "Nothing, since you stayed the night in my house: you're my guests."

' "Oh, madame, not at all!"

'So there we were making all these protests and paying each other compliments! Say what you like, old man, we're just poor buggers, but it was amazing all that polite toing and froing.

' "Right, let's be going, shall we?"

'They were off, one by one. I stayed till last.

'At that moment another passer-by started to bang on the window, yet another dying for a cup of coffee. Mariette leaned out of the open door and shouted: "One moment!"

'Then she took a parcel that she was keeping ready and gave it to me.

' "I bought a ham. It was for the two of us to have for supper, with a bottle of decent wine. But when I saw there were five of you I didn't want to share it with everyone and still less now. Here's the ham, the bread and the wine. You can have them and enjoy them all by yourself, my boy. We've given them quite enough!" she said.

'Poor Mariette,' Eudore sighed. 'It was fifteen months since I'd seen her. And when will I see her again? And will I see her again?

'It was a nice idea of hers. She stuck all that in my kitbag.'

He opened his grey canvas bag.

'Here they are! There's the ham and the bread, and here's the plonk. Well now, since I've got it, d'you know what we're going to do? We're going to share it, aren't we, me old mates?'

9
Mighty Anger

When he got back from his convalescent leave, after two months away, we clustered round him. But he was sullen and taciturn, edging into the corners.

'Come on then, Volpatte! Haven't you got anything to say for yourself? Is that it?'

'Tell us what you saw in hospital and on sickie, you old clot, starting with the day when you left all bandaged up with your head in parentheses. They say you were in the offices, so tell us about it for heaven's sake!'

'I don't want to say a word about my lousy life,' he said at last.

'What? What's he on about?'

'I'm sick of it, that's what I am. People! They turn my stomach, so they do, and you can tell them so!'

'What have they done to you?'

'They're a load of bastards,' said Volpatte.

There he was, looking just as he always did, with his ears stuck back on and his high Mongol cheekbones, stubborn as a mule, in the midst of this circle of inquisitive men trying to get the story out of him. You could feel that deep down he was seething, his mouth shut tight against the bitter silence inside.

In the end the words spilled out. He turned round, towards the rear, and waved his fist towards the infinity of the sky.

'There are too many!' he said, between his grey teeth. 'Too many!'

In his imagination he seemed to be threatening and driving back a rising tide of ghosts.

A short time afterwards we questioned him again. We knew very well that his annoyance would not stay inside and that his savage silence would burst asunder at the first opportunity.

It was in a deep rear trench where we had gathered for a meal after a morning's digging. The rain was coming down in buckets, a flood that muddied and drenched and harried us, and we were standing up to eat, in a line, with no shelter from the open liquid sky. You had to perform acrobatics to keep the bully beef and the bread from the torrents that poured down on all sides and we were finding what shelter we could as we ate, with our hands and our faces under our hoods. The rain clattered down, splashing and streaming across our soft shells of canvas or linen until eventually, at times in frontal attack and at others slyly insinuating itself, it soaked through us and our food. Our feet sank further and further, taking root in the stream running along the bottom of the clayey trench.

A few men were laughing, rain pouring off their moustaches, while others scowled at having to eat bread like a sponge and meat that had been washed over, while at the same time under fire from the raindrops battering their skin through the slightest chink in their thick muddy armour.

Barque, pressing his mess tin to his chest, yelled to Volpatte:

'So, a load of bastards was it you saw there where you were?'

'Give us a f'r'instance,' Blaire shouted through a new squall that lifted his words and scattered them. 'What kind of bastards did you see?'

'There are . . .' Volpatte began. 'And then . . . There are too many of them, for heaven's sake! There are . . .'

He tried to say what there were, but could only repeat: 'Too many.' He was gasping for breath. He gulped down a sodden piece of bread and then threw up a confused lump of the memories that were choking him.

'Are you talking about the shirkers in the rear?'

'You bet I am!'

He had thrown the remains of his bully beef over the parapet and this shout, this sigh, burst out of his mouth like a head of steam.

'Don't get all het up about shirkers, old griper,' Barque advised him, in a bantering tone, but with a hint of bitterness. 'What's the use?'

Crouching and hidden by the fragile and uneven roof of his oilskin hood, as the shining water poured off it, Volpatte held his empty tin out in the rain to clean it and muttered:

'I'm not a complete halfwit; I know quite well that we've got to have some blokes in the rear: I can see we need a few lazybones. But there are too many of them, and the many are always the same, and not the best ones, either!'

Relieved by this announcement which cast a little light over the dark jumble of furies that he had brought back to us, Volpatte spoke in fits and starts through the relentless sheets of rain:

'In the very first little village where they sent me I saw one shitload of them after another, and they started to get my goat. All kinds of services and sub-services, directorates and centres and bureaus and groups. At first, when you're there, every new guy you meet belongs to a different service with a different name. It's enough to drive you potty. I tell you, old man, the bloke that thought up all those names has got to be a bloody genius!

'Well, I got sick to death of it. It blew me away and, try as I may, even when I'm half doing something else, I'm half dreaming about it!

'Let me tell you,' our comrade went on. 'All those buggers ambling around and paper scribbling, done up to the nines in their officers' kepis and greatcoats and their boots – which don't leave any traces, huh? – who eat those delicacies and can stick a tumbler of gut rot down their gullets when they feel like it, take baths twice a day, go to church, smoke like chimneys and tuck up in a feather mattress at night to read the paper . . . And when it's all over they'll be saying: "Oh, yes, I was in the war." '

One thing had struck Volpatte particularly, as it emerged from his confused, angry account:

'All those *poilus*, they don't take their eating-irons and their ration of wine and eat on the hoof. No, they have to be comfy. They'd rather go and settle down with some bint from roundabouts at a table just for them where they can eat their veg while the old cow puts their dishes away in her dresser where she keeps their tins of food and all the other stuff they need to scoff their fill – in a word, they've got all the comforts of wealth and peacetime in that fucking rear of theirs!'

The man standing next to Volpatte shook his head in the torrents of rain pouring down on it and said:

'Good luck to them.'

'I'm not a complete . . .' Volpatte starts saying again.

'Maybe not, but you're not being fair either.'

Volpatte felt insulted by this term. He started and threw back his head in fury, so the rain, which had been waiting for just such an opportunity, slapped into his face.

'Fair? What d'you mean, fair? To those buggers . . .'

'Yes indeed, sir,' said the other man. 'What I say is, you're grousing but you'd leap at the chance to join them, those lazy bastards.'

'Of course I would, but what does that prove, bum-face? For a start, we've been in danger and it'll soon be our turn. It's always the same ones, I tell you, and worse than that, there are some young blokes there who are as strong as oxes and built like all-in wrestlers; and it's worse still because there are too many of them. You see, "too many" – I keep coming back to it because it's the truth.'

'Too many! What do you know about it, you peasant. Do you know what all those services are?'

'I don't know what they are,' said Volpatte, 'but I tell you . . .'

'D'you think it's a doddle running everything in the Army?'

'I don't give a shit, but . . .'

'But you'd like to do it, huh?' muttered his invisible neighbour who, under a hood that was having all the bucketloads in the sky emptied over it, concealed either a great deal of indifference, or else a pitiless desire to wind Volpatte up.

'Don't know how,' Volpatte said simply.

'There are people who know for you,' Barque's sharp voice cut in. 'I knew one of them . . .'

'I've seen one, as well,' Volpatte shouted desperately through the storm. 'Why, not far from the front, God knows the name of the place, where they have the evacuation hospital and an assistant quartermaster's office, that's where I met the rat.'

The wind as it blew over us asked jerkily: 'What's that?'

At that moment there was a lull and the weather allowed Volpatte to get out a few words:

'He guided me round all the jumble at the depot like he was showing me round a fair, even though he was one of the curiosities of the place himself. He took me along the corridors, inside houses and auxiliary barrack rooms. He would open a door with a label on it, show me inside and say: "Get a look at this, and this, look there!" I went round it with him but he didn't come back to the trenches like I did, don't you worry. And he wasn't on his way back from them neither, don't you worry. The first time I saw that rat he was marching calmly across the yard. "Expenses department," he says. So we got chatting. Next day he got himself made orderly, so as not to have to go, seeing like it was his turn to leave since the war started.

'On the doorstep of the room where he'd slept all night in a real bed, he was waxing his boss's boots – a queer customer that one. Lovely yellow pumps he had. There he was sticking polish on them, gilding them, he was, mate. I stopped to take a look and the chap told me his story. Believe me, I don't recall much more of that *Arabian Nights'* tale he told than I do of the history of France and the dates they taught us at school. Not once had he been sent to the front, mate, even though he was class three and built like a side of beef. But he was not going to risk his life or tire himself out or have any of that ugliness of war; that was for other people, not for him, no. He knew that if once he put his foot on the line of fire then all the rest would go too, so he dug all his hooves in to stay in the same place. They'd tried everything to get hold of him, but you wouldn't believe – he'd slipped through the fingers of all the captains and colonels and majors, even though they got mad as hell with him. He told me about it. D'you know how he did it? He just let himself fall. He took on a silly look and did his falling over bit and behaved like a parcel of dirty washing. "I've got this kind of general fatigue," he'd snivel. They didn't know what to do with him and after a while they let him go; everyone spewed him out. There you have it. And he'd change his game according to circumstances, you get me? Sometimes it was his foot that hurt; he was a clever bugger with his feet. As well as that he was up with everything, on to every angle and how to grab every opportunity. Now there's a guy who was in the know. You could see him slipping unobtrusive like into a group at the depot where they were on some cushy number and stay there, always without anyone noticing but really putting himself out to make himself useful. He'd be up at three in the morning to put the kettle on, go to fetch water while the others were eating, in a word, wherever he went – the lousy bastard, the rotten swine – he'd make himself part of the family. He'd do everything to avoid doing anything. To me, he was like a bloke that might have earned an honest hundred francs with all the trouble and toil he put into forging a fifty-franc note. But there you are: he'll save his skin, that one will. At the front he would just be one of the crowd, but he's not that stupid. He doesn't give a damn about those who have to eat their grub off the ground and he'll care even less when they're six feet under it. When they've all finished fighting he'll go back home and tell his friends and neighbours: "Here I am, safe and sound!" And they'll all be pleased because he's a good sort, with a pleasant way about him, bastard as he is, and – here's the idiotic thing – you swallow it, he takes you in, the louse.

'You mustn't think that he's the only customer like that around: there are loads of them in every depot who twist themselves around and cling to their point of departure and say: "I'm not going," and they don't and no one can ever get them as far as the front.'

'This is all stale news,' said Barque. 'We know about it, we all know.'

'And the offices!' Volpatte went on, now launched into his travelogue. 'There are whole houses, streets, districts! All I saw was my little corner of the rear, one dot, and it blew my mind. No, I'd never have thought that in wartime there were so many men sitting on their arses.'

Somewhere, from the line of men, a hand reached out and felt the air.

'It's not pissing down anymore.'

'Then we'll be off, you can bet.'

And, sure enough, there was a shout of: 'Fall in!'

The rain had stopped. We were walking down the long narrow pond lying in the bottom of the trench which, a moment before, had been shaking with the sheets of rain. Volpatte began to mutter again in the clatter of moving men and the squelch of paddling feet. I could hear him as I watched the swinging shoulders in front of me, wrapped in some poor coat, drenched to the bone. It was the police that Volpatte had it in for now.

'The more you turn away from the front, the more of them you see.'

'They're not fighting the same war as we are.'

Tulacque had an old grudge against them.

'Just watch how they make out in a billet to get the best lodgings and the best grub. Then, when their creature comforts are seen to, they'll be out looking for the illegal drinking dens. You can see them at the door of some joint, looking out of the corner of their eye to see if there aren't any *poilus* slipping out, leering left and right, the two-faced sods, and licking the ends of their moustaches.'

'There are some decent ones. Where I come from in the Côte d'Or I know one . . .'

'Belt up!' Tulacque snapped. 'They're all the same. There's not one who can make up for another.'

'Yeah, they're in clover,' said Volpatte. 'But do you think they're happy? Not at all. They're always grousing.' Then he corrected himself: 'Well, I knew one who used to grouse. He got really pissed off with the manual. "There's no sense in learning up the regulations," he'd say. "They change them all the time. Take police duty. Well, you learn up the main lines of the thing, then it turns out it's something else altogether. Ah, when will this lousy war be over?" he'd say.'

'They do what they're told to do, those guys,' suggested Eudore.

'Of course they do. In short, it's not their fault. But for all that, the fact remains that these professional soldiers, who've been pensioned off and given their medals – while us lot, we're just civilians – will have had a bloody funny way of fighting the war.'

'That reminds me of a forester I saw, too,' says Volpatte, 'who grumbled away about all the fatigues they dumped on him. "It's a crying shame," the bloke said, "what they're doing to us. We're former NCOs, soldiers with at least four years' service. Now, I admit, they pay us on a higher scale, that's true, but what about it? We're officials! In HQ, they make us clean up the garbage and take it out. Civilians see the way we're treated and look down on us. And if you dare to complain, they almost talk about sending you to the trenches, like infantry! What'll it do to our position? When we go back to our villages as wardens and keepers after the war – always assuming we do get back from the war – people in the countryside and forests will say: 'Ah! Weren't you the one who was sweeping the streets in X . . . ?' If we're to get back the prestige that we have lost as a result of human injustice and ingratitude, I know," he said, "that we're going to have to report people, and report some more, and report till we're blue in the face, even against the local bigwigs and the rich!" he said.'

'Now me,' said Lamuse, 'I did see a gendarme who was fair. "On the whole," he said, "your gendarme is a sober sort of fellow. But there are always some rotten apples, aren't there? Now it's a fact," he said, "that the gendarme puts the wind up the people and I have to admit, there are some who take advantage of it; and those ones – they're the scum of the gendarmerie – get the landlord to give them a drink or two. If I was chief of police or brigadier, I'd come down on those characters like a ton of bricks," he said, "because public opinion blames the whole force for the misdeeds of one sergeant."'

'One of the worst days of my life,' said Paradis, 'was once when I saluted a gendarme, thinking he was a sub-lieutenant with those white stripes of his. Fortunately – and I say this not to console myself, but because I think there may be some truth in it – fortunately, I don't think he saw me.'

Silence.

'Yeah, of course,' the men muttered. 'But what's to be done? You have to get used to it.'

A bit later when we were sitting beside a wall, with our backs to the stone and our feet dug into the ground, Volpatte continued to offload his impressions:

'I went into one room that was an office in the depot, the accounts office. It was swarming with tables. There were people in there like in a market. Clouds of words. All along the walls on each side and in the middle there were blokes sitting with their stuff spread out in front of them, like old paper merchants. I'd put in a request to be returned to my regiment and they told me: "You take care of it yourself." I came across this sergeant, giving himself airs with his gold pince-nez – specs with a stripe – fresh as a daisy. He was young, but since he had joined up again he had the right not to go to the front. I said: "Sarge!" But he wasn't listening. He was too busy ticking off some clerk. "It's too much, my lad," he was saying. "I've told you a dozen times that you have to send one for action to the squadron commander, provost marshal of the army corps, and one for information, with no signature, but indicating where the signature goes, to the provost of the Amiens Force Publique and the regional centres on your list – in envelopes, naturally, of the general officer commanding in the region. It should be quite simple," he said.

'I stepped back a few paces and waited for him to finish telling the man off. Five minutes later I went over to the sergeant. He said: "My dear chap, I don't have time to bother about you, I've plenty of other things to think about." Sure enough, the idiot, he was having a fit over his typewriter because, he said, he'd forgotten to press down the shift key and instead of underlining the title on the page he'd put a line of 8s all the way through it. So he wasn't listening to anyone, just cursing the Americans, because that's where the typewriter came from.

'After that he started grumbling at some other pen-pusher because, so he said, the man had forgotten to put the ration department, the cattle troop and the administrative convoy of the 328th Division on the form for the distribution of maps.

'Next to him some blockhead was insisting on trying to get more copies off a duplicator than it would take and was sweating blood to make it produce some barely legible ghosts. Others were talking: "Where are the paper clips?" one dandy was saying. And then they wouldn't call things by their right name: "Please could you tell me where the elements billeted at X are?" The elements! What kind of jargon is that?' Volpatte said.

'At the end of the large table where these characters were, the one that I'd gone up to, with the sergeant at the top of it behind a whole mound of papers, rushing around, giving orders – he would have done better to put some order in things – there was one gent doing nothing, just tapping his hand on his blotter. This was the chap in charge of leave and since the big push had started and all leave was cancelled, he hadn't got anything to do. "Great!" he said.

'And that was one table in one room in one department in one depot. I saw others, and still others, and more and more of them. I lost count: it would drive you bananas, I tell you.'

'Were there any long-service stripes?'

'Not too many, but they all have them in the departments in the second line. There are whole collections of veterans' stripes there, flower beds full of 'em.'

'The nicest set of long-service stripes I ever saw,' said Tulacque, 'was on a chauffeur dressed up in cloth that looked like satin, with fresh stripes and an English officer's leathers, even though he was only a private. And he was leaning, with his finger on his cheek, on this gorgeous motor car with mirrors all over it that he was in charge of. You'd have died laughing. Bowing and scraping he was, that fine-feathered rascal.'

'That's just the kind of *poilu* they show you in those ladies' papers, the naughty ones.'

Each man had his own memories, his own verse to contribute to this poem on lead-swingers, and they started to boil over, all talking at once. A babble of voices enveloped us under the miserable little wall where we were heaped up like bundles in the grey, muddy, downtrodden landscape in front of us, sterilized by the rain.

'. . . ordered his clothes from a tailor, not from the quartermaster . . .'

'. . . orderly in the road department, then at the stores, then cyclist in the supply depot of the 11th Group . . .'

'. . . every morning he's got a folder to take round to the quartermaster's, to the firing range, to the bridges department, then in the evening to the AD and the AT. That's it!'

'. . . "when I got back from leave," this orderly used to say, "these women used to cheer us at all the level crossings." "They must've thought you were soldiers," I told him . . .'

'"So!" says I. "You've been called up, then, have you?" says I.

"You bet I have," says he, "since I've been on a lecture tour in America with a team from the ministry. If that's not called up, what is? And apart from that, my friend," he tells me, "I don't pay rent, so I must be called up."'

'And I . . .'

'To sum it all up,' said Volpatte, silencing all this hum of voices with the authority of a traveller who'd just come back from there, 'I saw, in one fell swoop, a whole heap of them at a binge. For two days I was an assistant, like, in the kitchen of one of the army canteens, because they couldn't leave me doing nothing while they waited for my reply to come through, and it took its time, since they'd added a re-request and super-enquiry and, what with comings and goings, it had to stop loads of times at each office.

'In short, I was cookie in that joint. Once, when the chief cook had just got back from leave and was feeling tired, I waited at table. I could hear those people, every time I went into the dining room which was in the *préfecture**** and the heat and light and noise hit me in the face.

'They were all auxiliaries in there, but some among them were from the armed service as well, and they were all exclusively old men, with one or two young ones sitting here and there.

'I started to laugh when one of those clots said: "Better close the shutters, just to be on the safe side." There we were, in a room two hundred kilometres from the front line and this prick was trying to make us think they were in danger from air attack . . .'

'I've got my cousin writing to me,' said Tirloir, hunting through his pockets. 'Yes, here we are, here's what he says: "Dear Adolphe, I've been definitively assigned to Paris as attaché to Guard Room No. 60. So while you're there, I'm in the capital at the mercy of a *Taube*† or a Zeppelin!"'

'Ha ha! Ho!'

The remark causes great hilarity and is savoured like a delicacy.

---

* Main administrative centre of a *département*, region. [trans.]
† Camouflaged observation plane, which the French called 'the invisible aircraft'. The name is derived from the German word for 'dove'. [trans.]

'After that,' Volpatte went on, 'I had an even better laugh while those shirkers had their grub. It wasn't a bad dinner, either: cod, since it was Friday, but done up like a *sole Marguerite* or whatever. And the table talk!'

'They call a bayonet Rosalie, don't they?'

'They do, the halfwits. But what those gents talked about at dinner was mainly about themselves. Each of them, to explain why he wasn't somewhere else, more or less said – even while he was saying something else and eating like an ogre: "I'm ill, I'm weak, look at the wreck I am, I'm gaga." They hunted around for illnesses that they might have that they could give themselves: "I wanted to go to the front, but I've got a hernia, two hernias, three hernias!" Oh, no, that meal! "The orders that talk about sending everybody to the front," one joker was saying. "It's like a comedy," he said. "There's always a last act that sorts out all the to-do in the rest of the play. And the third act here is the paragraph that says *unless otherwise required by the service.*" There was one of them who was saying: "I've got three friends I was counting on to give me a lift up. I tried to contact them and one after the other, after I put in my application, they went and got killed at the front. Would you believe my bad luck!" he said. Another of them was explaining to his neighbour that in his case he'd really like to have gone, but that the MO had put an armlock on him to keep him in the auxiliaries at the depot by force. "Well," he said, "I'm resigned to it. After all, I'll be of more use putting my intelligence in the service of the country than carrying a knapsack." And the bloke next to him said: "Yes," with his cap and the feathers on it. He had agreed to go to Bordeaux just as the Boche were getting close to Paris, when Bordeaux was the smart place to be, but after that he jolly well came back to Paris, saying something like: "I'm of more use to France with my talents and I've really got to preserve them for the country's sake."

'They talked about other people who were there, about the commandant who was starting to be a real pain in the arse and who, the softer he got, the harder he was with them; about a general who made surprise inspections to try and catch people out, but who'd been in bed for a week, very ill: "He's going to die, sure as sure – his condition no longer gives any cause for concern," they said, smoking the fags that society gents sent to the depot to be passed on to the lads at the front. "Y'know," someone said, "dear little Frazy, who's such a lovely boy, a real cherub, finally found an excuse to stay behind: they were asking for men to kill cattle in the slaughterhouse and he got himself taken on just to be safe, even though he's got a law degree and is the son of a solicitor. As for young Frandrin, he managed to be appointed a roadmender." "Him? A roadmender? D'you think they'll keep him there?" "Of course they will," said one of these pricks. "Mending roads takes a long time." '

'Talk about idiots,' muttered Marthereau.

'And they were all jealous, I don't know why, of some bloke called Bourin: "Once upon a time he mixed with the best of Parisian society: he lunched out and dined out, he called on a dozen and a half people a day, he would flutter around drawing rooms from tea-time to dawn. He was indefatigable when it came to leading the dance, organizing a party, going out to the theatre – not to mention outings by motor car, all washed down with champagne. Then the war comes and it turns out he's not capable of sentry duty on a look-out or cutting a bit of wire. He has to keep quiet and stay warm. And then, do you expect him, a Parisian, to go out to the provinces and bury himself in a trench? Never!" "I sympathize," this bloke said. " 'Cos I'm thirty-seven and I've reached an age when I ought to look after myself." And while he was saying that I kept thinking of Dumont, the gamekeeper, who was forty-two, who copped it right next to me on Hill 132, so close in fact that after that load of bullets hit him in the head, my body was left shuddering from the shaking of his.'

'And how did they treat you, these animals?'

'They didn't care much for me, but they tried not to show it. But from time to time, when they couldn't restrain themselves, they gave me a sidelong glance. Most of all they tried not to touch me as I went past, because I was still filthy from the war.

'It did make me a bit sick to be in the middle of all those good-for-nothing twits, but I'd say to myself: "You're only here for a while, Firmin." Only once did I nearly lose my rag and that's when this one guy said: "Later, when we go home – if we go home!" Now that was too much! To say things like that you have to earn the right: it's like a decoration. I don't mind them swinging the lead, but pretending to be in danger when you've taken to your heels before even getting there. And if you could hear them talking about the battle, because they're more in the know than you are when it comes to the big picture and how the war's being fought and afterwards, when you get home – if you get home – you'll be the one in the wrong with that crowd of jokers, with your little truth of what happened.

'Oh, that evening, man! All those heads in the smoke from the gaslights and those people living it up and enjoying life, enjoying some peace! You'd think you were in a play, some kind of a fantasmagoria. There were so many, and more . . . There's a hundred thousand more,' Volpatte concluded, unable to continue.

But these men whose strength and whose lives were paying for the safety of those others were amused by the anger that stifled him, trapping him in a corner and submerging him beneath the spectres of the draft dodgers.

'Just as well he's not telling us about the factory workers who did their apprenticeship in wartime and all those who stayed behind on some pretext of national defence that they rustled up in five secs!' said Tirette. 'He'd be twisting our ears with that until kingdom come.'

'You say there are hundreds of thousands of them, fish-face,' Barque teased him. 'Well, in 1914, don't you know, Millerand, the Minister for War, told Parliament: "There are no draft-dodgers."'

'Millerand!' Volpatte muttered. 'I don't know the man, but if he said that he's a real bastard!'

'Other people can do what they like in their own country, but among us, even in a front-line regiment, there are cushy numbers and unfairnesses.'

'You're always a shirker to someone,' said Bertrand.

'That's true. No matter who you are, there's always, always, someone less of a rascal and someone more of a rascal than you are.'

'All those who don't go into the trenches, or those who don't ever go in the front line, or even those who only go sometimes – they're all shirkers, if you like, and if they only gave stripes to the real soldiers, you'd see how many of them there are.'

'Two hundred and fifty, per regiment of two battalions,' said Cocon.

'There are the orderlies, and a short while ago there were even the adjutant's batmen.'

'Cooks and assistant cooks.'

'Sergeant-majors and quartermaster-sergeants, often as not.'

'Mess corporals and mess fatigues.'

'A few pen-pushers and the colour guard.'

'Baggage-masters.'

'Drivers, workers and all the section, with its NCOs and even the sappers.'

'Cyclists.'

'Not all of them.'

'Almost all the medical corps.'

'Not the stretcher-bearers, of course, because not only do they have a lousy job, but they live with the front-line troops and go over the top with their stretchers; but nurses . . .'

'Almost all padres, especially in the rear, because I must say I've not seen too many padres with knapsacks at the front, have you?'

'No, not a lot. In the newspapers, but not here.'

'They say there were some.'

'Huh!'

'It comes to the same thing. The infantry has a job in this war.'

'There are others who are in the firing line. It's not just us.'

'Yes, it is,' Tulacque snapped. 'It is just us, more or less!'

He added: 'You're going to tell me – I know what you'll say – that the drivers and heavy artillery took a battering at Verdun. That's true, but they still have an easy job compared to us. We're always in the firing line like they were one time (and we even have rifles and grenades, which they don't). The heavy artillery raise rabbits near their dugouts and they were making omelettes for a year and a half. But we're really in danger – and those who are partly in danger or only once, aren't really. If that wasn't so, then everyone would be: the children's nanny who wheels her pram through the streets of Paris would be at risk as well, as there are always the *Taubes* and Zeppelins, as that prick said that our friend was talking about just now.'

'In the first Dardenelles expedition there was a chemist who got wounded by a shell. Don't believe me? But it's true – and an officer with green on his jacket, wounded!'

'It's a matter of chance, as I wrote to Mangouste, driver of a horse for the section who was wounded, but him, it was by a lorry.'

'Why, yes, that's how it is. After all, a bomb might fall on an avenue in Paris or Bordeaux.'

'Yes, you're right. So it's too easy to say: "Let's treat all danger as the same!" But hang on. Since the outbreak there have been some people killed by an unfortunate chance, while among us there are a few who are still alive by a fortunate chance. It's not the same thing, especially since you're a long time dead.'

'Yep!' said Tirette. 'But you're starting to get on my nerves with your stories about shirkers. When you come to something you can't change, the best thing is to see how you can make a fresh start. It reminds me of a former town warden in Cherey where we were last month, who was walking up and down the streets spying out any civilians of military age and who could sniff out a draft-dodger like a bloodhound. So he stops in front of a well-built dame with a moustache and, just looking at the moustache, bawls at her: "And what are you doing not at the front?"'

'As far as I'm concerned,' says Filon, 'I'm not worried about dodgers and shirkers, since it's a waste of time, but when I can't abide them is when they show off. I agree with Volpatte: let them swing the lead if they can, that's only human, as long as they don't come back afterwards and say: "I fought in the war." Now, the regulars, for example . . .'

'That depends on what regulars they are. Those who signed up unconditionally in the infantry I respect, just as I respect those that have got killed; but the volunteers who opt for the clerical jobs or the special services, even heavy artillery – they are starting to get on my wick. You know the kind. The ones who will say, in the polite society where they mix: "I signed up for the war." "Oh, what a splendid thing to do: you defy the machine-guns all alone!" "Yes, Madame la Marquise, that's the sort of chap I am." Pah! Bullshitter!'

'I know one gent who signed up for the aerodromes. He had a lovely uniform: he might as well have joined the Opéra Comique.'

'Yes, but it's always the same old story. He couldn't have come back to the drawing rooms and said: "Here I am! Take a look at a prize volunteer!"'

'What do I mean, "might as well"? He would have done a lot better. Because then at least he'd have been giving people a decent laugh instead of making them snigger at him.'

'They're all a load of fake china that is newly painted and well decorated, with all sorts of decorations, but doesn't go in the fire.'

'If it was just types like that, the Germans would be in Bayonne.'

'When there's a war on you've got to risk your skin, haven't you, Corporal?'

'Yes,' said Bertrand. 'There are times when duty and danger are precisely the same. When your country, and when justice and freedom are in danger, you don't defend them by running for cover. On the contrary, war means deadly peril and sacrifice for everyone, *everyone*: no one is sacred. So you have to go straight at it, right to the end, and not just pretend, wearing some fancy uniform. Services in the rear, which are necessary, should automatically be manned by those who are genuinely infirm or really old.'

'You see, there are too many rich and well-connected people who shouted: "Save France! – and let's start by saving ourselves!" When war was declared, there was a mad rush to get out of it, that's what there was. The strongest succeeded. I noticed, in the little place I come from, that it was above all those who shouted loudest about patriotism before ... In any case – as we were saying before – the worst thing you can do if you do manage to get into a shelter, is to pretend that you've taken a risk. Because those who do really take risks, as I said, deserve to be respected as much as the dead.'

'Then what? It's always the same, old man, you won't change people.'

'Nothing to be done about it. Grumble, complain? Huh, when it comes to complaining, did you ever know Margoulin?'

'Margoulin, that decent sort who was one of us, who they left to die on the Crassier because they thought he was dead?'

'Well, he tried to complain. Every day he was talking about making a complaint about all that stuff to the captain and the commandant, and asking if they couldn't make it a rule that everyone took his turn in the trenches. You could hear him saying after dinner: "I'll say it, as sure as that jug of wine there." And a moment later: "If I don't say it, then there's never a jug of wine there." And when you came back, you heard him again: "Well, that's a jug of wine, eh? You see if I don't say something." In short, he never said a word. Now, you'll tell me: "He got killed." That's true, but before he copped it, he'd had plenty of chance to do it a thousand times if he'd dared.'

'It all pisses me off,' said Blaire, darkly, with a sudden flash of fury.

'As for us, we've seen nothing – since we don't see anything . . . But if we did!'

'Listen to what I'm saying, old man,' said Volpatte. 'Those depots, what they ought to do is channel the Seine, the Garonne, the Rhône and the Loire through them to clean them out. And meanwhile they're living in there and living very well, and they go and grumble calmly every night, every bloody night!'

The soldier fell silent. In the distance he saw those nights that one spends, bent double, trembling with vigilance in the dark, at the bottom of the listening hole which appears all round in silhouette like a broken jawbone every time a shell burst throws its light into the sky.

Cocon said bitterly: 'It doesn't make you keen to die.'

'Yes, it does,' someone remarked placidly. 'Yes, it does . . . Don't exaggerate now, me old kipper.'

10

Argoval

The evening twilight was approaching across the countryside and with it came a noise as soft as a whisper.

In the houses along the village street – a main road dressed up for a few yards as a main street – the rooms, no longer supplied by the light of day, were starting to be lit by lamps and candles, so that the evening emerged from them to go outside: you could see light and dark gradually change place.

On the edge of the village, towards the fields, soldiers wandered without equipment, sniffing the air. We were ending the day in peace. We were enjoying that vague idleness that one appreciates when one is really exhausted. It was fine; we were at the start of our rest and dreaming. The evening light seemed to exaggerate faces before darkening them and our foreheads reflected the serenity around.

Sergeant Suilhard came over and took my arm to lead me away. 'Come on,' he said. 'I want to show you something.'

At the edge of the village were rows upon rows of tall calm trees; we walked alongside them. From time to time, the huge branches chose to make some majestic movement, pushed by the breeze.

Suilhard was in front of me, leading us towards a sunken road that twisted along between banks; on each side there was a tightly packed hedgerow. We walked for a while, surrounded by soft greenery. A last ray of light slanting across the path scattered bright yellow dots among the leaves like golden coins.

'It's pretty,' I said.

He said nothing, but looked to one side. Then he stopped.

'It must be here.'

He made me climb up a little bit of path into a field surrounded by a huge square of tall trees and full of the scent of new-mown hay.

'Look!' I said, seeing the ground. 'It's all been trampled around here. There's been some kind of parade.'

'Come on,' Suilhard said.

He led me into the field, not far from the entrance. There was a group of soldiers, speaking in low voices. My companion pointed.

'There it is,' he said.

A low post, barely a metre high, was standing a few feet from the hedge which at this point consisted of young trees.

'That's where they shot the soldier of the 204th this morning,' he said. 'They set up the stake overnight. They brought the fellow at dawn and it was the men of his squad who killed him. He tried to get out of the trenches. At the relief he stayed behind and quietly went back to the billet. He didn't do anything else. No doubt they wanted to make an example of him.'

We went close to the others who were talking.

'No, not at all,' one of them was saying. 'He wasn't a bandit, he wasn't one of those tough types you sometimes see. We joined up together. He was a bloke like us, no different, a bit of a loafer, that's all. He'd been in the front line since the start, mate, and I never saw him drunk, either.

'You have to admit, unfortunately, that he had a bad record. There were two of them at it, you know. The other one got two years in quod. But Cajard*, because he had a conviction in civilian life, didn't benefit from extenuating circumstances. He did something silly in civvy street when he was drunk.'

'If you look you can see a little blood on the ground,' said one man, leaning over.

'They gave it the full works,' said another. 'The whole ceremony from A to Z, the colonel on horseback, the stripping of rank. Then they tied him to that little post, something you'd tie an animal to. He must have been forced to kneel or sit on the ground with a stake like that.'

---

* I have changed the soldier's name, as well as that of the village. [H.B.]

'It's unbelievable,' a third man said after a pause. 'Except for that thing the sergeant was saying about making an example.'

On the stake, scribbled by the soldiers, were inscriptions and protests. A rough Croix de Guerre, cut out of wood, had been nailed to it and on it were the words: 'To Cajard, called up in August 1914. With the gratitude of his country.'

As I was going back to the billet I saw Volpatte talking, with a crowd around him. He was telling some new story about his stay with the happy folks in the rear.

II

The Dog

The weather was dreadful. Wind and water attacked the passers-by and riddled, flooded and broke up the roads.

Coming back from fatigue I reached our billet on the edge of the village. Through the thick rain, the countryside that morning was a dirty yellow and the sky quite black, slate-coloured. The rainstorm was whipping the drinking trough with rods. Along the walls, figures crouched and shrank along, bent double, shameful, paddling through the water.

Despite the rain, the low temperature and the harsh wind, a group had gathered at the door of the barn where we were lodging. Pressed together, back to back, from a distance the men looked like a huge heaving sponge. Those who could see over the shoulders and past the heads were staring wide-eyed and saying:

'He's got a nerve, that lad!'

'He certainly doesn't have the wind up, I'll say that.'

Then the onlookers scattered, with red noses and drenched faces, in the lashing rain and pinching wind, letting the hands that they had raised up in astonishment fall to their sides, before putting them in their pockets.

In the centre, streaming with rain, stood the object of their curiosity: Fouillade, naked from the waist up, washing himself. Thin as an insect, waving long slender arms, frenzied and agitated, he was soaping and rinsing his head, neck and chest right down to the prominent grill of his ribs. Across his sunken cheek this energetic operation had spread a snowy beard and on the top of his head, a viscous fleece had gathered that was being perforated with little holes by the rain.

As a bucket the man was using three large mess tins that he had filled with water – though there was no telling where he got it, in this village that had none; and since, beneath this universal streaming from the heavens and on the earth, there was nowhere to put anything down, he had tucked his towel into the belt around his trousers after using it and put his soap in his pocket.

Some who had stayed behind were still admiring this heroic defiance of the intemperate weather and kept saying, with a shake of the head:

'It's a sickness, keeping clean like that.'

'You know he's going to get a mention in dispatches, so they say, for that business in the shell hole with Volpatte.'

'Well, he doesn't get them for nothing, his mentions in dispatches.'

Without quite realizing it they mingled the two exploits, the one in the trench and this one now, considering him the hero of the day, while he went on puffing, sniffing, panting, grunting, spitting and trying to dry himself under the shower of rain, in quick movements, as though hoping to take it by surprise. Then, finally, he got dressed.

When he has finished washing, he is cold.

He turns on his heels and takes up his post in the entrance to the barn where we are billeted. The icy wind makes spots and patches on the skin of his long, hollow, sunburned face, bringing tears and scattering them across his cheeks, formerly tanned by the Mistral; his nose too is weeping and dribbling.

Defeated by the constant burning of the wind that catches him on the ears, despite the scarf knotted around his head, and on the shins, despite the yellow leggings wrapped around his cockerel's legs, he goes back inside the barn, but immediately comes back out, rolling his ferocious eyes and muttering: 'Holy bitch!' and 'Thief!' with the accent that burgeons in throats a thousand kilometres from here in that corner of the country from which war drove him.

He remains standing, outside, more out of place than ever in these northern climes. And the wind comes, enters into him and returns with sudden movements, shaking and tossing his slight and fleshless scarecrow figure.

It's almost uninhabitable, by God, the barn they've allocated for us to live in during this rest period. Our refuge is falling down, murky, leaking and narrow as a well. The whole of one half is flooded – you see the rats floating in it – and the men have gathered in the other half. The walls, made of slats held together with dried mud, are broken, split and holed all the way round, with wide openings in the upper part. The night we arrived we blocked those gaps that were within reach as best we could – working through until morning, ramming them with leafy branches and hurdles. But the openings at the top and in the roof continue to gape. And while only a dim, feeble light hangs there the wind, by contrast, manages to burst through and blow from all sides with all its strength, so that the squad is subject to a continual draught.

When we are inside we remain standing, in this miserable half-light, groping around, shivering and moaning.

Fouillade, who has come back again, driven by the cold, now regrets his wash. He has a pain in his back and sides. He wants to do something, but what?

Sit down? No hope. It's too dirty inside there. The ground and the flagstones are covered in mud and the straw put down for us to sleep on is damp through because of the water that gets in and the boots that have wiped themselves on it. In any case, if you sit down, you freeze, and if you lie down on the straw, you are assailed by the smell of manure and nauseated by the whiff of ammonia. Fouillade merely stares at his place and yawns fit to unhinge his long jaw, made longer by a little beard in which, if daylight were really daylight here, you could see white hairs.

'You mustn't imagine,' says Marthereau, 'that our mates and pals are any better or more well off than we are. After supper I went to visit some guy of the 11th, in the farm, near the infirmary. You have to climb over a wall by a ladder that is too short – nearly doing the splits,' Marthereau observed, seeing he's a bit short in the leg. 'And once you're in the chicken run and rabbit hutch you're pushed about on all sides and you keep bumping into people. You don't know where to put a foot. I got out of there, pretty sharpish.'

'Now, me,' said Cocon, 'when we'd finished grub, I tried to go to the blacksmith's for something warm, that you can buy there. Yesterday he was selling coffee, but this morning some coppers came by so he's got the wind up and locked his door.'

Fouillade saw them return with bowed heads and slump down at the foot of their bedding.

Lamuse tried to clean his rifle, but you can't clean a rifle here, even if you sit on the ground near the door and lift up the damp, hard, icy sheet of canvas hanging in front of it like a stalactite; it's too dark.

'And then, my old mate, if you drop a screw, you may as well hang yourself for all the hope you've got of finding it, especially when your hands are numb with cold.'

'I've got some sewing to do, but damn that!'

There's one alternative: you can lie down on the straw, wrap your head in a handkerchief or a towel to keep out the aggressive stench that rises out of the fermenting straw, and sleep. Fouillade, who is not on fatigue or on guard duty today, and is free to do what he likes, decides to do just that. He lights a candle to search through his things, unrolls his scarf and you can see his emaciated form in black silhouette bending and unbending.

'Potato peeling inside there, my little lambs!' a sonorous voice brays from a hooded figure at the door. It's Sergeant Henriot. He's a sharp-eyed fellow and, even as he jokes with crude sympathy, he is supervising the evacuation of the billet so that no one can escape the fatigue. Outside, in the endless rain on the streaming road, are the scattered elements of the second section, which is also being driven to work by the adjutant. The two sections mingle. We walk up the street and up the little hill of clayey soil where the kitchen wagon is smoking.

'Come on, children, let's get down to it. It doesn't take long when everyone does his bit. Now then, what are you grumbling about? It won't get you anywhere.'

Twenty minutes later we go back at the double. In the barn, whatever your hands meet now as you feel around is an object or a body that is soaked and frozen, while an acrid scent of damp animals mingles with the whiff of slurry rising from our bedding.

We gather around the posts holding the barn up and around the lines of water that are falling vertically downwards through the holes in the roof – vague columns with a kind of pedestal of splashes.

'Here they are!' someone shouts.

One after the other two masses block the door, drenched in water which is pouring off them: Lamuse and Barque have been to look for a brazier. Now they are back from the expedition, empty-handed and utterly fed up and vicious: 'There's not a hint of a stove. Apart from which, there's not wood or coal, at any price.'

No fire to be had.

'It was a wrong order, 'cos if I can't get one, nobody can,' says Barque, with a pride supported by a hundred exploits.

We stay still or move slowly around in the little space we have, depressed by so much misery.

'Whose paper's this?'

'Mine,' says Bécuwe.

'What's it say? Damn and blast, you can't read in this light!'

'They now say they've done all that's needed for the soldiers to keep 'em warm in their trenches. They've got all they need: woollens, shirts, stoves, braziers and buckets of coal. That's how it is in them front line trenches.'

'God Almighty!' mutter some of the poor prisoners of the barn, shaking their fists at the emptiness outside and at the newspaper.

But Fouillade is not interested in what they are saying. He has bent his great, bluish Don Quixote body in the darkness and is reaching out with a neck where the veins stand out like violin strings. There is something there on the ground which has caught his eye.

It is Labri, the other squad's dog.

Labri, a sort of mongrel sheepdog with a clipped tail, is lying curled up on a tiny patch of straw dust. Fouillade looks at Labri and Labri looks at him.

Bécuwe comes over and, with that sing-song accent of his from around Lille, says: 'Him's not eatin' 'is grub. There's somethin' wrong with that dog. Now now, Labri, what's up? 'Ere's your biscuits and your meat. Get outside that, then. It's good when it's in your belly. He's not 'appy, somethin's up. One of these fine mornin's, we'll be findin' 'im like that, dead.'

Labri is not lucky. The soldier who has the job of looking after him is hard on him and frequently treats him badly; apart from which, he doesn't care for him. The animal is tied up all day. From time to time he has hopes of a walk when he sees movement around, so he gets up, stretches and wags what is left of his tail. But it's an illusion. He lies down again, pointedly looking past his almost full mess tin.

He is bored; life is a burden to him. He is in as much danger as we are from bullets and shrapnel, but even if he escapes those, he will eventually die here.

Fouillade pats the dog's head with his thin hand, and the dog stares back at him. They have the same look on their faces, with the only difference that one is looking up, the other down.

Fouillade sits down anyway – too bad! – in a corner, his hands protected by the folds of his coat and his long legs bent like a folding bed.

He is thinking, his eyes closed under their bluish lids. He is seeing something again. This is one of those moments when the home that one has left behind assumes in the distance the gentleness of a person; the Hérault, coloured and scented, the streets of Cette. He can see it so well and so nearby that he can hear the sound of the barges on the Canal du Midi and the goods being unloaded in the docks, and the familiar sounds are calling clearly to him.

At the top of the road, where the perfume of thyme and *immortelles* is so strong that it fills your mouth and almost becomes a taste, under the sun, in a good warm breeze, full of scents stirred by the wings of the day, on Mont Saint-Clair, the flowers and greenery flourish around his family home. From there you can see both the Etang de Thau, bottle green, and the sky-blue Mediterranean joined together; and at times you can also glimpse the ghostly silhouette of the Pyrenees against the indigo sky.

This is where he was born, where he grew up, happy and free. He used to play on the red and golden earth; he would even play at soldiers. His round cheeks, now ravaged and scarred, would light up with the eager thrill of wielding a wooden sword ... He opens his eyes, looks around him, shakes his head and yields to regret for a time when he had a pure, exalted, sunny feeling about war and glory.

The man puts his hand in front of his eyes, to hold back his inner vision. Now things are quite different.

It was there, at the same spot, that he met Clémence. That first time she was walking by, glorious in the sunshine. She was carrying a sheaf of straw in her arms and seemed so blonde that beside her head the straw looked brown. The second time she had a friend with her. They both stopped to look at him; he could hear them whispering and turned round towards them. When they realized he was aware of them the two girls fled in a swish of petticoats, laughing like partridges.

There, too, is the place where both of them later set up home. On the front of the house is a vine which he prunes, wearing a straw hat, regardless of the time of year. At the garden gate is the rose bush which he knows well and which uses its thorns only in an attempt to hold him back a little as he goes by.

Will he return to all that? Oh, he has seen too deep into the past not to see the future with horrifying precision! He thinks of how the regiment is decimated at every tour of duty, of all the hard blows he has taken and will take again, and also about illness, exhaustion . . .

He gets up and shakes himself, to throw off what has been and what will be. He falls back into the icy, windswept shadows, among these scattered, uneasy men who are blindly waiting for night to fall; he slips back into the present and continues to shiver.

Two steps of his long legs and he comes across a group of men who, to distract or to console themselves, are talking about food.

'Back home,' someone is saying, 'they make huge loaves, round ones, as big as car wheels, believe me!'

And the man gleefully opens his eyes wide, to see the bread they make where he comes from.

'Where I live,' the poor Southener says, 'feasts go on for so long that the bread which is fresh at the start of the meal is stale by the end!'

'There's a little wine from around us – a little innocent-looking wine . . . Well, my friend, if it's not fifteen degrees that wine, it isn't one!'

Then Fouillade tells us about a red that is almost violet, which takes so well to being diluted that it might have been made for it.

'We have Jurançon,' says a chap from Béarne. 'But the real thing, not what they sell as Jurançon and send up to Paris. As it happens, I know the owner of one of the vineyards.'

'While we're on the subject,' says Fouillade, 'I've got muscats of all kinds at home, and all the colours you can find; you'd think they were samples of silk. Stay with me for a month and I'll give you a different one every day, my lad.'

'There's a feast for you!' said the soldier, gratefully.

Fouillade is quite stirred by these memories of wine, which also remind him of the luminous scent of garlic from his distant table. The emanations of strong red and delicately varied liqueur wines rise to his head in the sad, slow storm raging in the barn.

Suddenly he remembers that there is a cabaret owner who comes from Béziers in the village where we are billeted. Magnac told him: 'Come and see me, comrade, one of these fine mornings and we'll drink some wine from there, you old bugger! I've a few bottles I'd like your opinion about.'

At once this prospect amazes Fouillade. A shudder of pleasure runs through him from one end to the other, as though he had found the answer . . . To drink some wine from the South – and even from his own special South – and drink a lot of it . . . How great it would be to see life in the best of colours again, if only for a day! Ah, yes! He needs wine! He dreams of getting drunk!

Unable to contain himself, he leaves the group of speakers to go immediately and sit down with Magnac.

But on the way out, in the entrance, he runs into Corporal Broyer who is galloping down the street like a pedlar, shouting through every opening: 'On parade!'

The company assembles and forms a square, on the slippery hill where the camp kitchen empties its soot into the rain.

'I'll go for a drink after parade,' Fouillade tells himself.

Filled with this idea he listens absent-mindedly to the report. But however absent-mindedly he listens, he hears the officer say: 'It is absolutely forbidden to leave your billets before seventeen hundred hours and after twenty hours,' and the captain who, without heeding the murmur that runs around the *poilus*, comments on this order from above:

'This is the Headquarters of the Division. As long as you are here, don't show yourselves. Hide. If the general sees you in the street, he will immediately put you on fatigue. He doesn't want to see a soldier. Stay hidden all day in your billets. Do what you like as long as no one sees you – no one!'

And we went back to the barn.

It is two o'clock. Only in three hours' time, when night has completely fallen, will he be able to risk going out without being punished.

Should he sleep meanwhile? Fouillade isn't sleepy; his hope of wine has woken him up. In any case, if he sleeps in daytime he won't sleep at night. No, no! Staying awake at night is worse than a nightmare.

The weather is getting worse. The wind and rain are getting fiercer, inside and out . . .

So what? If one cannot stay still, sit down, lie down, go for a walk or work, then what can one do?

An increasing feeling of misery falls over the group of tired, chilled soldiers, who are itching to do something and really can't think what to do with themselves.

'God in heaven, this is awful!'

The abandoned men shout this as a lamentation, a cry for help.

Then, instinctively, they do the one thing that is possible for them in this world: they stamp up and down to prevent their limbs stiffening and ward off the cold.

Now they have started to walk back and forth very quickly, up and down, in these cramped quarters which can be crossed in three paces, going round in circles, weaving in and out, brushing against one another, leaning forward, their hands in their pockets, tapping their soles on the ground. These creatures, with the wind blowing even on their straw beds, look like a group of urban down-and-outs under a low winter sky, waiting for the door of some charitable institution to open. But no door will open for them, except in four days, one evening when their rest period is over, for them to return to the trenches.

Cocon is crouching alone in a corner. He is eaten up with lice, but weakened by cold and damp. His morale is too low to change his clothes, so he stays there, silent, eaten up . . .

As five o'clock approaches, in spite of everything, Fouillade once more starts to indulge in his dream of wine, and waits, with this light in his soul.

'What time is it? Quarter to five . . . Five to five . . . Off we go!'

He is outside in the darkness. With great lapping skips, he heads towards Magnac's place, towards the generous, loquacious man from Béziers. It is very hard for him to find the door in the darkness and ink-black rain. Dear God, it's not lit! Dear God Almighty, it's closed! The light of a match, which he shelters in his great skinny hand like a lampshade, reveals the fatal notice: 'Out of bounds to troops.' Magnac has committed some breach of the rules and been exiled to darkness and idleness.

Fouillade turns his back on the tavern which has become a prison for the solitary landlord. He has not given up his dream. He will go elsewhere, and have ordinary wine and pay, that's all.

He puts his hand in his pocket to feel his wallet. It's there. He should have one franc eighty-five. It's not a fortune, but . . .

Then suddenly, he jumps and stops dead, banging his hand on his forehead. His long face gives a horrible grimace, concealed by the shadows. No, he hasn't got one franc eighty-five! Silly bugger that he is! He's forgotten the tin of sardines that he bought the day before, so disgusted was he by the macaroni at the mess, and the drinks he bought for the cobbler who put some nails back in his boots. Blast! He can't have more than thirteen sous – sixty-five centimes!

If he wants to give himself the high he needs and take revenge on his present life, he has to get at least a litre and a half, dammit! Here, a litre of red costs twenty-one sous. He's a long way from having enough.

He searches the darkness around him. He is looking for someone. Perhaps there is a mate who will lend him some money or buy him a bottle.

But who? Who? Not Bécuwe, who only has a 'soldier's friend' who sends him some tobacco and writing paper every fortnight. Not Barque, who wouldn't agree, or Blaire who is too mean to understand. Not Biquet, who seems to hold something against him, or Pépin, who is always scrounging himself and doesn't pay back, even when it's his round. Oh, if only Volpatte was here! Of course there is Mesnil André, but Fouillade already happens to be in debt to him for several rounds. Corporal Bertrand? He ticked him off severely after Fouillade had spoken out of turn and now they are not on good terms. Farfadet? He doesn't usually talk to him. And, as for that, why does he bother to search for guardian angels in his imagination, for heaven's sake? Where are all these people when he needs them?

Slowly he walks back towards the billet. Then, mechanically, he turns round and returns hesitantly. He'll have a try, even so. Perhaps, on the spot, some comrades sitting round a table . . . He reaches the central part of the village just as the night has buried the earth.

The lighted doors and windows of the taverns shine across the mud in the main street. There is one every twenty yards. You can glimpse the heavy ghosts of soldiers, most of them in groups, walking down the street. When a car passes they move to the side of the road to let it go by, dazzled by its headlights and spattered by the liquid mud that the wheels splash the full width of the road.

The taverns are full; through the misted glass you can see that they are packed with a solid cloud of helmeted men.

Fouillade goes into one, at random. As soon as he passes the door the warm breath of the boozer, the light, smell and noise touch his soul. This sitting around is, after all, a fragment of the past in the present.

He searches from table to table, pushing forward and disturbing the chairs until he has checked everyone in the room. Ay! He doesn't know any of them.

In the next tavern it's the same story. He's not having any luck. However much he cranes his neck and searches for a familiar head among all these uniforms which, in groups or in couples, are drinking and chatting, or sitting alone and writing . . . He looks like a beggar and no one pays any attention.

Finding no one to come to his assistance he decides to spend at least what he has in his pockct. He slithers over to the counter . . .

'A jug of wine and a good one . . .'

'White?'

'Uh huh.'

'You come from the South, my lad,' says the barmaid, giving him a small full bottle and a glass, while putting his twelve sous in the till.

He sits down at the end of a table already crowded with four drinkers playing a hand of manille. He fills the glass to the brim and empties it, then fills it again.

'Hey there, good health, don't break the glass!' a new arrival barks in his face. The man is dressed in sooty blue fatigues and has a thick band of eyebrows across the middle of his pale face, in a conical head with a half-pound of ears attached.

It's Harlingue, the armourer.

He is not exactly covered with glory, Fouillade, finding himself alone in front of a jug in the presence of a comrade who is showing every sign of thirst. But he pretends not to understand the need of this gent who hovers around in front of him with an engaging smile and quickly empties his glass. The other man turns his back, while muttering that they are 'not too keen on sharing and a bit greedy, these Southerners'.

Fouillade puts his chin on his hands and looks, without seeing it, into a corner of the tavern where the *poilus* are piled together, pressed against one another, pushing and shoving to get past.

As a matter of fact, it was quite nice that little white, but what good are those few drops in the desert of Fouillade? His depression did not go far away and it is back already.

The man from the South gets up and goes, with his two glasses of wine in him and one sou in his purse. He musters the courage to visit one more tavern, look all around it and leave, muttering by way of excuse: 'Sonofabitch! He's never there, the brute!'

Then he goes back to the billet. There are still as many streams and gusts as ever. Fouillade lights his candle and, by the flame that flickers desperately as though trying to fly away, he goes to see Labri.

He crouches down, his little light in his hand, in front of this poor dog which may die before he does. Labri is sleeping, but not deeply, because he opens one eye and wags his tail.

The Cettois strokes him and whispers: 'Nothing to be done, nothing . . .'

He doesn't want to tell Labri any more than that, for fear of making him sad, but the dog agrees, shaking his head, before closing his eyes again.

Fouillade gets up with some discomfort because of his rusty joints, and goes to lie down. Now he only hopes for one thing: to sleep, so that this dreary day will expire, this nothing day, this day like so many to come which he will have to endure heroically, to get by, until he reaches the last day of the war, or of his life.

12
The Doorway

'It's foggy. Do you want to go?'

Poterloo asks me the question, turning his honest blond head towards me, his two clear blue eyes seeming to make it transparent.

Poterloo comes from Souchez, and now that the *chasseurs* have finally retaken Souchez he wants to see the village where he used to live happily, in former times, when he was a man.

It's a dangerous pilgrimage. Not that we are far away: Souchez is just over there. For the past six months we have been living and working in trenches and lines almost within hailing distance of it. All we have to do is climb out of here directly on to the Béthune road, which the trench follows and under which are the honeycombs of our dugouts, then keep on the road for four or five hundred metres as it heads off for Souchez. But all those places are the object of regular and dreadful attention. Since they sank back, the Germans have gone on bombarding us with huge shells, which thunder from time to time, shaking us in our basements, and throwing up great black geysers of earth and rubble, and vertical heaps of smoke as high as churches, visible here and there above the embankments. Why are they bombing Souchez? We don't know. There is nobody and nothing left in the village which has been taken and retaken, grimly disputed between one side and the other.

But this morning, as Poterloo said, we are wrapped in thick fog and, under cover of this great blanket that the sky has cast across the earth, we might risk it . . . At least we are sure not to be seen. The fog has hermetically clamped the perfect retina of the observation balloon that must be somewhere up there, enshrouded in cotton wool, and it has placed its light but opaque wall between our lines and the observation posts at Lens and Angres, from where the enemy spies on us.

'Right-ho,' I tell Poterloo.

Adjutant Barthe is informed and nods his head, with his eyelids down, to show that he is turning a blind eye.

We clamber up out of the trench and here we are, the two of us, on the Béthune road.

This is the first time that I have walked here in daylight. We have only ever seen it from a distance, this terrible road, which we have so often travelled down or crossed in leaps, bent double in the dark, with bullets whistling around us.

'Well, are you coming, old man?'

After walking for a bit Poterloo has stopped in the middle of the road where the cottony fog stretches out in strands, and he is standing with his eyes wide open and his scarlet mouth almost gaping.

'Oh my, oh my!' he is muttering.

As I turn to look at him he indicates the road and says, shaking his head:

'This is it, good Lord – to think that this is it! I know this spot where we are so well that if I close my eyes – or even if I don't – I can see it just as it used to be. It's frightful, old man, to see it like this now. It was a lovely road, with tall trees planted all along it . . . And now what is it? Just look at that: a sort of long thing, broken, sad, sad . . . Take a look at those two trenches on either side, all open, and the pavement ploughed up and pitted with holes . . . These trees, torn up, sawn, blackened, broken into logs, scattered in all directions, riddled with bullets . . . And this sieve here! – Oh, my dear man, you can't imagine how disfigured this road is!'

And he walks forward, looking about him at every step, with fresh amazement.

The truth is that it is fantastic, this road on either side of which two armies have crouched and dug in, across which they have been trading blows for a year and a half. It is a great dishevelled highway, travelled only by bullets and by ranks and rows of shells, which have furrowed it, lifted it up, covered it with soil from the fields, dug it and ploughed it down to the bone. It seems like a passage of the damned, colourless, flayed and aged, sinister and magnificent to look at.

'If only you could have seen it! It was clean and level,' says Poterloo.

'All the trees were there, all the leaves, in every colour, like butterflies, and under them there was always someone to greet as you went by: some good women swaying between two baskets, or people chatting loudly on a cart, with their smocks bellowing out in the wind. Oh, how good life was in the old days!'

He sets off towards the bank of the misty river that follows the road, towards the earthworks of the parapets. He leans over and stops at some vague bulges in the ground on which you can make out crosses – graves, set at intervals in the wall of fog, like the stations of the cross in a church.

I call to him. We won't get there, if we carry on at this funereal pace. *Hurry up!*

We reach the spot, me first with Poterloo lagging behind, his head muddled and heavy with thoughts, vainly trying to exchange a look with the objects around him or with a dip in the ground. Here, the road is lower and hidden by a fold of ground to the north. In this sheltered place there is a bit of traffic.

On a patch of wasteland, dirty and sick, where the dried grass is mired with black mud, the dead are lined up. They are brought here when the trenches and no man's land are emptied during the night. They are waiting – some have done so for a long time – until they are transported, again by night, to the cemeteries in the rear.

We go over to them quietly. They are pressed against one another, each making a different gesture of death with his arms or his legs. Some exhibit half-mouldy faces, their skin rusted or yellow with black spots. Several have faces that have turned completely black, tarred, their lips huge and swollen: Negro heads blown up like balloons. Between two bodies, belonging to either one or the other, is a severed hand with a mass of filaments emerging from the wrist.

Others are shapeless, fouled larvae with vague pieces of equipment or fragments of bone. A little further on a corpse has been brought in in such a state that, to avoid losing it on the way, they had to pile it on a wire rack which was afterwards fixed to the two ends of a stake. He was brought here in this metal hammock and left. You can't tell the top of this corpse from the bottom; all that can be recognized in the pile is a gaping trouser pocket. An insect is going in and out of it.

Around the dead, letters that fell out of their pockets or their ammunition belts when they were being placed here are fluttering around. On one of these plain white scraps of paper, flapping in the breeze but held down by the mud, I can read, if I lean over a little, the sentence: 'Dear Henri, what fine weather for your birthday!' The man is lying on his belly, his back is split from one side to the other, his head is half turned. You can see his hollow eye and a kind of moss that has grown on the temple, the cheek and the neck.

The wind carries a sickening breath around these dead bodies and the heaps of debris close to them: canvas or clothing, in some kind of cloth, stained and stiffened with dried blood, blackened by the burning of shells, hardened, earthy, already rotten, with a layer of living things seething and burrowing on it. It turns our stomachs. We look at one another, shaking our heads and not daring to admit aloud that it smells bad. Yet it is only slowly that we walk away.

Now, through the fog, we can see the bent backs of men who are joined together by something they are carrying. They are stretcher-bearers bringing a new body. They come towards us with their haggard faces, panting, sweating and grimacing with the effort. For two people to carry a dead man in the trenches when it is muddy is an almost superhuman task.

They put down the body which is cleanly dressed.

'It's not long since he was on his feet, this one,' says one of the stretcher-bearers. 'He got his bullet in the head two hours ago when he tried to fetch a German rifle from no man's land. He was off on leave on Wednesday and wanted to take it home. He was a sergeant in the 405th, class of '14. A decent little bloke, too.'

He shows him to us, lifting off the handkerchief covering the face. The man is quite young and seems to be asleep, except that the eyeballs are rolling upwards, his cheeks are waxen and there is a pink liquid around the nostrils, mouth and eyes.

This body, sounding a clean note in the charnel house, has not stiffened yet – when moved it turns its head to one side, as though looking for a more comfortable position – so it gives a childish illusion of being less dead than the others. As it is less disfigured, it seems more pathetic, closer and more attached to whoever is looking at it.

If we were to say anything in front of this whole mass of obliterated beings it would be: 'Poor lad!'

We get back on the road, which from here starts to go down into the dip where you find Souchez. In the whiteness of the fog this road under our feet seems like a terrifying vale of misery. Heaps of rubbish, remains and filth accumulate on the broken spine of its pavings and on its muddy edges, becoming indistinguishable. The trees strew the ground or have vanished, torn up, their stumps shattered. The embankments are turned over or broken by shell bursts. All along either side of the highway, where only the crosses of graves are still standing, are trenches twenty times filled in and dug out again, holes, passages into holes, duckboards on quagmires.

The further we go the more everything appears turned over, terrifying, full of rottenness and smelling of disaster. We are walking on a path paved with shrapnel. Your foot hits a piece of it at every step, it trips you up and you stumble among the jumble of broken weapons, sewing machines, parcels of electric wire, French and German equipment, torn to shreds in their skin of dry mud, and suspect heaps of clothing, stuck together with reddish-brown glue. And you must watch out for unexploded shells, their points sticking out everywhere, or their bottoms or their sides, painted red, blue and brown.

'That's the old Boche trench that they gave up eventually . . .'

In some places it is blocked, in others riddled with mortar holes. The sandbags have been split, gutted, emptied, shaken in the wind; the wooden props have shattered and are sticking out in every direction. The dugouts are filled to the brim with earth and heaven knows what else. It looks like the half-dried bed of a river, smashed, widened and slimy, abandoned by water and by men. At one place the trench has been truly obliterated by cannon fire: the blocked ditch ends and is just a field of fresh earth, with holes placed symmetrically beside one another in length and breadth.

I point out this extraordinary field, where some gigantic plough seems to have passed, to Poterloo. But he is entirely taken up by the change that has taken place in the landscape as a whole.

★

He points towards a space in the plain, with an astonished air, as though emerging from a dream.

'The Cabaret Rouge!'

It's a flat field, paved in broken bricks.

'And what's that?'

A milestone? No, it isn't a milestone. It's a head, a black head, tanned and waxed. The mouth is askew and you can see the moustache bristling on either side: a large, scorched cat's head. The body, a German one, is underneath, buried upright.

'And that?'

It's a sorrowful whole made up of a white skull, then two metres away from it, a pair of boots and between the two, a heap of frayed leather and rags, held together with brownish mud.

'Come on. The fog's thinning. Let's get a move on.'

A hundred metres ahead of us, in the transparent layers of fog which shift along as we do and give us less and less cover, a shell whistles and bursts . . . It falls at the place we are heading for.

We carry on down. The slope levels out. My companion says nothing, but looks to the right and the left. Then he stops again as he did on the crest of the road. I hear him stammer, in a low voice:

'Well, that's it! We're there . . . We've reached it . . .'

And indeed we haven't left the plain, the huge sterilized, cauterized plain – yet we are in Souchez!

The village has disappeared. Never have I seen such a disappearance of a village. Ablain-Saint-Nazaire and Carency still preserved some semblance of locality, with their gutted and truncated houses and their courtyards filled with plaster and tiles. Here, framed by the shredded trees – which, in the midst of the fog, surround us with a ghostly sort of decor – nothing has any shape; there is not even a fragment of wall or railing or gate still standing, and we are amazed to discover, under the heap of beams, stones and ironmongery, that there are paving stones – here there used to be a street!

You would think it was a patch of untended waste ground, swampy, where some nearby town for years had been regularly emptying its mess, its litter, its building rubble and its worn-out utensils without leaving a clear spot, just a uniform layer of muck and rubbish into which we go, walking slowly and with a great deal of difficulty. The bombardment has changed things so much that it has changed the course of the mill stream which is flowing at random and forming a pond on the remains of the little square where the cross used to stand. A few mortar holes where swollen horses are rotting, others in which are scattered the remains of what used to be humans, distorted by the massive injury of the shells . . .

Here, lying across our path, which we are following upwards like a disaster, like a flood of debris beneath the dense sadness of the sky, lies a man who seems to be sleeping; but he is flattened against the ground in a way that distinguishes a dead body from a sleeping one. He was a man on soup fatigue, with his rosary of loaves threaded into a belt and a bunch of his comrades' mess tins held to his shoulder by a tangle of straps. He must have been hit the previous night, his back holed by a piece of shrapnel. We must be the first to find him: an obscure soldier who died in obscurity. Perhaps he will be scattered before anyone else comes across him. We hunt for the identity disc which is stuck in the clotted blood where his right hand is lying. I copy down the name on it in letters of blood.

Poterloo left me to do this by myself. He is like a sleepwalker, but looking, looking desperately all round. He is looking towards infinity among all these gutted, vanished things; in this void he is staring towards the misty horizon.

Then he sits down on a beam, lying there aslant, after kicking a twisted saucepan off it. I sit down next to him. There is a slight drizzle. The dampness of the fog is condensing into droplets and putting a film of varnish over everything.

He murmurs: 'Oh damn, damn!'

He wipes his forehead, and looks at me with supplicating eyes. He is trying to understand, to grasp the destruction of this whole corner of the world, to take in his loss. He murmurs some meaningless phrases and exclamations. He takes off his large hat and you can see his head steaming. Then he says painfully to me: 'Old man, you can't imagine, you can't . . .'

He sniffs.

'The Cabaret Rouge, where that Boche's head was and all the rubbish around, that sort of drain, it used to be a brick house at the side of the road and two low buildings, next to it . . . How often, at the same place where we stopped, how many times have I said goodbye to the good woman having a laugh on her doorstep, as I was wiping my lips and looking towards Souchez, where I was headed! And after taking a few steps you'd turn back to shout some joke out to her! No, you can't imagine . . .

'But that! I mean, that!'

He makes a sweeping gesture to indicate the absence all around him.

'We mustn't stay here too long, old man. The fog is lifting, you know.'

He gets up, painfully.

'Come on . . .'

The most serious part is still to come. His house . . .

He hesitates, finds his bearings and goes . . .

'It's here. No, I've gone past. It's not here. I don't know where it is . . . where it was . . . Oh, misery!'

He wrings his hands, despairing, finding it hard to stand upright in the midst of the rubble and the timbers. At one moment, completely lost in this cluttered plain, with no landmark, he looks up at the sky, like a thoughtless child or a madman. He is looking for the homeliness of rooms scattered in infinite space, their internal shape and half-light cast on the winds.

After searching in several directions he stops at one point and steps back a little.

'This is where it was. No mistake. You see, it was that stone that convinced me. There was a fanlight: you can see the traces of an iron bar from the fanlight before it was blown away.'

He sniffs and thinks, slowly shaking his head, unable to stop.

'It's when you have nothing that you realize how happy you were. Oh, we were happy!'

He comes over to me, laughing nervously.

'It's something strange, no? Huh? I'm sure you've never seen that before – not being able to find one's own house, the place where you've always lived, all your life . . .'

He turns about and now he's the one taking me away.

'Right, let's get going, since there's nothing here. We could be looking for where things are for an hour! Let's be off, old man.'

And off we go. We are the two living creatures haunting this vaporous, illusory place, this village razed to the ground so that we can walk over it.

We carry on upwards. The weather is lifting and the fog dispersing very quickly. My comrade, who is striding forward in silence, head down, shows me a field.

'The cemetery,' he says. 'It was there, before being everywhere, before taking over everything, like a sickness in the world.'

Halfway up we are walking more slowly. Poterloo comes over to me.

'It's too much, all this, d'you see? It's wiped out too much of my life up to now. It scares me, so much has been wiped out.'

'Come on, your wife is safe and sound, as you know, so is your little girl.'

He gives me an odd look.

'My wife . . . I'm going to tell you something. My wife . . .'

'Yes?'

'Well, I've seen her again.'

'Seen her? I thought she was in the occupied areas.'

'Yes, she's in Lens, with her parents. Well, I saw her . . . Oh, hell, what of it . . . I'll tell you the whole thing. I went to Lens, three weeks ago. It was the 11th. Twenty days ago, to be precise.'

I'm looking at him in amazement, but he seems to be telling the truth. He mumbles, walking along beside me in the increasingly clear air:

'They said, you may remember . . . But you weren't there, I think . . . They said we'd got to strengthen the barbed wire forward of the Billard Parallel. You know what that means. No one has been able to do it up to now. As soon as you leave the trench you are spotted on the downward slope, which has a funny sort of name.'

'The Toboggan.'

'That's the one! And the place is difficult enough at night or in the fog as well as in broad daylight, because of the rifles which have been pre-aimed and set up on stands and the machine-guns which they adjust during the day. When they can't see, the Boche spray everything.

'They took the pioneers of the Compagnie Hors Rang, but some of them had scarpered so they were replaced by *poilus* chosen from the ranks. I was one. Fine. Off we went. Not a shot was fired! "What's all this?" we asked one another. And what next, except we see a Boche, then another and another – ten Boche – coming up out of the ground, with their devilish grey uniforms, waving at us and shouting: "*Kamarad!* We're from Alsace!" – that's what they said, as they came up out of their International Trench. "We won't shoot," they said. "Don't worry, friends. Just give us a chance to bury our dead." So there we were, working side by side, and even chatting to each other, since they were Alsatians. In fact, they were cursing the war and their officers. Our sergeant knew damned well that you're not allowed to enter into conversation with the enemy and we've even been read out something saying that you can only chat to them down the barrel of a rifle. But the sergeant thought it was a unique opportunity to reinforce the wire and, since they were letting us work against them, we might as well take advantage.

'Then one of these Boche started to say: "Perhaps there's someone among you who's from the occupied lands and would like to have news of his family?"

'Old man, that was too much for me. Without thinking if it was right or not, I went over and said: "Yes, there's me." The Boche asked me some questions. I replied that my wife was in Lens, at her parents', with the girl. He asked me where in Lens. I described where and he said he knew just where it was. "Listen," he said, "I'll take a letter for you, and not only a letter, 'cos I'll even bring you back the reply." Then, all of a sudden, this Boche strikes his forehead and comes over to me: "Listen, old man, I'll do better than that. If you do what I tell you, you can see your wife, and your children, and everything, just as I'm seeing you now." He told me that all I had to do was to go with him at a particular time with a Boche coat on and a forage cap that he'd get for me. He'd fit me into the coal fatigue for Lens; we'd go all the way to our place. I could see, as long as I laid low and didn't show myself, since he could answer for the blokes on the fatigue but in the house there were some NCOs who he couldn't be sure of. Well, old man, I agreed.'

'That's serious.'

'Of course it's serious. I made up my mind on the spur of the moment, without thinking or wanting to think, so staggered was I at the idea that I was going to see my folks again. And if after that I was shot, well, too bad: tit for tat. It's the law of supply and demand, as the bloke says, isn't it?

'Actually, it all went without a hitch. The only problem was they had a hard time finding a big enough cap for me, 'cos, as you know, I've got a pretty hefty head. But in the end they even fixed that and they found a flea-trap large enough to stick my head in. And I've even got Boche boots already – Caron's, you remember? So off we went into the Boche trenches – which are a bloody lot like our own – with these sort of Boche comrades telling me in very decent French – as good as what I talk myself – that I wasn't to worry.

'There was no alarm, nothing. Going out, no problem. Everything went so easily and simply that I didn't feel such a bad Boche after all. We got to Lens at nightfall. I remember going past the Perche and taking the Rue du Quatorze-Juillet. I saw townspeople going around the streets as they do in our billets. I didn't recognize them because of the dark, and they didn't recognize me, because of the dark too, and because the thing was unimaginable. It was too dark to stick a finger in your eye when I got to her parents' garden.

'My heart was pounding; it was shaking me from head to foot as though I was nothing but a kind of heart on legs. I was so happy and excited I had to restrain myself not to shout out loud, and in French, too. The *kamarad* told me: "Walk past once, then again, looking through the door and the window. Don't let anyone see that you're looking . . . And mind out . . ." So I got a grip on myself and swallowed my feelings, hup, in a single gulp. He was a decent bloke that Boche, because he would really have got it in the neck if I'd been caught, wouldn't he?

'You know, in our house, like everywhere in the Pas-de-Calais, the front doors of the houses are divided into two: at the bottom is a kind of gate up to your waist and above it what you might call a shutter. That way you can close just the bottom part of the door and be half at home.

'The top part was open and the room, which is the dining room and the kitchen as well, of course, was lit and you could hear voices.

'I went by, craning my neck. Beside the round table and the lamp there were men's and women's heads, lit up in the pinkish light. I looked at them, at Clotilde. I saw her clearly. She was sitting between two men, NCOs I think, who were talking to her. And what was she doing? Nothing. She was smiling, her head prettily on one side, and surrounded by a little light frame of blonde hair shining gold in the lamplight.

'She was smiling, she was happy. She seemed contented beside these Boche corporals, that lamp and the fire which was giving off the warmth of home. I went by, then I turned round and went past again. I saw her again, still with the same smile. It wasn't a forced smile, or a grateful smile, no, a real smile, from the heart, which she was giving them. And in the fraction of time when I went by in each direction I managed to see my kid holding out her hands to a fat gent in a braided uniform and trying to climb on his lap; and next to them, who else did I see? Madeleine Vandaërt, the wife of Vandaërt, my mate in the 19th who was killed on the Marne, at Montyon.

'She knew that he'd copped it, because she was in mourning. And there she was, joking, laughing openly, I tell you . . . And she looked from one to the other as though to say: "How nice it is here!"

'Oh, boy! I got out of there and ran up against the *kamarads* who were waiting to take me back. How I got back I can't tell you. I was done in. I walked along, stumbling like one of the damned. Just as well no one bothered me at that moment, because I'd have shouted out loud. I'd have made a scandal just to get myself shot and have done with this rotten life!

'Do you get it? She was smiling, my wife, my Clotilde, on that day of the war! So! You only have to go away for a while and you don't count any more. You leave your home to go off to war and everything seems to be done for; but while you're thinking that, they're getting used to you being away and learning to do without you, to be as happy as before and have a laugh. Bloody hell! I'm not talking about that other tart who was laughing but my Clotilde, my own, whom I happened to see then by chance, for that one moment, and, say what you like, she didn't care a damn about me!

'Even so, if she'd been with friends or relations. But no, she was with German NCOs. Tell me, wasn't that as good a reason as any to jump into that room, give her a good hiding and ring the neck of that other bird in her black dress!

'Yes, yes, I did think of doing it. I know I was getting worked up. I was in a real state.

'Mind you, I don't want to imply any more than I'm saying. She's a good lass, Clotilde. I know her and I trust her; no mistake, you know, if I was bumped off, she'd cry all the tears in her body for a start. She thinks I'm alive, I know, but that's not the point. She can't help being comfortable and satisfied and letting herself go, as soon as she's got a nice fire, a nice lamp and people around her, whether I'm there or not.'

I dragged Poterloo along.

'You're exaggerating, old chap. Come now, you're imagining ridiculous things . . .'

We had been walking slowly. We were still at the bottom of the slope. The fog was turning silver before disappearing altogether. The sun was going to come up. The sun was up.

Poterloo looked and said: 'We'll go round on the Carency road and come up from behind.'

We went off at an angle into the fields. After a moment or two he said: 'D'you think I'm making too much of it? D'you think I am?'

Then he thought for a while and said: 'Ah!' And he added, with that shake of the head that he'd been giving all morning: 'But even so! Even so, there's one thing . . .'

We were climbing up the slope. The cold had changed to warmth. When we got to a flat piece halfway up he suggested: 'Let's sit here for a bit more before we go in.'

He sat down, heavy with a world of reflections piled one on another. His forehead wrinkled. Then he turned towards me with an embarrassed look as though he had a service he wanted to ask of me.

'Listen, old man, I wonder if I'm right.'

But after looking at me, he turned to looking at the things around him, as though he wanted to consult them rather than me.

A transformation had taken place in the sky and on earth. The fog was nothing more than a dream. Distances were being revealed. The narrow dreary grey plain was growing larger, driving away its shades and taking on some colour. Clear light was covering it little by little, from east to west, like two wings.

Now, down there at our feet, we could see Souchez between the trees. With the help of distance and light the little village was reconstituted before our eyes, new in the sunlight.

'Am I right?' Poterloo repeated, more hesitant, more uncertain.

Before I could say anything he answered himself, at first almost whispering in the sunlight:

'She's quite young, you know, twenty-six. She can't help her youth, it bursts out of her everywhere and when she is resting by the lamp, in the warm, she has to smile; and even if she were to start laughing, it would simply be her youth singing in her throat. It's not really because of others, it's because of herself. It's life. She's alive. Yes, she's alive, that's all. It's not her fault if she's alive. You don't want her to die, do you? So what do you expect her to do? Cry, on account of me and the Germans, all day long? Grumble? You can't cry all the time and grumble all the time for eighteen months. It's not possible. It's too long, I tell you. That's the whole trouble.'

He paused to look at the panorama of Notre-Dame-de-Lorette, now fully illuminated.

'It's just the same as the kid who, when she is next to a bloke who's not talking about sending her away, she eventually tries to get up on his knees. She might prefer it if it was her uncle or a friend of her dad, p'raps, but she still tries with the only one who always happens to be there, even if it's some fat pig in glasses.

'Oh!' he cried, getting up and gesticulating in front of me. 'Here's what you could answer me. If I didn't come back from the war, I'd say: "Old man, you're done for, no more Clotilde, no more love! One day or another someone will replace you in her heart. There's no getting away from it; your memory and the portrait of you that she has inside her will gradually vanish and another will be placed on top of it and she'll start a new life." Oh, if I weren't to come back!'

He laughed loudly.

'But I do mean to come back! Oh yes, you've got to be here! Otherwise . . . You've got to be here, see?' he went on more seriously. 'Otherwise if you're not here, even if you're dealing with saints and angels, you'll end up in the wrong. That's how it is. But I am here.'

He laughed.

'I'm even a little bit up here, as they say!'

I got up too and clapped him around the shoulder.

'You're right, old man. It'll all end one day.'

He rubs his hands. Now he can't stop talking:

'Oh, it'll end all right, don't worry. And everything will have to be remade. So we'll remake it. The house? All gone. The garden? Nowhere. Well, we'll remake the house, we'll remake the garden. The less there is, the more we'll remake. After all, that's life. We were made to remake, weren't we? We'll remake our life together, too, and our happiness. We'll remake the days, we'll remake the nights.

'And the other lot, too. They'll remake their world. Do you want the truth? It may take longer than you think . . .

'Now I can very well see Madeleine Vandaërt marrying someone else. She's a widow, but she's been a widow for eighteen months, old man. Don't you think it's a gap, that – eighteen months? I think it's even around that time you have to stop wearing mourning. People don't think of that when they say: "She's a tart!" and when, in effect, what they want is for her to commit suicide. But you forget, old man, you're bound to forget. It's not other people who do it, it's not even ourselves, it's just forgetting, that's all. I come across her suddenly and see her having a laugh and it turns me over, as though her husband had been killed yesterday – it's human – but then! It's been an age since he snuffed it, poor devil. An age, too long in fact. No one's the same. But hang on, we've got to go back, we've got to be there! We will be there and we'll set about becoming again.'

As we went he looked at me, winked and said, cheered up at finding an idea on which to hang his ideas: 'I can see it now, after the war, everyone from Souchez getting back to work and to life ... What a business! There was Old Ponce – what a character he was! So finicky that you could see him sweeping the lawn in his garden with a horse-hair brush or else down on his knees, cutting the grass with a pair of scissors. Well, he can do it again! And Madame Imaginaire, the one who lived in one of the last houses on the side towards the Château de Carleur, a large woman who seemed to be gliding along the ground as though she had roller skates under the wide folds of her dress. She produced a kid every year. Regular as clockwork – a real machine-gun of kids. Well, she can go back to that like a shot.'

He stopped, thought, gave a bit of a smile and said, almost to himself:

'Hey, one thing I noticed ... It's nothing very important,' he insisted, as if suddenly embarrassed by the pettiness of the parenthesis, 'but I did notice – as you do notice things out of the corner of your eye when you're looking at something else – that it was cleaner at home than it used to be in my day.'

We come across some small rails on the ground, buried beneath the hay which has dried where it grew. With his boot Poterloo shows me this length of abandoned line and smiles:

'Now that's our railway. A branch line they called it. That must mean something that's out on a limb. It didn't go fast! A snail could have kept up with it. We'll remake it. But it won't go any faster, that's for sure. It's not allowed!'

When we got to the top of the hill he turned back and took a last look over the devastated places where we had just been. Even more than before, distance recreated the village through the remains of the trees which, cut down and trimmed, looked like young saplings. Even more than then, the fine weather stamped an appearance of life and even a semblance of thought on this group of white and pink materials. The stones underwent a transfiguration of rebirth. The beauty of the sun's rays announced what was to come and showed us the future. The face of the soldier looking at the scene was also lit up with a light of resurrection. Spring and hope made it smile and his rosy cheeks, clear blue eyes and golden-yellow eyebrows seemed to have been painted afresh.

We go down into the communication trench. The sun is shining into it, making it yellow, dry and sonorous. I admire its beautiful geometrical depth and its smooth sides polished by shovels, and I feel joy at hearing the honest, clear sound of the soles of our boots on the hard ground or on the duckboards, little frames of wood placed end to end to make a floor.

I look at my watch. It informs me that it is nine o'clock and also shows me a face delicately coloured, reflecting a blue and pink sky and the fine outlines of the bushes planted above the edges of the trench.

Poterloo and I look at one another with a sort of troubled joy. We are pleased at seeing each other, as though we were meeting again! He talks to me; and though I'm quite used to the sound of his singing northern accent, I discover how it sings.

We've had bad days, tragic nights, in the cold, damp and mud. Now, even though it's still winter, this first fine morning tells us and convinces us that spring will soon be here once again. Already the upper part of the trench is decked with soft green grass and, in the new-born shudders of this grass, there are flowers awakening. The shrunken, narrow days are done. Spring is coming from above and below. We breathe in with joyful hearts, we are uplifted. Yes, the bad days are going to end. The war, too, will end, devil take it! No doubt it will end in this fine season that is coming and which already brings us light and starts to caress us with its breeze.

A whistle. Huh! A stray bullet.

Bullet? Come now! It's a blackbird.

Funny how alike they are. Blackbirds, singing softly, the country-side, the ceremony of the seasons, the intimacy of rooms, dressed in light . . . Oh, the war will end and we shall see our folks again, for ever: wife, children, or the one who was both wife and child, and we are smiling at them in this burst of youth that already unites us.

★

At the junction of the two communication trenches, in the field, at the edge, there is a sort of gateway. It consists of two posts leaning against one another, with a tangle of electric wires hanging like creepers. It looks good. You'd think it was set up there on purpose, like a theatrical decor. A slender plant – a real creeper – winds around one of the posts and if you follow it upwards you can see that it has already dared to cross over to the other one.

Soon, by following this trench – with its grassy flanks shivering like the flanks of a fine, live horse – we get to our trench on the Béthune road.

This is our position. All our comrades are here in a group. They are eating, enjoying the warmth.

When the meal is over we clean the mess tins or aluminium plates with scraps of bread . . .

'Hey, the sun's gone in!'

True. A cloud has spread across the sky and is hiding it.

'It's going to start pissing down, lads,' says Lamuse.

'Just our luck! Just as we're leaving.'

'Damned country,' says Fouillade.

The truth is that this northern climate is not much to write home about. You get mist, fog, drizzle and rain. And when there is a bit of sun it soon gets swallowed up in this great damp sky.

Our four days in the trenches are over. The relief comes with nightfall. We are gradually getting ready to leave, filling our kitbags and satchels and putting them ready, cleaning our rifles and wrapping them up.

It's four o'clock already. The mist is coming in fast. We're finding it harder to see one another.

'Jesus! Here comes the rain!'

A few drops, then a shower. Oh la la! We dive under our hoods or canvas sheets. We make for shelter, sliding and getting mud on our knees, hands and elbows, because the bottom of the trench is starting to get sticky. In the dugout we barely have the time to light a candle on a bit of stone and shiver around it.

'Off we go then!'

We emerge into the damp and windy darkness outside. I can see

Poterloo's powerful form: we are still next to one another in the line. As we start to march, I give him a shout:

'You there, old man?'

'Yep, in front of you!' he shouts back, turning round.

As he does so he gets a slap of wind and rain in the face, but he laughs. He still has the good, happy look of this morning. No mere shower will take away the contentment that he carries in his strong, firm heart; no dull evening will extinguish the sunlight that I saw, a few hours ago, enter into his mind.

We march on, bumping into one another. We stumble once or twice. The rain is not letting up and water is running along the bottom of the trench. The duckboards sway on the soft ground, a few leaning to left or right, and slipping. And, in the dark, they are hard to see, so that it is easy at a bend to put your foot to one side or the other, into a puddle.

I keep my eyes fixed, in the grey of the night, on the slate-like glimmer of Poterloo's helmet, streaming like a roof in the rain, and his broad back, which has a shiny square of waxed cloth on it. I follow in his footsteps and from time to time I call out to him; he answers me, still in a good mood, always calm and strong.

When the duckboards end we splash through thick mud. It is dark now. Suddenly we stop and I am thrown against Poterloo. Ahead of us we hear an almost angry shout:

'Can't you get a move on? We'll be left behind!'

'I can't get my feet unstuck,' says a pitiful voice.

Finally the trapped man succeeds in getting his feet out and we have to run to catch up with the rest of the company. We start to pant and groan and curse those who are at the front. We put our feet wherever we can. Sometimes we stumble, support ourselves against the wall and get our hands covered in mud. The march becomes a stampede, accompanied by the noise of ironmongery and curses.

The rain is getting heavier. Another sudden halt. Someone has fallen over. Chaos.

He gets up. We set off again. I'm making an effort to follow close behind Poterloo's helmet, which shines feebly through the night in front of my eyes, and from time to time I shout to him:

'Okay?'

'Yes, yes, I'm okay,' he answers, puffing and blowing, but in that same deep, sing-song voice of his.

The haversack drags on your shoulders and hurts them, tossed around in this pitching race under attack from the elements. The trench is blocked by a fresh landfall, which we plunge into. We have to drag our feet out of the soft, sticky mud, lifting them very high at every step. Then, once we have struggled through this piece of the landscape, we immediately drop down into a slippery river. At the bottom boots have made two narrow ruts where your foot is caught as in a tram line, and puddles where it splashes. At one point you have to bend very low to pass beneath a large, muddy bridge across the trench, and we only just manage it. We have to kneel down in the mud, get close to the ground and crawl along on hands and knees for a few steps. A little further on we have to contort ourselves, grabbing a post that the softening of the earth has caused to lean over, across the middle of the gangway.

We reach a crossroads.

'Come on, forward! Get a move on, boys!' says the adjutant, who has flattened himself into a recess to let us go past and talk to us. It's not a good spot.

'We're done in!' bellows a voice, so hoarse and panting that I cannot recognize whose it is.

'Damn it, I've had enough! I'm staying here,' moans another, breathless and exhausted.

'What do you expect me to do?' says the adjutant. 'It's not my fault, eh? Come along, get moving, this is a bad place. It was shelled at the last relief.'

We go on in the midst of a tempest of wind and water. It seems we are going down, always down, into a hole. We slip, fall and bang against the wall, then throw ourselves back upright. Our march is a sort of long fall in which we keep upright as best we can and where we can. You just have to stagger on, as straight as possible.

Where are we? I look up, despite the waves of rain, out of this gulf in which we are struggling. Against the barely visible background of the cloudy sky I can see the edge of the trench, then suddenly in front of my eyes, hanging over this edge, is a sort of sinister postern composed of two black posts leaning against each other, in the midst of which is what looks like a skein of hair. It is the gateway.

'Forward! Forward!'

I lower my head. I can't see anything now, but I can once more hear the boots going into the mud and coming out of it, the click of the bayonet sheaths, the muttered exclamations and the heavy breathing of chests.

Once again there are violent shudders. We stop suddenly and as before I am thrown against Poterloo. I lean against his back, his strong back, solid as a tree trunk, as solid as health and hope. He calls out to me: 'Cheer up, old man, we're getting there!'

We stop. We have to go back. In heaven's name! No, we're going forward again.

Suddenly a tremendous explosion hits us. I shudder from head to foot and a metallic resonance fills my ears, while a burning, suffocating smell of suphur enters my nostrils. The ground has opened up in front of me. I feel myself being lifted up and thrown to one side, bent, stifled and half blinded in this flash of lightning. And yet I remember clearly: in the second when, vaguely, instinctively, I searched for my comrade-in-arms I saw his body rising, upright, black, his two arms fully outstretched and a flame in place of his head!

13
Swearwords

Barque sees that I am writing. He crawls over to me across the straw and offers me his wide-awake face, his straw-like reddish forelock and his quick little eyes with two circumflex accents rising and falling above them. His mouth is twisting in every direction because he is biting and chewing a bar of chocolate, holding the damp stump of it in his hand.

His mouth full, he gives me a whiff of sweetshop as he stammers:

'Hey you, the writer! Later on you'll write about soldiers and talk about us, won't you?'

'Certainly, I'll talk about you, our pals and our lives.'

'So tell me . . .'

He nods towards the papers where I was taking notes. With my pencil hanging in the air I look at him and listen. He wants to ask me something.

'So, tell me. Without wanting to tell you what to do, there is something I'd like to ask. Here it is: if you get the squaddies in your book to speak, will you make them speak like they really do, or will you tidy it up and make it proper? I'm talking about swearwords. Because, after all, though we're good pals and all, and we're not actually swearing at each other, you won't ever hear two *poilus* chat for a minute without them saying something or repeating something that the printers won't much like to print. Huh? So if you don't put it in, your picture won't be very accurate; it's like you wanted to paint them and didn't put in one of the most glaring colours wherever it appeared. But it's not done, even so.'

'I'll put the swearwords in, because it's the truth.'

'But tell me, if you do put them in, won't people like you, but who don't care about truth, say that you're a foul-mouthed pig?'

'Probably, but I'll do it even so and not bother about those fellows.'

'D'you want my opinion? Though I don't know much about books, that's brave, that, because it's not done, and it would be great if you did dare, but at the last moment you''ll find it hard, 'cos you're too polite. It's one of the faults I've noticed since we first met. That, and the filthy habit you've got when they hand round the hooch, on the grounds that it's not good for you, instead of giving your share to a mate, of pouring it on your head to wash your barnet.'

14
Kit

At the back of the courtyard of the Muets' farm the barn gapes like a cave in the low building. It's always caves for us, even in houses! When you have crossed the courtyard, where the manure gives way under your boots with a spongy sound, or else walked round the outside, trying to keep your balance on the narrow stone pavement, and you are standing in front of the opening of the barn, you can't see a thing inside . . .

Then, if you try hard, you may perceive a misty recess where misty black shapes are crouching or lying down or moving from one side to the other. At the far end, to right and left, are two pale candles with round halos like distant red moons, and they finally allow you to make out the human shape of these masses whose mouths are breathing out either condensation or thick cigarette smoke.

This evening our hazy den – into which I cautiously introduce myself – is in a state of excitement. Tomorrow morning we leave for the trenches and the shadowy tenants of the barn are starting to pack.

Under attack from the dark, which, after the pale light of evening, blocks my eyes, I still manage to avoid the trap of cans, mess tins and equipment lying on the ground, but I stumble over the lumps piled right in the middle, like stones in a builder's yard . . . I reach my corner. A creature, with a huge, spherical, woolly back, is crouching down, leaning over a number of small objects shining on the ground. I clap him on his shoulder, with its sheepskin mattress. He turns round and, in the obscure flickering light of the candle, held in a bayonet stuck into the ground, I can see half his face – an eye, a piece of moustache, a half-open corner of mouth. He grunts, in a friendly way, and goes back to looking at his kit.

'What are you up to there?'

'I'm tidying up, tidying up my things.'

This fake brigand who appears to be counting over his spoil is my comrade Volpatte. I see what is going on: he has spread out his piece of canvas, folded in four, on his bed – that is to say on the strip of straw allocated to him – and then emptied and displayed the contents of his pockets.

It's a whole shop that he is examining, with the solicitude of a housewife, while carefully and aggressively making sure that no one steps on it . . . I cast an eye over the rich display.

Alongside the handkerchief, the pipe, the tobacco-pouch, which also contains a notebook, the knife, the wallet and the lighter (the necessary and indispensable minimum), there are two pieces of leather strap tangled together like worms around a watch inside a case of transparent celluloid, which has gone curiously dull and white with age. Then there is a little round mirror and another square one; the second of these is broken, but of better quality, with a bevelled edge. A flask of turpentine essence, another (almost empty) of mineral oil and a third, entirely empty. A German belt buckle with the device *Gott mit uns*, and a dragoon's tassel of similar origin; an aviator's dart, shaped like a steel pencil and pointed like a needle, half wrapped in some paper; folding scissors, and a fork and spoon set, also folding; a piece of pencil and a piece of candle; a tube of aspirin also containing some opium tablets; and several tin boxes.

Seeing that I am giving his personal fortune a detailed inspection, Volpatte helps me by identifying certain objects:

'That's an old leather officer's glove; I cut the fingers off to stick up the muzzle of my blunderbuss. That's telephone wire, the only thing to keep your coat buttons on with, if you don't want them to fall off. Are you wondering what's in here? White thread, strong, not the kind they use to tack new clothes together when they deliver them and which you pull out with a fork like macaroni cheese . . . And there's a set of needles on a card. The safety pins are there, separate . . . And here we have the papers. Talk about a lib'ry.'

Indeed, in the array of objects that came out of Volpatte's pockets there was an amazing accumulation of papers. There was the violet-coloured set of writing paper in its mangy printed envelope; the military passbook with its cover, dusty and desiccated, like the skin of an old tramp, worn away and shrinking all over; a moleskin notebook, frayed and stuffed with papers and portraits: in the middle reigns the picture of Volpatte's wife and children.

He takes the photograph out of the bundle of yellowed or blackened papers and shows it to me once more. I renew my acquaintance with Madame Volpatte, a lady with a generous bosom and soft, gentle features, with two lads in white collars, one on each side, the elder one slim, the younger round as a ball.

'Now I've only got photos of old people,' says Biquet, who is twenty.

He shows us the picture of a couple of old folk, placing it close to the candle; they are looking at us with the well-behaved look of Volpatte's children.

'I've also got mine with me,' says someone else. 'I never let go of the picture of my brood.'

'Well, everyone takes his folks along,' somebody else chips in.

'It's a funny thing,' Barque observes, 'but a portrait gets worn with looking at it. You mustn't eyeball it too often or spend too long with it, because in the long run, I don't know how it happens, but the likeness goes.'

'You're right,' says Blaire. 'I find exactly the same thing.'

'I've also got a map of the area in my papers,' Volpatte adds.

He unfolds it in the light. Worn through and transparent on the folds, it looks like one of those blinds made of squares sewn together.

'I also have a newspaper' (he unfolds a newspaper article about the *poilus*), 'and a book' (a twenty-five centime novel, *Twice a Virgin*). '. . . Ah, and there's another piece of newspaper, *The Bee*, from Etampes. I don't know why I kept that. There must be a reason. I could find it if I had time. Then there's my pack of cards and a paper draughts board with pieces in a kind of sealing wax.'

Barque, who has come over, looks at this scene and says:

'I've got even more than that in my pockets.'

He turns to Volpatte.

'Have you got a Boche *Soldbuch*, flea-head, phials of iodine and a Browning? I have, and I've got two knives.'

'No,' says Volpatte. 'I haven't got a revolver, or a German pay-book, and I could have had two knives or even a dozen, but I only need one.'

'That depends,' says Barque. 'Do you have any mechanical buttons, fish-face?'

'I've got some of them in my pocket!' Bécuwe shouts.

'A private can't do without them,' Lamuse insists. 'Otherwise there's no way to keep your braces attached to your trousers.'

'I always keep my case of rings in my pocket,' says Blaire. 'Within reach.'

He gets it out, wrapped in a gas-mask bag, and shakes it. The three-cornered file and the flat file clang and you can hear the aluminium rings clinking.

'I always keep some string, that's what's useful,' says Biquet.

'Not as much as nails,' says Pépin; and he shows us three of them in his hand, one large, one small and one medium.

One by one each of the others comes over to take part in the conversation, even as they carry on packing. You do get used to the half-light. But Corporal Salavert, who has a justified reputation for being good with his hands, hangs up a candle in the fitting that he has cobbled together out of a Camembert box and some wire. They light it and around this chandelier everyone describes what he has in his pockets, with the partiality and preferences of a mother with her offspring.

'First of all, how many do we have?'

'Pockets? Eighteen,' says someone who must be Cocon, the statistics man.

'Eighteen pockets! You're kidding us, rat-face,' says big Lamuse.

'Not at all: eighteen,' Cocon replies. 'Count them, if you're so clever.'

Lamuse wants to argue about it, so, placing both hands near the candle, the better to count, he enumerates on his fat fingers, the colour of dusty bricks: two pockets in the greatcoat, hanging at the back; the pocket with the field dressing that is used for tobacco; two inside the greatcoat, at the front; the two pockets outside on each side, with flaps; and three in the trousers – or even three-and-a-half, because there's the little one in front. . . .

'I put a compass in there,' says Farfadet.

'Some scraps of tinder.'

'And I've got a teeny whistle,' says Tirloir, 'that the wife gave me, and said: "If you're wounded in battle, you can whistle for your comrades to come and save your life."'

We laugh at the naivety of the idea.

Tulacque joins in, and says indulgently to Tirloir:

'They don't know what war is, back home. If you tried to talk about what it's like in the rear, you'd say some stupid things.'

'Let's not count that one, it's too small,' says Salavert. 'That makes ten.'

'And four in the jacket. That's still only fourteen.'

'There are the two cartridge pockets, those new ones which are fastened with straps.'

'Sixteen,' says Salavert.

'Now, miserable infant, pig-head, turn my jacket over. You didn't count those two pockets! So what do you expect? They're pockets, in the usual place – the civilian pockets where you stick your snot-rag, your baccy and the address where you were going to make a delivery, when you were a messenger in civvy street.'

'Eighteen!' Salavert goes, as serious as a tax inspector. 'There are eighteen, no mistake. That's settled.'

At this point in the conversation someone stumbled noisily several times on the pavings near the door, like a horse pawing the ground, and cursed.

Then there was silence and a resonant voice barked authoritatively:

'Well now, in there, are you getting ready? Everything's got to be prepared by this evening and, as you know, good solid packets. We're going to the front line this time and things might even hot up a bit.'

'Right-ho, right-ho, sir,' voices reply to the adjutant, absent-mindedly.

'How do you write "Arnessed"?' Benech asks. He is down on all fours working on an envelope with a pencil.

While Cocon is spelling out 'Ernest' for him and the adjutant, who has moved on, can be heard repeating his homily some way off, at the next doorway, Blaire takes the floor and says:

'Now then, lads, listen up to what I have to say. You must always put your mug in your pocket. I've tried sticking it here, there and everywhere, but only the pocket is really practical, believe me. If you are on the march fully kitted up, or making your way along the trench without your kit, you'll always have it with you when the opportunity arises – a mate who's got some wine and is well disposed towards you and says: "Give us yer mug!", or else a bloke peddling the stuff. So, me young bucks, just listen to me, you'll always be on top of things if you've got your mug in your pocket.'

'It's not often,' says Lamuse, 'that you'll catch me with my mug in my pocket. If you want a silly idea, try putting hedgehog grease on your finger and go fishing with it. I'd much rather hang mine up with a hook on my braces.'

'Much better is to stick it on a greatcoat button, like your gas-mask holder. Because if you take your gear off, you're ready and waiting in case the wine goes round.'

'Now I've got a German mug,' says Barque. 'It's flat, it goes in your side pocket if you want and it fits very well into your cartridge belt, once you've fired off the cartridges or else stuck them in your kitbag.'

'A German mug's not that brill,' says Pépin. 'It don't stand up. It just gets in the way.'

'You wait, maggot-face,' says Tirette, who has some grasp of psychology. 'This time, if we attack, like the warrant off. seemed to be saying, then maybe you'll find a Boche mug and then suddenly it'll be brill after all!'

'The warrant off. said that, but he doesn't know,' Eudore remarks.

'It holds more than a quarter litre, the Boche quarter-litre mug,' Cocon observes. 'Seeing that the exact quarter is marked on the side, three-quarters of the way up the quarter-litre. And it's always a good thing to have a big one, because if you have a mug that holds just a quarter, to get a quarter of coffee or wine, or holy water or whatever you like, it has to be filled to the brim and they never do that when they're doling the stuff out, or if they do you spill some.'

'I'll say they never bloody do it,' says Paradis, whose hackles rise as he thinks about it. 'The quartermaster sticks his finger in the tin mug and gives it a couple of thumps on the bottom. Result, you're palmed off with one-third of a mugful and you've been fooled all along the line.'

'Yes,' says Barque, 'that's true. But at the same time you don't want a mug that's too big, because then the guy who's serving you is on his guard and he pours out a drop or two at a time, so as not to give you more than the right amount, and ends up giving you less – so you're shafted, with your soup plate in your paws.'

Meanwhile Volpatte was putting back the objects that he had spread out, one by one, into his pockets. When he got to the wallet he regarded it with a look full of pity.

'He's bloody flat, poor old boy.'

He counted.

'Three francs! I'd better set about refilling this one, old man, or I'll be broke by the time we come back.'

'The soldier spends more than he earns, no mistake. I wonder what would become of a bloke who only got his pay.'

Paradis answered with a simplicity worthy of Corneille:

'He'd snuff it.'

'Look what I've got in my pocket, which I don't let go.'

Pépin, his eyes glittering, produced a silver knife and fork.

'These belonged,' he says, 'to the old bag where we were billeted in Grand-Rozoy.'

'Perhaps they still belong to her?'

Pépin gave a vague gesture in which pride mingled with modesty, then, a little more confident, he smiled and said:

'I know her, the old hoarder. She'll spend the rest of her life for sure looking all over for her silver cutlery, in every corner.'

'I've never been able to steal more than a pair of scissors,' says Volpatte. 'Some people have all the luck. Not me. So naturally I guard them preciously, those scissors, though I have to say they're not a lot of use.'

'I've nicked a few things here and there, but what of it? The sappers have always beaten me to it when it comes to theft, so what?'

'Do what you can and what you like, someone else always gets there first, old man! Don't let it bother you.'

'Hey, in there,' says the medical orderly, Sacron. 'Who wants some iodine?'

'Now, I keep my wife's letters,' says Blaire.

'And I send them back to her.'

'I keep them. Here they are.'

Eudore displays a packet of shiny, worn sheets, the writing on them modestly concealed by the gloom of evening.

'I keep them. Sometimes I reread them. When we're cold and uncomfortable I reread them. It doesn't warm you up, but it seems like it does.'

This odd phrase must have some deep meaning, because several men look up and say: 'Yes, that's right.'

The conversation continues, ranging from one topic to another, in the depths of this fantastic barn, crossed by great moving shadows, with heaps of darkness in the corners and the sickly light of a few scattered candles.

I can see them coming and going, strangely silhouetted, then bending, sinking to the ground, these busy removal men with their burdens, talking or calling out to one another, stumbling against the objects under their feet. They show one another their prized possessions.

'Here, look at this!'

'I'll say!' someone replies, enviously.

They want whatever they don't have. And, in the squad, there are some treasures that everyone envies: for example, the two-litre water bottle belonging to Barque that a well-judged shot with a blank from a rifle has expanded to contain two and a half litres; or Bertrand's famous big knife with the horn handle.

In the tumult of comings and goings sideways glances hover on these museum pieces, then everybody looks straight ahead again, attending to his own stuff, busy putting it in order.

Sad stuff it is, indeed. Everything made for soldiers is ordinary, ugly and of poor quality, from their cardboard boots, with their uppers held on by cats' cradles of bad thread, to their ill-cut, ill-made, ill-sewn, ill-dyed clothes of flimsy, transparent cloth – blotting paper – that a day's sunshine discolours, an hour's rain soaks through, not to mention their thin leather straps, brittle as wood shavings, torn by the buckles, their flannel underclothing thinner than cotton and their tobacco which looks like straw.

Marthereau is beside me. He gestures to our comrades:

'Look at 'em, these poor beggars hoarding their clutter. They're like a clutch of mothers keeping an eye on their kids. Listen to 'em. They call them their things. Like that one, when he says "my knife" it's like he was saying: "Léon, Charles or 'Dolphe." And it's impossible, you know, for them to lighten the load. It's incredible. It's not that they don't want to – seeing that the job's not one that builds up your strength, huh? It's that they can't. They love them too much.'

The load we have to carry! It's massive, and we know perfectly well, of course, that every object makes it a little heavier, every tiny thing is another wound. Because there's not only what you stick in your pockets and your pouches; to complete the burden there is what you have to carry on your back.

The pack is the trunk, even the wardrobe. The old soldier knows the art of enlarging it almost miraculously by the judicious arrangement of his things and his household provisions. In addition to the obligatory regulation baggage – two tins of bully beef, twelve biscuits, two tablets of coffee and two packets of condensed soup, one sachet of sugar, fatigues and spare boots – we manage to put in a few tins of food, some tobacco, chocolate, candles, espadrilles, even soap, a spirit lamp, solidified spirits and woollens. Together with the blanket, sheet, groundsheet, portable tool, mess tin and camping tool, it grows, widens and spreads to become monumental, crushing . . . My neighbour is right: every time he reaches his post after so many kilometres by road and so many through the trenches the *poilu* does swear that next time he will get rid of a mass of stuff and relieve his shoulders from some of the weight. But every time he gets ready to set off he takes up this same exhausting, almost superhuman burden, and never gives it up, though he curses it.

'There are some clever buggers who are on to a good thing,' says Lamuse. 'They find a way to stick something in the company truck or the medical truck. I know one who's got two new shirts and a pair of drawers in an adjutant's canteen – but, you see, with two hundred and fifty lads in the company, once the trick gets out there's not a lot can take advantage of it, especially privates! The more NCOs there are, the more they've got some trick for laying off their packs. Not to mention the fact that the commandant sometimes goes round the trucks without warning and he'll chuck your stuff out in the road if he finds it in a truck where it doesn't belong: hey, hup, off you go! And that's apart from the ticking off you'll get and prison.'

'In the early days it was straightforward, old man. There was some – and I've seen 'em – who stuck their pouches and even their wardrobe in a pram and pushed it along.'

'Oh yeah, I remember! That was the good time in the war! But all that's changed.'

Volpatte, deaf to all this, wrapped in his blanket like a shawl, which makes him look like an old witch, is hovering around something lying on the ground.

'I'm wondering,' he says, to no one in particular, 'if I should take that darned bottle. It's the only one in the squadron and I've always had it. Yep! But it leaks like a sieve.'

He can't make up his mind. This is a real parting.

Barque is looking sideways at him and teasing him. You can hear him saying: 'Nutter! Poor sap!' Then he stops making fun and says: 'But then, if we were in his place, we'd be as daft as he is.'

Volpatte delays his decision until later:

'I'll see about it tomorrow morning, when I'm saddling up Shanks's pony.'

After the inspection and filling of pockets it's the turn of the pouches, then the cartridge belts. Barque gives a lecture on how to fit the regulation two hundred cartridges into the three belts. It's not possible to manage it with them in packets. You have to undo them and put them upright one next to the other, head-to-tail. In this way you can fill each cartridge belt without leaving any space and make the whole lot weigh around six kilos.

The rifles are already cleaned. We check the wrapping round the breech and the plug in the muzzle; these are essential precautions, given the dirt in the trenches.

You need a sign to recognize your weapon.

'I've made some nicks in the sling. Look, I've cut the edge.'

'I've rolled a shoelace round the top of the sling and that way I can recognize it in the dark.'

'I've got a mechanical button. No mistakes there. In the dark I feel it at once and say: "That's my rifle." 'Cos, you know, there's some blokes that don't care, that'll sit around doing bugger all while their mate is cleaning his, then they quietly snitch the clarinet that he's just cleaned and have the nerve to say: "Captain, my rifle's okay." Now, I don't go along with that. That's swinging the lead and sometimes I've had all I can take of lead swinging, my old matey.'

Rifles, which are all alike, are as individual as handwriting.

'It's curious and odd,' Marthereau tells me. 'Tomorrow we're going up to the trenches and there's no drunks around yet this evening, or future hangovers and – odder still – no arguments yet! Now, in my view . . .

'Now, of course,' he immediately concedes, 'I'm not saying those two over there aren't a bit tanked up or lit up neither . . . Without being quite sozzled they're a trifle pissed, huh . . .'

'It's Poitron and Poilpot, of Broyer's squad.'

They are lying down and talking in low voices. You can see the round nose of one of them shining like his mouth, right next to a candle, and his hand, with one finger raised, making little explanatory gestures which are closely followed by the shadow it casts.

'I can light a fire, but I can't relight it after it goes out,' Poitron is saying.

'Nonsense!' says Poilpot. 'If you can light it, you can relight it, since if you light it, that means it'd gone out. And when you're lighting it, you could say you were relighting it.'

'That's all a load of codswallop. I'm no genius and I don't give a toss for all your patter. I tell you and I'll say it again: if you need someone to light a fire, I'll do it, but when it comes to relighting it once it's gone out, no go! That's all there is to it.'

I can't hear what Poilpot replies to that.

'But for God's sake, you blockhead,' Poitron croaks. 'I've told you thirty times, I can't do it. Can't you get that into your pig's head? I ask you!'

'This is starting to get boring,' says Marthereau. Obviously he spoke too soon just now.

A kind of fever, helped by some farewell libations, reigns in the hovel full of cloudy straw where the tribe – some standing up and wavering, others on their knees and banging like miners – is repairing, piling up and fastening its provisions, clothes and tools. A growling of words, a confusion of gestures. Out of the smoky lights you can see bits of faces and dark hands moving above the shadows like puppets.

Apart from that, in the next-door barn, which is only separated from ours by a wall the height of a man, you can hear drunken cries. Two men there are settling some argument with desperate violence and fury. The air hums with the foulest language you can imagine. But one of them, a stranger from another squad, is thrown out by the inhabitants and the other man's stream of curses weakens and flickers out.

'Now, as for us, we behave ourselves,' says Marthereau, with some pride.

He's right. Thanks to Bertrand, who is obsessed with his hatred of alcoholism, that poisonous curse that decides the fate of multitudes, our squad is one of the least affected by wine and spirits.

All around they are shouting, singing and boasting. And they laugh endlessly. Laughter is like cogwheels turning in the human organism.

You try to discover the meaning of certain physiognomies that rise up with moving relief out of this menagerie of shadows, this aviary of reflections. But you cannot. You see them, but see no depths behind them.

'Ten o'clock already,' says Bertrand. 'We can finish packing tomorrow. Time to hit the sack.'

So everyone goes to bed, slowly. The chatter continues. The soldier takes all his time whenever he's not absolutely obliged to hurry. Everyone comes and goes with something in his hand – and I see the outsized shadow of Eudore gliding across the wall as he goes in front of a candle, with two bags of camphor hanging from the ends of his fingers.

Lamuse tosses and turns, looking for a comfortable position. He seems uncomfortable: whatever his capacity may be, he has clearly eaten too much today.

'There's some people here that wants to sleep! Belt up, you herd of elephants!' Mesnil Joseph shouts from his place.

For a short while, this appeal does calm them, but it doesn't stop the murmur of voices or the comings and goings.

'It's true we're going up the line tomorrow,' says Paradis, 'and that in the evening we'll be going into the front line. But no one's thinking about that. We know it, that's all.'

Little by little everyone goes to his place. I am stretched out on the straw. Marthereau is wrapped up next to me.

A colossal mass enters, taking care not to make any noise. It's the medical sergeant, a Marist brother, a huge bloke with a beard and glasses. When he takes off his coat and stands there in his jacket, you sense that he feels embarrassed about showing his legs. You see the bearded hippopotamus shape hurrying discreetly. He pants, sighs and mutters.

Marthereau nods towards him and whispers to me:

'Take a look. Those chaps always have to kid you around. When you ask him what he does in civvy street he doesn't say: "I'm a brother in a school," he looks at you under his specs with half his eyes and says: "I'm a teacher." When he gets up early to go to Mass, and notices that he's woken you up, he doesn't say: "I'm going to Mass." He says: "I've got a tummy ache. I've got to go to the bog, that's for sure."'

A little way off Old Ramure is talking about his home.

'Where I come from it's a little village, not large at all. All day long my old man is seasoning a pipe. Whether he's working or resting he's blowing that smoke into the air or into the smoke from the stove.'

I'm listening to this rural tale, which suddenly takes on a specific and technical character:

'For that he prepares a straw wrapper. D'you know what I mean by that? You take a stalk of green wheat and strip off the outer layer.

You split it in two, then in two again, and you have different sizes, like different numbers. Then with a thread and these four lengths of straw, he wraps the stem of his pipe.'

The lesson ends, since no one appears to be listening.

There are now only two candles alight. A great wing of shadow covers the prone mass of humanity.

Individual conversations still flutter around the primitive dormitory. My ears catch a few snatches.

Old Ramure is sounding off against the commandant.

'Now the commandant, old man, with his gold braid, I've noticed that he doesn't know how to smoke. He draws on his pipes one after the other and burns them. It's not a mouth he has in his head, it's a stove. The wood cracks open, grills and ends up not as wood but charcoal. Clay pipes are stronger, but even so he roasts them. What a stovepipe. Just listen to me, old fellow, when I tell you: something will happen to him that doesn't often happen which is that his pipe, after being driven to the edge and cooked through and through, will explode in his face, in front of everybody. You'll see.'

Bit by bit calm, silence and darkness settle across the barn, smothering the worries and hopes of its inhabitants. The line of similar parcels formed by these creatures rolled up one beside the other in their blankets is like a huge organ emitting a variety of snores.

With my nose already in my blanket I can hear Marthereau telling me about himself.

'I'm in the rag trade, you know,' he says. 'A rag-and-bone man, rather, but in my case I'm in wholesale. I buy off the little rag-and-bone men in the street and I have a shop – a loft, huh – which serves me as a warehouse. I do everything in cast-offs from cloth to tin cans, but especially broom handles, sacks and old shoes. And, of course, I specialize in rabbit skins.'

A little later, I hear him telling me:

'As for me, though I'm small and not well-built, I can carry a hundred-kilo bin into the warehouse, up the ladder, with clogs on. Once I came up against one shady character who was a white slaver, so they said, well . . .'

'Boy, oh boy, what I can't stand,' Fouillade suddenly exclaims, 'is those exercises and marches that they stick on us when we're resting. My back's all done in by them and I can't get any shut-eye with the aches and pains I've got.'

There is a metallic noise from Volpatte's direction. He has decided to pick up his dixie can, while telling it off for having a hole in it.

'Oh la la, when will all this war be over?' groans one man, half asleep.

A stubborn, uncomprehending cry of revolt bursts out:

'They want our hide!'

Then there's a 'don't worry' as vague as the cry of revolt.

I wake up a long time later, as two o'clock is striking, and in a dim light, which no doubt comes from the moon, I see the troubled silhouette of Pinégal. In the distance, a cock has crowed. Pinégal is sitting half upright. I hear his grating voice:

'What now? It's the middle of the night and there's a cock bellowing away. He's a bit premature, that cock.'

And he laughs, repeating: 'A bit premature, the cock!' before twisting round in his woollen blanket and going back to sleep with a gargling sound in which a laugh mingles with his snores.

Pinégal has woken up Cocon, so the statistics man starts to think aloud:

'The squad had seventeen men when it set out for the war. Now it still has seventeen with the replacements. Every man has already worn out four greatcoats, one of the first blue and three of the cigar smoke blue, two pairs of trousers, six pairs of boots. For each man one must allow two rifles, but you can't count the overalls. We have replaced our emergency rations twenty-three times. Among the seventeen of us we have been mentioned in dispatches fourteen times, including two at brigade level, four at division and one at army level. We once stayed for sixteen days on end in the trenches. We have been billeted and housed in forty-seven different villages so far. Since the start of the campaign, twelve thousand men have gone through the regiment which is two thousand strong.'

A strange lisping sound interrupts him. It is Blaire who can't talk with his new set of false teeth – any more than he can eat with them.

But he puts them in every evening and keeps them in all night with dogged persistence, having been promised that eventually he would get used to this object inserted into his head.

I sit half upright, as though on a battlefield. Once again I contemplate these creatures who have ended up here together, after drifting through events and places. I look at all of them, sunk in the depths of inertia and forgetfulness, a few still clinging to the edge of the abyss with their pitiful concerns, their childish instincts and their slavish ignorance.

The intoxication of sleep is overcoming me. But I remember what they have done and what they will do. And, faced with this profound vision of the poor human night that fills this cave under its shroud of darkness, I dream of some great light, I know not what.

15
The Egg

We were utterly lost. We were hungry and thirsty and there was nothing in this lousy camp!

Provisions, which usually came regularly, had failed to turn up and our deprivation was becoming acute.

A haggard group is grinding its teeth, surrounded by the thin square with its slender doors, its bony houses, its bald telegraph poles. The group remarks on the absence of everything:

'The grub's gone AWOL, there's no meat and we've got to tighten our belts.'

'Cheese? Nothing doing! And no more jam than there is butter, by God!'

'There's not a crumb, no kidding, and all the grousing in the world won't alter that!'

'Talk about a manky camp! Three billets and not a thing to eat in any of them, just water and draughts!'

'No point in having any cash here. You might as well have just the memory of a franc in your purse, since there's no shops anyway.'

'You could be Rothschild – or even a military tailor. What good would your money do you?'

'Yesterday there was a little moggy mewing around near the 7th. I'm sure they've eaten it.'

'Yes, I bet they have – and it was so thin you could see it had a good ribbing.'

'Don't get all het up, that's the way it is.'

'There's some blokes,' says Blaire, 'who slipped in smartish when we got here and found a few cans of plonk for sale at the shop on the corner.'

'Oh, the bastards! What lucky sods they are, being able to chuck that down their throats.'

'Well, it was lousy stuff, even so – wine that would leave your mug as black as a pipe.'

'They say that there are even some who scoffed a bat!'

'Crickey!' says Fouillade.

'I've hardly had a bite, myself. I had one sardine left and some tea leaves at the bottom of a packet which I chewed with some sugar.'

'There's no hope even of getting a drink.'

'It's not enough, even if you don't eat a lot and your belly's flat.'

'In the last two days, some soup: a yellow something or other, shining like gold. Not bouillon, frying oil. No one ate it.'

'They moulded it for candles, I suppose.'

'The worst is you can't light a pipe.'

'Right, it's misery! I've no more wick left. I had a few ends of it, but that's all gone. I've looked through all the pockets of my flea-pit – nothing! And, if you want to buy a bit, like you said, no hope.'

'I've got a tiny bit of wick that I'm keeping.'

It is hard indeed and pitiful to see *poilus* who can't light a pipe or a cigarette, and who, resigned to the fact, stick their hands in their pockets and wander around. Fortunately Tirloir has his petrol lighter with a tiny amount of fuel still in it. Those who know this cluster around him carrying their pipes, filled but cold. And there is not even any paper to light from the lighter; you have to use the flame from the wick itself, with the liquid that remains in its tiny insect's belly.

I have a bit of luck. I see Paradis wandering around, his face in the wind, humming away and chewing on a bit of wood.

'Hey!' I tell him. 'Take this!'

'A box of matches!' he exclaims, amazed, looking at the object as one might look at a jewel. 'Now that's really great! Matches!'

A moment later, you can see him lighting up his pipe, his ruddy face splendidly empurpled by the glow from the flame and everyone shouts:

'Paradis has got some matches!'

★

Around nightfall I meet Paradis near the triangular remains of a façade on the corner of two streets of this most miserable of all villages. He signals to me:

'Psst!'

He has an odd look, a bit embarrassed.

'I say,' he tells me, in an affectionate tone of voice, staring at his feet. 'Just now you gave me a box of sparklers. Well, I'm going to reward you for it. Look!'

He puts something into my hand.

'Careful!' he whispers. 'Or it'll break.'

Dazzled by the splendour and whiteness of his present and hardly believing what I can see, I recognize . . . an egg!

16
Idyll

'Honest,' says Paradis, who was next to me on the march. 'Believe it or not, but I'm exhausted, I'm played out . . . I've never hated a march like I hate this one.'

His feet were dragging and he was leaning forward in the evening light, his square form burdened under a pack which looked fantastic with its broad, complicated, extended silhouette. Twice he tripped and stumbled. Paradis is tough, but all night he had been running around as a messenger while the others were sleeping and he had good reason to be exhausted.

So he grumbled:

'Are they made of elastic, these kilometres? That's the only explanation.'

He was sharply adjusting his pack every three steps, with a heave of his back, dragging and panting, and with his parcels, swinging and groaning, he looked like an old overloaded wagon.

'We're nearly there,' said an NCO.

NCOs always say that, about everything. Well, despite this assurance from the NCO, we were indeed arriving in the village where, in the evening light, the houses seemed to be drawn in chalk and crudely inked in against the blue paper of the sky; the church, with its pointed steeple flanked by two more slender and more pointed towers, had the outline of a tall cypress tree.

But when he has got into the village where he is to bed down, the trooper's troubles are still not over. It's rare for the squad or the section to be housed in the place which has been assigned to them. Misunderstandings and cross purposes tangle and re-entangle on the spot and it is only after several quarters of an hour that each of us is conducted to his definitive provisional lodgings.

So, after the usual wandering around, we were admitted to our night camp: a hangar held up by four poles and with the four compass points as its walls. At least it did have a good roof – a notable advantage. It was already occupied by a wagon and a plough, next to which we settled in. Paradis, who had been continually complaining and groaning during the whole hour of tramping backwards and forwards, threw his bag on the floor and himself after it and stayed there for a while, stunned, complaining that his limbs were numb and the soles of his feet were hurting, and all his joints as well.

But now the house, to which the hangar belongs, which we can see right in front of us, lights up. Nothing attracts a soldier like a window with a lamp behind it in the monotonous grey of evening.

'Let's go and have a look,' Volpatte suggests.

'Why not?' says Paradis.

He sits up and stands up. Limping with exhaustion, he goes over to the golden window which has appeared in the darkness, and then towards the door. Volpatte follows him and I go after.

We go inside and ask the old man who opened to us if he has any wine for sale. His head sparkles and is as worn as an old hat.

'No,' he says, shaking his skull, which has a few patches of white cotton wool scattered over it.

'No beer? No coffee? Something or other . . .'

'No, my friends, not a drop of anything. We don't come from here, we're refugees, you know.'

'Well, since there's nothing here we'll be off.'

We about turn. Even so, for a brief moment, we have enjoyed the warmth in the room, the sight of the lamp. Volpatte is already at the door and his back is vanishing into the dark. However, I have noticed the old woman, slumped in the bottom of a chair in the far corner of the kitchen, who seems very taken up with her work.

I pinch Paradis's arm:

'There's the beauty of the house. Go and flirt with her.'

Paradis gives a proud gesture of indifference. He has cared very little for women in the past year and a half when none of those he has seen has been for him. In any case, even if they were for him, he wouldn't bother.

'Young or old, huh!' he says, starting to yawn.

Out of boredom and because he is in no hurry to leave, he goes over to the old woman.

'Evening, grandma,' he mutters, stifling his yawn.

'Good evening, children,' the old woman quavers.

Close up you can see her more clearly. She is wizened, bowed and heaped in her old bones, and has the dead white face of a clock.

What is she doing? Wedged between her chair and the edge of the table, she is trying to clean some shoes. It's a heavy job for her child's hands; her movements are uncertain and from time to time the brush goes off to one side. Moreover, the shoes are very dirty.

Seeing that we are watching her, she whispers that she really has to wax her granddaughter's boots this very evening, because the girl is a dressmaker in town and will be going there tomorrow morning.

Paradis has leant over to get a closer look at the boots and suddenly reaches out a hand towards them.

'Don't you do that, grandma. I'll get them polished in no time, your girl's bootees.'

The old woman shakes her head and shoulders. But Paradis insists on taking the shoes, while the old woman struggles impotently, showing us a ghost of protestation.

Paradis takes one boot in each hand, holds them gently and looks at them for a moment; he even seems to squeeze them a little.

'How small they are!' he says, in a voice different from the one that he usually has when talking to us.

He has grasped the brushes and starts to rub eagerly and carefully; I can see that his eyes, fixed on the work, are smiling.

Then, when he has got the mud off the boots, he takes some shoe polish on the end of the pointed double brush and caresses them with it, very attentively.

The shoes are of good quality, the shoes of a smart young lady, with a row of little buttons shining on them.

'Not one missing, not one button,' he whispers to me, and there is pride in his voice.

There is no more tiredness, no more yawning. On the contrary, his lips are pressed together. A ray of youth and springtime lights up his face and this man who was on the point of falling asleep looks as though he has just woken up.

He runs his fingers, with fine black wax on the ends of them, along the uppers which widen considerably at the top, giving a suggestion of the shape of the leg. His fingers, which were so agile in cleaning, have a kind of awkwardness as he turns the shoes round and round, smiling at them and thinking, deep down inside . . . until the old woman lifts her arms in the air and turns to me as witness: 'Now there's a very helpful soldier!'

It's done. The boots are cleaned and polished up until they shine. Nothing left to do . . .

He puts them back on the edge of the table, very gently, as though they were relics. Then, finally, he takes his hands off them. Yet he does not take his eyes off them. He looks at them, then looks down at his army boots and mine. I remember that as he made the comparison this large lad, with the destiny of a hero, a gypsy and a monk, smiled once more with all his heart.

The old woman moved around in her chair. She'd had an idea.

'I'll tell her! She can thank you herself, monsieur. Hey, Josephine!' she shouted, turning towards one of the doors.

But Paradis stopped her with a wide gesture that I found magnificent:

'No, don't bother, old woman. Leave her where she is. We'll be leaving. It's not worth bothering her!'

He believed so strongly in what he was saying that his voice had the accent of authority and the old woman obeyed him, reverting to stillness and silence.

We went off to bed in the hangar, in the arms of the plough that was waiting for us there.

And now Paradis started to yawn again; but, in the light of the candle in the manger, a little while later, you could see that he still had a happy smile on his face.

17
The Sap

In the shambles of a distribution of mail, from which the men come away, some with the joy of a letter, some with the half-joy of a post-card, some with a new burden (quickly remade) of waiting and hope, one comrade, waving a sheet of paper, tells us an astonishing story.

'You remember old weasel-face in Gauchin?'

'That ancient ruin who was looking for a treasure?'

'Well, he's found it!'

'No! You're having us on . . .'

'No, I'm telling you, you great pillock. What do you want me to say? Mass? Well, I don't know it . . . The courtyard outside his room was shelled and it brought up a box full of coins near a wall. He got his treasure full in his face! Even the curé turned up quietly and talked about claiming credit for a miracle.'

Our jaws were hanging open.

'A treasure! Ah, I ask you! Well, I never, that old coot!'

The unexpected revelation brought out a wealth of reflections.

'You never do know!'

'Remember how we made fun of the old fart, when he kept on and on about his treasure and bent our ears and banged our heads with it!'

'And we used to tell him, when we were there, that you never know, remember? We didn't know how right we were!'

'Even so, there are some things that are for sure,' said Farfadet, who, all the time we were talking about Gauchin, had had a dreamy, absent-minded look, as though some much-loved face was smiling at him. 'But I'd never have believed that,' he added. 'He's going to be so proud, the old man, when I go back there after the war.'

★

'They're asking for a volunteer to help the sappers to do a job,' says the big adjutant.

'Not likely!' the men mutter, without budging.

'It's something useful for evacuating men if we need to,' says the adjutant.

At that we stop grumbling and a few heads look up.

'Present!' says Lamuse.

'Get your gear on, fatty, and come with me.'

Lamuse fastens the buckle on his bag, rolls up his blanket and secures his pouches. Now that his crisis of unrequited love has passed he has become more moody than before, and though he seems unable to stop putting on weight he is taken up with himself, isolated, hardly ever talking to anyone.

That evening something approaches down the trench, rising and falling as it crosses the heaps and pits on the floor, a form that seems to be swimming in the darkness and from time to time holds out its arms, as though appealing for help.

It is Lamuse. He comes up to us. He is covered in soil and mud. Shivering, pouring with sweat, he looks as though he is afraid of something. His lips are moving and he is mumbling: 'Meu, meu!', unable to say a comprehensible word.

'Well?' we ask in vain. 'Well?'

He slumps into a corner between us and lies down flat.

We offer him some wine. He makes a gesture of refusal. Then he turns towards us and calls me over with a move of the head. When I'm next to him he whispers, very quietly, as though in church:

'I saw Eudoxie again.'

He is trying to catch his breath. His chest is wheezing and he continues, his eyes staring at some nightmare:

'She was rotting.'

'It was at the place we lost,' Lamuse continues, 'the one the colonial troops took back with bayonets ten days ago.

'First of all we dug a hole for the sap. I really went to it. As I was working harder than the rest I found myself at the front. The others were widening and consolidating behind. Then I came across a jumble of beams. I'd got into some old trench that was filled in, obviously. Well, half filled in, 'cos there were gaps and spaces. In amongst the bits of wood, all lying one on another, which I was taking away one by one in front of me, there was like a large bag of earth standing on end, straight up, with something hanging out of it.

'Then a beam gave way and this odd kind of bag fell right on top of me. It was weighing me down; I was stuck – with this smell of corpse getting me in the gullet . . . And at the top of the packet there was a head. What I'd seen hanging down was the hair.

'I tell you, it wasn't easy to see much in there, but I recognized the hair, 'cos there's not two heads of hair like that on earth; then the rest of the face, all sunk in and rotted, the neck like dough and the whole lot of it dead for a month, probably. It was Eudoxie I tell you.

'Yes, it was that woman I couldn't never get near to before, you know – that I saw from a distance without being able to touch, like diamonds. She ran here, there and everywhere, you know. She used to wander around the lines. One day she must have got hit and stayed there, dead and lost, until we happened to make that sap.

'You see how it was? I had to hold her up with one arm as best I could and work with the other. She kept trying to fall on top of me with all her weight. I tell you, old man, she wanted to kiss me, but I didn't want to, it was ghastly. It was like she was saying to me: "You wanted to kiss me, well then, come on, come on!" On her . . . She had fastened there the remains of a bunch of flowers, which was rotten too and that bouquet hit me in the nose like the corpse of some small animal.

'I had to take her in my arms and turn round, the two of us together, gently, to put her down on the other side. It was so close, so narrow, that for a moment as I turned I had her pressed against my chest without wanting to, with all my strength, just as I would have held her before – if she'd wanted to . . .

'I was half an hour cleaning myself up from the touch of her and that smell she gave me, in spite of herself, and in spite of me. Oh! Thank God I'm as tired as a poor old horse.'

He turns over on his belly, clenches his fists and falls asleep, his face buried in the earth, in his dream of love and decay.

18
The Matches

It is five o'clock in the evening. You can see all three of them moving at the bottom of the dark trench.

They are frightful, black and sinister in the earthy diggings around the extinguished fire. It has been killed off by rain or neglect and the four cooks are looking at the corpses of firewood buried in the ashes and these cooling remains of a pyre from which the flame has vanished, fled away.

Volpatte staggers over to the group and unloads a black lump that was on his shoulder.

'I pulled it out of a dugout where it doesn't show too much.'

'We've got wood,' says Blaire. 'But we've got to light it. Otherwise how can we cook this gristle?'

'It's a fine piece,' says one of the black men. 'Flank. Now in my view that's the best bit of beef, the flank.'

'A light!' Volpatte demands. 'No matches, no nothing.'

'We need a light,' grumbles Poupardin, swaying and swinging around uncertainly with his bear's shape in the depths of this place which is like a dark cage.

'There's no getting round it, that's what we need,' says Pépin emphatically, emerging from his dugout like a sweep from a chimney. He comes out, a grey mass, appearing like night into twilight.

'Don't worry, I'll get some,' Blaire announces in tones of fury and determination.

He has not been cook for long and he is determined to show himself capable of dealing with difficulties in the exercise of his duties.

He spoke as Martin César used to speak, when he was alive. He lives to imitate the great legendary figure of the cook who always found a light – just as others, among the NCOs, try to imitate Napoleon.

'If need be, I'll go and strip every bit of wood off Company HQ; I'll requisition the commandant's matches; I'll . . .'

'Let's go and fetch a light.'

Poupardin marches off ahead. His face is dark, like the bottom of a saucepan which the fire has gradually browned. As it is wickedly cold, he is wrapped up in every direction. He is wearing a cape, half goat, half sheep, half brown, half whitish, and this double skin with its geometrically divided shades of colour makes him look like some strange arcane creature.

Pépin has a cotton cap so black and so shiny with dirt that it becomes a traditional black silk bonnet. Volpatte, inside his balaclava and his woollens, looks like a walking tree trunk. A square opening reveals his yellow face at the top of the huge, thick bark on the trunk he forms, dividing into two legs.

'Let's go towards the 10th. They always have what you need. It's on the Route des Pylônes, beyond the Boyau-Neuf.'

The four terrifying creatures get going like a cloud floating down the trench that winds away in front of them, a blind alley, dangerous, badly lit and unpaved. As a matter of fact it is uninhabited at this point, being a passage from front to rear lines.

The cooks hunting for a light meet two Moroccans in the dusty evening. One of them has the complexion of a black boot, the other of a yellow shoe. A glimmer of hope shines in the hearts of the cooks.

'Any matches, lads?'

'No hope!' the black one replies, his laugh displaying his long porcelain teeth against the havana-coloured leather of his mouth.

The yellow-skinned man comes over and asks:

'Tobacco? A pinch of baccy?'

He holds out his grey-green sleeve and his wooden paw stained with walnut, which has settled in the lines on the palm, ending in violet nails.

Pépin mutters something, searches about his person and brings out of his pocket some shreds of tobacco mixed with dust which he gives to the Moroccan.

A little further on they meet a sentry who is half asleep in the middle of the evening, in a heap of loose earth. Half awake, he tells us:

'To the right, then right again, then straight on. Don't get lost.'

They walk. For a long time they walk.

'We must have come a long way,' says Volpatte, after half an hour of useless walking and enclosed solitude.

'Hey, we seem to be going downhill pretty damned fast, don't you think?' says Blaire.

'Don't worry, old stick,' Pépin teases him. 'But if you've got the wind up, you can leave us.'

They carry on as night falls. The trench, still deserted, a frightful, horizontal desert, is taking on a strangely dilapidated look. The parapets are in ruins and slippages of earth have made the ground like a roller-coaster.

A vague sense of unease starts to grip the huge fire-hunters as the darkness deepens and they go further and further along this monstrous roadway.

Pépin, who is now in the lead, stops and holds his hand up for them to follow suit.

'Footsteps . . .' they say, under their breath, in the gloom.

Now, in their guts, they are afraid. They made a mistake, all leaving their shelter for so long. They are in the wrong. And one never knows.

'Quick!' says Pépin. 'In here! Quick!'

He points to a rectangular hole, level with the ground.

When they feel it with their hands the rectangular shadow turns out to be the entrance to a shelter. They go in one after another; the last, impatient, pushes the others and they squeeze together in the dense blackness of the hole.

The sound of footsteps and voices grows clearer and gets nearer.

Out of the mass of the four men pressed into the narrow bolt hole, fumbling hands reach out and feel around. Suddenly Pépin is murmuring in a strangled voice:

'What's this?'

'What?' the others ask, heaped up beside him.

'Cartridge clips!' Pépin says very quietly. 'German cartridge clips on the duckboard! We're in one of the Boche trenches!'

'Let's get going.'

The other three men shove to get out.

'Look out, for Christ's sake! Don't move! Footsteps . . .'

They hear someone walking. The steps are the quick tread of a man on his own.

They don't move and hold their breath. Their eyes, fixed on the ground, see the darkness move on the right, then a shadow with legs emerges from it, approaches and goes on by . . . The shadow has a shape. It is surmounted by a helmet with a cover under which one can see the point. There is no noise other than the footsteps of this passer-by.

Hardly has the German passed than the four cooks, with a single movement, not prearranged, leap forward, jostling each other, running like idiots, and pounce on him.

'*Kamarad, messieurs!*' he says.

But you can see the blade of a knife glitter and vanish. The man slumps down as though sinking into the earth. Pépin grabs the helmet as the man falls and keeps it in his hand.

'Let's get out of here!' Poupardin mutters.

'We've got to frisk him, huh?'

They lift him up, turn him over, supporting the soft, damp, warm body. Suddenly he coughs.

'He's not dead.'

'Yes he is. It's the air.'

They shake him by the pockets. The four black men can be heard breathing fast as they crouch over their work.

'The helmet's mine,' says Pépin. 'I stuck him. I want the helmet.'

They deprive the body of his wallet, with its still warm papers, his binoculars, his purse and his gaiters.

'Matches!' Blaire exclaims, shaking a box. 'He's got some.'

'Oh, the rotten sod!' Volpatte says, softly.

'Now, let's put our skates on as fast as we can.'

They heap the body up in a corner and race away, seized by a kind of panic, without worrying about the noise made by their head-long dash.

'Over here! This way! Come on, lads, quick as you can!'

Without saying any more they rush along the maze of the astonishingly empty trench, which seems to go on and on.

'I'm puffed out,' says Blaire. 'I'm done for . . .'

He staggers and comes to a halt.

'Come along! Make an effort, old thing,' Pépin growls in a harsh, breathless voice.

He takes his sleeve and pulls him forward, like a reluctant nag.

'Here we are!' Poupardin says suddenly.

'Yeah! I recognize that tree.'

'It's the Route des Pylônes!'

'Ah!' Blaire groans, his chest heaving like a motor. He throws himself forward in one final spurt and sinks to the ground.

'Halt! Who goes there?' a sentry cries.

'But what . . . !' the man stammers then, seeing the four *poilus*. 'Where are you coming from, in that direction?'

They laugh and jump around like puppets, streaming with sweat and covered in blood, which makes them seem blacker than ever in this light. The German officer's helmet is shining in Pépin's hands.

'Oh shit!' the sentry mutters, his jaw dropping. 'But what . . . ?'

An exuberant reaction makes them leap wildly.

They are all speaking at once. Bewildered, they hastily reconstruct the drama from which they are just waking, without yet knowing it. As they were leaving the half-asleep sentry they took the wrong road and got into the International Trench, part of which belongs to us, part to the Germans. Between the French and German sections there is no barricade or fence to separate them. There is just a sort of neutral zone, at the two ends of which two lookouts are permanently stationed. No doubt the German lookout was not at his post, or he had hidden when he saw the four shadows, or he retreated and did not have time to bring reinforcements. Or else it could be that the German officer had advanced too far forward into the neutral zone. In short, they realize what happened without really understanding.

'And the funniest thing is,' says Pépin, 'that we knew all that and didn't think to take care when we set out.'

'We were looking for a light!' says Volpatte.

'And we got one!' Pépin shouts. 'You haven't lost the matches, you old lump?'

'Not a chance!' says Blaire. 'German matches are better quality than ours. And then, they're all we've got for a light. Lose the box! They'd have to cut off my hand!'

'We're late. The dinner water is starting to freeze. Let's get back quick. After that, in that drain where the boys are, we'll tell them about the little joke we played on the Boche.'

19
Bombardment

In flat, open country, in the immensity of the mist.

The sky is dark blue. Towards dawn a little snow falls, powdering the shoulders and folds in the sleeves. We are marching along, in ranks of four, with our hoods up. In the opacity of the half-light we might be some vague population group emigrating from one northern country to another.

We have been following a road through the ruins of Ablain-Saint-Nazaire. We caught glimpses of the whitish heaps of houses and the vague spiders' webs of hanging roofs. The village is so long that, though it was deep night when we went into it, when we saw its last buildings they were starting to blanch with the frost of dawn. In one cellar, through a grill, on the edge of the waves of this petrified ocean, we made out the fire that the guardians of this dead place keep alight. We waded through marshy fields, we got lost in silent regions where the mud grabbed us by the feet, then we more or less managed to regain our balance on another road, the one leading from Carency to Souchez. The tall poplars lining it are broken, their trunks shredded; at one place there is a huge colonnade of shattered trees. Then, accompanying us on either side through the darkness we can see dwarf phantoms of trees, split into palms or completely wrecked into chopped wood or string, bent over on themselves, as if kneeling. From time to time potholes interrupt the march and make the column wobble unevenly; or the road becomes a pond which we cross on our heels, making a sound of splashing oars with our feet. Planks have been put down in the mud at intervals. When, slippery with mud, they veer to one side our feet slide on them, and sometimes there is enough water for them to float. Then, under a man's weight, they go 'flack!' and sink. The man falls or staggers, with a frenzied stream of oaths.

It must be five in the morning. The snow has stopped, and the naked, fearsome scene is emerging; but we are still surrounded by a great fantastic circle of mist and darkness.

Onward we go, and onward. We reach a place where you can see a dark mound with some humans teeming around its base.

'March on by twos,' says the leader of the detachment. 'Every team of two will pick up, alternately, a plank and a wicket.'

The order is obeyed. One of the two men takes his teammate's rifle with his own, while the other man, with some difficulty, separates out of the heap a long plank, slippery with mud, weighing at least forty kilos, or else a wicket of leafy branches, as big as a door, which he can just manage to carry on his back, with his hands in the air, gripping the edges.

We resume our march, scattered across the road, which is now greyish, very slow and very encumbered, accompanied by groans and dull curses which sheer effort stifles in the throat. After a hundred metres the two men in each team exchange loads, so that after two hundred metres, despite the sharp, brightening wind of early morning, everyone except the NCOs is pouring with sweat.

Suddenly a very bright star appears ahead of us in the vague place towards which we are marching: a flare. It lights up a whole section of the sky with its milky halo, outshining the constellations before descending gracefully, with something of the fairy about it.

A quick flash ahead of us, over there. A flash, a bang.

A shell. By the horizontal light that the explosion has spread for an instant across the lower part of the sky we can clearly see the crest of a ridge crossing in front of us from east to west, perhaps a kilometre away. In all the part visible from where we are this ridge is ours right up to the summit, which is occupied by our troops. On the far slope, a hundred metres from our front line, is the German front line. The shell fell on the summit, in our lines. It is the other lot who are firing.

Another shell, then another, and another, planting trees of violet tinted light at the top of the hill, each dully illuminating the whole horizon.

Soon there is shimmering of bursting stars and a sudden forest of phosphorescent plumes on the hill; a magic mirage of blue and white hangs lightly before our eyes over the deep gulf of night.

Those among us who are devoting all the strength in their bowed arms and legs to preventing their over-heavy, muddy burdens from slipping off their backs – and with keeping themselves from slipping to the ground – see nothing and say nothing. The rest, shivering with cold, trembling, sniffing, wiping their noses, damp handkerchiefs hanging from their paws, cursing the obstacles on this broken road, look and comment.

'It's like seeing a firework display,' they say.

To complete the illusion of our hunched black troop crawling, swarming and stamping in front of a grand opera set, at once enchanting and sinister, there is a red star, then a green one; then a red bunch, much slower.

In the ranks they cannot refrain from murmuring, in mingled tones of popular admiration, while the available half of the pairs of eyes gazes at this: 'Oh, a red one! Oh, a green!'

The Germans are signalling; so are our people, calling for artillery fire.

The road twists and climbs upwards. At last, day has decided to break. Everything looks dirty. Around the road, which is covered by a layer of pearl-grey paint, with white impasto, the real world sadly emerges. We are leaving Souchez behind us, destroyed, its houses no longer anything except platforms piled with building materials and its trees like shredded brambles heaped on the ground. We proceed on the left down a hole; it is the entrance to the trench.

We put down the stuff we are carrying in a circular area designed for that purpose and, at once warmed up and ice-cold, our hands wet, grazed and bent with cramp, we settle into the trench and wait.

Buried in our holes up to the chin, our chests pressed against the earth, protected by its might, we watch the dazzling and profound drama unfold. The bombardment gets heavier. On the ridge the luminous trees have, in the paleness of dawn, become like parachutes of vapour, pale medusas with a point of fire. Then, more clearly marked as the daylight spreads, plumes of smoke – white and grey ostrich feathers – suddenly arise out of the mournful and tumbled soil of Hill 119, five or six hundred metres in front of us, then, slowly, fade away. This is truly a pillar of fire and a pillar of smoke mingled together and thundering at the same time. At that moment, on the side of the hill, we see a group of men running for cover. They vanish one by one, swallowed up by the anthills planted there.

Now we can see the shape of the 'incomers'; at each shot, a sulphurous white puff, with a black edge under it, forms in the air, about sixty metres up, expands, mottles, and in the burst you can hear the whistling of the bunch of shrapnel that the yellow puff is furiously ejecting towards the ground.

They explode in groups of six, in succession: pan, pan, pan, pan, pan, pan! They're 77s.

We despise the shrapnel of the 77mm gun – which didn't stop Blesbois from being killed by one, three days ago. But they almost always burst too high.

Barque explains it to us, even though we already know.

'Your chamber pot will protect your nut well enough against lead. A bullet will put your shoulder out and knock you down, but it won't do for you. Of course, you've got to look out for yourself, even so. Try not to get caught with your head over the parapet when there's some bother going on, or stick your hand out to see if it's raining. Whereas our 75s . . . !'

'There's not only the 77s,' Mesnil André interrupts. 'You've got all sorts. Give me a light here.'

There are shrill, quavering and grinding whistles, and lashing whines. On the vast slopes now appearing in front of us, where our boys are sheltering, clouds of every description are gathering. Among the huge fiery nebulous clouds are immense tufts of steam, plumes casting out straight filaments and feathery towers of smoke that spread as they fall back to earth. All in white or grey-green, coal or copper, with golden glints, or as though stained with ink.

The last two explosions were quite close. Above the beaten earth they have formed huge balls of black and fawn-coloured dust, which, now that they are unfolding and drifting off calmly, their work done, take on the shapes of fabulous dragons.

Our line of faces, level with the ground, turns towards them and follows them from the depths of the trench in the midst of this country peopled with ferocious, luminous apparitions and these landscapes crushed by the sky.

'Now, those are 150mm howitzers.'

'Could even be 210s, halfwit!'

'There are high explosives too, the bastards! Get a load of that!'

A shell burst on the ground and we saw the earth and debris that it threw up, in a fan of dark cloud. Through the shattered soil it sounded like the frightful crashing of a volcano which had been gathering in the bowels of the earth.

A diabolical noise surrounds us. You have the incredible impression of a constant increase, an incessant multiplication of universal fury. A tempest of hoarse, dull crashes, of furious yells, of the piercing cries of beasts rains down on the earth, entirely covered with shreds of smoke, where we are buried up to our necks as the force of the shells seems to push it and rock it.

'My word!' Barque yells. 'And there was me saying that they had no more munitions!'

'Oh la la! We've heard that one before! That and the other fibs that the papers chuck at us by the bucket load.'

A dull tick-tock rises out of this jumble of sounds. Of all the noises of war, this slow rattle is the one that most grips the heart.

'The coffee grinder! One of ours, listen: the shots are regular while the German ones don't have the same interval between them. They go tick . . . tick-tock-tick . . . tick-tock . . . tock . . .'

'You're way off, thickhead! It's not the unsewing machine, it's a motorcycle driving along the road towards Shelter 31, way over there.'

'If you want my opinion, it's some chap up on high taking a peep out of his broomstick,' Pépin sniggers, looking skywards in search of an aircraft.

A debate starts. Who can tell? That's how it is. In the midst of all these various dins, accustomed though we are, one gets confused. It actually happened to one section, the other day, going through the wood, that for a moment they thought they heard the hoarse croak of incoming shells in the voice of a mule which had started to bray a little way off.

'By God, there's a lot of sausage in the air this morning,' says Lamuse.

We look up and count the balloons.

'Eight of ours and eight of the Boche's,' says Cocon, who had already counted them.

Floating at regular intervals above the horizon, opposite the group of captive enemy balloons, smaller and further away, are the eight oblong eyes of the army, light and sensitive, tethered to the command centres by living filaments.

'They can see us as we see them. How do you expect to escape them, those God Almighties up there?'

'There's our answer!'

Suddenly, behind us, we hear the sharp, strident booming of the 75. It blasts away without pause. The thunderous sound lifts us, intoxicates us. We are shouting at the same time as the guns and watching one another without hearing – except for the extraordinarily piercing voice of that loudmouth Barque – in the midst of this fantastic drum roll, each crack of which is a cannon shot.

Then we look forward, stretching our necks, and see on top of the hill the upper part of a black row of trees out of hell, the frightful roots of which are plunging into the invisible slope where the enemy is hiding.

'What's that?'

While the battery of 75mm guns a hundred metres behind us carries on with its shrieking – the sharp blows of an enormous hammer on an anvil, followed by a cry which is dizzying in its power and fury – a prodigious gurgling dominates the concert. This is also coming from our side.

'That's Big Daddy, that one!'

The shell blasts through the air some thousand metres above our heads. Its noise covers everything as though with a dome of sound. The noise of its passing is slow: you can feel that this is a plumper, vaster projectile than the rest. We hear it go past, we hear it coming down with the heavy, mounting vibration of an underground train coming into a station; then we hear its heavy whistling fade. Opposite us, we watch the hill. After a few seconds it is covered by a salmon-coloured cloud which the wind draws across a whole half of the horizon.

'That's a 220 from the battery at point gamma.'

'You can see them,' says Volpatte. 'Those shells, you can see them when they come out of the gun. And if you're under the line of fire, you can see them with the naked eye, even a long way from the gun.'

Another one goes by.

'There! Look! Look! Did you see it that time? You didn't look fast enough. You've got to keep your eyes open. There! Another one! Did you see it?'

'No.'

'Slowcoach! D'you have to have a drawing? Your dad was a painter. Look, quick, there's one! You must have seen that, didn't you, clown?'

'Yes, I saw it. Is that all?'

A few of them have seen a small black object, slender and pointed like a blackbird with folded wings, diving down in a curve from the top of its flight with its beak forward.

'That weighs a hundred and eighteen kilos, that does, my old flea-brain,' Volpatte says proudly. 'And when it lands on a dugout it kills everyone inside. Those who aren't torn apart by the shrapnel are stunned by the blast or drop down asphyxiated before they can say *ouch*.'

'You can also see the 270 shell – and that's some lump of metal – when a howitzer chucks it up: off you go!'

'And the 155 Rimailho, though that one you lose sight of because it goes too straight and too far. The more you watch it, the more it fades in front of your eyes.'

Amid a smell of sulphur, gunpowder, burnt materials and charred earth, which spreads in waves around the countryside, the whole menagerie is released, in full cry. Bellows, roars, strange fierce rumblings, caterwaulings that tear through your ears and turn your stomach, and a long piercing wail like the siren of a boat in trouble at sea. Sometimes these exclamations even cross in the air, their odd changes of tone giving them a sort of human accent. Here and there the landscape lifts and falls back. Before us, from one horizon to the other, it presents an extraordinary tempest of events.

The very big guns, in the distance, produce rather subdued, muffled growls; but you can feel their strength by the displacement of the air that hammers your eardrums.

And now a heavy parcel of green cotton wool fizzes and lands on the target area, spreading in every direction. This splash of colour clashes with the general picture and attracts our attention. All the faces of the caged prisoners turn towards the frightful burst.

'That looks like mustard gas. Get your face sacks ready.'

'Pigs!'

'That's a really unfair move,' says Farfadet.

'What is?' says Barque, jeering.

'Yes, not decent, I mean, gas . . .'

'Don't make me laugh,' says Barque, 'you and your fair and unfair weapons. When you've seen men cut open, chopped in half or split from top to bottom, spread around in pieces by ordinary shells, their bellies gaping and the contents dug out, skulls driven right into the lungs as if from a blow with a mallet or a little neck in place of the head with a blackcurrant jam of brains dripping all round it, on the chest and back . . . When you've seen that then come and tell me about clean, decent weapons of war!'

'All the same, shells are allowed, accepted . . .'

'Oh la la! Let me tell you this: you'll never make me weep like you make me laugh, mate!'

And he turns his back.

'Hey! Watch out, boys!'

We listen out. One of us has dropped flat on his belly, while others are instinctively looking, with a frown, towards the shelter which we do not have time to reach. For those two seconds each of us bends his head. There is a screeching noise of giant scissors getting nearer and nearer, then, at last, it ends in a deafening crash of falling metal.

That's one that didn't fall far away – two hundred metres, perhaps.

We bend down in the bottom of the trench and keep crouching there until the wave of small fragments has lashed the spot where we are.

'You don't want that in your bread basket, even at this distance,' says Paradis, picking out a fragment that has just buried itself in the wall of the trench. It looks like a small piece of coke, bristling with sharp edges and points. He tosses it in his hand, so as not to burn himself.

Suddenly he bends down. We do the same.

Bsss, bsssss . . .

'The fuse! It's gone over.'

The shrapnel fuse goes straight up and comes down vertically while the percussion fuse falls out of the shattered shell after the explosion and usually remains buried at the point of impact; but sometimes it takes off and goes wherever it wants, like a huge incandescent pebble. You have to be careful. It can attack you a long time after the explosion and in incredible ways, passing over the parapet and diving into holes.

'Nothing as nasty as a fuse. Now, what happened to me was . . .'

'There's worse than that,' Bags, of the 11th, interrupts. 'Austrian shells: the 130 and 74. Now, they do put the wind up me. They are nickel-plated, so they say, but all I know – and I was there – is that they go so fast that there's nothing you can do to get out of the way. As soon as you hear it snore it's exploding around you.'

'That's like the German 105: you don't have time to lie down and get your chops close to the ground. I heard all about them once from some gunners.'

'Let me tell you about marine shells: you don't have time to hear them; you've got to get out of the way first.'

'There's also that bastard of a new shell which only blows up after ricocheting on the ground and going up and down once or twice, over six metres. When I know they've got those up ahead I shit myself. I remember once . . .'

'That's nothing, all that, mates,' says the new sergeant, who has stopped as he was passing by. 'You should see what they chucked at us in Verdun, where I've just come back from, as it happens. Nothing except ginormous stuff: 380s, 420s, the two kinds of 44. When you've had a proper shelling down there then you can truly say: "I've been shelled!" Trees mown down like corn, all the shelters picked off and stove in even with three thicknesses of beams, every crossroads sprayed, and the roadways thrown into the air and changed into these sorts of long lumps of shattered convoys, smashed guns and bodies twisted together as though they'd been piled up with a shovel. You could see thirty blokes laid out at once on a crossroads; you could see chaps twisting around as they went up in the air, always to a height of some fifteen metres, and pieces of trouser leg caught right at the top of whatever trees were left. In Verdun you saw one of those 380s hit a storeroom, on the roof, go through two or three floors and burst on the ground floor, and the whole bloody lot go sky-high. And, in open country, whole battalions scattering and flattening themselves under the shower like poor little defenceless partridges. At every step, in the fields, you found splinters as big as your arm and as wide as this, bits of iron that it took four *poilus* to lift. The fields looked like ground full of rocks. And it didn't stop for months. Oh, you tell me about it, tell me . . .' the sergeant repeated as he went away, no doubt intending to tell the same story somewhere else.

'I say, corporal, look at those guys over there; are they nuts?'

In the position under bombardment we can see small human figures rushing out and running towards the explosions.

'Gunners,' says Bertrand. 'As soon as a shell bursts, they run out to look for the fuse in the hole, because the way that the fuse is sticking in the ground shows the direction the shot came from, see? As for the distance, you just have to read it off, 'cos it's marked on the scale around the fuse that's set before firing.'

'Don't care if it is, they've got a nerve to go out in a storm like this, those idiots.'

'Gunners, my man,' says a chap from another company who was walking along the trench, 'gunners are either all good or all bad. Either they're the tops, or they're crap. Now, I can tell you . . .'

'That's true of all soldiers, what you're saying.'

'Maybe, but I'm not talking about all soldiers. I'm talking about gunners, and I'm also saying that . . .'

'Hey, boys! Why don't we look for a hole to slip into? We might very well finish by getting a lump of iron on our heads.'

The outsider walking past takes his story somewhere else and Cocon, who likes to be different, says:

'We might go off our heads in *your* dugout, since it's already not too much fun out here.'

'Look, over there, they're firing torpedoes,' says Paradis, pointing at our higher positions on the right flank.

Torpedoes go straight up, or almost, like skylarks, fluttering and rustling, then stop, pause and fall right back down, letting you know that they are coming in the last seconds of their fall with a 'baby cry' which is easy to recognize. From here, the people on the crest of the ridge are like invisible players lined up, playing at ball.

'In the Argonne,' says Lamuse, 'my bro' writes me, they have what they call turtle doves. They're great heavy things, fired from close to. They make a cooing noise as they come in and go off with a hell of a fart, so he says.'

'There's nothing worse than a trench mortar, which seems to run after you and jump on top of you, then bursts inside the trench, level with the parapet.'

'Listen! Listen! Did you hear it?'

A whistle had been coming towards us, then suddenly stopped. The shell failed to go off.

'A shell that said: "Dammit!",' Paradis remarks.

We listen out to have the satisfaction of hearing – or not hearing – others. Lamuse says:

'All the fields, the roads, the villages around here are covered with unexploded shells of every calibre; including some of our own, I have to say. The ground must be full of them, which you can't see. I wonder what they'll do later, when the moment comes and they say: "It's not over yet, but we've got to start ploughing again."'

And still, in their frenzied monotony, the squalls of fire and iron continue: the shrapnel with its whistling as it goes off, powered by a furious metallic soul, and the heavy artillery, with their thunder like a plunging locomotive suddenly crashing into a wall, and loads of rails or steel girders tumbling down a hill. In the end the atmosphere becomes opaque and leaden, crossed by weighty gusts of breath; and all around the massacre of the earth goes on, ever deeper, ever more complete.

There are even more guns joining in. These are ours. They have an explosion that is similar to that of the 75, but louder, with a long, resounding echo like thunder rumbling around the mountains.

'Those are the long 120s. They're at the edge of the wood, a kilometre away. Terrific guns, old man, which look like greyhounds. They are slim and narrow-snouted; you want to call them "madame". They're not like the 220 which is just a mouth, a coal scuttle, which spits out its shell from the bottom upwards. They do their job, but in an artillery convoy they look like legless beggars on trolleys.'

A lull in the conversation. Here and there someone yawns.

The size and extent of this bombardment is wearying for the spirit. Voices struggle to be heard, drowned out.

'I've never seen one like this!' Barque shouts.

'That's what people always say,' says Paradis.

'Even so,' Volpatte bawls. 'They've been talking about an attack recently. I'm telling you: it's the start of something.'

'Oh!' the others go, simply.

Volpatte announces that he's going to take forty winks and settles down on the ground, his back to one wall, his feet braced against the opposite one.

There is talk about this and that. Biquet tells us about a rat he saw once.

'He was a cheeky little joker, you know. I'd taken off my shoes and this rat decided he wanted to eat his way round all the uppers! Admittedly, I had greased them.'

Volpatte, who had gone still, shifts around and says:

'Hey, chatterboxes! You're keeping me awake!'

'You're not telling me, you old fraud, that you could go drop off and get some kip with all the row and buggery that's going on round here,' says Marthereau.

'Grooo,' replies Volpatte, snoring.

★

'Fall in! March!'

We're changing place. Where are they taking us? No one knows. The most we know is that we are in the reserve and they are moving us around to consolidate certain points one after another or to free the communication trenches – where managing troop movements is as complex as organizing the coming and going of trains in a railway station, if you want to avoid blockages and collisions. It is impossible to work out the meaning of the vast manoeuvre in which our regiment turns like a little cogwheel, or to know what is happening in the vast expanse of the sector. However, lost in the network of depths where there is an interminable coming and going, exhausted, broken and stiff from long periods on our feet, stupefied by boredom and noise, poisoned by smoke, we do realize that our artillery is taking an increasingly active role and that the offensive seems to have changed sides.

'Halt!'

An intense, furious, atrocious burst of gunfire was smashing against the parapets of the trench where they had just stopped us.

'Fritz is having a go. He's afraid of an attack, he's going crazy! What a go he's having!'

A dense hail of metal was pouring down on us, slicing its frightful way through the air, scratching and brushing across the plain.

I looked through a slit, and had this strange, brief vision:

Ahead of us, some ten metres away at most, there were motionless, outstretched bodies, one beside another, a row of soldiers, mown down; and, from every direction, clouds of bullets and shells were riddling this row of dead men with holes.

The bullets that swept across the ground in straight lines, raising little linear clouds, were holing and battering the bodies rigidly pinned to the ground, breaking the stiffened limbs, pounding into pale, empty faces, bursting liquefied eyeballs, splattering them around. Beneath the onslaught one could see the row of dead men move a little, shifting around in places. You could hear the dry noise made by the plunging dots of copper as they ripped through clothing and flesh: the sound of a ferocious knife or a noisy blow from a stick on clothes. Above us rushed a host of sharp whistling sounds, with the descending tone, always lower down the scale, of ricochets. We bent our heads beneath this extraordinary barrage of cries and voices.

'We've got to get out of the trench! Hurry!'

We leave this tiny corner of the battlefield where the gunfire is tearing, wounding and killing corpses all over again. We head right and to the rear. The communication trench goes uphill. At the top of the ravine, we pass in front of a telephone post and a group of artillery officers and gunners.

Here we halt once again. Kicking our heels we listen to the observer gunner shouting orders which the telephonist, buried beside him, picks up and relays.

'First gun, same height. Two tenths to the left. Three rounds a minute!'

A few of us have ventured to put our heads above the edge of the parapet and manage for a fraction of a second to take in the whole of the battlefield around which our company has been vaguely marching ever since this morning. I see a vast grey plain, across which the wind seems to be blowing light, mixed waves of dust broken at intervals by a sharper drift of smoke.

This huge expanse, across which the sun and the clouds spread patches of black and white, flashes here and there; those are our guns firing, and for a moment I saw it entirely sprinkled with brief bursts of fire. A moment later part of the countryside has been smothered in a blanket of whitish vapour, a kind of hurricane of snow.

In the distance, on the interminable and sinister fields, half concealed and the colour of rags, pitted with holes like a necropolis, you can see the slender skeleton of a church, like a piece of torn paper, and, from one side of the picture to the other, vague ranks of vertical marks, close together and underlined, like pages of schoolchildren's writing; these are tree-lined roads. Thin winding lines cross the plain backwards and forwards, chopping it up, and these lines are dotted with men.

You can see the fragments of lines formed by these human dots who, emerging from the depressions, are moving over the plain beneath this frightful, savage sky.

It is hard to believe that each of these minute smudges is a being of flesh, trembling and fragile, infinitely vulnerable, but full of deep thoughts, full of long memories and full of a host of images. It is dazzling, this sprinkling of men as small as the stars in the sky.

My poor fellow men, poor unknown brothers, it is your turn for sacrifice. Another time it will be ours. Tomorrow, perhaps, it will be our turn to feel the skies bursting over our heads and the ground opening beneath our feet, to be assaulted by a prodigious army of missiles and to be swept aside by blasts a hundred thousand times more powerful than a hurricane.

They push us into the rear shelters. The field of death is extinguished from our eyes. In our ears, the thunder is deadened against the mighty anvil of the clouds. The noise of universal destruction falls still. Egotistically, the squad wraps itself in the familiar sounds of life and sinks into the caressing smallness of the shelters.

20

Fire

Suddenly roused, I open my eyes in the darkness.

'What? What is it?'

'It's your turn on watch. It's two in the morning,' says Corporal Bertrand whom I can hear, without seeing him, at the entrance to the hole in the depths of which I am lying.

I mutter that I am coming, shake myself and yawn in the narrow tomb-like shelter. I reach out and my hands touch the soft, cold clay. Then I scramble through the heavy darkness blocking the entrance, pushing through the thick smell as I walk between the slumped bodies of deeply sleeping men. After tripping once or twice and stumbling on pieces of equipment, bags and limbs stretched out in every direction, I put a hand on my rifle and find myself standing in the open air, only partly awake, unsteady on my feet, bitten by the sharp black north wind.

Shivering, I follow the corporal who makes his way between high dark embankments, the pit between which narrows oddly around where we walk. He stops. Here we are. I see a large mass detach itself from halfway up the ghostly rampart and come down. The mass gives out a yawn. I pull myself up into the niche he was occupying.

The moon is hidden by the mist, but there is a very vague light on things that the eye gets used to bit by bit. This glimmer is extinguished by a wide strip of darkness lowering across the sky. I can barely make out the framework and the peephole in front of my face after touching them with my hand; the same experienced hand finds a bundle of grenade handles in a specially designed hollow.

'Keep your eyes peeled, mate,' Bertrand says, in a whisper. 'Don't forget our listening post is up ahead there on the left. Bye, see you soon.'

His footsteps move off, followed by the sleepy tread of the watchman whom I have just relieved.

Rifle shots are cracking on all sides. Suddenly a round lands smack in the earth of the wall against which I am leaning. I put my face to the peephole. Our line twists along the top of the ravine and the ground slopes away sharply in front of me. You can't see a thing in that gulf of darkness. However, your eyes do eventually manage to make out the regular line of stakes for our wire standing on the brink of the sea of shadow and, here and there, the round wounds of shell holes: small, medium or huge. A few of these, nearby, are full of mysterious baggage. The wind is blowing straight in my face. Nothing moves except the wind as it goes by and the vast humidity dripping everywhere. It is so cold that you could shiver forever. I look up, searching here and there. A dreadful melancholy crushes the earth. I have the impression of being all alone, shipwrecked, in the midst of a world devastated by some cataclysm.

The air suddenly lights up: a flare. The scenery in which I am lost appears clearly around me. You can see the crest of our trench, jagged, dishevelled, and, plastered along the forward wall, every five metres, like vertical larvae, the shadows of those on watch. A few drops of light show where their guns are beside them. The trench is shored up with sandbags; it has been enlarged everywhere and in lots of places is broken by landslides. The sandbags, lying flat and disjointed on top of each other, have the appearance, in the astral light of the flare, of those vast dismantled slabs of ancient monuments in ruins. I look through the peephole. In the pale misty light spread by the flare I can see the rows of stakes and even the slender lines of barbed wire crossing over from one stake to the next. It's right in front of me, like pen-strokes scribbled and hatching the pallid pock-marked field. Further down, in the nocturnal ocean filling the ravine, silence and immobility gather.

I get down from my observation post and grope my way towards my nearest neighbour on watch. With hand outstretched, I reach him.

'Is that you?' I ask him in a low voice, without recognizing him.

'Yes,' he answers, without knowing me either, being as blind as I am.

'It's calm right now,' he went on. 'Just now I thought they were going to attack. Maybe they tried to, on the right, where they launched loads and loads of grenades. There was a barrage of 75s: vrrrrom, vrrrrom! I said to myself: "Mate, those 75s, they've got to have a reason for firing off like that. If the Boche have emerged, they must have taken a good hiding." There! Listen! All the lead flying around. Can you hear it?'

He paused, uncorked his bottle and took a swig. His last sentence, still in a whisper, smells of wine:

'Oh la la! What a bloody awful war this is. Don't you think we'd be better off at home? Hold on! What's that idiot up to?'

A shot has just rung out near us, suddenly leaving a brief, phosphorescent trace. Others go off, here and there, along our line. Firing is contagious at night.

We feel our way along the trench to find out from one of the men who fired, groping through the thick darkness that has suddenly fallen back on us like a roof. Swaying, sometimes thrown on to one another, we reach the man and touch him.

'What's up?'

He thought he saw a movement, then nothing. My neighbour and I go back through the deep blackness along the narrow road of sticky mud, uneasy, with difficulty, bent over, as though each of us was carrying a heavy weight.

On one point of the horizon, then another, all around us, the guns are crashing and their heavy din mingles with the chattering of rifle fire that sometimes increases and sometimes stops, and the clusters of grenade bursts, more sonorous than the cracking of the Lebels and Mausers, which have almost the sound of old-fashioned, classical gunshots. The wind has risen some more; it is so strong that we have to protect ourselves against it in the darkness. Huge banks of cloud are passing across the moon.

There we are, this man and I, walking close and bumping into one another without knowing who we are, revealed, then hidden in sudden flashes by the light of the gunfire; we are there, weighed down with the darkness, in the centre of a vast cycle of fires which appear and disappear in this landscape for witches' sabbaths.

'There's a curse on us,' the man says.

We separate and each go to our posts where we strain our eyes against the immobility of things. What dreadful, terrifying tempest is about to break?

The tempest did not break that night. At the end of my long watch, in the first light of day, there was even a fall in activity.

While dawn came on us like a stormy evening I once again saw the sort of sharp, sad, dirty edges – infinitely dirty, embossed with debris and garbage – the edges of our trench emerging and redefining themselves under the sooty scarf of the low clouds.

The livid pallor of the clouds makes the sandbags white and leaden, with their vaguely shining and swelling shapes, like a long heap of giant viscera and entrails opened upon the earth.

In the wall behind me is a hollow recess with things heaped up in it, horizontally like logs. Are they tree trunks? No: they are corpses.

As the birdsong rises from the furrows, the faint outlines of the fields reappear and the light buds and blossoms in each blade of grass, I look into the ravine. Lower than the bumpy field with its high swells of earth and its burned hollows, beyond the bristling stakes, there is still a lake of stagnant darkness and, in front of the opposite hill, still a wall of black rising.

Then I turn and look at the dead who are gradually being exhumed from the night, showing their stiffened, spattered forms. There are four of them. They are our companions, Lamuse, Barque, Biquet and little Eudore. They are decomposing there, right beside us, half obstructing the wide, twisting, muddy furrow that the living still care to defend.

They have been set down as best we could; they are supporting each other and crushing each other. The top one is wrapped in tarpaulin. The faces of the others did have handkerchiefs on them, but as we brushed past at night without seeing them or by day without paying attention, we knocked the handkerchiefs off and now we live face to face with these dead men, piled there like a blazing funeral pyre.

★

They were killed together four nights ago. My memories of that night are vague, like a dream I may have had. We were on patrol: them, me, Mesnil André and Corporal Bertrand. We had to reconnoitre a new German listening post that the artillery observers had spotted. Around midnight we came out of the trench and crept down the slope, in line, three or four paces apart. We went a long way into the ravine until we could see in front of us, like some stranded sea creature, the embankment in front of their International Trench. After making sure that there was no listening post in this sector we went back up, with an infinite amount of care. I could vaguely see my comrades on the right and left of me, like moving shadows, pulling themselves upwards, slowly sliding, rolling in the mud in the depth of the night, pushing their rifles like needles in front of them. Bullets were whistling above us, but casually, not looking for us in particular. When we got in sight of the mound of our line we paused for breath. One of us gave a sigh, another said something, and another turned right round, the sheath of his bayonet clanking against a stone. Immediately a flare shot hissing out of the International Trench. We hugged the ground, closely, desperately, keeping absolutely still and waited, with that terrible star hanging over us, bathing us in daylight, twenty-five or thirty metres from our trench. Then a machine-gun on the far side of the ravine sprayed the area where we were. Corporal Bertrand and I had the good luck, at the moment when the flare went up, red, before it burst into light, to be right in front of a shell hole where a broken trestle was lying in the mud. The two of us flattened ourselves against the edge of the hole and sank as far as we could into the mud, so that the miserable skeleton of rotten wood hid us. The machine-gun raked the ground several times. We could hear a piercing whistle in the middle of each report, the powerful dry blows of the rounds hitting the ground, and also dull soft snaps followed by groans, by a little cry and, suddenly, by a great snoring noise rising then gradually receding. Bertrand and I, with the horizontal hail of bullets brushing a few centimetres above our heads as they traced their pattern of death and sometimes scorched our clothing, pressed ourselves further and further into the ground, not daring to make any movement that might raise a part of our bodies up a little; and we waited. Finally the machine-gun fell silent, a vast silence. A quarter of an hour later the two of us slid out of the shell hole, crawling along on our elbows and finally fell like two sacks into our listening post. We were just in time, because at that moment the moon came out. We had to stay at the bottom of the trench until morning, then until the following evening. Machine-guns were constantly spraying all round it. Through the spyholes of the post we could not see the bodies lying there because of the slope; only, perhaps, right on the edge of our field of vision, a shape that looked like the back of one of them. In the evening a sap was dug to get to the point where they had fallen. The work could not be carried out in a single night. The pioneers took over the following night because we were totally exhausted and could not stay without sleep any longer.

When I woke up after a leaden sleep I saw the four bodies that the sappers had reached in no man's land from underneath, before tying them up and dragging them with ropes through the sap. Each one had several wounds next to one another, the bullet holes a few centimetres apart: the machine-gun had concentrated its fire. They hadn't found Mesnil André's body. His brother Joseph did everything he could to find it. He went out alone into no man's land, which was constantly being swept this way and that by the crossed fire of the machine-gunners. In the morning, dragging himself along like a slug, he re-appeared over the parapet with a face blackened with dirt and showing signs of dreadful distress.

We dragged him in, his cheeks scratched by the barbed wire, his hands bloody, with heavy lumps of mud in the folds of his clothing and stinking of death. He kept repeating like a madman: 'He isn't anywhere.' He slumped in a corner with his rifle and started to clean it, without hearing what anyone said to him, merely repeating: 'He isn't anywhere.'

That was four nights ago and now I can see the shapes of the bodies appearing in the dawn, which has come once again to wash over this hell on earth.

Barque is rigid and seems extended. His arms are stuck to his sides, his chest has collapsed, his belly has sunk into a bowl. With his head raised on a pile of mud he watches over the top of his feet those who approach from the left, with his darkened face, smudged by the viscous stain of hair that has fallen across it, thickly encrusted with black blood, and his scalded eyes, looking bloodshot and as though cooked. Eudore, by contrast, looks very small and his little face is completely white, so white that it could be a clown's face made up with flour; it is heart-rending to see it there, like a circle of white paper in the grey and bluish tangle of corpses. Biquet the Breton, stocky, square as a paving stone, seems to be stretching in some great effort, as though trying to lift the fog: this enormous strain becomes a grimace on his rugged face with its prominent cheekbones and forehead, and twists it hideously, seeming in places to make his dry, earthy hair stand on end, opening his jaw with a ghost of a cry and pulling back the lids from his wide-open eyes, his flinty eyes, now drab and troubled. His hands are clenched from clawing at the void.

Barque and Biquet have been shot in the belly, Eudore in the throat. They were further damaged by being moved and dragged along. Big Lamuse, emptied of blood, had a face that was swollen and creased, its eyes gradually sinking into their sockets, one more than the other. He has been wrapped in a piece of tarpaulin which is getting a blackish stain around the neck. His right shoulder was chopped through by several bullets and the arm is only hanging on by some threads of material from his sleeve and the string that was tied round it. The first night that they put him here the arm hung out of the pile of bodies and his yellow hand, clasping a fistful of earth, brushed against the faces of those going by. So the arm was pinned to the greatcoat.

A pestilential cloud is starting to hang around the remains of these creatures with whom we lived so closely and suffered for so long.

When we see them, we say: 'All four of them are dead.' But they are too misshapen for us to really think: 'This is them.' And you have to turn away from these motionless monsters to feel the void that they have left and the shared things that are broken.

Those from other companies or regiments, strangers who come by here during the day – because at night one leans on whatever is within reach, dead or alive – are repelled by these bodies lying one on top of the other in the open trench. Sometimes it angers them:

'What are they thinking about, leaving these stiffs here?'

'It's a disgrace!'

Then they add:

'Of course, you can't move them.'

Meanwhile they were only buried by night.

Morning has come. Opposite us we can see the far side of the ravine: Hill 119, scraped, skinned and grated, veined with twisting trenches and lined with parallels which have bared the mud and the chalky soil. Nothing is moving there and our shells, which burst here and there, seem to strike resounding blows against a great breakwater, ruined and abandoned.

My watch is over and with the others who have been on watch, wrapped in damp streaming tarpaulins, striped and patched with mud, with livid faces, I emerge from the earth in which we have been encased, move out and go down. The second squad is coming to take over the firing post and the loopholes. We can rest until evening.

We yawn and walk around. We see one comrade go by, then another. Officers are wandering about with periscopes and binoculars. We go back to normal, we start to live again. The usual remarks are exchanged, the usual arguments. If it were not for the dilapidated appearance and broken lines of the ditch in which we are buried on the edge of this ravine, as well as the need to keep our voices down, we might think we were in the rear. Yet there is a weariness on all of us, our faces are yellow, our eyelids red: we have stayed awake so much that we have the faces of people who have been crying. All of us in the last few days have sagged and aged.

One after another the men of my squad have gathered at a bend in the trench. They collect where the soil is chalky and where, under the crust of earth bristling with cut roots, the diggings have exposed layers of white stones which had been lying in darkness for more than a hundred thousand years.

This is where, in the widened part of the trench, Bertrand's squad ends up. It is considerably diminished now because, without including the dead who were killed the other night, we no longer have Poterloo, who was killed in a relief, or Cadilhac, wounded in the leg by a piece of shrapnel on the same evening as Poterloo (how long ago it seems already!), or Tirloir or Tulacque, who have been evacuated, one with dysentery, the other with a pneumonia that is turning bad, according to the postcards he writes to us to kill his boredom in the hospital in the Centre of France where he has nothing to do all day.

Once again I see them coming together as a group, dirtied by their contact with the earth, dirtied by the grey smoke of space, with their familiar physiognomies and familiar stances, those who have still not been separated since the beginning, fraternally welded and chained one to another. Yet there is less dissimilarity than at the start in the appearance of the cavemen.

Old Blaire exhibits a row of new teeth in his worn mouth, shining so much that in his poor face all one can see is this brand new jaw. The arrival of his foreign teeth, which he is gradually taming and which he now sometimes uses for eating, has profoundly altered his character and his behaviour. He is hardly ever, now, smeared with black; he is hardly ever neglected. Now that he is handsome he feels the need to be a bit of a dandy. For the time being he is gloomy, perhaps – oh, miracle! – because he cannot get a wash any longer. Slumped in a corner he half opens a dull eye, chewing and biting his old soldier's moustache, once the only ornament of his face. From time to time he spits out a hair.

Fouillade is shivering with a cold, or else yawns, depressed and shabby. Marthereau has not changed: still bearded, with round blue eyes and such short legs that his trousers seem constantly to be leaving his belt and falling on to his feet. Cocon is still Cocon with his dry, parchment-like head that has the figures working inside it, but for a week now a fresh bout of lice, the ravages of which can be seen emerging at his neck and wrists, has isolated him in prolonged struggles and makes him savage when he afterwards returns among us. Paradis has maintained the same degree of fresh colouring and good humour intact: he is unchanging and impossible to wear down. You smile when you see him approaching from a distance, standing out against the sandbags like a new poster. Nor has anything altered Pépin whom you can see wandering around with his placard of red-and-white checked tarpaulin on his back and, from the front, his knife-edge face and his cold grey look like the reflection of a revolver. Nor Volpatte with his gaiters, his blanket over his shoulders and his mandarin's face tattooed with dirt; nor Tirette, even though for some time he has been excited, with bloodshot eyes – no one knows why. Farfadet stays to one side, thoughtfully waiting. When the post comes he awakes from his reverie to fetch it, then slumps back into himself. His office clerk's hands meticulously write numerous postcards. He does not know what happened to Eudoxie. Lamuse had told no one about how he clasped her body in that supreme and terrifying embrace. Lamuse, I realize now, regretted having whispered that confidence to me one evening and hid the frightful, virginal thing inside him, with modest obstinacy, until his death. This is why one can see Farfadet still living with the vague, live image of her blonde hair, which he abandons only to make contact with us in brief monosyllables. When he is with us, Corporal Bertrand still has the same serious military attitude, always ready to smile at us calmly, to give a clear explanation whenever you ask for one, and to help each of us to do his duty.

We chat as we always did, before. But the need to keep our voices down means that our exchanges are rarer and gives them a funereal calm.

There is one odd thing: for the past three months each unit has been spending four days in the front line trenches. Now, we have been here for five, and there is no mention of a relief. A few rumours of a forthcoming attack are going round, circulated by liaison men and the fatigue party that brings our rations every other night – though it's not regular or guaranteed. Other clues support this talk of an offensive: leave is cancelled, letters stop arriving and the officers have changed visibly – they are serious, more pally. But any conversation on the topic always ends with a shrugging of shoulders. No one ever tells a soldier what is going to be done with him; his eyes are bandaged and the cloth lifted only at the last moment. So:

'We'll see.'

'We've just got to wait!'

This is a way of detaching ourselves from the tragic event that we guess is coming. Is it the impossibility of understanding it entirely? Or is it discouragement at being unable to fathom orders that are a closed book to us? Calm resignation? Or a tenacious belief that, once again, one will escape from danger? Whatever it may be, despite the signs and the voice of prophecies that seem to be coming true, we slip mechanically into our immediate concerns and cling to them: hunger, thirst, lice – crushing them leaves blood on your nails – and the immense weariness that undermines us all.

'Seen Joseph this morning?' asks Volpatte. 'He's in a bad way, poor lad.'

'He'll get carried away, I know it. He's had it, that kid, believe me. Sure as sure, as soon as he gets the chance, he'll step in front of a bullet.'

'It's enough to drive you crazy for the rest of your life. They were six brothers, you know. Four of them have bought it: two in Alsace, one in Champagne and one in Argonne. If André has been killed, that'll be five.'

'If he had been killed, we'd have found his body or someone would have seen it from the observation post. There's no two ways about it, mate. What I think is that the night they went out on patrol he got lost on the way back. He went off at an angle, poor bugger, and ended up in the Boche lines.'

'He might have got all chopped up in their wire.'

'We'd have found him, I tell you, if he'd been tied up in the wire, because you bet if he had the Boche wouldn't have bothered to take his body in. Truth is, we've looked everywhere; and since we haven't found him, the only answer is that, wounded or not, he got nicked by the Jerries.'

This hypothesis is logical, so we accept it; and now that we know Mesnil André is a prisoner we lose interest. But we still feel sorry for his brother:

'Poor old chap, he's so young!'

And the men of the squad quietly keep an eye on him.

'I'm famished!' Cocon says suddenly.

As it is past dinner-time we demand our food. It's there already, because it's the remains of what we had last night.

'What's the corporal thinking of, leaving us hungry? Here he comes. I'm going to get hold of him. Hey! Corporal! Why aren't you giving us any grub?'

'Yes! Yes! Grub!' repeats the chorus of the ever-hungry.

'I'm coming,' says Bertrand, who never stops bustling around, day or night.

'So what!' says Pépin, always difficult. 'I don't feel like macaroni again. Half a sec and I'll have a tin of bully beef open.'

The daily comedy of dinner resumes, coming to the forefront of the drama.

'Don't touch your emergency rations,' says Bertrand. 'As soon as I've been to see the captain, I'll give you something.'

When he returns he brings and hands out a salad of potatoes and onions, which we eat. And as we chew our faces relax and our eyes soften.

Paradis is sporting a policeman's hat while he eats. This may not be either the time or the place, but the hat is brand new and the tailor, who had been promising it to him for three months, only handed it over on the day we came up line. The soft, irregularly shaped hat in bright blue cloth sitting on his splendid round head makes him look like a cardboard gendarme with painted cheeks. While he is eating, however, Paradis is looking closely at me. I go over to him:

'You look good.'

'Don't bother about that,' he says. 'I'd like a word. Come over here.'

He reaches out towards his half-full mug which is sitting next to his knife and other things, hesitates, then decides to put the wine down his throat, for safe keeping, and the mug in his pocket. Then he moves off, with me following him. As he goes by he takes his helmet which is gaping on the earth bench. After a dozen yards he comes back to me and says very softly, with an odd manner about him, without looking at me, as he does when he's upset:

'I know where Mesnil André is. D'you want to see him? Come on.'

As he says this he takes off his policeman's hat, folds it and puts on his helmet. He sets off again. I follow him in silence.

He takes me a hundred metres on towards the place where we have our shared dugout and the bridge of sandbags under which we slide, each time with the feeling that this arch of mud is going to fall on our backs. After the bridge there is a hollow in the side of the trench, with a step made out of a hurdle stuck in the clay. Paradis gets up on it and signals to me to follow him on to this narrow, slippery platform. There used to be a spyhole for a sentry here, but it has been destroyed. The spyhole has been remade lower down with two bullet screens. You have to crouch down to avoid your head going above this structure.

Paradis, still in a very low voice, tells me:

'I'm the one who arranged those two shields, to see . . . Because I had an idea, and I wanted to see. Put your eye to the hole in this one.'

'I can't see a thing. It's blocked. What's that bundle of cloths?'

'That's him,' said Paradis.

Oh! It was a corpse, a corpse sitting in a hole, horribly close by.

When I pressed my face to the steel plate and put my eye up against the hole in the bullet shield I saw all of him. He was crouching, his head bending forward between his legs, his two arms on his knees, his fists half clenched, in hooks; and near, so near! He was recognizable despite the squinting of his bulging, opaque eyes, the mass of his muddy beard and the teeth showing in his twisted mouth. He seemed at one and the same time to be smiling and grimacing at his rifle, which was stuck upright in the mud in front of him. His hands, reaching forward, were quite blue on the top and scarlet underneath, made crimson by a damp light from hell.

It was him, washed with rain, smeared with mud and with a sort of foam, fouled and horribly pale, four days dead, right against our embankment, which the shell hole where he had gone to ground had broken into. We hadn't found him because he was too close!

Between this dead man, abandoned in his superhuman solitude, and the men who lived in the dugout there was only a slender earth partition, and I realize that the place where I put my head to sleep is the very same as the one against which this awful corpse is resting.

I take my face away from the hole. Paradis and I look at one another.

'Mustn't tell him yet,' my comrade whispers.

'No, that's right, not right away . . .'

'I mentioned it to the captain so that we could dig him out and he also said: "Don't say anything for the moment to the lad."'

A light breeze went past.

'You can smell him!'

'You're telling me!'

We sniff it, it enters into our souls and turns them over.

'That way,' Paradis says, 'Joseph is the only one of six brothers to survive. And I'll tell you something else, I don't think he'll be the only one for long. That kid won't look after himself, he'll get himself bumped off. What he needs is for God to send him a lucky wound, or else he's buggered. Six brothers is too much, don't you think? Don't you think it's too much?'

He adds:

'It's amazing he was just beside us.'

'His arm is resting exactly at the point where I put my head.'

'Yes,' says Paradis. 'His right arm with the watch on the wrist.'

The watch . . . I pause . . . Is it an idea? Was it a dream? I think, yes, I'm pretty sure that before I fell asleep three days ago, the night when we were so tired, I thought I heard something like the tick-tock of a watch. I even wondered where it was coming from.

'Yeah, it could well have been that watch you heard through the earth,' says Paradis, when I tell him what I'm thinking. 'It carries on telling the time and working even when the bloke has stopped. Hell, a mechanism like that doesn't know about you; it just keeps going round and round.'

I ask him: 'He's got blood on his hands, but where was he hit?'

'I don't know. In the belly, I think, 'cos I think there was black underneath him. Or else the face. Didn't you see a little mark on the cheek?'

I picture the dead man's hairy, greenish face.

'Yes, you're right, there was something on his cheek, here. Or perhaps it entered there . . .'

'Look out!' Paradis says to me suddenly. 'Here he is. We shouldn't have stayed here!'

But we stay, even so, hovering uncertainly, while Joseph Mesnil walks directly towards us. Never has he seemed so frail. From a distance you can see his pale face and its drawn, strained features. He walks along slowly with back bent, overwhelmed with an infinite tiredness and one fixed idea.

'What's wrong with your face?' he asks. He has seen me showing Paradis where the bullet entered.

I pretend not to understand, then give him some kind of evasive reply.

'Ah!' he says, without seeming to hear.

At that moment, one thing bothers me: the smell. You can't escape it or mistake it: it is the smell of a corpse. And he may just guess . . .

Suddenly I have the feeling that he has smelt this sign, the pitiful appeal of the dead man. But he says nothing, carries on his solitary way and vanishes round the corner.

'Yesterday,' Paradis tells me, 'he was right here with his can full of rice that he didn't want to eat. As though on purpose, the silly bugger, he stopped right there and, hup! He said something and made as though he was going to throw the rest of his food over the embankment, just at the spot where the other one is. Now, that I couldn't take. I grabbed his arm just as he was chucking his rice over and it all spilled here, in the trench. I tell you, old man, he turned on me in a fury, red in the face: "What's up with you? Are you mad or something?" he asked. I looked a real idiot and I mumbled how I didn't do it deliberately and all. He shrugged his shoulders and looked at me as though I was daft. He went off muttering and saying to Montreuil who was there: "No, but did you see what he did! What an arsehole!" You know he's got a short fuse, that lad, and even though I told him: "Okay, okay!", he kept on. And I wasn't pleased, see, since I was put in the wrong over it all, even though I was right.'

We go back together in silence to the dugout where the others had gathered. It's a former command post and spacious.

As we are going in Paradis stops to listen.

'Our guns have been going at it pretty hard for the past hour, haven't they?'

I know what he's thinking, and make a vague gesture:

'We'll see, old man, we'll soon see!'

In the dugout, with an audience of three, Tirette is telling soldiers' tales. Marthereau is snoring in a corner; he is close to the entrance and, to get in, you have to step over his short legs which seem to have shrunk back into his body. A group of card players kneeling around a blanket are playing manille.

'My turn!'

'40, 42! – 48! – 49! – Good!'

'Look at the luck of that rotter! It's not possible! You've trumped me three times! I'm not playing with you. You've skinned me this evening, you did the same the other day. You've been squinting at my cards, you twat!'

'Why didn't you discard, dickhead?'

'I only had the king, nothing else.'

'He'd got the ten of spades.'

'It's not the only time he had it, gob-skin!'

'Whatever you say,' murmured someone who was eating in the corner, 'this Camembert costs twenty-five sous but you can't imagine what garbage it is: there's a layer of putty on top that stinks and inside it's plaster that crumbles.'

Meanwhile Tirette is describing the humiliations that a certain commandant-major made him suffer during his basic training:

'The fat pig: he was the biggest swine that ever walked the earth. We didn't look like anything much, all of us, when he walked past, or when you saw that bulk in the officers' mess spread out over a chair that you couldn't see underneath him with his vast belly and his huge kepi with the stripes going all round it from top to bottom like a barrel. He came down hard on the private soldier, he did. His name was Loeb – a Boche, huh?'

'I knew him!' Paradis exclaims. 'When war broke out he was declared unfit for active service, of course. While I was doing my stint he already knew how to lay an ambush – at every street corner, to trap you. One day in clink he'd give for a button not buttoned, and on top of all that he'd give you a bawling out in front of everyone if there was the slightest little thing in your uniform which wasn't according to the book – and everybody laughed. He thought they were laughing at you, but you knew it was at him. But it didn't do you a damned bit of good, you were still going to the nick.'

'He had a wife,' Tirette goes on. 'This old . . .'

'I remember her, too,' Paradis says. 'Talk about an infectious disease!'

'Some people have a puppy dog that they take around with them. He took this poisonous creature . . . She was yellow, you know, like one of those apples, with her hips like a broom handle and a filthy look. She was the one who would work the old chump up against us. Without her he was stupid rather than wicked, but whenever she was there he became more wicked than stupid. So, you can guess what rows there were . . .'

At that moment Marthereau, who is sleeping close to the entrance, wakes up with a faint groan. He sits up on his straw bedding like a prisoner, and you can see his bearded profile silhouetted in the half-light and his round eye turning. He is looking at what he has just dreamed. Then he puts a hand over his eyes and, as though it had something to do with his dream, he conjures up a picture of the night when we came up to the trenches.

'Even so,' he says, in a voice heavy with sleep and reverie, 'what a wind there was in the sails that night! Oh, what a night it was! All those troops, whole companies, whole regiments, shouting and singing as they came up all the way along the road. In the clear night you could see the soldiers coming, on and on – it was like the waters of the sea – waving their arms at all the artillery convoys and ambulance cars that we passed that night. I'd never seen so many convoys in the night, never!'

Then he strikes himself a blow on the chest, slumps right back down, grunts and doesn't say another word.

Blaire's voice rises, expressing the unadmitted hope that haunts each man: 'It's four o'clock. It's too late for there to be anything on our side today.'

One of the card players, in the opposite corner, is barking at another:

'What now? Are you playing or not, worm-face?'

Tirette carries on with the story of his commandant:

'Would you believe, one day they'd served us up suet soup in the mess. A proper plague it was. So this chap asks to talk to the captain and sticks his mess plate under his hooter.'

'Clodhopper!' someone exclaims in the other corner, very angry. 'Why didn't you trump it then?'

' "Oh my gosh!" this captain says. "Take that away from my nose. It don't half stink." '

'It wasn't my turn to play,' quavers a dissatisfied but uncertain voice.

'And the captain makes a report to the commandant. But now the commandant flies off the handle and shows up, waving this report in his fist. "So where," says he, "is the soup which caused this mutiny, so that I can taste it?" They bring him some in a clean tin. He sniffs it. "So!" says he. "It smells good! You shan't have it then, soup as rich as this!" '

'Not your turn! And he was leading, the halfwit! Pea-brain! It's pitiful, you know that?'

'So at five o'clock, as we were coming out of barracks, these two phenomena come over and plant themselves in front of the soldiers, trying to see if there wasn't some small thing out of place, saying: "Oh yes, my pretty lads, you wanted to make a fool out of me by complaining about the excellent soup that I ate myself, and the commandant too, so just you wait and see what I'll get you for . . . Hey, you there, with the long hair, the great artist, come over here a moment." And while the bastard was talking like that the old scrag, dead upright, stiff as a post, was nodding her head.'

'It depends, since he didn't have an ace, it's a special case.'

'Then suddenly she goes as white as a sheet, puts her hand on her guts, is shaken by God knows what and all at once, in the middle of the square and all the fellows that were in it, she drops her umbrella and starts to spew!'

'Hey, look out!' Paradis says suddenly. 'They're shouting something in the trench. Can't you hear it? Aren't they calling "Alarm!"?'

'Alarm? Are you crazy?'

No sooner have the words been spoken than a shadow falls across the low entrance of our dugout and shouts:

'Alarm, the 22nd! To arms!'

★

There was silence, then a few exclamations.

'I knew it,' Paradis mutters through his teeth, and drags himself on his knees towards the entrance of the molehill where we are lying.

Then words cease. We have become dumb. Hastily we half rise. Bent over or kneeling we hurry about, buckling belts, with shadows of arms flying left and right, and we thrust things into our pockets, before going out, pell-mell, dragging our packs behind us by their straps, with our blankets and pouches.

Outside the noise is deafening. The din of the bombardment has increased a hundredfold and wraps us around, on the left, on the right and ahead. Our artillery is firing continuously.

'Do you think they're attacking?' someone asks.

'How do you expect me to know?' another voice answers, abruptly, with irritation.

Our jaws are clenched. We lock in what we are thinking. We hurry around, push each other aside, bump into each other and grunt without speaking.

The order goes out: 'Packs on!'

'There's a counter-order!' shouts an officer dashing down the trench with great strides, elbowing people out of the way. The rest of the sentence vanishes with him.

Counter-order! A visible shudder ran through the ranks, a shock to the heart which raises every head and halts everyone in an extraordinary attitude of expectation. But no: it's only a counter-order for packs. No packs. Blankets rolled around the body, excavating tool at the belt.

We unbuckle our blankets, take them out and roll them. Still not a word; everyone is staring with his mouth as though impulsively shut.

The corporals and sergeants, slightly feverishly, go here and there, pressing the men even in their silent haste:

'Come on, hurry up! Come on, come on, what are you doing? Are you going to get a move on, or what?'

A detachment of soldiers, wearing the insignia of crossed axes on their sleeves, make their way through us and quickly dig holes in the wall of the trench. We look askance at them while we finish putting on our equipment.

'What are those blokes doing?'

'It's so we can get up.'

We are ready. The men line up, still in silence, with their blankets across their backs, their chin straps on, leaning on their rifles. I look at their tense, pale, profound faces.

These are not soldiers, these are men. They are not adventurers or warriors, designed for human butchery – as butchers or cattle. They are the ploughmen or workers that one recognizes even in their uniforms. They are uprooted civilians. They are ready, waiting for the signal for death or murder, but when you examine their faces between the vertical ranks of bayonets, they are nothing but men.

Each one knows that he will be presenting his head, his chest, his belly, the whole of his body, naked, to the rifles that are already fixed, the shells, the heaps of ready-prepared grenades and, above all, the methodical, almost infallible machine-gun – to everything that is waiting in frightful silence out there – before he finds the other soldiers that he must kill. They are not careless of their own lives, like bandits, or blind with fury, like savages. Despite all the propaganda, they are not inflamed. They are above any instinctive reaction. They are not drunk, either physically or spiritually. Fully conscious of what they are doing, fully fit and in good health, they have massed there to throw themselves once more into that madman's role that is imposed on each of them by the folly of the human race. One can see what vision and what fear and what farewells are in their silence, their immobility, the mask of calm that inhumanly grasps their faces. They are not the sort of heroes that people think they are, but their sacrifice has greater value than those who have not seen them will ever be able to understand.

They wait. The wait grows longer, seems to go on for ever. From time to time one man or another in the ranks shudders a little when a bullet, fired from in front of us, grazes the embankment protecting us and buries itself in the soft earth of the wall behind.

Evening casts a sombre and grandiose light on this strong whole mass of human beings, only some of whom will live until nightfall. It is raining – the same rain that, in my memory, attaches to all the tragedies of the Great War. Evening is getting itself ready, like a faint, icy threat. It is about to spread out its trap, a trap as large as the world, in front of men.

New orders are spread by word of mouth. Grenades are handed out, strung on wire hoops. 'Each man take two grenades!'

The commandant walks along the line. He is restrained in his gestures, in undress, buttoned up tight, without his medals. You can hear him saying:

'One good thing, lads, the Boche are buggering off. It'll be a walkover, huh?'

News passes among us like the wind:

'The Moroccans and the 21st are ahead of us. The attack has been launched on the right.'

The corporals are called over to the captain. They come back with arms full of metal. Bertrand feels my chest and fastens something to the button of my coat. It's a kitchen knife.

'I'm giving you this,' he says.

He looks at me, then goes off in search of others.

'Me!' says Pépin.

'No,' Bertrand replies. 'It's not permitted to take volunteers for this.'

'Get stuffed,' Pépin growls.

We are waiting, in the depths of the rainy vastness, hammered with blows, with no boundary except the huge and distant shelling. Bertrand has finished handing things out and comes back. A few soldiers have sat down, some are yawning.

The cyclist Billette slips past us, carrying an officer's waterproof over his arm and clearly turning his head away.

'What's this? Aren't you coming?' Cocon shouts at him.

'No, I'm not,' he replies. 'I belong to the 17th. The 5th Battalion isn't attacking.'

'Oh, they get all the luck, the 5th. They never have to fight like us.'

Billette is already far away and men grimace a little as they watch him go.

A man arrives at the double and says something to Bertrand. Bertrand turns to us.

'Let's go,' he says. 'It's our turn.'

Everyone moves off at once. We put our feet on the steps that the sappers have made and, elbow to elbow, we lift ourselves out of the shelter of the trench and go up on to the embankment.

Bertrand is standing on the sloping field. He surveys us with a quick glance and, when we are all there, says:

'Right! Advance!'

Voices resonate oddly. It has all happened very quickly, unexpectedly you might say, as if in a dream. There is no whistling through the air. Amid the huge pounding of the guns, one can clearly perceive the extraordinary absence of the noise of bullets around us.

We set off down the slippery, uneven ground with automatic gestures, at times steadying ourselves with our rifles, made longer by their bayonets. The eye mechanically takes in some details of the slope, its wrecked earth, the occasional stake pointing upwards, the wreckage in the shell holes. It is incredible to find oneself in full daylight on this hill where a few survivors can remember flattening themselves so cautiously in the darkness and on which the others have only cast the odd furtive glance through a spyhole. No, they are not firing at us. The extensive exodus of the battalion out of the earth seems to have gone unnoticed! This truce is full of ever-increasing menace. We are dazzled by the pale light.

On all sides the embankment is covered with men who are emerging at the same time as we are. On the right is the outline of a company that is reaching the ravine through Trench 96, an old German earthwork, now in ruins.

We cross our wire through the gaps. Still no one is firing at us. Some clumsy men stumble and get up. We form up on the far side of the barbed wire, then start to go down a slope a little faster; there is an instinctive acceleration in the advance. Now a few bullets come in between us. Bertrand shouts to us not to waste our grenades, to wait until the last moment.

But the sound of his voice is drowned. Suddenly, in front of us and along the whole breadth of the hill, dark flames burst out, striking the air with appalling explosions. Across the line, from left to right, timed shells fall from the sky and explosives rise from the earth. They form a terrifying curtain that separates us from the world, separates us from the past and the future. We stop, rooted to the ground, stupefied by the sudden cloud pounding from all directions. Then, with a simultaneous effort, the mass of troops rises and plunges forward, very fast. We stagger, support one another, in great waves of smoke. At the bottom, towards which we are dashing helter-skelter, we can see craters opening here and there, some inside others, with strident din and cyclones of broken earth. Then we no longer know where the rounds are falling. Bursts of gunfire clatter out with such monstrous resonance that one feels annihilated by the very noise of these thunderclaps, these great stars of debris forming in the air. One can see, one can feel the chunks of shrapnel whizzing past one's head with the sound of red-hot iron hitting the water. At one point my hands are so burnt by the blast from an explosion that I drop my rifle. I pick it up, swaying on my feet, and set off again through the storm with its savage lights, through the crushing rain of molten things, stung by jets of dust and soot. The screeching of the fragments going past makes your ears hurt, hits you in the nape of your neck and bangs at your temples; it is impossible to keep from crying out. You feel sick, your stomach turned by the smell of sulphur. The blast of death pushes us, carries us onward, rocks us this way and that. We leap on, without knowing where we are going. Your eyes blink, are blinded, weep. In front of us everything is obscured by a blazing avalanche that occupies the whole horizon.

This is the barrage. We have to go through this whirlwind of flames and those frightful upright clouds. We pass, or we are passed, by chance. Here and there I saw shapes spin round, rise up and fall down, lit by a vague flash of the beyond. I glimpsed strange faces giving sorts of cries that one could see without hearing them in the annihilating din. A blazing inferno with huge and furious masses of red and black was falling around me, digging into the earth, cutting it away from under my feet and throwing me to one side like a bouncy toy. I remember stepping over a burning corpse, entirely black with a sheet of vermilion blood crackling on him; and I also recall that the tails of the coat moving along beside me had caught fire and were leaving a furrow of smoke. On our right, along the whole length of Trench 97, one's eye was attracted and dazzled by a line of ghastly illuminations, pressed one against the other like men.

'Forward!'

Now we are almost running. You can see some men falling like logs, head first, while others drop, humbly, as though sitting down on the ground. You step suddenly this way or that to avoid the dead, prone, stiff and well behaved, or else rearing upwards, and also, more dangerous snares, wounded men struggling and clinging on to you.

The International Trench!

We've reached it. The barbed wire has been uprooted with its long spiralling stems, cast aside and rolled up, swept away and pushed into huge piles by the guns. Between these great iron bushes, wet with rain, the earth is open and free.

The trench is not defended. The Germans have abandoned it, or else a first wave has already passed over it . . . The inside is bristling with rifles placed along the embankment and at the bottom there are scattered bodies. Hands emerge out of the debris in the long ditch, reaching from grey sleeves with red piping, or booted feet. In places the embankment has been smashed and its wooden shoring broken: the whole side of the trench blown apart and submerged in an indescribable jumble. At other places there are gaping wells. What I most remember from that moment is the vision of a trench oddly in tatters, covered with multicoloured rags: to make their sandbags, the Germans had used sheets, cotton cloths, woollens with motley designs, pillaged from some furnishing shop. All this mishmash of coloured scraps, chopped up and frayed, is hanging, waving and flapping in front of one's eyes.

We have spread along the trench. The lieutenant, who has jumped over to the far side, leans over and calls to us, waving his hands:

'Don't stay there! Forward! Keep going forward!'

We clamber up the side of the trench with the help of the bags, weapons and backs piled there. At the bottom of the ravine, the earth is ploughed up with shell holes, cluttered with wreckage and seething with outstretched bodies. Some have the immobility of things; the others are moving gently or twitching convulsively. The barrage continues to accumulate its infernal explosions behind us, in the place where we have been. But the point we have reached at the foot of the hill is a dead point for artillery.

A slight, brief moment of calm. We recover a little from our deafness. We look at one another. There is fever in our eyes and red on our cheeks. We are gasping for breath and our hearts are pounding in our breasts.

We recognize one another, hastily, confusedly, as if in a nightmare we were to find ourselves face to face at the far side of the river of death. In this hellish glade we exchange a few hasty words:

'It's you!'

'Oh la la! They're really handing it out!'

'Where is Cocon?'

'Dunno.'

'Have you seen the captain?'

'No . . .'

'Okay?'

'Yeah . . .'

We have crossed the bottom of the ravine. The other side rises up in front of us. We climb it in single file, by a rough stairway cut into the ground.

'Look out!'

A soldier has reached the halfway point up the stairway and been struck in the back by a piece of shrapnel from the other side; he is falling, like a swimmer, with no helmet, both arms in front of him. You can see the shapeless outline of the mass diving into the gulf and I glimpse the detail of his tousled hair above the black profile of his face.

We come out on to the heights.

In front of us is a great colourless void. At first we see nothing except a chalky, pebbled steppe, yellow and grey as far as the eye can see. There is no human wave preceding ours; no one alive in front of us, though the ground is peopled with the dead, recent bodies still in poses of suffering or of sleep, and ancient remains already discoloured and scattered by the wind, almost digested by the earth.

As soon as our line, pushing and shoved, emerges I feel that two men beside me have been hit, two shadows have dropped to the ground, rolling under our feet, one with a sharp cry, the other in silence, like an ox. Another vanishes with a crazy gesture, as though carried away. Instinctively, we close ranks as we press forward, ever forward. In our mass the scar heals itself. The adjutant stops, raises his sabre, drops it and kneels. His kneeling body leans jerkily backwards, his helmet falls on his heels and he stays there, his head uncovered, looking up at the sky. The line parts suddenly in its forward dash, respecting his immobility.

But we can no longer see the lieutenant. So: no more leaders. A vague hesitation holds back the human flood as it starts to flow over the plateau. Amid the tramp of feet one can hear the hoarse breath from our lungs.

'Forward!' shouts some private soldier.

So we all resume our forward rush into the abyss, with growing haste.

'Where is Bertrand?' the voice of one of those running forward moans, struggling to get out the words.

'There! Here . . .'

He had bent over a wounded man as he went by, but soon leaves him. The man reaches out with his arms, apparently sobbing.

It is just as he rejoins us that we hear the tock-tock-tock of a machine-gun ahead, coming from a sort of hump. It is a worrying moment, even more serious than when we crossed the blazing earthquake of the barrage. The well-known voice speaks clearly and terrifyingly to us through the air. But we don't stop.

'Forward! Forward!'

Panting gives way to hoarse groans as we continue to dash towards the horizon.

'The Boche! I can see them!' someone suddenly yells.

'Yes! Their heads, above the trench . . . That's where the trench is, that line. It's just ahead. Oh, the bastards!'

We can indeed make out the little grey caps, rising then falling back, at ground level, fifty metres or so ahead beyond a black strip of earth, furrowed and humpy.

A shudder runs through those who now make up the group around me. So close to our goal, unharmed so far, surely we'll make it? Yes, we'll make it! We take great strides, no longer hearing anything. Each man throws himself forward, attracted by the dreadful trench, going onward rigidly, almost unable to turn his head to right or left.

You have the feeling that many are losing their footing and falling down. I jump to one side to avoid the bayonet of a tumbling rifle that rises before me. Farfadet, right beside me, his face bloody, pushes me and falls on Volpatte, who is next to me, clinging to him. Volpatte bends and, plunging forward, drags him with him for a few steps then shakes him off, without looking, without knowing who it is, shouting in a strangled voice, almost choking with the effort:

'Let me go! For God's sake, let me go! Later on we'll pick you up. Don't worry.'

The other man sinks back, his head, covered in a vermilion mask, all expression wiped off it, turns this way and that – while Volpatte, already far off, continues to mutter mechanically: 'Don't worry!', his eyes staring ahead at the German line.

A hail of bullets spurts around me, increasing the number of sudden stops, delayed, resisting, gesticulating falls, plunges all of a piece with the full weight of the body, cries, dull, furious or desperate exclamations, or else those dreadful, hollow sounds of *huh!* as all of life is exhaled in a single breath. And those of us who have not yet been hit look right ahead, march or run, amid the games of death as it strikes at random in the flesh of us all.

The barbed wire. There is an area intact. We go round it. It has been gutted by a wide, deep path, a vast funnel formed by funnels next to one another, a fantastic volcano's mouth dug there by the guns.

The sight of this upheaval is astonishing. It really seems that this has come up from the centre of the earth. The appearance of these layers of soil ripped open stimulates our thirst for the attack and some, even at this moment when it is hard to thrust the words from one's throat, cannot restrain themselves from shouting, with a grave shaking of the head:

'Crikey! Look what we laid on them there! Oh, crikey!'

As if driven by the wind we go up and down, over the dips and the mounds of earth, through this huge fissure soiled, blackened and cauterized by the furious flames. The soil clings to the feet and we angrily shake it off. The equipment and materials that cover the soft earth, the linen spread there out of eviscerated packs, prevent us from sinking and we are careful to put our feet on these remains when we jump into the holes or climb up the little mounds.

Behind us, voices urging us on:

'Forward, lads, forward! For God's sake!'

'The whole regiment is behind us!' they shout.

We don't turn round to look, but this assurance gives still greater impetus to our charge.

There are no longer any helmets visible behind the embankment of the trench in front of us. Bodies of dead Germans are stretched in front of it, heaped up in clumps or extended in lines. We are getting there. The embankment is clearer, with its cunning shapes, its details: the spyholes . . . We are prodigiously, incredibly close . . .

Something falls in front of us. A grenade. With a kick, Corporal Bertrand lobs it back so well that it jumps forward and explodes inside the trench.

On this lucky note the squad reaches the ditch.

Pépin has thrown himself on his belly. He goes round a corpse, reaches the edge and plunges in. He is the first. Fouillade, shouting, making great gestures, jumps into the void almost at the same moment as Pépin slides into it . . . In a flash I glimpse a whole row of black demons, bending down, crouching on the top of the embankment before descending into the black trap.

A terrible volley bursts in our faces, at point-blank range, throwing a sudden ramp of flames the whole length of the parapet. After a moment's surprise, we shake ourselves and burst out laughing diabolically; the salvo has gone over our heads. Then straightaway, with shouts and roars of deliverance, we slide, roll or fall, alive, into the belly of the trench!

We are submerged in an incomprehensible cloud of smoke. At first, in the tight gulf, I can only see blue uniforms. We go this way and that, driven by one another, grumbling, searching. We turn round and at first, our hands encumbered by knives, grenades and rifles, we don't know what to do.

'They're in their dugouts, the bastards!' someone shouts.

Dull explosions shake the ground, coming from underneath, in the shelters. Suddenly we are separated by monumental clouds of smoke so thick that it plants a mask on your face and you can see nothing. We struggle like drowning men, through this murky acrid air, in a piece of night. We stumble against reefs of creatures kneeling, curled up, bleeding and shouting below us. We can barely see the walls, which are upright here and made of white linen sandbags, torn everywhere like paper. At times the heavy fog sways and grows lighter, and you can see the swarming mass of attackers. A fragment torn out of this dusty picture: an outline of a hand-to-hand struggle silhouetted against the embankment, in a mist, sinks slowly downwards. I hear a few harsh cries of '*Kamarad!*' from one group with haggard faces and grey jackets driven into a corner made enormous by a shell burst. Under the ink cloud the storm of men turns back, goes up in the same direction towards the right, jumping and twisting, along the dark, destroyed jetty.

Suddenly you sense that it is over. We see, we hear, we realize that our wave, which rolled forward here through the barrage, did not meet an equal counter-wave and that they retreated as we came. The human battle melted in front of us. The slender curtain of defenders disappeared into their holes where we capture them like rats or kill them. There is no more resistance: a void, a great void. We are advancing, in a mass, like a terrible line of spectators.

Here the trench is shattered. With its crumbled white walls it seems at this point like the muddy, unclear outline of a vanished river between stony banks with, here and there, the flat rounded hole of a pond that has also dried up, and on the edge, on the embankment and the bottom, lies a long glacier of bodies – all of this fills up and overflows with the new waves of our troops when they arrive. In the smoke pouring out of the shelters and the air shaken by underground explosions I come across a compact mass of men who are attached to one another and turning round in a wide circle. As I come up the whole mass dissolves and this remnant of a battle dies away. I see Blaire getting out of it, his helmet hanging round his neck close to the jugular, his face skinned, giving a savage yell. I bump into a man who is crouching at the entrance to a dugout. Keeping away from the treacherous gaping hole, he is supporting himself with his left hand on a beam, while with the right hand he swings a grenade for several seconds. It is about to explode. It vanishes into the hole and explodes at once. A frightful human echo replies from the bowels of the earth. The man grabs another grenade.

Someone else, with a pickaxe that he has found on the spot, is hitting and smashing the beams of another dugout. There is a landslide and the entrance is blocked. You can see several shadows trampling and gesticulating above this tomb.

One side and the other . . . In the band of the living who have got this far, up to this trench that we have been aiming at for so long, after crashing through the invincible shells and bullets thrown against it, I have trouble recognizing those that I know, as if all the rest of life had suddenly become very far away. Something is working inside them and changing them; a frenzy has taken hold of them all and lifted them out of themselves.

'Why are we stopping here?' one asks, grinding his teeth.

'Why don't we go as far as the next one?' another asks me, full of rage. 'Now that we've got here, in a few steps, we'd be there!'

'Me too, I want to go on.'

'Me too . . . The bastards!' They shake themselves like flags, carrying their luck at having survived as a badge of glory, implacable, bubbling, intoxicated by themselves.

We do nothing, trampling round the conquered earthwork, that odd, half-demolished roadway that snakes across the plain and goes from one unknown to another.

'By the right, advance!'

So we continue to flow in the same direction. No doubt the movement has been coordinated on high, over there, by our leaders. We trample soft bodies, some of which shift and slowly change their position, giving out little cries and rivulets of blood. Corpses are piled up lengthwise, crosswise, like beams and rubble, even on top of the wounded, pressing down on them, stifling, strangling them and taking their life. I push to get past a torso with its throat cut. Its neck is a stream of gurgling blood.

In the cataclysm of collapsed or excavated earth and massive debris all we find now are blazing faces, bloody with sweat, their eyes shining, above the groaning of the wounded and the dead who move together behind the moving forest of smoke pouring across the trench and the whole area around. Some groups of men seem to be dancing, waving knives. They are happy, enormously relieved and savage.

Imperceptibly the battle ends. A soldier asks:

'What do we have to do now?'

Suddenly it flares up again at one point. Twenty metres ahead on the plain, towards a circle made by the grey embankment, a bunch of rifle shots crackles, laying scattered fire around a machine-gun that is buried there, firing intermittently, apparently putting up a struggle.

Under the sooty wing of a sort of bluish and yellow nimbus cloud, men are surrounding the blazing machine and closing in on it. Near me I can see the silhouette of Mesnil Joseph. He is standing up without trying to conceal himself and walking towards the place from which a succession of short bursts of fire is coming.

A shot rings out from a corner of the trench between us. Joseph stops, sways, leans over and falls on one knee. I run over to him and he watches me as I come.

'Nothing, my thigh. I can crawl along by myself.'

He seems like a well-behaved, docile child. He is swaying gently towards the hollow . . .

I can still see exactly the point from which the shot came that brought him down. I slide over there, to the left, making a detour.

No one there. The only person I meet is one of our own who is also looking: Paradis.

We are being jostled by men carrying lumps of iron of every shape on their shoulders or under their arms. They are blocking the sap and separating us.

'The machine-gun has been taken by the 7th!' someone shouts. 'It won't be barking any more. It was rabid, the dirty beast! Dirty beast!'

'What is there to do now?'

'Nothing.'

We stay there, in a muddle. We sit down. The living have ceased to pant, the dying have ceased to croak, surrounded by smoke and light and the din of the guns, pounding at every end of the earth. We still don't know where we are. There is no more earth or sky, there is still only a sort of cloud. A first interval appears in the drama of chaos. There is a universal slowing down of movements and noises. The gunfire lessens; and it is further away now, shaking the sky like a cough. Exaltation is calmed and there is nothing left except an infinite fatigue that rises up in us, drowning us, and the endless waiting that resumes.

Where is the enemy? He has left bodies everywhere and we saw lines of prisoners: there is one still, not far away, outlined against the dirty sky, monotonous, indefinite and shrouded in smoke. But most of them appear to have vanished into the distance. A few shells are fired towards us, inaccurately; we laugh at them. We are delivered, calm, alone in this sort of desert where an immense expanse of bodies ends in a line of living men.

Night has fallen. The dust has cleared, but it has given way to half-dark and darkness, above the disorder of the crowd spread out in a line. Men come together, sit down, get up and walk around, leaning on one another or holding each other by the arm. Between the shelters, which are blocked by the heaps of dead, they crouch in groups. Some have put their rifles down and are wandering around the edges of the trench, their arms dangling; but close up one can see that they are blackened, burnt, red-eyed and spattered with mud. Few people talk, but they have started to search.

One can see stretcher-bearers, in silhouette as they hunt, bend over or march forward, two by two, clutching their long burdens. Over there, on the right, we can hear picks and spades.

I am wandering around in the midst of this dark chaos.

At one point, where the embankment of the trench has been crushed by the bombardment to make a gentle slope, someone is sitting. There is still some light left. I am struck by the calm attitude of this man, looking straight ahead and thinking; he looks like a sculpture. Leaning over I recognize him. It is Corporal Bertrand.

He turns and I can feel that he is smiling at me through the darkness with his thoughtful smile.

'I was going to look for you,' he said. 'We're organizing the guard for the trench, until we get news of what the others have done and what is going on ahead. I'm going to put you on sentry duty with Paradis in a hole that the sappers have just dug.'

We watch the silhouettes of men going by and others standing still, like blots of ink, bent over, twisted into various poses against the grisaille of the sky along the ruined parapet. They move strangely, darkly, as small as insects and worms, in these hidden landscapes of shadows, pacified by death, where for the past two years battles have made towns of soldiers wait and wander over deep, outsized cities of the dead.

Two dark shadows pass by in the dark, a few steps away from us. They are speaking in hushed voices.

'You bet, mate, instead of listening to him, I stuck me bayonet in his belly so far I couldn't pull it out.'

'Well, I found four of them at the bottom of the trench. I called to them to come out and each one, as he came, I bumped him off. I was red right up to my elbows. My sleeves are sticky with it.'

'Ah,' the first one said, 'when we tell them about it, if we ever get back home, by the stove or the candle, who'll believe us? It's a bleeding shame, innit?'

'I don't give a toss, as long as we do get home,' said the other. 'The end, and quick, and that's all!'

Usually Bertrand was very reserved and never spoke about himself. But now he said:

'I had three of them to deal with. I hit out like a maniac. Oh, we were all like beasts when we reached here!'

His voice rose, with a slight quaver.

'We had to,' he said. 'We had to – for the future.'

He crossed his arms and shook his head.

'The future!' he exclaimed suddenly, like a prophet. 'Those who come after us, when progress – which is coming with the inevitability of fate – has finally set people's consciences at rest . . . how will they think of these massacres, these deeds, when even we who commit them don't know whether they are like the exploits of heroes from Plutarch and Corneille or the doings of bandits!

'And yet,' he went on. 'Look! There is someone who has risen above the war and who will shine out for the beauty and extent of his courage . . .'

I listened, leaning on a stick, bending over him, listening to this voice in the silence of the dusk, emerging from a mouth that was almost always silent. He exclaimed in a clear voice: 'Liebknecht!'*

He got up, his arms still folded. His fine head, as profound and serious as that of a statue, bent forward on to his chest. But once again he came out of his chiselled silence and repeated:

'The future! The future! The work of the future will be to efface this present and to efface it more than we think, to efface it as something abominable and shameful. And yet this present was necessary! Necessary! Shame on military glory, shame on armies, shame on the soldier's profession, which changes men, some into stupid victims, others into base executioners. Yes, shame, that's true – but it's too true, it's true in eternity, but not yet for us. Take care of what we think now. It will be true when there will be a whole, true bible. It will be true when it is written among other truths that a purified mind will allow us to grasp at the same time. We are still lost, exiled, a long way from that future time. In these present days, in these moments, this truth is almost an error, nothing more: this holy word is mere blasphemy!'

He gave a laugh full of echoes and dreams.

'I told them once that I believed in prophecies – just to kid them!'

I sat down beside Bertrand. This soldier, who always did more than his duty and yet managed to survive, took on at that moment in my eyes the aspect of those who are the incarnation of some high spiritual ideal and have the strength to rise above the hustle and bustle of contingency – those who, provided they move into the spotlight of events, are destined to dominate their age.

* Karl Liebknecht (1871–1919), German Communist. [trans.]

'I've always thought all those things,' I murmured.

'Ah!' Bertrand went.

We looked at one another without a word, with a certain surprise and reverence. After this great silence, he resumed:

'It's time to go back on duty. Take your rifle and come with me.'

From our listening post we can see a light in the east spreading, like the light of a fire, but more blue and sadder than a fire. It streaks the sky with a long extended black cloud, hanging like the smoke from an extinguished bonfire, a huge blot on the world. It is the return of morning.

The cold is such that one cannot stay motionless despite the chains of sleep. We shiver, we shake, our teeth chatter, our eyes water. Little by little, desperately slow, day escapes from the sky into the narrow framework of black clouds. Everything is icy, colourless and void; the silence of death reigns everywhere. Frost and snow, under a blanket of mist. Everything is white. Paradis moves, a thick, pallid ghost. We are white all over as well. I have put my shoulder bag on the far side of the parapet in front of the listening post and it looks as though it is wrapped in paper. At the bottom of the trench a little snow floats, grey-tinted and eaten away, on the black foot bath. Outside the hole, on the mounds, in the dips, over the throng of the dead, there is a thin scarf of snow.

Two crouching masses, blurred and mamillated, emerge from the fog; they speed up and hail us as they arrive. These are the men who have come to relieve us. Their tanned faces are reddened and damp with the cold, their cheekbones are like enamelled tiles, but their coats are not dusted with snow: they have slept underground.

Paradis heaves himself out. Behind him, across the empty field, I follow his Father Frost back and the duck waddle of his shoes as they pick up white lumps of soft soles. Bent double, we get back to the trench; the steps of those who came to take over from us have left a black trail in the thin powdering of white on the ground.

Watchers are standing in the trench, above which in places there are tarpaulins, stretched with the help of pegs to make vast, irregular tents, brocaded with white velvet or iridescent with frost. Between them are crouching shapes, groaning, trying to struggle against the cold and to defend the poor hearth of their chests from it – unless they are already frozen. A body has slipped slightly to one side from upright, his chest and two arms resting against the embankment. He was moving some earth when he died. His face, raised to the sky, is covered with a leprous layer of rime, his eyelids are white and his moustache covered with hard spittle.

Other bodies are sleeping, not as whitened as the rest; the layer of snow only stays intact on things: objects and the dead.

'Must sleep.'

Paradis and I are looking for a shelter, a hole where we can hide ourselves and close our eyes.

'Too bad if there are a few corpses in a dugout,' Paradis murmurs. 'In this cold they'll keep it in, they won't misbehave.'

We carry on, so exhausted that we can hardly look up.

I am alone. Where is Paradis? He must have gone to sleep in some ditch. Perhaps he called to me and I didn't hear.

I come across Marthereau.

'I'm looking for somewhere to sleep; I've been on guard,' he says.

'Me too. Let's look.'

'What's up with all that noise and hullabaloo?' Marthereau asks.

A shuffle of tramping feet, mingled with the sound of voices, is coming out of the trench that joins ours at this point.

'The trenches are full of blokes and guys . . . Who are you?'

'We're the 5th Battalion.'

The newcomers stop. They are in full kit. The man who spoke sits down, to get his breath back, on the swelling side of a sandbag sticking out of the wall and puts his hand grenades down at his feet. He wipes his nose on his sleeve.

'What're you doing here then? Did they tell you?'

'You bet they told us. We've come to attack. We're going thataway, right to the end.'

He nods in a northward direction.

Our curiosity fixes on one detail:

'You've brought all your gear with you?'

'We preferred to keep it with us, that's all.'

'Forward!' comes the command.

They get up and advance, only half awake, their eyes puffy and their faces heavily lined. There are young ones with thin necks and empty expressions, and old ones, and in between, ordinary blokes. They march with quiet, ordinary steps. What they are going to do seems beyond human strength to us, even though we did it yesterday ourselves. And yet off they go, northwards.

'The awakening of the condemned,' says Marthereau.

We step aside to let them pass with a kind of admiration and a kind of terror.

When they have gone Marthereau shakes his head and mutters:

'And on the other side there are blokes getting ready too, in their grey uniforms. D'you think they're feeling eager for an attack? Don't be crazy. So why did they come? I know it's not them, but it is them even so, since they're here. I know, I know . . . but it's pretty odd, the whole thing.'

The sight of someone going by redirects his thoughts.

'Hey, there's Thingamy, Whatsit, you know, the tall one . . . Look at the height on him, and how pointed he is! No, I know that I'm not quite as tall as I might be, but he really has taken it a bit far. He always knows what's going on, that yardarm! There's no one can beat him when it comes to being in the know. We'll go and ask him about a funk hole.'

'Wanna know if there are any digs?' the outsized individual says, leaning over Marthereau like a poplar. 'Of course there are, my old Carpathian. Dozens of 'em. Look there . . .' (and, unfolding his elbow, he makes a gesture like a signals telegraph) '. . . Villa Von Hindenburg, and over here you've got Villa Glücks Auf. If you're not happy with 'em then you're a pair of fusspots. There may be some tenants in the back rooms, but they won't be noisy neighbours and you can say whatever you like without them overhearing.'

'God in heaven!' Marthereau exclaimed, quarter of an hour after we had settled into one of these square-cut graves. 'There are tenants here he didn't mention, that great lightning conductor, that go-on-forever . . .'

His eyes had shut, but now they were open again and he was scratching his arms and sides.

'I'm dog tired! But there's no hope of any shut-eye, not with these bastards!'

We started yawning and sighing; finally we lit a little piece of candle that was wet and reluctant to burn, even though we cupped it in our hands. Then we watched each other yawn.

The German shelter had several rooms. We were up against a partition of badly fitting planks and on the other side, in Cellar No. 2, there were other men who couldn't sleep; you could see light between the planks and hear voices rustling.

'It's the other section,' said Marthereau.

Then we started to listen, without meaning to.

'When I was on leave,' an invisible speaker was murmuring, 'at first we were sad, 'cos we thought of my poor brother who vanished in March, dead no doubt, and my poor little Julien, from the class of 1915, who was killed in the October attacks. Then, bit by bit, she and I found we were enjoying life together again: you know how it is. Our little nipper, the youngest, who's five, took up a lot of our time. He wanted to play soldiers with me. I made a little gun for him. I explained to him about the trenches and he would fire at me, fluttering with joy like a little bird. I tell you, that little chap, he really loved it; he'll make a hell of a soldier when he grows up. He's got the makings of a proper *poilu*, old man!'

A pause. Then, a vague hum of conversation in which we hear the word 'Napoleon', followed by another voice – or the same – which is saying:

'That Kaiser Bill, he's a stinking bastard for wanting this war. But Napoleon, now, there was a great man!'

Marthereau is on his knees in front of me, in the scant and feeble rays of our candle, at the bottom of this dark, draughty hole through which a shudder of cold passes from time to time, where vermin teem and the unhappy pile of living bodies gives off a faint odour of the tomb . . . Marthereau looks at me. Like me, he can still hear the voice of that anonymous soldier saying: 'Kaiser Bill's a stinking bastard, but Napoleon's a great man' – and celebrating the warlike spirit of the one remaining child. He drops his arms, shakes his tired head . . . and the faint, yellow light throws the shadow of this double gesture on the partition, making a rapid caricature out of it.

'Oh, we're none of us such bad sorts,' says my humble companion. 'And we're also unfortunates, sad types. But we really are too bloody stupid! We really are!'

He looks back at me. In his unshaven face, a spaniel's face, he has two fine, shiny dog's eyes with a look of astonishment in them, thinking – though still in a confused way – about this and that, and in the purity of his obscurity, he is starting to understand.

We leave the uninhabitable shelter. The weather has grown a little milder, the snow has melted and everything is dirty again.

'The wind has licked off the sugar,' says Marthereau.

I am the one picked to accompany Joseph Mesnil to the Pylônes First Aid Post. Sergeant Henriot delivers the wounded man to me and hands me his evacuation papers.

'If you meet Bertrand on your way,' he says, 'you'd better tell him to get a move on, could you? He was sent on a liaison mission last night and we've been waiting for him for an hour. The old man is getting impatient and may go off the deep end any moment.'

I set out with Joseph, who is a little paler than usual but just as silent; he walks along slowly. From time to time he stops, with a look of pain on his face. We are following the communication trenches.

Suddenly someone appears: it is Volpatte. He says: 'I'll go with you as far as the hill.'

Having nothing particular to do he is swinging a splendid cane, twisted like a corkscrew, and in his other hand he has the precious pair of scissors that never leaves him, which he is shaking like a pair of castanets.

All three of us leave the trench as soon as the slope of the hill allows us to without the risk of being hit by sniper fire. The guns are silent. No sooner are we in the open than we come across a group of men. It is raining. Through the thick legs, standing like sad tree trunks in the mist on this grey-brown plain, we can see a dead body.

Volpatte makes his way through to the horizontal shape around which all these vertical shapes are waiting, then turns round and shouts to us: 'It's Pépin!'

'Oh!' Joseph says, almost fainting already.

He leans against me. We go closer. Pépin is outstretched, with his hands and feet taut and twisted; his face, with the rain running down it, is swollen, bruised and horribly grey.

A man with a spade, whose sweaty face is full of little black lines, tells us about the death of Pépin:

'He'd gone down into a dugout where the Boche had hidden. But our lads didn't know that and they smoked the hole out to clear it, so we found the poor old chap after the operation, a goner, all stretched out like catgut in the middle of this Boche meat that he'd bled – and very properly bled, I can tell you, me that was a butcher by trade, near Paris.'

'One less in the squad,' said Volpatte as we were leaving.

Now we are at the top of the ravine, at the point where the plateau over which we charged crazily yesterday evening begins – and which is now unrecognizable. The plain, which gave me the impression of being level, in reality slopes quite considerably, and now it is an astonishing charnel house. There are bodies everywhere: it's like a cemetery with the topsoil taken off. Gangs are walking over it, identifying the dead from the day and the night before, turning over the remains, recognizing them by some detail, despite their faces. One of these enquirers is taking a torn, erased photograph out of the hand of a dead man, a killed portrait.

Black smoke from shells twists upwards, then bursts on the horizon, in the distance. Armies of crows drift across the sky in a vast sweep of dots.

Down below, among the mass of those who do not move, recognizable by the way they are wasted and eroded by time, are Zouaves, African infantry and legionaries, from the May attack. At that time the furthest edge of our line was in the Berthonval Wood, five or six kilometres from here. In that attack, one of the most tremendous of this or any other war, they had managed to reach this point in a single push, just by running. But by then they were too far ahead of the main wave of the assault and were attacked from the flanks by machine-gunners to the right and left of the lines they had broken through. For months death has been pitting their eye sockets and eating away their cheeks; but even in their scattered remains, spread around by the weather and already almost dust and ashes, one can detect the ravages made by the machine-guns which killed them, holing their backs and sides, cutting them in half. Beside the waxy black heads, like Egyptian mummies, clotted with maggots and the remains of insects, with white teeth showing through the gaps, beside the poor, darkened stumps which swarm there, like a field of uptorn roots, you can see skulls, polished clean, yellow, wearing red fezzes with grey covers that are crumbling away like papyrus. Femurs stand up out of a heap of clothes stuck together with reddish mud, or a fragment of spinal column emerges from a hole filled with frayed material, covered in a sort of tar. Ribs dot the ground like old, broken birdcages and nearby float stained leather belts or mugs and tins, holed and flattened. There are some white dots in a regular pattern around a slit bag, lying on some bones and on a tuft of pieces of clothing and equipment: if you lean over it, you can see that the dots are the finger and toe bones of what once was a body.

At times, among the outstretched bulges in the soil – because all these unburied dead eventually go back into the ground – only a piece of cloth sticks up, showing that a human being was obliterated at this spot on the earth's surface.

The Germans, who were here yesterday, have abandoned their soldiers beside our own, without burying them, as we can see from these three putrifying corpses, one on top of another, one in another, with their grey forage caps, the red border hidden by grey piping, their grey-yellow jackets and their green faces. I look for the features on one of them; from the depth of his neck to the tufts of hair stuck to the brim of his cap he is an earthy mass, his face an anthill, with two rotten fruit in place of eyes. The other, empty, dry, is flat on his belly, his back in half-detached rags, his hands, feet and face rooted in the earth.

'Look, this one's recent!'

In the middle of the field, under the rainy, ice-cold sky, in the midst of this pale aftermath of an orgy of killing, there is this head on the ground, damp and drained of blood, with a thick beard.

One of ours: his helmet is just beside him. Behind the swollen eyelids one can make out a little of the bleak glaze of his eyes and one lip is shining like a slug in the dark beard. He must have fallen into a shell hole which was then filled in by another shell, burying him up to his neck, like the German with the cat's head at the Cabaret Rouge.

'I don't recognize him,' says Joseph, going over very slowly and talking with difficulty.

'I do,' says Volpatte.

'This bearded bloke?' says Joseph, in a monotonous voice.

'He hasn't got a beard. You'll see.'

Crouching down, Volpatte puts the end of his cane under the chin of the body and knocks off a chunk of mud in which the head was set like a stone in a brooch: this is what we had taken for a beard. Then he picks up the dead man's helmet, puts it on the body and holds the two rings of his famous scissors in front of the eyes for a moment, like glasses.

'Oh!' we both exclaim. 'It's Cocon!'

'Ah . . .'

When you learn or see the death of one of those who had been fighting alongside you and living the very same life it gives you a direct shock which hits you before you understand. It really is almost like suddenly learning of one's annihilation. Only afterwards do you start to feel grief.

We look at this ghastly head, this Aunt Sally, this fairground head which is already cruelly blotting out our memories of the man. One comrade less . . . We stand there around him, intimidated.

'It was . . .'

We feel the need to talk a little, but we don't know how to say anything that will be serious enough, important or true enough.

'Come on,' Joseph groans, completely overwhelmed by his own physical suffering. 'I'm not strong enough to keep stopping all the time.'

We leave poor Cocon, the former statistics man, with a last brief and almost absent-minded glance.

'You can't imagine . . .' says Volpatte.

No, you can't imagine. All these deaths at once crush the soul. There are not enough of us left. But we have a vague idea of the grandeur of these dead. They have given everything; they gave it little by little, with all their strength, then finally they gave themselves, altogether, all at once. They outdistanced life, and there is something superhuman and perfect in what they did.

'Hang on, this one here's just copped it. Though . . .'

There is a fresh wound on the neck of an almost skeletal corpse.

'It's a rat,' says Volpatte. 'The funny fellers may be quite old, but the rats keep them going . . . You see dead rats – they could well be poisoned, for all I know – near to each body or under it. Here, this poor chap will show us his.'

He lifts up the flattened remains with a foot and we can indeed see two dead rats lying there.

'I'd like to find Farfadet,' says Volpatte. 'I told him to wait, when we were running and he caught hold of me. Poor bugger, I hope he did wait!'

So he goes up and down, a strange curiosity drawing him towards the dead. Not that they care: they send him on from one to another, and he keeps his eyes to the ground all the time. Suddenly, he gives a cry of distress. He beckons to us and kneels down beside a body.

'Bertrand!'

A sharp and deeply rooted emotion takes hold of us. Ah, so he too has been killed like the rest, the one who had the most authority over us because of his energy and clear-sightedness! He was killed, he got killed in the end, because he was always doing his duty. He finally found death where it was waiting for him.

We look at him, then turn away from the spectacle and look at each other.

'Ah . . . !'

The shock of his disappearance is made worse by the sight of his remains. He is frightful to look at. Death has given the look and gestures of a grotesque to this man who was so handsome and so calm. With his hair flopping down over his eyes, his moustache drooping in his mouth and his face swollen, he is laughing. One eye is wide open, the other shut and he is sticking his tongue out. His arms are extended in the shape of a cross, with open hands and fingers stretched. His right leg is reaching to one side while the left, which was broken by a piece of shrapnel, causing the haemorrhage that killed him, is completely turned round, dislocated, soft, with nothing to support it. A sad irony made the last twitches of his dying agony look like the gesticulations of a clown.

We arrange him, lying him out straight and adjusting his frightful mask. Volpatte has taken the wallet out of Bertrand's pocket, to hand it over at the office, and he places it reverently among his own papers, next to the portrait of his wife and children. Then he shakes his head.

'He was really someone, that one. When he said something, that proved it was true. Oh, we really needed him!'

'Yes,' I say. 'We always would have needed him.'

'Oh la la,' says Volpatte, shaking. And Joseph keeps saying quietly: 'Oh for God's sake! Oh for God's sake!'

The whole area is covered with people, like a market square. There are burial parties and isolated individuals. Patiently, and in a small way, the stretcher-bearers are starting their huge and immeasurable task.

Volpatte leaves us to go back to the trench, to report our new losses, in particular the great absence of Bertrand. He tells Joseph:

'We won't lose sight of each other, will we? Write from time to time – just a word: "All's well, signed: Camembert." Okay?'

He vanishes among all those people who go back and forth in an expanse that is now entirely in the grip of a melancholy drizzle of rain.

Joseph leans on me and we go down into the ravine.

The slope along which we are walking is called the Alvéoles des Zouaves, or 'Zouaves' Cells'. This is because the Zouaves in the May attack started to dig out one-man shelters, before being killed beside them. You can see some, brought down beside the start of a hole, who still have their entrenching tools in their fleshless hands or are staring at it with the deep hollows in which the remains of their eyes are shrivelling. The ground is so full of bodies that landslides uncover places bristling with feet, half-clothed skeletons and ossuaries of skulls, one beside the other in the sheer wall, like china jars.

In the earth here there are several layers of dead bodies and in places the pounding of the shells has brought up the oldest and placed them or scattered them across the newer ones. The bottom of the ravine is completely carpeted with debris: weapons, clothing or utensils. You stumble against fragments of shells, pieces of iron, loaves of bread and even biscuits which have fallen out of kitbags and not yet been dissolved by the rain. Billy cans, tins and helmets are riddled with bullet holes so that they look like skimming ladles or sieves of every shape and kind; and the posts that survive, knocked this way and that, are dotted with holes. The trenches running across this valley look like seismic rifts, so that you might think that cartloads of diverse objects had been tipped over the ruins left by an earthquake. Where there are no dead the earth itself is corpselike.

We cross the International Trench, still fluttering with many-coloured bits of cloth – this shapeless trench, which, with its jumble of torn rags, looks as though it has been assassinated – to a place where the uneven and winding ditch bends sharply. All along it, until you reach an earthwork barricade, German corpses are twisted and knotted together like torrents of the damned, some of them emerging from muddy grottoes in the midst of an incomprehensible pile of beams, cords, steel ropes, gabions, hurdles and screens. By the barrier we see one body standing upright in the rest; in the same spot another body is lying sideways across this dismal place. The whole looks like a section of a huge wheel stuck in the mud, or the broken sails of a windmill. And over it all, across this rout of debris and flesh, is spread a profusion of religious images, postcards, pious tracts and leaflets with prayers written in Gothic script, which have tumbled in streams out of torn clothes. The words seem to make this pestilential shore, this valley of annihilation, flower with their lying, sterile whiteness.

I look for solid ground over which to guide Joseph who is gradually being paralysed by his wound; he can feel it spreading through his whole body. While I support him and he looks at nothing I take in the macabre devastation over which we are walking.

A *Feldwebel** is sitting, leaning against the shattered planks that used to form a sentry's post, where we are now stepping. He has a little hole under his eye: a bayonet thrust pinned him to the planks by his face. In front of him, also seated with his elbows on his knees and his fists on his neck, is a man with the whole top of his head taken off like the shell of a boiled egg. Beside them a ghastly watchman – or rather half a man – is standing, a man sliced in two from the top of his skull to his hips, leaning, upright, against the earth wall. You can't tell where the other half of this sort of human post has gone; his eye is hanging out and his bluish entrails are wound around his leg.

On the ground, once your foot is unstuck from a clot of dried blood, you notice French bayonets, twisted, bent and torn by the shock.

Through a breach in the broken wall you see a pit in which the bodies of soldiers from the Prussian guard are kneeling, it seems, like suppliants, holed from behind with bloody, impaling holes. From this group they have dragged to the edge a huge Senegalese infantryman, who, petrified in the position in which he died, is leaning against the void, gripping with his feet and staring at his two severed wrists, cut off no doubt by the explosion of the grenade he was carrying. His whole face moves, so that he seems to be chewing worms.

'Here,' a *chasseur alpin* tells us as he goes by, 'they tried out the white flag, as though they were dealing with darkies. D'you suppose we let them get away with it? There, look, that's the white flag the shits used.'

He picks up a long stick which is lying there, with a square of white cloth attached to it, which unfolds innocently as he shakes it.

A procession of shovel-carriers advances along the devastated trench. They have been ordered to shovel the earth into the remains of the trenches, blocking everything so as to bury the bodies where they lie. So, at this spot, these helmeted workers will act as the righters of wrongs, giving the countryside back its shape and levelling out

---

* *Feldwebel*: sergeant (German). [trans.]

these holes which have already been half filled by the attacks of the invaders.

Someone is calling me from the far side of the trench, a man seated on the ground leaning against a post. It's Old Ramure. Through his open coat and his unbuttoned jacket, you can see the bandages around his chest.

'The orderlies came to put my dressings on,' he says, in a hollow, light voice, full of wheezing. 'But they won't be able to take me away from here until this evening. Though I know quite well that I'm going to peg out any moment.'

He shakes his head.

'Stay for a bit,' he asks.

He is emotional. Tears are running down his cheeks. He reaches out and takes my hand. He wants a long chat, almost a confession.

'I was a decent bloke before the war,' he says, fighting back his tears. 'I worked morning to night to feed my tribe. Then I came here to kill Germans. Now they've killed me. Listen, listen, don't go, listen to me . . .'

'I've got to take Joseph, he can't manage any more. After that I'll be back.'

Ramure turned his streaming eyes towards the wounded man.

'Not only alive, but wounded! Freed from death! Oh, there are some women and children whose luck's in! Well, take him and come back. I hope I'll be able to wait.'

Now we have to go up the far side of the ravine. We set off along the shapeless and battered depression that is the old Trench 97.

Suddenly a frenzied whistling tears through the air. A burst of shrapnel up above us. In the heart of ochre clouds meteorites thunder and burst in fearful storms. Revolving missiles tear through the sky before breaking up and smashing into the slope, digging into the hill and throwing up the old bones of the world. And the thundering flashes build up along an even line.

It's another barrage starting.

Like children we scream: 'Enough! Stop!'

There is something that outstrips our strength and willpower, something supernatural, in this relentless fury of the machines of death, this mechanical cataclysm that hounds us through space. Joseph, standing with his hand in mine, looks back over his shoulder at the hail of lethal bursts. He is turning his head like a terrified, hunted beast.

'What! Again! Forever then!' he groans. 'After all we've done, all we've seen . . . And now it's starting again. Oh no! No!'

He sinks to his knees, panting, with a futile look full of hatred in front of him and behind. Again he says: 'So it's never going to end, never!'

I take his arm and lift him up:

'Come on, for you it is going to end.'

We have to wait there, before going up. I think about going to the dying Ramure who is waiting for me. But Joseph is clinging to me and I see a crowd of men bustling around where I left Ramure and I guess from this that there is no longer any point in going.

The ground shudders in the ravine where we two are clasped together under the storm and we feel every thud of the dull simoom of shells. But in the dip where we are there is no risk of being hit. As soon as there is a lull men who had been waiting as we are move away from the group and start to go up: stretcher-bearers who make repeated, incredible efforts to climb up carrying bodies and remind you of obstinate ants pushed back by successive waves of grains of sand; and others, alone or in pairs, wounded men and messengers.

'Come on,' says Joseph, his shoulders hunched, measuring the extent of the hill, the last stage in his calvary.

There are trees there, a line of willows, their trunks stripped, some as wide as a human head, others hollowed, gaping, like standing coffins. The landscape through which we struggle is churned up and ripped open, with dark hills, gulfs and swellings, as though all the storm clouds had rolled over here. Above this tortured, blackened land the rout of tree trunks stands out against a streaky brown sky, milky in places, vaguely scintillating – an onyx sky.

Across the entrance to Trench 96, the great body of a felled oak.

A corpse is blocking the trench. Its head and legs are buried and the muddy water that flows along the bottom has covered the rest with a sandy glaze. Under this damp veil you can see the swelling of the chest and belly covered by a shirt.

We step over these remains, iced, viscous and clear as the belly of some kind of beached reptile – and it is no easy task because of the soft, slippery ground. We have to stick our hands up to the wrists in the mud of the trench wall.

At that moment a hellish whistling sound falls upon us. We bend like reeds. The shrapnel bursts, deafening and blinding, in the air ahead of us, and buries us in a mountain of dark smoke, full of fearful hisses. One soldier who was coming up waves his arms and vanishes, cast into some pit or other. Shouts rise and fall like debris. At the same time, through the great black veil, which the wind tears off the earth and tosses into the sky, we see the stretcher-bearers put down their burden and run towards the point of the explosion where they pick up something that is lying there, inert – and I recall the unforgettable image of the night when my brother-in-arms Poterloo, whose heart was full of hope, seemed to fly away, both arms outstretched, in the flame of a shell.

We finally reach the top of the hill where, like a signal, a frightful wounded man marks the place. He is there, standing in the wind, shaken but upright, rooted to the spot, in his overcoat which flaps in the air. We can see his face, screaming and convulsed, as we walk past this sort of shouting tree.

We have reached our former front line, the one from which we set off for the attack. We sit down on a firing post with our backs against the steps that the sappers dug at the last moment for us to go over the top. The cyclist Euterpe goes by and wishes us a good morning, but when he has passed he retraces his steps and takes an envelope out of the cuff of his sleeve where its edge had been making a white stripe on his uniform.

'It's you, isn't it,' he asks me, 'who's taking letters for Biquet, deceased?'

'Yes.'

'Here's one that's been returned. The address has got lost.'

The envelope, which has no doubt been exposed to the rain on top of a bundle of letters, is smudged and you can no longer read the address on the now dry, frayed paper among the stains of violet ink. All that remains readable is the sender's address in one corner.

I take the letter out, carefully: 'Dear mother . . .'

'Now I remember!'

Biquet, who is lying in the open in this same trench where we have paused now, wrote the letter not long ago in our billet at Gauchin-l'Abbé, on a marvellous, blazing afternoon, replying to a letter from his mother, whose needless anxieties were making him laugh.

'You think I'm suffering from the cold and rain and in danger. Not at all, on the contrary. All that's over. It's hot, we're sweating and we have nothing to do except walk around in the sun. Your letter made me laugh . . .'

I open the fragile, spoiled envelope and put back this letter which, if chance had not intervened to prevent this further irony, would have been read by the old peasant woman at a moment when the body of her son, in the cold and the storm, was nothing more than a little damp ash, trickling like a dark rivulet across the embankment of the trench.

Joseph has leant back. At one moment his eyes shut, his mouth half opens and he gives an irregular, gasping sigh.

'Strength!' I tell him.

He opens his eyes.

'Oh,' he says, 'I'm not the one who you should say that to. Look at them, they're going back. And you're going back there too. For the rest of you it will go on. My God! You have to be really strong to go on and on like that!'

21

The First-Aid Post

From this point on we are in view of the enemy observers and must not leave our trenches. First of all we follow the Route des Pylônes. The trench runs alongside the road – though this has vanished: its border of trees has been uprooted, the trench has half eaten into and swallowed it over its whole length and whatever remained has been invaded by soil and grass, eventually becoming part of the fields. At some points along the trench, where a sandbag has broken and left only a muddy cavity, you find at eye level the stone ballast of the old road gnawed away, or the roots of the bordering trees, cut down and incorporated into the mass of the embankment. The embankment itself is choppy and uneven like a wave of earth, debris and dark foam, spat up and driven by the vast plain right to the edge of this ditch.

We reach a crossroads of trenches. At the top of the damaged mound that you can see against the grey sky a mournful signboard is stuck sideways to the wind. The network of trenches gets narrower and narrower and the men who are making their way towards the first-aid post from all parts of the front are multiplying and gather in the deep-dug roads.

These pitiful roads are lined with bodies. At irregular intervals the wall is broken from top to bottom with new holes, funnels of fresh earth that break into the sick ground beyond them, and here muddy corpses are crouching, their knees against their teeth, or leaning on the wall, silent and upright like their guns waiting beside them. A few of these dead men who are still on their feet turn their blood-spattered faces towards the survivors, or else, with heads facing in another direction, stare at the emptiness of the heavens.

Joseph stops to draw breath. I tell him, as you might a child:

'We're nearly there, we're nearly there.'

The road of desolation, with its sinister ramparts, gets narrower still. You have a feeling of suffocation, a nightmare of descent into a narrowing space, of strangling . . . and in these depths where the walls seem to be constantly getting nearer to one another, closing in, we have to stop, push our way past the dead, disturbing them as we go, while being shoved by the disordered file of those who are in continual movement towards the rear: messengers, the maimed, moaners and groaners, in desperate haste, purple with fever or pale-faced and visibly racked with pain.

This whole crowd finally pours, crushes and groans at the crossroads where the dugouts of the first-aid post open.

A doctor is waving and shouting to keep a little space free from this mounting tide as it breaks against the doors of the shelter. In the open air, at the entrance, he is putting on emergency dressings, and they say that neither he nor his assistants have stopped all night and all day and that his labours are superhuman.

As they come out of his care some of the wounded are taken into the dugouts of the post while others are evacuated to the rear, to the larger clearing station in the trench by the Béthune road.

We have been waiting for two hours in the narrow dip at the crossing of the trenches, as though at the bottom of a sort of beggars' kitchen, tossed around, squeezed, stifled and blinded, climbing over one another like cattle, in a stench of blood and butcher's meat. Faces grow more strained and hollow by the minute. One of the patients, unable to hold back his tears, lets them pour out and, shaking his head, sprinkles them on his neighbours. Another, bleeding like a fountain, cries: 'Hey, look after me!' A young man, his eyes aflame, raises his arms and cries like one of the damned: 'I'm burning!', groaning and blowing like a furnace.

Joseph's wound is dressed. He pushes his way across to me and holds out his hand.

'It seems it's not serious,' he says. 'Farewell.'

Immediately we are separated by the throng. My last look at him shows me Joseph with wasted features, concentrating on his pain, absent-minded, as he lets himself be led away by a stretcher-bearer who has put a hand on his shoulder. All at once he is gone.

In wartime life as well as death separates you without even giving you the time to think about it.

Someone tells me not to stay there but to go down into the first-aid post and rest before going back.

There are two entrances, each very low and tight, at ground level. One of them gives way to the mouth of a sloping gallery, as narrow as a drain. To reach the post you first have to turn round and start backwards down this constricted pipe, bending your body and feeling with your feet for steps: every third one is widely spaced.

Once you have started down there you feel trapped, and your first impression is that you will not have room either to go on down, or to get back up. The further you descend into this pit the more you continue the nightmare of suffocation, which you have gradually endured as you came further into the entrails of the trenches, before ending here. You bump yourself on all sides, rubbing against the wall, gripped by the narrowness of the passage, halted, stuck. You have to change the position of your cartridge pouches, sliding them around your belt, and take your shoulder bags in your arms, pressing them against your chest. On the fourth step the grip tightens still further and you have a moment of panic; just lifting your knee to go backwards pushes your back against the roof. Here you have to go on all fours, still backwards. As you sink into the depths a pestilential atmosphere, heavy as the earth itself, surrounds you. Your hand feels the clay wall, cold, sticky, sepulchral. This earth weighs on you from all sides, wrapping you in dismal solitude, touching your face with its blind, mouldy breath. When you finally reach the last steps you are assailed by the eerie noises rising from the hole, which is as hot as some kind of kitchen.

At last you reach the bottom of this laddered tube, which squeezes and pushes you at every step; the nightmare is not over. You find yourself in a dark cavern, very long but narrow, nothing more than a corridor and a mere one metre fifty high. If you stop bending over and try to walk with your legs straight, you hit your head sharply on the beams which make up the roof of the shelter, and, invariably, you hear new arrivals grumble – more or less loudly according to their mood and state of health: 'Huh! Lucky I had my helmet on!'

In a corner a crouching man is making a sign with his hand. He is a duty nurse who is telling each new arrival in a monotonous voice: 'Take the mud off your shoes before you come in.' In this way a heap of mud has accumulated at the bottom of the stairs and you slip and sink into it, on the threshold of this hell.

In the hubbub of groans and lamentations, in the strong smell given off by innumerable wounds, in the flickering light of this cavern, teeming with confused and incomprehensible life, the first thing I try to do is find my bearings. Weak candle-flames shine along the walls of the shelter, only piercing its darkness in their immediate surroundings. At the back, far away, as in the far corner of a dungeon, there is a vague hint of daylight; by this clouded window one can make out the main objects stationed along the corridor: stretchers as low as coffins. Then moving around and above them broken and leaning shadows, while lines and clusters of ghosts swarm against the walls.

I turn round. Next to the wall opposite the one through which the distant light is filtering a crowd has gathered, in front of a canvas stretched from the roof to the ground. This tenting forms a compartment with a lamp inside it, which can be seen through the brown, oily-looking canvas. Inside the compartment, by the light of an acetylene lamp, injections are being given against tetanus. When the canvas is raised, to let someone in or out, the light floods crudely over the scruffy, tattered clothing of the wounded who are stationed in front, waiting for their injections, and who, bent over beneath the low ceiling, sitting, kneeling or crawling, push so as not to lose their turns or to take someone else's, with shouts of: 'Me!' 'Me!' 'Me!', like barking dogs. In this corner, with this constant struggle going on, the warm stench of acetylene and of bleeding men is frightful to endure.

I move away from it, looking for somewhere else to stop and sit down. I go forward a little, groping, still bent, hunched, hands reaching out.

Thanks to a pipe that a smoker is lighting I can see a bench in front of me, full of people.

My eyes are getting used to the half-light stagnating in the cellar and I can more or less make out this line of people whose dressings and bandages make pale shapes on their heads and limbs.

Lame, scarred and deformed, motionless or agitated, clinging to this kind of boat, they seem stuck here, like the emblems of a varied collection of sufferings and miseries.

Suddenly one of them shouts out, half gets up, then sits down again. His neighbour, bare-headed, wearing a torn overcoat, looks at him and says:

'Why worry?'

And he repeats the phrase several times, randomly, his eyes staring ahead and his hands on his knees.

A young man sitting in the middle of the bench is talking to himself. He says he's an aviator. He has burns down one side of his body and on his face. In his fever he is still burning and believes that he is being licked by the sharp flames pouring out of the engine. He mutters: '*Gott mit uns!*' and then: 'God is with us!'

A Zouave with his arm in a sling, leaning to one side, carries his shoulder like a terrible burden; he turns to the other man:

'You're the aviator who came down, aren't you?'

'I saw some things,' the aviator replies, painfully.

'Me too,' the soldier interrupts him. 'I've seen some too. There are people who'd go crazy if they saw what I've seen.'

'Come and sit down,' one of the men on the bench says to me, making a place. 'Wounded?'

'No, I brought a wounded man here. I'm going back.'

'Worse than wounded then. Come and sit down.'

'I'm the mayor in my village,' one of the seated men informs us. 'But when I go home no one will recognize me, I've been so sad for so long.'

'Four hours I've been sitting on this bench,' groans a kind of beggar with shaking hands, his head bowed, his back bent, holding his helmet on his knees like a trembling begging bowl.

'We're waiting to be evacuated, you know,' a fat wounded man informs me. He is panting and sweating, so that he seems to be boiling with all his bulk; his moustache is hanging down as though half unstuck by the dampness of his face. He has two large opaque eyes and no visible wound.

'That's right,' says another. 'All the wounded from the brigade come and pile up here, one after another, not counting those from elsewhere.'

'Yeah, just take a look at it: this hole is the rubbish bin of the whole brigade.'

'I've got gangrene, I'm crushed, I'm all in pieces inside,' chants one wounded man who has his head in his hands and is talking through his fingers. 'And yet a week ago I was young and clean. They've changed me: now I have only this filthy old body to drag around.'

'I was twenty-six yesterday,' says another. 'How old am I today?'

He tries to get up so that we can see his rickety withered face, worn out in a single night, emptied of flesh, with its sunken cheeks and sockets, and a flame like a night light fading in his oily eye.

'It hurts!' says some invisible creature, humbly.

'Why worry?' says the other man again, mechanically.

There was silence. Then the aviator cried: 'The priests were trying on both sides to disguise their voices!'

'What's that?' said the Zouave in astonishment.

'Are you taking leave of your senses, old chap?' asked a *chasseur* with a wound on the hand, one arm tied to his body, turning away from his mummified hand for a moment to look at the aviator.

He was staring into space, trying to explain the mysterious picture he had in front of his eyes.

'From up there in the sky you don't see much, you know. Among the squares of the fields and the little heaps of villages, roads are like white thread. You can also see some hollow filaments which look as though they were traced with the point of a pin scratched into fine sand. These traces festooning the plain with regular wavy lines are the trenches. On Sunday morning I was flying over the front. Between the edges, between the outer fringe of the two vast armies that are there, one against the other, looking and not seeing one another as they wait, there is very little distance: forty metres in some places, sixty in others. It seemed to me that it was only a step because of the great height at which I was flying. And I could make out two similar gatherings among the Boche and ourselves, in these parallel lines that seem to touch one another: a crowd, a hub of movement and, around it, what looked like black grains of sand scattered on grey ones. They weren't moving; it didn't seem like an alarm! I circled down a bit to get a closer look.

'Then I understood. It was Sunday and these were two services being held in front of my eyes: the altars, the priests and the congregations. The nearer I got the more I could see that these two gatherings were similar – so exactly similar that it seemed ridiculous. One of the ceremonies – whichever you liked – was a reflection of the other. I felt as though I was seeing double.

'I went down further. No one fired at me. Why not? I don't know. Then I heard it. I heard a murmur – a single one. I could only make out one prayer rising up in a single sound, a single hymn rising to heaven and passing through me. I went backwards and forwards in space listening to this vague mixture of songs, one opposing the other, but mingling despite that – and the more they tried to surmount one another the more they were unified in the heights of the sky where I was suspended.

'I was fired at just as, flying very low, I made out the two terrestrial cries of which their one cry was made up: "*Gott mit uns!*" and "God is with us!" – and I flew off.'

The young man shook his head, which was swathed in bandages. It was as though the memory were driving him insane.

'I thought at that moment: "I'm mad!"'

'It's the reality of things that is mad,' said the Zouave.

His eyes blazing with folly, the storyteller tried to convey the great emotion that he felt and against which he was struggling.

'No! Come on!' he exclaimed. 'Imagine those two identical crowds shouting identical yet contrary things: hostile cries that have the same form. What must the good Lord be saying, after all? I realize that he knows everything but even if he does, he can't know what to do.'

'What rubbish!' said the Zouave.

'He doesn't give a damn about us, don't worry.'

'And after all, there's nothing odd about it. Guns speak the same language, don't they, but that doesn't stop countries arguing with them, and how!'

'Yes,' said the aviator. 'But there's only one God. It's not where the prayers come from that bothers me, it's where they go to.'

There was a pause.

'There's a whole heap of wounded lying in there,' the man with the dull eyes told me, pointing. 'I wonder, yes, I just wonder how they managed to bring them down here. It must have been terrible, their journey to the bottom.'

Two colonials, hard and thin, supporting one another like two drunks, came along, bumped against us and stepped back, looking for a place on the ground where they could fall.

'Old man,' one of them concluded, in a hoarse voice, 'in that trench I was telling you about we stayed for three days without provisions, three whole days with nothing, nothing at all. Well, we drank our own piss, but that was it.'

The other, in reply, described how he had once had cholera:

'Ah, that's a filthy business! Fever, vomiting, colic. Now that really made me ill.'

'But another thing,' the aviator suddenly growled, determined to carry on investigating the great enigma, 'what's he thinking about, this God, if he lets everyone believe that he's on their side? Why does he allow us all to shout like idiots and animals, one next to another: "God is with us!" "No, not at all, you've made a mistake; God's with *us!*"'

A groan rose from a stretcher and for a moment hung all alone in the silence, as though answering the question.

'Me,' said a voice full of pain, 'I don't believe in God. I know he doesn't exist – because of suffering. They can give us all the claptrap that they like and deck it out in all the words they can find or invent; the idea that all this innocent suffering comes from a perfect God is just a load of bleeding trickery.'

'Well, I don't believe in God,' said one of the other men on the bench, 'because of the cold. I've seen men become corpses bit by bit, just through the cold. If there was a good God, there wouldn't be any cold. You can't get round that.'

'If you were to believe in God, there wouldn't have to be anything that there is. So we're a long way off it.'

Several wounded men, simultaneously, without seeing one another, communicated in a shaking of the head.

'You're right,' said another man. 'You're right.'

These shattered men, scattered and isolated, vanquished in victory, are starting to have a revelation. In the tragedy of events there are moments when men are not only sincere, but true, and one can see the truth on them, face to face.

'Now me,' said a new speaker, 'I don't believe, but that's because . . .'

The sentence ended in a terrible attack of coughing. When he stopped, exhausted, his cheeks scarlet, bathed in tears, someone asked:

'Where are you wounded?'

'I'm not wounded, I'm ill.'

'Oh well,' was the reply, in a tone of voice that meant: you're not interesting.

He felt this and put in a word for his illness:

'I'm done for. I'm spitting blood. I've no strength left, and, you know, you don't get it back when it's gone like that.'

'Huh, huh,' his comrades murmured, undecided, but still convinced despite everything of the inferiority of civilian diseases to wounds.

He bent his head in resignation and said very quietly to himself:

'I can't walk any longer. Where do you want me to go?'

Something is stirring, no one knows why, in the horizontal gulf that extends from stretcher to stretcher, getting smaller as it goes until it is lost to sight in the pale orifice of daylight, in this disordered hallway where the miserable flames of candles flicker here and there, growing red, as though feverish, and across which winged shadows fall from time to time. You can see the clutter of limbs and heads moving, you can hear calls and cries awakening one another and spreading like invisible ghosts. The prostrate bodies undulate, bend double and turn over.

In this hovel, amid this swell of captives, degraded and punished by pain, I can make out the thick bulk of a medical orderly whose heavy shoulders sway like a sack carried crossways and whose stentorian voice reverberates rapidly through the cellar.

'You've been touching your bandage again, you pig, you vermin!' he roars. 'I'm going to do it again for you, because it's you, my sweetie, but just try touching it and see what'll happen!'

Here he is in the half-light twisting a strip of cloth around the head of a little chap, almost standing, with his hair on end and his beard sticking forward, who lets him do it in silence, with hanging arms.

But the orderly leaves him, looks on the ground and exclaims loudly: 'What's this then? Hey, you there, my good man, are you crackers? I've never seen anything like it, lying on top of a wounded man!'

His vast hand shakes a body and, amid panting and cursing, disentangles a second limp body on which the first had been lying as though on a mattress – while the midget with the bandage, as soon as he is freed, puts his hands to his head without saying a word and once more tries to take off the dressing.

There is a scuffle, some shouts: some shadowy figures, visible against a light background, seem to be misbehaving in the darkness of the crypt. There are several of them around a wounded man, lit by a candle, and they are shaking as they try to keep him down on his stretcher. The man has no feet. He has horrific dressings on his legs with tourniquets to stop the bleeding. His stumps have bled into the cloth bandages wound around them and it looks as though he is wearing red breeches. His face is devilish, glowing and dark, and he is in a delirium. They are pushing down on his shoulders and knees: this man, whose legs have been cut off, wants to get up off the stretcher and go away.

'Let me go!' he croaks, in a voice quivering with breathless anger, low, but with sudden sonorities, like a trumpet that someone is trying to blow too softly. 'God in heaven, let me get out of here, I tell you! Huh! You don't expect me to stay here, do you? Out of my way, or I'll stamp on your hands.'

He is springing backwards and forwards so violently that the men who are trying to restrain him with their clinging weight are dragged this way and that with him, and you can see the zigzagging candle held by a kneeling man who has his other arm round the truncated maniac. He is waking any sleeping patients with his shouts and shaking the rest from their drowsing. People turn towards him on all sides, half rise and attend to these incoherent complaints, which do eventually trail off into the darkness. At the same time, in another part of the cellar, two wounded men, crucified on the ground, are exchanging insults and one has to be carried away to break up their frantic argument.

I make my way towards the place where light from outside is shining through the crossed beams as though through a broken grill. This means stepping over the endless lines of stretchers that occupy the whole width of this subterranean alley, which is strangling me with its stifling low roof. The human forms lying on the stretchers have fallen still now under the flickering light of the candles and are stagnant amid their dull groaning and croaking.

A man is seated on the edge of a stretcher, leaning against the wall. Amid the darkness of his half-open, torn clothing appears the white, emaciated chest of a martyr. His head, leaning right back, is in shadow, but you can see the beating of his heart.

The daylight that filters through, drip by drip, at the end of the room comes from a landslide: several shells landing on the same spot have finally broken through the thick earth roof of the first-aid post.

At that point a few white highlights fall on the blue of the coats, at the shoulders and along the folds. A herd of men, paralysed by the dark as much as by weakness, can be seen pushing their way towards this hole to taste a little pale air and separate themselves from the necropolis, like half-awakened dead. At the end of the darkness this patch is like a bolt hole, an oasis where you can stand upright, angelically touched by the light of heaven.

'There were some chaps that were blown apart when those shells showed up,' says one man, who was waiting with his mouth half open in the miserable ray of light buried there. 'Talk about a shambles. Look, there's the padre gathering up the bits of them that were scattered around.'

The huge sergeant-orderly, in a brown hunter's waistcoat that makes his upper half look like a gorilla, is scraping guts and entrails that are hanging, twisted around the beams of the shattered roof. For this job he is using his gun with its bayonet fixed, because there wasn't a stick long enough, and the bald, bearded, wheezy giant is not very skilled at the work. He has a gentle face, kindly and sad, and while he tries to catch hold of these fragments of intestines in the corners, he mutters a rosary of 'Ohs!' like sighs, with an air of distress. His eyes are hidden behind blue glasses, his breath is noisy, he has a small head on a neck so vast that it is conical.

Seeing him like that, sticking and waving strips of entrails and scraps of flesh in the air, with his feet in the bristling ruins, at the end of this long, groaning cul-de-sac, you would think he was a butcher engaged in some diabolical task.

But I have let myself sink into a corner, my eyes half closed, barely observing what is extended, shivering or falling around me.

I do catch a few confused scraps of conversations: the absurd monotony of stories about wounds.

'By God Almighty, at that point I truly think there was no gap at all between the bullets . . .'

'His head was shot through from one temple to the other. You could have put a piece of string through it.'

'It was an hour before those lousy bastards eased up and stopped sniping at us.'

Closer to where I am someone is mumbling through the end of a story: 'When I sleep, I dream, and it's as though I was killing him all over again.'

Other tales well up among the wounded who are buried here, like the humming of the numberless wheels of some machine grinding on and on . . .

And I can hear the same man on his bench at the end repeating: 'Why worry about it?' in every possible way, imperious or pitiful, now like a prophet, now like a shipwrecked sailor, beating time with his cry for this chorus of stifled or plaintive voices raised in the ghastly song of their pain.

Someone is coming towards me, blindly, tapping the wall with a stick. It's Farfadet! I call out to him. He turns more or less towards me and tells me that he has lost one of his eyes. The other one is also bandaged. I give up my place to him and make him sit down, holding his shoulders. He does as I tell him and, sitting with his back to the wall, waits patiently, with the resignation of an office worker in a waiting room.

I fetch up a little further on, in a space. Here two men are talking in low voices, but they are so close to me that I can hear them without listening. They are two Foreign Legionnaires, with dark-yellow helmets and coats.

'No sense in pretending,' one of them is saying, in a jocular tone. 'I've had it this time. It's over. I've got it in the gut. If I was in a hospital, in town, they'd operate in time and might be able to stick me together. But here! Yesterday I bought it. We're two or three hours from the Béthune road, no, and how many hours will it take from the road to get to an ambulance where they can operate? You tell me. And then, when will they pick us up? It's no one's fault, mind, but you've got to see things as they are. Oh, at the moment, I know, it's not too bad. But it won't last, since I've got a hole right through the guts. Now you, your foot'll get better, or they'll stick another one on you. But I'm going to die.'

'Ah!' said the other man, persuaded by the logic of this.

The other man continued:

'Listen here, Dominique, you've led a rotten life. You were a right boozer and you couldn't hold your wine. You've got a police record as long as your arm.'

'Can't say that's not true, 'cos it's true,' said the other. 'But what's it got to do with you?'

'You'll go back to your old ways after the war, of course, and then they'll be on to you about that business with the barrel maker.'

His companion flares up aggressively:

'Keep your trap shut! That's none of your bloody business!'

'Now, I've got no more family than you do. No one, except Louise – and she's not family since we're not married. But I don't have a record, apart from some small military stuff. There's nothing against my name.'

'So what? I don't give a fuck.'

'What I'm telling you is: take my name. Take it, I'm giving it to you. Since neither of us has any family.'

'Your name?'

'Call yourself Léonard Carlotti, that's all. It's no great shakes. What harm can it do you? And straightaway you've a clean record. You won't be a wanted man and you can be as happy as I would have been, if this bullet hadn't got me in the belly.'

'Well, I'll be buggered!' says the other. 'You'd do that? Now that, old chap, that beats everything!'

'Take it. It's there, in my passbook, in my greatcoat. So take it and pass me yours, your pass, and let me take it all with me! You can live where you like, except at home in Longueville, where a few people know me, and in Tunisia. You can remember it, and in any case it's all written down. Just read the passbook. I won't tell a soul. For something like this to work you have to keep mum about it.'

He pauses, then says in a trembling voice:

'Maybe even so I'll tell Louise, so she'll reckon I did something good and think the better of me for it . . . when I write to her to say goodbye.'

However, he has second thoughts about this and shakes his head in a final effort.

'No, I won't say anything, even to her. I know it's her, but women are such chatterboxes.'

The other man is looking at him and repeating:

'Well, I'll be darned!'

Without them noticing I leave this drama to unfold in that pitiful corner, with its pushing and shoving and noise.

I catch a fragment of the calm, convalescent chatter of two miserable wretches:

'Oh my God! The way he loved those vines! You wouldn't find a thing between the roots . . .'

'That little nipper, that nipper, when I went out with him and held his little hand, it was like holding the warm neck of a swallow, you know what I mean?'

'Do I know the 547th? You bet I do. It's a bloody funny regiment.

There's a *poilu* in that regiment who's called Petitjean, and another called Petitpierre, and another called Petitlouis . . . I swear there is! That's the kind of regiment it is.'

As I am starting to make my way out of the depths there is a huge sound of someone falling and a chorus of exclamations.

The person who has fallen is the sergeant-orderly. A bullet has passed through the hole that he was clearing of its soft bloody remains, and hit him in the throat. He is stretched out, full length, rolling his great astonished eyes and foaming at the mouth.

His mouth and the bottom of his face are soon surrounded by a cloud of pink bubbles. They put his head on a bag of dressings and it, too, is immediately covered in blood. An orderly yells that they are spoiling the packets of dressings, which are needed, so they look for somewhere else to put this head, which is constantly producing its light, coloured foam. The only thing they can find is a loaf of bread, which they slide under the spongy hair.

Someone takes the sergeant's hand and they talk to him, but he simply goes on blowing out fresh bubbles which gather around his large, unshaven head, so that you see it through this pink cloud. Lying like this, on his back, he seems to be a panting sea monster, as the transparent foam gathers and covers as far as his large clouded eyes, shorn of their glasses.

Then he croaks. His death rattle is that of a child and he dies, moving his head from one side to the other, as though trying very gently to say: 'No.'

I look at this huge immobile mass, and think: this was a good man. His heart was pure and sensitive. I really regret having sometimes abused him for his naive narrow-mindedness and a certain ecclesiastic impertinence that he brought to what he did. How pleased I am, in the distress I feel – yes, so pleased that I almost shudder with joy – that I restrained myself one day when he was reading a letter that I was writing over my shoulder and I almost said something that would have unfairly hurt him. I remember how he infuriated me one day with something he said about the Virgin Mary and France. It seemed impossible to me that he could sincerely hold such ideas. But why should he not be in earnest? He was killed in earnest today, wasn't he? I also recall certain signs of devotion and kindly patience in this big man, as out of place in war as in life; and the rest is merely detail. Even his ideas are only details beside his heart, which is there on the ground, in ruins, in this corner of Hell. And how powerfully I miss this man, who was as different from me as could be!

This is when the thunder falls upon us. We are thrown violently against each other by the terrible shuddering of the ground and the walls. It is as though the earth above has collapsed and fallen in on us. A section of the wooden shoring collapses, enlarging the hole in the roof of the cellar. Another crash: another section is pulverized and collapses with a roar. The body of the big sergeant-orderly is rolled like a tree trunk against the wall. The whole framework of the cellar, those thick black vertebrae, cracks with an ear-splitting din and all the prisoners in this dungeon give a simultaneous gasp of horror.

More explosions ring out one after another, throwing us in all directions. The bombardment is shredding and eating up the first-aid post, breaking through it and shrinking it. While this whistling shower of shells is hammering on the gaping end of the post, crushing it with claps of thunder, daylight bursts through the gaps. In it you can see faces flaming or mortally pale, eyes closing in agony or blazing with fever, bodies wrapped in white, patched with monstrous bandages. All these things that were hidden are brought into the light. Haggard, blinking, twisted, confronted by this flood of shrapnel and charcoal along with storms of light, the wounded men get up, scatter and attempt to flee. This whole terrified population rolls along in compact groups, down the low gallery, as in the tossing hold of a great ship breaking up.

The aviator, rising as far as he can, the back of his neck against the vault, is waving his arms and calling on God to tell him His name, His real name. Blown along by the wind you can see the man who, with his clothes hanging loose like a great wound, was showing his heart like Christ throwing himself on the others. The coat of the man who was crying monotonously: 'Why worry?' appears entirely green, bright green, no doubt because of the picric acid given off by the explosion that addled his brain. Others, the rest, helpless, crippled, move, squeeze, crawl and creep into corners, taking on the shape of moles, of poor vulnerable creatures pursued by the terrifying hounds, the shells.

The bombardment slows down and stops, in a cloud of smoke still shuddering with the din, in a palpitating, burning atmosphere of firedamp. I climb out of the breach and arrive, still wrapped, still tied up in the desperate noise, under the open sky, on the soft ground where there are sunken beams tangled with legs. I clutch at the wreckage. Here is the embankment. Just as I am plunging into the depths I see the trenches, in the distance, still moving and dark, still filled by the crowd that, overflowing from the ground, pours endlessly towards the first-aid post. For days and nights you can see long streams of men flowing and mingling, men torn from the battlefields, from the plain with its entrails bleeding and rotting down there, to infinity.

22

The Jaunt

After going down the Boulevard de la République, then the Avenue Gambetta, we come out into the Place du Commerce. The nails on our polished boots chink on the cobbles. The sun is shining. The bright sky shimmers and shines as though through the glass of a greenhouse, making the shopfronts sparkle in the square. Our great-coats are well brushed and their tails are down; since they are usually raised this means that you can see two squares on these flapping skirts where the cloth is bluer.

Our band of strollers pauses for a moment, hesitantly, in front of the Café de la Sous-Préfecture, also known as Le Grand-Café.

'We've got a right to go inside!' says Volpatte.

'There are too many officers there,' Blaire replies. He has taken a cautious glance, raising his face above the lace curtain that adorns the café and looking between the gold letters through the glass.

'And then,' says Paradis, 'we haven't seen enough yet.'

We set off again and, simple privates that we are, take a look at the rich shops lining the sides of the square: drapers', stationers', chemists' and, like the bemedalled uniform of a general, the jeweller's window. We bring out our smiles like ornaments. We have no work to do until the evening, we are free, we are fully in possession of our time. Our legs take gentle, restful steps; our hands, empty, swinging, walk up and down as we do.

'You can't deny we're enjoying our leave,' says Paradis.

The town that opens before us is most impressive. We make contact with life, people's life, life in the rear, normal life. How often have we felt that we would never get here from where we were!

We see gentlemen, ladies, couples with children, English officers, aviators (who can be recognized from a distance by their trim elegance and their decorations) and soldiers, who parade their worn clothes and rubbed skins, with the single jewel of their identity discs flashing in the sun on their greatcoats as they venture cautiously through this beautiful scene, emptied of all nightmares.

We exclaim aloud, like visitors from some distant land.

'What a crowd!' says Tirette, in amazement.

'Oh, it's a rich town,' says Blaire.

A factory girl goes past, glancing at us.

Volpatte elbows me, drinking her in with his eyes, his neck outstretched, then points out two other women approaching further away. His eyes shining, he takes in the fact that the town has an abundance of this female element:

'By God, there's a lot of arse!'

Just now Paradis had to overcome a certain amount of timidity before going up to a group of splendidly decked-out cakes, touching them and eating one of them; and we are forced to stop every minute in the middle of the pavement while we wait for Blaire, who is attracted by the shop windows with their displays of fancy jackets and kepis, ties in soft blue drill and boots as red and shiny as mahogany. He has reached the apogee of his transformation – Blaire, who used to hold the record for neglect and dirt, is now certainly the best turned-out of us all, especially since the complication of having his teeth shattered in the attack and remade. He affects an offhand manner.

'He looks young and juvenile,' says Marthereau.

Suddenly we are confronted by a toothless hag smiling with wide-open mouth. A few black hairs bristle around her hat. Her face, with its big ugly features and pitted with smallpox, looks like one of those faces crudely painted on the backdrop to some booth in a funfair.

'She's beautiful,' says Volpatte.

Marthereau, the one she smiled at, is struck dumb.

This is the conversation of *poilus* suddenly transported to the wonder of a town. They enjoy more and more the lovely neat surroundings, so incredibly clean. They once again pick up their lives, calm and peaceful, and the concepts of comfort and even happiness, for which houses, when it comes down to it, were made.

'After all, one could easily get used to this, you know!'

Meanwhile a crowd is gathering around a window where an outfitter has produced a ridiculous group scene with the aid of wood and wax puppets: on a piece of ground dotted with little pebbles, such as the ones you find in an aquarium, a German is kneeling in a new uniform, with sharp creases, and even wearing a cardboard Iron Cross, holding his pink wooden hands out to a French officer, whose curly wig forms a cushion for a child's kepi. His cheeks are plump and pink, and his unbreakable baby eyes are looking into the distance. Beside the two figures is a gun borrowed from the stock of some toyshop. A board carries the title of this lively composition: '*Kamarad!*'

'Well, I'll be damned! What about that!'

Faced with this childish assemblage, the only thing here to remind one of the immense war that is raging somewhere under the sky, we shrug our shoulders and start to laugh bitterly, offended and deeply wounded in our recent memories. Tirette steps back and prepares to launch some offensive sarcasm, but this protest takes time to mature in his mind because of our complete transplantation and our astonishment at being somewhere else.

Meanwhile a very elegant lady, rustling and radiating in black and violet silks, in a cloud of scent, notices our group and reaches out with her little gloved hand to touch Volpatte's sleeve, then Blaire's shoulder. The two men are instantly frozen to the spot, bewitched by direct contact with the enchantress.

'Tell me, gentlemen, you who are real soldiers from the front, you've seen this in the trenches, haven't you?'

'Eh . . . yes . . . yes . . .' the two men reply, hugely intimidated and flattered to the depths of their being.

'Ah! You see! And they've been there!' people are muttering in the crowd.

When we are alone together, on the even stones of the pavement, Volpatte and Blaire look at each other and shake their heads.

'After all,' says Volpatte, 'that's more or less it, huh?'

'Well, yes, just about.'

That day, those were their first words of false witness.

We go into the Café de l'Industrie et des Fleurs. A mat of esparto grass runs along the middle of the floor. Painted across the walls, up the square pillars supporting the ceiling and over the front of the counter are violet convolvulus flowers, light red poppies and roses like red cabbages.

'You can't deny we've got good taste, in France,' says Tirette.

'It must have taken a deal of patience to paint all that,' says Blaire, looking at this variegated blossoming.

'In these places,' Volpatte adds, 'you don't enjoy just the pleasure of drinking.'

Paradis informs us that he is used to cafés. Often, in the old days, he used to hang around on Sundays in cafés as splendid, or even more so, than this one. However, that was a long time ago and he had forgotten what they were like. He points to a little enamel basin, decorated with flowers, on the wall.

'You can wash your hands.'

We go politely over to the basin. Volpatte nods to Paradis to turn on the tap.

'Get the plumbing going!'

Then all five of us go into the room, which already has a fair sprinkling of customers around its edge, and sit at a table.

'Five vermouth-cassis, no?'

'We'll soon get used to it again, after all,' we tell one another.

Some civilians get up and come over to us. They are whispering:

'Look, Adolphe, they've all got the Croix de Guerre . . .'

'They're real *poilus*.'

My comrades have heard and are only talking among themselves absent-mindedly, their attention elsewhere, unconsciously lapping it up.

A moment later the man and woman who were making these comments lean over towards us, their elbows on the white marble, and ask:

'Life in the trenches is hard, isn't it?'

'Hum . . . Yes . . . Well, darn it, it's not always a bundle of laughs.'

'How splendidly tough you must be, physically and morally! You manage to get used to the life, I suppose?'

'Why yes, one does, one does get quite used to it.'

'Even so, it's a dreadful existence . . . and such suffering,' the lady mutters, leafing through an illustrated magazine showing some dismal scenes of devastation. 'They shouldn't publish such things, Adolphe! There is the dirt, the lice, the fatigues . . . Splendid chaps though you are, it must get you down.'

She is addressing Volpatte, who blushes. He's ashamed of the misery from which he comes and to which he will return. He bows his head and lies, perhaps without fully realizing the extent of his deception:

'No, in the end, we're not too badly off . . . It's not as dreadful as all that, you know!'

The woman thinks the same.

'Of course,' she says, 'I realize there are compensations. A charge must be magnificent, no? All those ranks of men marching as though on parade! And the trumpet sounding *Y'a la goutte à boire là-haut!* And the young lads who can't be stopped, shouting *"Vive la France!"*, or who die with a smile on their lips! Oh, we civilians, we don't share in the glory like you do. My husband is at the town hall, though at the moment he's off work because of his rheumatism.'

'I'd like to have been a soldier now,' says the gentleman. 'But I didn't have that good fortune. My boss can't do without me.'

People come and go, elbowing past or stepping aside for one another. The waiters slip through with their shining, fragile burdens of green, red and bright yellow fringed with white. The crunch of footsteps on the sanded floor mingles with the exclamations of regulars meeting, some standing, others leaning on their elbows, or the noises of dominoes and glasses on marble . . . At the back of the room the clink of ivory balls attracts a ring of spectators, pressed together, emitting the usual jokes.

'Each man to his own job, my good chap,' a man with a face blotched in many colours says to Tircttc from the far end of the table. 'You're heroes, while we're working for the economic life of the country. It's a battle like yours. I'm useful – I'm not saying more useful than you – but as much.'

I can see Tirette, the joker of the squad, wide-eyed through the cigar smoke and barely hear him through the din answer in a humble, stunned voice:

'Yes, that's right . . . Each man to his job.'

We creep away furtively.

We don't speak as we leave the Café des Fleurs. It seems to us that we cannot speak any longer. A sort of discontent cramps and disfigures my companions. They seem to be becoming aware that in crucial circumstances they have not done their duty.

'All the stuff they told us in their patois, those cuckolds!' Tirette grumbles at last, with a bitterness that emerges and grows stronger the more we are alone together.

'We should've got pissed today!' Paradis answers aggressively.

We carry on without saying a word. Then, after a while, Tirette resumes:

'They're vermin, filthy vermin. They tried to have us on, but I'm not taken in by it. If I see them again I'll know what to say to them,' he adds, his voice rising to a crescendo.

'You won't see them again,' says Blaire.

'In a week we may be done for,' says Volpatte.

Approaching the square we run into a mob pouring out of the town hall and some other public monument with a classical portico and pillars. It's time for the offices to empty, with civilians of every sort and every age emerging, as well as young and old soldiers who, from a distance, are dressed more or less like us. Closer up, though, you can detect their identity as shirkers and runaways from the war through their military disguise and their *brisques* – the arm badges showing their length of service.

Women and children are waiting for them, clustered together like pretty bouquets of happiness. The shopkeepers lovingly shut up their shops, smiling towards the day that has ended and the tomorrow to come, revelling in the intense, unending thrill of their accumulated profits and the mounting clatter of the till. They have stayed right there at home; they have only to bend down to kiss their children. And in the first lights of the street we can see all these rich people as they get richer, all these tranquil souls who are tranquillized more every day and filled, in spite of everything, with one unutterable prayer. They all go home quietly, by grace of evening, and settle into well-designed houses and cafés where they are served. Couples – young women and young men, civilians or soldiers, bearing some preservative sign on their shoulders – are formed and hurry off, under cover of the rest of the crowd, towards the dawn of their room, towards a night of rest and of caresses.

Walking past a half-open ground-floor window we see the breeze lift the lace curtain and give it the light, soft shape of a chemise.

The advancing crowd drives us back like the poor strangers that we are.

We are wandering around on the cobbles, as dusk falls, as dusk starts to deck itself out with lights; in towns, the night clothes herself in jewels. The sight of these people has finally brought us the revelation of a great reality, one that we cannot avoid: a Difference between people, a Difference far deeper and with far more uncrossable boundaries than race, the distinct, clear-cut and truly inexorable distinction among the people of one country, between those who profit and those who toil . . . those who have been asked to sacrifice everything, who take their names, their strength and their martyrdom right to the end, and over whom the others trample, march forward, smile and enjoy success.

A few mourning clothes stand out from the mass and speak to us, but the others are rejoicing, not mourning.

'There's not just one country, it's not true,' Volpatte says suddenly, with peculiar accuracy. 'There's two. I'm telling you, we're divided into two foreign countries: the front, over there, where there are too many unhappy people, and the rear, here, where there are too many happy ones.'

'What d'you expect? They do their bit . . . You've got to have it . . . It's the rear . . . Anyway . . .'

'Yes, yes, I know, but even so, even so, there are too many of 'em and they're too well off, and then, it's always the same ones . . . and then, there's no reason . . .'

'What d'you expect?' says Tirette.

'Too bad!' Blaire adds, even more simply.

'In a week's time we may all be bloody dead!' is the only thing that Volpatte has to say, again, as we go off with heads hanging.

23
The Fatigue

Night is falling over the trenches. All day long, invisible as fate, it has been approaching and now it encroaches on the embankments of the long ditches like the lips of an unending wound.

Since morning, in the depths of the crevasse, we have talked, eaten, slept and written. With the arrival of evening a stir has spread along the limitless hole, shaking and unifying the inertia and the solitudes of the men scattered along it. This is the hour when we rise up and go to work.

Volpatte and Tirette approach each other.

'One more day gone, a day like the rest,' Volpatte says, looking at the darkening cloud.

'That's what you think,' says Tirette. 'Our day's not over.'

A long experience of misfortune has taught him that where we are, one should not tempt fate by predicting the outcome even of an evening that has already started on its ordinary way.

'Come on now! Muster!'

We collect with the absent-minded sluggishness of habit. Each man brings his rifle, his cartridge cases, his water bottle and his bag with a little bread. Volpatte is still eating, his cheek bulging and heaving. Paradis growls, his nose violet and his teeth chattering. Fouillade drags his rifle along like a broomstick. Marthereau examines a miserable, well-used, stiff handkerchief, then puts it back in his pocket.

It is cold and drizzling. Everyone shivers.

A short way off you can hear the chant of: 'Two spades, one pick, two spades, one pick . . .'

The line shuffles towards this equipment store, hesitates at the entrance and then sets off, bristling with tools.

'Everyone here? Gee up!' says the corporal.

We hurry on, rolling forwards. We are advancing, none of us know where. We know nothing, except that the sky and the earth are mingling into the same abyss.

We emerge from the trench, which is already blackened like an extinct volcano, and find ourselves on open ground at dusk.

Great grey clouds, full of water, are hanging from the sky. The land is grey too, palely lit, with muddy grass and watery scars. Here and there, stripped trees have nothing left to them except sorts of limbs and contortions. In the dank mist one cannot see far in any direction; and, in any case, we only look at the ground, at the slippery mud.

'Blimey, what crud!'

Across the fields we knead and pound a dough with a viscous consistency that makes it constantly spread and slide back under our feet.

'Chocolate cream! No, coffee cream!'

On the stony parts, which are former roadways, wiped off the map and as sterile as the fields, the marching troop crunches the flint through a sticky layer which makes it slither and crackle under our nailed boots.

'It's like walking on buttered toast!'

Sometimes, on the slope of a hill, there is thick black mud with deep crevices in it, such as you find in villages around a horse-pond. In the dips are puddles, ponds and lakes with irregular, ragged edges.

The comedians who cried 'quack, quack!' whenever they saw some water, while they were fresh and jolly at the start, find that these witty sallies are now becoming rarer as their mood darkens. Little by little they fall silent. Rain starts to fall in torrents. You can hear it. Daylight fades and the foggy space around us draws in. A lingering fragment of livid yellow light wallows in the water, on the ground.

In the west the misty silhouette of monks appears through the rain. It's a company of the 204th, wrapped in tarpaulins. As they pass we see the sunken, colourless faces and black noses of these great waterlogged wolves. Then they disappear.

We are following a track in the middle of the vaguely grassed fields, the track itself a muddy field marked with innumerable parallel ruts, ploughed in the same direction by the feet and wheels travelling towards the front or the rear.

We jump across gaping trenches – not always an easy task: the edges have become sticky, slippery, and they have been widened by falls of earth. Moreover, tiredness is starting to weigh down our shoulders. Vehicles pass by us with a lot of noise and splashing of mud. The limbers of gun carriages bounce past and spray us with mud-laden water. Motor trucks sail by on liquid wheels turning around their solid ones and throw off water in tumultuous spokes.

As night draws on, the jolted horse teams are silhouetted in a still more fantastic manner, the necks of the animals and the profiles of their riders with their floating cloaks and carbines slung across their backs standing out against the cloudy sky. At one point there is a hold-up among the ammunition trucks. The horses stop and paw the ground as we go by. You can hear a confusion of screeching axles, voices, arguments, contradictory orders and the great oceanic sound of the rain. Above the dark mêlée you can see the horses' flanks and their riders' cloaks steaming.

'Careful!'

On the ground, to the right, something is spread out. It is a row of dead men. Instinctively, as we go past, we step aside, but our eyes search it. We notice pointing feet, necks outstretched, the hollowness of vague faces, and the hands half grasping in the air above the black jumble of corpses.

And on and on we go, across these fields still footworn and livid, under a sky where the clouds unfurl, shredded like rags, across the blackening expanse that seems to have been dirtied by its long contact, for so many days, with so much poor humanity.

Then we go back down into the trenches.

They are further down the hill and to reach them we have to make a wide circle, so that those at the rear can see the whole company extending through the half-light over a hundred metres, dark little manikins clinging to the side of the hill, following one another as they trickled past with their rifles or their tools raised on either side of their heads, a slender, insignificant line of suppliants, with raised arms, going down into the earth.

These second-line trenches are still occupied. Outside the shelters animal skins or grey cloths flap or hang still. Crouching unshaven men watch us go by with expressionless eyes, as though staring into space. From under other cloths, which have been lowered to the ground, emerge feet and snores.

'Good God! It's a bleeding long way!' some of the marching men start to moan.

A shudder and a backward movement.

'Halt!'

We have to halt to let others go by. Cursing, we press back against the sloping sides of the trench. It's a company of machine-gunners with their strange burdens.

It goes on and on. These long pauses are irritating. Your muscles start to ache. The endless tramping is wearing us down.

No sooner have we set off again than we are obliged to go back as far as a side-trench to give way to a relief party of telephonists. Back we go, like awkward cattle.

We set off with heavier steps.

'Mind the wire!'

The telephone wire undulates above the trench, crossing it in some places between two pegs. When it is not tight enough it hangs down into the gap and tangles with the rifles of the men passing underneath, and the men who have been caught struggle to free their rifles, abusing the telephone engineers who never do attach their wires properly.

Then as the drooping cat's cradle of precious wires increases we hang our rifles by their straps from our shoulders, butt up, carry our spades head down and go forward with bent shoulders.

The march suddenly slows down. We are only advancing step by step now, pressed up against each other. The head of the column must have reached a difficult passage.

We get to the place: the ground slopes down to a gaping fissure. This is the Covered Trench. The others have vanished through this kind of low doorway.

'So, do we have to go inside this sausage?'

Each man hesitates before committing himself to the tight, underground gloom; it is the sum total of these hesitations and slow movements that reverberates to the rear portions of the column in waves, blockages and sometimes sudden halts.

As soon as we take our first steps inside the Covered Trench heavy darkness engulfs us and separates us, one by one, from each other. A smell of dank cellar and marshland penetrates us. On the ceiling of this earthy corridor all around us we can see a few pallid streaks and holes: these are the gaps and tears in the planks above us. In some places copious streams of water fall through them and, despite feeling our way with care, we stumble against heaps of wood while our sides brush the vague presence of the vertical supports.

The atmosphere in this interminable passageway vibrates dully from the searchlight generator which has been set up here; we have to pass in front of it. After a quarter of an hour drowned in this blackness, feeling our way, someone who has had enough of the dark and the damp, fed up with knocking against unknown objects, grumbles: 'Too bad, I'm lighting up!'

An electric torch sends out a dazzling stream of light. Immediately, the sergeant yells:

'Holy shit! Who is the utter imbecile who lit that! Are you crazy? Can't you tell that it can be seen through the roof, you nutter?'

The torch which had lit up the dark, streaming walls in its cone of light, sinks back into darkness.

'Not much chance of it being seen,' the man grumbles. 'After all, we're not in the front line!'

'No, no one could see it!'

The sergeant is caught up in the line and being carried forward all the time, but you guess that he is turning round as he walks and disjointedly trying to speak his mind:

'Halfwit! God Almighty on a trapeze!'

Then suddenly he flares up again:

'Another one's smoking! Holy shit!'

This time he tries to stop, but however much he struggles to press himself against the wall and stay there, he is forced to follow the drift and gets carried away along with his own muttered curses while the cigarette which has occasioned his fury vanishes in silence.

The jerky thudding of the machine grows clearer and the heat thickens around us. As we go forward the packed air in the trench shudders more and more. Soon the pounding of the machine hammers against our ears and shakes us through and through. The heat increases; it's like the breath of some monster in our faces. We are going along this buried ditch, down towards the din of some infernal laboratory, its dark red glow starting to tint the walls and throw our massive, crouching shadows on it.

In a diabolical crescendo of noise, hot wind and lights we move on towards the generator. We are deafened. It now seems as though it is the engine which is blocking the gallery and coming to meet us, like a speeding motorcycle, plunging forward with its headlights and its power.

Half-blinded, scorched, we pass in front of the red furnace and the black engine, its flywheel roaring like a hurricane. We have just time to notice men moving around before shutting our eyes, suffocated by the contact of this incandescent, bellowing breath.

At length the noise and heat carry on behind us and grow fainter. And my neighbour grumbles into his beard:

'And that idiot said my lamp might be visible!'

Open air at last. The sky is a very dark blue, hardly a lighter shade than the earth itself. The rain is falling still more heavily. We trudge on through these cloying muds. The whole shoe sinks into them and there is a sharp pain of exhaustion each time you withdraw it. Nothing can be seen through the darkness – though, on coming out of the hole, we did notice a heap of beams cluttering the widened trench: some shelter, now demolished.

At this moment the searchlight turns its great magic arm which swings through space and alights on us – and we discover that the jumble of poles, uprooted and driven into the soil, and broken frames is inhabited by dead soldiers. Quite close to me a head has been attached to a kneeling corpse with some kind of fastening and is hanging on its back; on its cheek is a black mark dotted with congealed drops. Another body has its arms round a post and has only half fallen. Another, curled round in a circle and stripped bare by the shell blast, is exposing its pale belly and back. Still another, lying at the edge of the piled earth, has one hand trailing on the path. In this spot, where you can only pass at night – the trench has been filled in by a collapsed wall and is inaccessible in daylight – everybody walks on the hand. I saw it clearly in the searchlight, skeletal and worn, like some kind of atrophied flipper.

The rain is belting down. The sound of its streaming dominates everything. The sense of desolation is appalling. You feel the rain on your skin, denuding you. We go down into the open trench while the night and the storm take the jumble of bodies back to themselves, fanning them where they lie, clasping this corner of earth like men stranded on a raft.

The wind ices the tears of sweat on our cheeks. It is nearly midnight. We have been walking for six hours in the ever-more-clinging mud. This is the time when, in the theatres of Paris, illuminated by chandeliers and bedecked with lamps, bursting with luxurious enthusiasm, the shimmering of dresses and the warmth of parties, a sweet-smelling, radiant and expansive throng chatters, laughs, smiles and applauds, gently stirred by the feelings that the play has evoked, or lolls around, pleased with the magnificence and richness of the military splendours that fill the stage at the music hall.

'Are we there yet? In God's name, will we ever get there?'

A groan rises from the long cavalcade jolting along through the gaps in the earth, carrying its rifles, spades and picks under the endless rain. We march, we march. Tiredness makes us drunk, throwing us to one side then another, as weighed down and soaked through we beat our shoulders against the earth which is as sodden as we are.

'Halt!'

'Is this it?'

'Why yes, it is. We're there!'

For the time being a powerful counter-flow appears, dragging us back, with a whisper running along the line:

'We're lost.'

The truth emerges in the confusion of the wandering horde: somewhere, at some fork in the road, we took the wrong turning and now it will be the devil's own job to find the right road.

More than that, the rumour spreads from mouth to mouth that behind us is a company fully armed on its way to the front. The road we took is blocked with men. There's a jam.

Whatever happens we must try to get back to the lost trench, which is said to be on our left, making our way through some kind of sap. The irritation of the men, who are exhausted and at the end of their tether, erupts in arm-waving and violent recriminations. They drag themselves along, then drop their tools and stay put. In places there are clusters of them – which can be seen in the white light of rockets – slumping to the ground. The troop waits, spread out from north to south, in the pitiless rain.

The lieutenant who is leading the column and who has managed to lose us makes his way past the men, looking for a way off to the side. A small slit opens, low and narrow.

'This is where we have to go, there's been no mistake,' the officer insists. 'Come on, friends, forward march!'

Each of us picks up his burden again, with a murmur of complaint. But a chorus of curses and swearwords pours out of the group which has started down the little sap.

'It's a latrine!'

A disgusting odour rises out of the passage, leaving no doubt about its nature. Those who have gone in stop, protest and refuse to go forward. We pile up on one another, causing a blockage at the entrance to these latrines.

'I'd rather go out in the open!' yells one man. But there are flashes breaking through the clouds overhead and the landscape is so awesome to look at from the shadows of this teeming pit, with those sprays of resounding flames in the sky above it, that no one takes up the madman's appeal.

Since we can't go back we must go through, whether we like it or not.

'Forward through the shit!' shouts the first man in line.

We set off, choking with disgust. The stench becomes intolerable. We are walking through filth and can feel its slithering softness against the earthy mud.

Bullets whistle overhead.

'Heads down!'

Since the passage is not deep we are obliged to crouch very low if we are not to be killed and have to advance, bent over, through the mire of excrement and paper under our feet.

Finally we reach the trench that we left by mistake. The march resumes. We keep on marching and never arrive.

The stream now running along the bottom of the trench wipes the foul and fetid muck off our feet as we wander forward, speechless, our heads empty, stunned and dizzy with fatigue.

The grumbling of the artillery becomes more and more frequent, until it forms a single rumbling of the whole earth. From all sides shells firing or bursting throw out rapid flashes of light that streak the black sky above our heads. Then the bombardment becomes so intense that the flashes merge into one. In the midst of this continual chain of thunder we can see each other directly, each helmet streaming like the body of a fish, the leathers drenched, the shiny black iron of spades and even the whitish drops of the eternal rain. Never before have I witnessed such a scene; it is like moonlight manufactured by cannon fire.

At the same time a host of rockets springs up from our lines and those of the enemy, mingling and merging in starry groups. At one moment there was a Great Bear of rockets in the valley of the sky we can see between the two parapets, lighting our fearsome journey.

We have lost our way again. This time we must be quite close to the front lines, but a dip in the ground on this part of the landscape makes a sort of basin, crisscrossed by shadows.

We have been along a sap in one direction, then the other. In the phosphorescent vibration of the cannon fire, as jerky as a cinema film, we can see two stretcher-bearers trying to get across the trench with a loaded stretcher.

The lieutenant, who does at least know the place to which he is meant to be conducting his party of workers, calls out to them:

'Where's the New Trench?'

'Dunno.'

From the ranks someone asks them a different question:

'How far are we from the Boche?'

They don't answer. They are talking to each other.

'I'm stopping here,' says the one in front. 'I'm too tired.'

'Come on, keep going, for heaven's sake,' says the other in a surly voice, floundering in the mud, his arms dragged over by the stretcher. 'We're not going to rot here.'

They put down the stretcher on the parapet, one end of it overhanging the trench. From underneath you can see the feet of the man who is lying there, and the rain falling on the stretcher is black when it drips off.

'Wounded?' someone asks from below.

'No, a goner,' the stretcher-bearer growls this time. 'And he must weigh at least eighty kilos. I don't mind the wounded ones – and over the past two days and nights we've done nothing but carry them. What I do mind is knocking yourself out lugging the dead ones around.'

And the stretcher-bearer, standing on the edge of the parapet, puts one foot on the base of the parapet opposite, above the hole, and with his legs doing the splits, precariously balanced, seizes the stretcher and tries to drag it across to the other side, calling on his comrade to help.

A little further on we see the shape of an officer with a hood over his head, stooping down. He puts his hand up to his face and two lines of gold braid appear on his sleeve. He will surely show us the way . . . But he says something: he is asking if we have seen his battery, which he has lost.

We'll never get there.

Yet we do.

We end up in a coal-black field with a few lone posts sticking out of it. We climb over them and spread out in silence. This is it.

Getting into place is another matter. Four times in succession we have to go forward, then back, until the company is regularly spaced along the full length of the trench that is to be dug, with the same space between each team of one pickman and two shovellers.

'Another three paces . . . No, that's too far. Back a little. Come on, back a little! Are you deaf? Halt! There!'

These instructions are being given by the lieutenant and an NCO of the Engineers who has emerged out of the ground. Together or separately they are exerting themselves, running along the line, shouting their orders in a growl in the faces of the men, while sometimes grabbing their arms to guide them. The operation, which started in an orderly fashion, is degenerating into a turbulent scramble because of the bad temper among the exhausted men, who constantly have to move away from the spot where they have come to rest.

'We're ahead of the front lines,' people are whispering around me.

'No,' other voices reply. 'Just behind them.'

We can't tell, though the rain is falling less heavily than at some times in our march. But who cares about rain! We are lying down, so comfortable with our backs and our limbs on the soft mud that we don't mind the water hitting our faces and slipping across our skin, or the spongy bed supporting us.

We hardly have time to draw breath. They are not going to let us slip into an unguarded ease. We have to start work and work flat out. It is now two in the morning; in four hours it will be too light for us to remain here. There is not a moment to lose.

'Every man' (they tell us) 'must dig one and a half metres along by seventy centimetres wide and eighty centimetres deep. So each team has its four and a half metres. And if you take my advice you'll put your backs into it, 'cos the sooner you're done, the sooner you'll leave.'

We've heard that one before. In the annals of the regiment there is not a single case of a team on trench-digging fatigue leaving before the time when everyone absolutely had to clear off – to avoid being seen, sighted and wiped out, with their trench.

We mutter: 'Yeah, yeah, thanks . . . Don't bother to spin us that line. Save your breath.'

However, apart from a few who are overcome with tiredness and forced to make a superhuman effort to keep working, everyone sets to it bravely.

We dig into the first layer of the new line: mounds of earth with stringy clumps of grass. The work starts so easily and quickly, like all digging work in open ground, that it gives the false impression that it will soon be over and we shall be able to sleep in our hole. This makes us work the harder.

Then, either because of the noise of the shovels or because a few people, despite demands to the contrary, are chattering almost in normal voices, our efforts awake a rocket which creaks directly upwards on our right, with its flaming tail.

'Get down!'

Everyone falls flat as the rocket hangs in the air, spreading its pale light wide over a sort of field of corpses.

When it goes out you can hear a few men in some places, then everywhere, shift out of their concealing immobility and stand up to carry on with the work, more cautiously now.

Soon another rocket rises on its gilded trail and pauses, its luminosity once more immobilizing the dark line of trench-diggers. Then another and another.

Shots tear through the air around us. Somebody shouts: 'Man wounded!'

He goes past, with his comrades supporting him. There even seem to be several wounded: you can see a group of men dragging one another along as they move away . . .

The spot is getting unhealthy. We bend down or crouch. A few people are kneeling as they scrape the earth; others work lying down, toiling away, turning from side to side, like men with nightmares. The first layer of soil was easy to remove, but now it is muddy and sticky, hard to lift, clinging to the tools like putty. With every shovelful you have to scrape the blade clean.

A slender line of excavated earth is already winding across the field and each digger deceives himself into thinking that he has strengthened this embryonic earthwork with his pouch and rolled coat, curling up behind the shade of this slight heap when a burst of fire starts.

As we work we sweat, but as soon as we stop the cold cuts through us, so we have to overcome our pain and fatigue and get back to it.

No, we won't get it done. The soil is getting heavier and heavier. A kind of spell seems to fall over us and paralyse our arms. The rockets are harassing us, hunting us down; they don't let us work for long. And after each one has petrified us with its light we have to resume an increasingly difficult task. Painfully, with desperate slowness, the hole advances into the depths.

The earth now is softer still: every shovelful runs off, sliding on to the ground with a slopping noise. At last someone shouts: 'Water!'

The cry echoes and spreads all along the row of diggers.

'There's water! Can't go on!'

'The team with Mélusson has dug deepest and reached water. We're getting into a swamp.'

'Can't go on!'

We stop, in confusion. In the darkness of the night we hear the sound of spades and shovels being cast aside like empty guns. The NCOs feel their way towards the officer to ask for instructions. And, here and there, without caring to discover what is happening, men have fallen deliciously asleep beneath the soft touch of the rain and the radiance of rockets . . .

It was more or less at this moment, as far as I remember, that the bombardment began.

The first shell came in with a terrible cracking of the air, which seemed to split in half, and the whistle of others was already converging on us when the explosion threw up the earth near the head of the detachment, in the grandeur of the night and the rain, revealing gesticulating silhouettes against a sudden red screen.

No doubt, with all their rockets, they had seen us and trained their guns in our direction.

Men dashed or rolled towards the little flooded ditch that they had dug. We fitted ourselves into it, bathed in it, burrowed into it, placing the blades of the shovels above our heads. Left, right, ahead, behind, shells were bursting, so close that each of them shook us and bounced us in our bed of muddy clay. Soon there was just one continuous trembling that rocked this sad little gutter full of men, bristling with shovels, beneath layers of smoke and flashes of light. Splinters, shrapnel and rubbish flew in all directions over the dazzling field with their criss-crossing web of noises. Not a second passed when we didn't all think what some were stuttering, their faces pressed to the ground:

'This time we're buggered!'

A little ahead of where I was a shape rose up and shouted:

'Let's get the hell out!'

Prone bodies half lifted themselves out of the shroud of mud which streamed off their limbs in liquid sheets, these macabre spectres shouting:

'Let's go!'

We were kneeling, on all fours, pushing in the direction of the rear.

'Forward! Come on, forward!'

But the long line did not budge. The frantic appeals did not move it. Those who were at the end did not shift and their immobility was blocking the rest.

Wounded men made their way over their companions, clambering across them as though over a pile of debris and sprinkling everyone with their blood.

Finally we learned the reason for the maddening immobility of the line:

'There's a blockage at the end.'

A strange panic of imprisonment, with inarticulate shouts and trapped gestures, took hold of the men. They writhed around on the spot and yelled. But, small though the shelter offered by the shallow ditch was, no one dared rise out of this dip that kept us below the level of the earth and run away from death towards the transversal trench that must be a short way off. The wounded who were able to clamber over the living took an exceptional risk in doing so and were constantly being hit and falling back.

It was a real rain of fire that poured down on us, together with the rain itself. We were shaking from head to toe, caught up in the supernatural din. The most hideous of deaths was falling and leaping and diving all around us in floods of light. Your attention was pulled and torn in every direction by the flashes as your flesh prepared for the monstrous sacrifice. The feelings tearing through us were so strong that only then, in that moment, did we remember that we had sometimes already felt this, suffered this metallic downpour with its screaming burns and its stink. Only during a bombardment do you really recall the ones you have already endured.

And, constantly, new wounded men were crawling, fleeing in spite of all; they terrified us; as they touched you, you groaned, thinking over and over:

'We won't get out of this, no one will get out of this.'

Suddenly a gap appeared in the mass of humanity and it shifted towards the rear: the way was cleared.

We started to crawl, then ran, bent double in the mud and the water glistening with flashes and purple reflections, stumbling and falling because of the uneven surface hidden beneath the water – and we ourselves were like heavy, splashing projectiles, dashing, hurled by thunder along the ground. We got to the end of the trench that we had started to dig.

'There's no trench. Nothing!'

There wasn't. The eye could find no shelter in the field where our work had been started. All you could see was emptiness, a vast, furious desert, empty even beneath the flashing of the rockets. The trench could not be far away, since we had come here along it. But in which direction should we search?

The rain grew heavier. We stayed there for a moment, hanging in glum disappointment, gathered on the edge of this smitten wilderness; then the rush began. Some set off to the left, others to the right, others directly ahead, all tiny and glimpsed only for a moment in the midst of the pouring rain, separated by curtains of blazing smoke and black avalanches.

The bombardment slackened over our heads, increasing chiefly near the place where we had been. But from one moment to the next it could come and destroy everything.

The rain was becoming more and more torrential. It was a deluge in the night. The darkness was so thick that the rockets only lit up fuzzy sections of it, streaked with water, in the depths of which distracted ghosts came and went, running in all directions.

I cannot say how long I wandered around with the group I joined. We had strayed into a quagmire. Our strained faces tried to feel their way in front of us towards the salvation of the parapet and the ditch, towards that trench which was somewhere in the depths like a port.

Finally a comforting shout was heard through the noise of war and the elements.

'A trench!'

But the embankment in front of this trench was moving, covered in a jumble of men who seemed to be crawling out of it, abandoning it.

'Don't stay here, lads,' these fugitives cried. 'Stay back! Don't come near! It's frightful! Everything's falling in, the trenches are going, the dugouts are collapsing. There's mud coming in everywhere. Tomorrow morning there won't be any trenches. All the trenches round here are done for!'

We went off. Where? We'd forgotten to ask for directions from these men who, as soon as they appeared, the rain pouring off them, were swallowed up in the dark.

Even our little group separated in the midst of this chaos. No one knew who they were with any longer. Each of us set off, now this one, now that, slipping into the night, vanishing with his chance of safety.

Uphill we went and down. In front of me I saw men bent and humpbacked, going up a slippery slope where the mud kept dragging them under, while the wind and the rain pushed them back, beneath a dome of dull flashes.

Then we were swept back into a bog where we sank up to our knees. We walked along, raising our feet high, making a sound as though we were swimming. Moving forward took a huge effort, getting agonizingly slower with each stride.

There we felt the approach of death. We had come out onto a sort of clay dike cutting through the marsh. We followed along the slippery back of this slender island and I remember that at one point, to avoid falling off its winding, crumbling ridge, we had to stoop down and guide ourselves by touching a group of dead bodies which had half sunk there. My hand felt shoulders, hard backs, a face as cold as a helmet and a pipe still gripped desperately in a jaw.

Emerging from there and vaguely looking up we heard a number of voices echoing not far away.

'Voices! Ah, voices!'

How sweet they were to us, those voices, as though calling us by name. We clustered together as we approached the brotherly murmurs of our fellow men.

The words became distinct; they were spoken quite near, on this little mound that we glimpsed as an oasis, yet we couldn't hear what they were saying. The sounds were jumbled, we couldn't understand it.

'What are they saying, then?' one of our number asked, in an odd voice. Instinctively we stopped looking for a way in.

A suspicion, a painful idea had come into our minds. And then we heard some echoing words spoken very clearly:

'*Achtung! . . . Zweites Geschütz . . . Schuss . . .*'

And from behind a cannon shot replied to this telephone order.

At first amazement and horror nailed us to the spot.

'Where are we? God Almighty! Where are we?'

We about turned, slowly for all that, dragged down by more exhaustion and disappointment, and fled, shot through with tiredness as with a mass of wounds, drawn towards enemy land, but keeping just enough energy to drive away the sweet temptation of allowing ourselves to die.

We arrived on a sort of vast plain. There we halted and threw ourselves on the ground beside a hillock. We leant back against it, unable to take a step further.

My chance companions and I no longer moved. The rain washed our faces, ran down our backs and across our chests and filled our shoes, getting through the material around our knees.

Perhaps one day we would be killed or taken prisoner. But we no longer thought about any of that. We were unable to move, unable to think.

24
Dawn

We waited for daylight at the place where we had stopped and slumped to the ground. It came little by little, icy, dark and sinister, spreading over the livid expanse.

The rain stopped. There was none left in the sky. The leaden plain, with its tarnished mirrors of water, seems to be emerging not only from night, but from the sea.

Half drowsing, half asleep, sometimes opening our eyes only to shut them again, paralysed, exhausted and cold, we experience the incredible renewal of light.

Where are the trenches?

We can see lakes and between them lines of stagnant, milky water. There is even more water than we thought. The water has got everywhere, spreading all around, and the prediction of the men last night has been realized: there are no trenches – the trenches are under those canals. The world is flooded. The battlefield is not asleep, it is dead. Somewhere over there life may go on, but we cannot see that far.

I half get up, painfully, swaying like an invalid, to look around. My coat weighs me down with its dreadful burden. Beside me are three monstrously shapeless forms. One of them – Paradis, under an extraordinary crust of mud, with a swelling around his waist in place of his cartridge belt – also rises. The others are asleep and motionless.

And then what is this silence? It is prodigious. There is no noise, except from time to time the falling of a sod of earth into the water, in the midst of this fantastic paralysis of the world. No one is shooting:

no shells, because they would not explode; no bullets, because the men . . .

The men! Where are the men?

Bit by bit we start to see them. There are some not far from us, spread out, asleep, caked in mud from head to foot, changed almost into things.

Some distance away I can make out others, curled up and stuck like snails along a rounded embankment half covered in water – a motionless line of crude shapes, parcels next to one another, dripping with mud and water, the colour of the earth that surrounds them.

Making an effort to break the silence I ask Paradis, who is also looking in that direction:

'Are they dead?'

'We'll go and look in a while,' he whispers. 'Let's stay here for a bit longer. In a while we'll feel more like going.'

We exchange a glance and then turn to those who have also come to rest here. Our faces are so weary that they are no longer faces: something dirty, smudged and bruised, with bloodshot eyes, on top of us. We have seen each other in every guise since the beginning, yet we can no longer recognize one another.

Paradis turns away and looks at something else. Suddenly I notice that he has started to tremble. He extends a huge arm, encrusted with mud.

'Look there . . . there . . .' he says.

There are shapes, round reefs floating on the water overflowing from one trench in the midst of a particularly uneven, humpy patch of ground. We drag ourselves over to it. They are men who have drowned.

Their heads and arms are underwater, but you can see their backs with the leather of their equipment emerging on the surface of the pasty liquid, while their blue cloth trousers are blown up with the feet attached crosswise to these balloon legs, like the rounded black feet stuck on the shapeless legs of clowns or puppets. From one sunken head the hair is standing upright like waterweed. Here there is a face almost emerging, its head stranded on the edge while the body vanishes into the murky depths. It is looking upwards, its eyes two white holes, its mouth one black one. The puffy yellow skin of this mask looks soft and wrinkled, like cold pastry.

The men there were on watch. They could not haul themselves out of the mud. All their efforts to escape from the ditch with its sticky embankment, slowly, fatally filling up with water, only served to drag them further back towards the bottom. They died holding on for support to the earth as it slid away from them.

Here are our front lines, and there the German ones, equally silent and submerged.

We go over to these soft ruins, passing through what was only yesterday a zone of terror, the dreadful space at the edge of which the forward thrust of our last attack had to come to a halt. Here, for a year and a half, bullets and shells were continually exchanged, their crossed fire furiously raking the ground from one horizon to another.

Now it is a supernatural field of rest. Everywhere the landscape is dotted with sleeping figures, or others who are gently moving, raising an arm, lifting their heads, starting to live again – or in the process of dying.

The enemy trench is finally collapsing into itself at the bottom of great undulations and marshy craters, filled with mud, through which it forms a line of puddles and wells. In places you can see the still overhanging edges move, break up and slide down. At one point you can lean over it.

There are no bodies in this whirlpool of mire, but over there, worse than a body, is a lone arm, naked and pale as stone, emerging from a hole that can be vaguely distinguished in the wall, under the water. The man was buried in his shelter and only had time to reach out his arm.

From close up one observes that some heaps of earth lined up against the remains of the parapet above this ditch are human beings. Are they dead? Are they asleep? There is no telling. In any case they are at rest.

Are they German or French? We do not know.

One of them opens his eyes and looks at us, shaking his head. We ask him:

'French?'

then:

'*Deutsch?*'

No reply. Instead he shuts his eyes and relapses into oblivion. We never found out who he was.

You cannot determine the identity of these creatures, not from the clothes buried under a layer of mud, nor from their headdress – they are bare-headed or swathed in wool under their liquid, stinking balaclavas, nor from their weapons – they do not have their guns, or else their hands are sliding across something which they have dragged here, a shapeless, sticky lump like some variety of fish.

All these men with their corpse-like faces, in front of us and behind, driven to exhaustion, emptied of words and will . . . All these men laden with earth, who, you could say, are carrying their own graves, are as alike as if they were naked. On either side a few ghosts are emerging from the ghastly night, dressed in precisely the same uniform of filth and misery.

It is the end of everything. For a moment it is the great stoppage, the epic cessation of war.

At one time I thought that the worst hell of war was the flaming of shells; then, for a long time, I thought it was the suffocation of underground passages that constantly close in on you. But no: hell is water.

The wind is rising. It is icy cold and its iced breath passes through our flesh. On the drowned and dissolving plain, dotted with corpses between its twisting watercourses and the islands of motionless men sticking together like reptiles, across this levelling and sinking chaos, slight hints of movement appear. You can see bands of men slowly advancing, sections of caravans made up of beings bent beneath the weight of their greatcoats and aprons of mud, dragging themselves along, separating and creeping along beneath the darkened light of the sky. The dawn is so foul that you would think day was already over.

These survivors are migrating across this desolate steppe, driven by a great unspeakable misfortune that exhausts and appals them, lamentable figures, a few dramatically grotesque when one gets close enough to see them, half undressed by the slime from which they are still escaping.

As they go by they look around, look at us, then perceive us as men and shout at us against the wind:

'It's worse over there than here. Blokes are falling into holes and you can't get them out. All the ones who stepped on the edge of a shell hole in the dark are dead . . . Over there, where we've come from, you can see a head and waving arms rooted in the ground. There's a walkway of duckboards that have caved in here and there, and have holes in them: it's a man mousetrap. Where there aren't any boards left there's two metres of water . . . Some people have never managed to uproot their guns. Look at those there: all the bottoms of their coats have been cut off – and too bad for the pockets – to get them out and because they didn't have the strength to carry all that weight. Dumas's greatcoat that they managed to get off him weighed a good forty kilos; two men were just able to lift it up with both hands. Look at him then, the one with the bare legs: it took everything off him, his trousers, his drawers, his shoes, the lot, all dragged away by the earth. No one's ever seen anything like it.'

And strung out in a line – because there are stragglers among these stragglers – they make their way through an epidemic of terror, their feet lifting huge roots of mud from the ground. We watch these gusts of men disappear, their bulk under their huge clothes gradually decreasing.

We get up. When we are standing the icy wind makes us shiver like trees.

We advance step by step. We diverge, attracted by the mass of two men, oddly jumbled together, shoulder to shoulder, their arms around each other's necks. Is this the close contact of two combatants who have dragged one another into death and are now fixed here, eternally unable to let go? No, these are two men who have leant against one another to sleep. Since they could not lie down on the ground, which was slipping away and wanted to lie over them, they bent towards one another, gripped their shoulders and fell asleep, up to their knees in mud.

We respect their immobility and carry on past this double statue to the misery of mankind.

Very soon we ourselves stop. We have overestimated our strength.

We cannot leave yet. It is not yet finished. We sink once more into a churned-up corner with a noise like a shovelful of muck.

We close our eyes. From time to time we reopen them.

People are staggering towards us. They lean over us and speak in low, weary voices. One of them says:

'*Sie sind tot. Wir bleiben hier.*'

The other replies *ja*, like a sigh.

But they see us move. So, at once, they sink down in front of us. The man with the toneless voice says to us:

'We raise our hands.'

And they do not move.

Then they flop over altogether, with relief. One of them, with mud pictures on his face like a tattooed savage, as though this were the end of their agony, gives a weak smile.

'Stay there,' Paradis tells him, without moving his head which is resting on a mound behind him. 'You can come with us presently, if you like.'

'Yes,' says the German. 'I've had enough.'

We do not answer.

He says:

'The others too?'

'Yes,' says Paradis. 'Let them stay if they wish.'

There are four of them, lying flat out.

One starts to gasp, a death rattle like a sobbing song rising from his throat. At this the others half kneel around him and roll their large eyes in faces streaked with dirt. We get up and watch the scene. But the rattle ends and the blackish throat, which was all that moved, like a little bird, in this great body, falls still.

'*Er ist tot*,' says one of the men.

He starts to weep. The others settle back to sleep. The weeping man falls asleep, still crying.

A few soldiers have arrived to take refuge here on the crest to which we are already clinging; they stumble, make sudden halts, like drunkards, or slip around like worms. We fall asleep, one on top of another in the mass grave.

*

We reawaken. We look at each other. Paradis and I remember. We come back into life and into the full light of day as though into a nightmare. The field of disaster is resurrected in front of us, with its blurred shapes of hillocks, swamped, its steely plain, rusted in parts, shining with lines and pools of water; and in its immensity, scattered here and there like garbage, the shattered bodies breathing or decomposing. Paradis says:

'That's war.'

'Yes, that's what it is, war,' he repeats, in a faraway voice. 'Nothing else.'

What he means – and I understand it like this myself – is:

'Rather than being a matter of charges that look like parades, more than visible battles unfurled like standards, even more than hand-to-hand fighting where men struggle and shout, this war is about appalling, superhuman exhaustion, about water up to your belly and about mud, dung and repulsive filth. It is about moulding faces and shredded flesh and corpses that do not even look like corpses anymore, floating on the greedy earth. It is this, this infinite monotony of miseries, interrupted by sharp, sudden dramas. This is what it is – not the bayonet glittering like silver or the bugle's call in the sunlight!'

So much was Paradis thinking of that, that he recalled something and grunted:

'Do you remember the old girl in the town where we walked around not long ago who was talking about an attack and drooling all over the idea, saying: "It must be a fine thing to see!"?'

A *chasseur*, lying on his belly, flat as a coat, raised his head out of the ignoble shade in which it had been plunged and cried:

'A fine thing! Oh shit! It's just as though an ox said: "It must be a fine thing, at the abattoirs in La Villette, to see all those hosts of oxen being driven forward!"'

He spat out some mud, his mouth smeared with it and his face covered in earth like an animal's.

'They can say, if they like: "It's necessary,"' he stammered in a strangely clipped and ragged voice. 'Fair enough. But a fine thing! Oh shit!'

He struggled against the idea. Then he burst out:

'It's when they say things like that about us that they don't give a bleeding shit about us!'

He spat again, but was so exhausted by the effort he had made that he fell back into his pool of slime and put his head back in his spittle.

Paradis, obsessed, his eyes staring, waved a hand over the expanse of the indescribable landscape and repeated:

'That's war, that is. That's it, everywhere. What are we, and what is this here? Nothing at all. Everything that you can see is a dot. Just tell yourself that, in the world this morning, there are three thousand kilometres of this sort of disaster, more or less, or worse.'

'And then,' said the comrade beside us – whom we did not recognize, not even by the voice emerging from him, 'tomorrow it will all start again. It did the day before yesterday and all the days before that!'

With an effort, as though tearing up the ground, the *chasseur* lifted his body off the ground where he had moulded an impression like a sweating coffin, and sat down in the hole. He blinked, shook his head with its fringe of mud, to clean it, and said:

'We'll pull through again this time. Who knows, perhaps tomorrow too, we'll pull through! Who knows?'

Paradis, his back bowed under carpets of mould and clay, was trying to describe his feeling that war is unimaginable and immeasurable in time and space.

'When you talk about the war,' he said, meditating aloud, 'it's as though you didn't say anything. It stifles words. We are here, looking at this, like blind men.'

A bass voice rumbled a little way off:

'No, you can't imagine it.'

A sudden outburst of laughter greeted this remark.

'To begin with, how could anyone imagine this, without having been here?'

'You'd have to be mad!' said the *chasseur*.

Paradis leant over a mass lying on the ground beside him:

'You asleep?'

'No, but I'm not moving,' stammered a frightened and stifled voice from within the heap, which was covered by a thick, silt-encrusted quilt, so deeply embossed that it seemed to have been trampled over. 'I'm telling you, I think my belly's been hit. But I'm not sure, I don't dare find out.'

'We'll take a look . . .'

'No, not yet,' said the man. 'I'd like to stay like this a bit longer.'

The others made vague slapping movements and pushed themselves up on their elbows to shift the accursed blanket of dough. Little by little the paralysis of cold was drifting off this cluster of sufferers, though there was no further increase in daylight on the great irregular pond of the battlefield. Desolation continued, under the same sky.

The one among us who spoke sadly, like a bell, said:

'I dunno, whatever you tell them they won't believe you. Not out of malice or because they want to give you the brush-off, but because they just won't be able. Later on, if you're still alive to get a word in, and you say: "We were on night work, we got shelled and we almost drowned in mud," they'll just go: "Ah!" Someone may say: "Can't have been much fun for you." That's all. Nobody's going to know. Just you.'

'No, not even us! Not even us!' someone shouted.

'I agree, mate. We'll forget. We're already forgetting, old man!'

'We've seen too much of it!'

'And everything we've seen is too much. We're not built to take all this in. It buggers off in every direction: we're too small.'

'You bet we won't remember! It's not just the length of the great misery – which, as you say, is incalculable, from the time when it started: the marching which tramples the earth backwards and forwards, bruises the feet and wears the bones under the weight of the load that seems to get bigger in the sky, under the unspeakable exhaustion, the moving about and the standing still that crushes you, the work that is beyond your strength, the endless nights without sleep, watching for an enemy who is everywhere in the darkness and fighting against sleep – and the pillows of dung and lice; but also the unpleasantness of shells and machine-guns, mines, poison gas and counter-attacks. We are full of the emotions of the moment, and we are right. But it all gets worn away inside you and goes, you can't tell how or where, leaving you only with the names, the words for things, like in a dispatch.'

'That's right, what he's saying,' a man said without moving his head in its collar of mud. 'When I was on leave I saw how I'd forgotten lots of things from my life before. There were letters from me that I read like opening a book. And yet, in spite of that, I also forgot what I'd suffered in the war. We are machines for forgetting. Men are things that think a little but, most of all, forget. That's what we are.'

'Not them, then, or us! So much misery lost!'

This prospect, coming on top of the desolation of these beings like the news of an even greater disaster, depressed them even further on the shore where they were stranded from the flood.

'Oh, if only one could remember!' one of them exclaimed.

'If people did remember,' said another, 'there wouldn't be any more war.'

A third declared grandly: 'Yes, if they remembered, war would be less useless than it is.'

But suddenly one of the survivors got up on his knees, shook his arms with the mud falling off them and, black as a great bat in a bog, cried out hoarsely:

'There mustn't be any wars after this one!'

In this slimy corner where, still weak and feeble, we were struck by blasts of wind that seized us so suddenly and so hard that the surface of the ground seemed to rock like a wrecked boat the cry of this man, who seemed to want to fly away, awoke other, similar cries:

'There must be no more war after this one!'

The dark, angry shouts of these men, chained to the earth, born of the earth, rose and drifted in the wind like flapping wings:

'No more war! No more war!'

'Yes, enough!'

'It's too stupid after all . . . It's too stupid,' they mumbled. 'In the end what does it all mean, all this . . . all this that we can't even name?'

They stammered and grumbled like wild animals on their kind of ice floe tossed by the elements, their dark faces streaked with mud. The protest rising in them was so huge that it stifled them.

'We're made for living, not to die like this!'

'Men are made to be husbands, fathers – men, in short! Not animals that hunt one another down, tear out each other's throats and stink in their own filth.'

'Yet wherever you look they're animals: wild beasts or stricken beasts. Look around! Look!'

I shall never forget the sight of this endless landscape across the face of which the filthy water had corroded colours, features, relief, its forms attacked by this liquid decay crumbling and draining off on all sides through the broken skeleton of posts, barbed wire and shoring – and above it all, amid the dark Stygian immensities, the vision of this thrill of reason and simple logic which suddenly began to shake these men like a fever of madness.

You could see that the idea tormented them: that trying to live one's life on earth and to be happy is not only a right but a duty – and even an ideal and a virtue. That social life is only designed to facilitate the inner life of each individual.

'Living!'

'Us! You . . . me . . . !'

'No more war. Oh no, it's too stupid! Worse than that, it's too . . .'

One statement echoed their vague thoughts, the various and half-formed murmur of the crowd . . . I saw a face crowned with mire emerge and the mouth declaring from the level of the ground:

'Two armies fighting is like one great army killing itself!'

'All the same, what have we become in the past two years? Poor unbelievable unfortunates, but also savages, brutes, bandits and bastards.'

'Worse than that!' chomped the man who seemed to know only that phrase.

'Yes, I admit it.'

In the desolate truce of this morning these men who had been crushed by tiredness, whipped by rain and overwhelmed by a whole night of thunder, these survivors of fire and flood could start to see how far war, morally as well as physically repulsive, was not only an outrage to good sense, a stigma on great ideas and a licence for every crime, but also how far it had developed every bad instinct in them and around them without a single exception: malice to the point of sadism, egotism to the point of ferocity and a lust for pleasure to the point of madness.

They are imagining all this, just as a short while ago they were vaguely conceiving of their own misery. They are filled with a curse that is trying to make its way out and blossom into words. They groan with it; they wail with it. You feel as though they are trying to escape from the error and ignorance that befoul them as much as the mud, that they want to know, at last, why they are being punished.

'So, what then?' one shouts.

'What?' the other man repeats, more grandly still.

The wind makes the flooded expanse shiver before our eyes, turns its anger against these human masses, lying or kneeling, motionless as paving stones or gravestones, and draws a shudder from them.

'There won't be any more war,' one soldier mutters, 'when there's no more Germany.'

'That's not what you ought to say!' another one cries. 'That's not enough! There won't be any more war when the spirit of war is defeated!'

As the moaning of the wind had half smothered these words he lifted up his head and repeated them.

'Germany and militarism,' another man angrily interrupted. 'It comes to the same thing. They wanted the war, they premeditated it. Militarism – that's what they are.'

'Militarism,' a soldier repeated.

'What's that?' someone asked.

'Well, it's brute force which is built up and suddenly, in a moment, attacks. It's being bandits.'

'Yes, today militarism means Germany.'

'Ah yes – but what will it mean tomorrow?'

'I don't know,' said a voice as grave as that of a prophet.

'If you don't kill the spirit of war you'll have conflict going on through every age.'

'We must . . . we must . . .'

'We must fight!' gurgled the hoarse voice of a body that had been petrified in the consuming mud since we woke up. 'We must!' And the body turned over heavily. 'We've got to give everything we have, our strength, our skins, our hearts, all our lives and the joys that remain to us. We must willingly accept the prisoners' lives that we lead. We must put up with everything, even injustice, which reigns everywhere, as well as the shameful disgusting things that we see, to devote ourselves utterly to war and to win. But if we have to make such a sacrifice,' the shapeless man added, turning over again, 'it's because we're fighting for progress, not for one country, and against error, not against a country.'

'We have to kill war,' said the first speaker. 'We have to kill war, in the belly of Germany!'

'Even so,' said one of those sitting there, rooted like a seed, 'even so, you do start to understand why we had to march.'

'All the same,' murmured the *chasseur*, who was kneeling up and struggling with a different idea in his head. 'I've seen a few young people who didn't give a toss for humanitarian ideas. For them what mattered was the national question, nothing else, and war was a matter of fatherlands; each one adds lustre to his own, that's all. They would fight, those ones, and fight well.'

'They're young, those you're talking about. They're young. You must make allowances.'

'You can do good things without knowing what you're doing.'

'It's a fact that men are mad! You can't repeat that enough!'

'Chauvinists are vermin,' growled a shadow.

They repeated several times, as though feeling their way in the dark:

'You've got to kill war. War, that's what!'

One of us, the one whose head was not moving in the carapace of his shoulders, kept one thought in his mind:

'All that's a load of claptrap. What does it matter what we think? We've got to win, that's all.'

But the others had started to search. They wanted to know and see beyond the present time. They were trembling as they tried to give birth to a light of will and wisdom in themselves. Scattered convictions sailed around in their heads and vague fragments of beliefs emerged from their lips.

'Of course, yes . . . But you've got to see things . . . You've always got to see the result, old man.'

'The result! Winning this war,' insisted the pillar man. 'Isn't that a result?'

Two voices replied simultaneously:

'No!'

At that moment there was a dull sound. Cries rose up around us and we shuddered.

A whole side of mud had become detached from the hillock against which we were leaning, unearthing right among us a seated corpse with its legs outstretched.

The landslide freed a pocket of water that had gathered at the top of the hillock and it sprayed out over the body, washing it as we watched.

Someone shouted:

'His face is all black!'

Another voice panted: 'What kind of a face is that?'

Those who could approached in a circle like toads. We could hardly bear to look at this head which appeared in bas-relief on the wall laid bare by the earth fall.

'His face? It's not his face!'

Instead of a face, there was hair.

It was then that we realized that the body, which had seemed to be seated, was in fact twisted, and broken backwards.

In dreadful silence we looked at this vertical back facing us from the dislocated remains, these hanging arms, bent backwards, and the two extended legs lying on the soft earth with their toes dug into it.

Reawoken by this frightful sleeper the discussion resumed. We shouted furiously, as though he were listening:

'No, winning is not a result! They're not the ones we've got to defeat, it's war!'

'Don't you realize yet that we've got to finish with war? If we start it again, everything that happened will serve no purpose. Look: it's pointless. It's two or three years, or more, of wasted catastrophe.'

'Oh my friend! If everything we've been through was not the end of this great misfortune – well, I love life, I have my wife, my family, with the house around them, I have ideas for my life afterwards, no? Well, even so, if that were the case, I'd rather die.'

'I'm going to die,' Paradis's neighbour said at that very moment, like an echo: no doubt he'd had a look at the wound in his belly. 'I'm sorry because of my children.'

'Now, it's because of my children that I'm not sorry,' said someone else. 'I'm going to die, so I know what I'm saying and what I tell myself is: "They at least will have peace!"'

'And maybe I won't die,' said another man, with a shiver of hope that he could not repress, even in front of his condemned comrades. 'But I'll suffer. And I say: too bad. I even say: so much the better and I can suffer still more if I know that it's for some purpose!'

'So we'll have to go on struggling after the war?'

'Yes, p'raps.'

'You want more of it, do you?'

'Yes, because I don't want any more of it!' he grumbled.

'And p'raps it's not against foreigners that we'll have to struggle?'

'P'raps, yes . . .'

A gust of wind stronger than the rest closed our eyes and stifled us. When it had passed and we saw it travelling over the landscape, at times catching up and shaking its load of mud and ploughing through the water of the trenches which gaped like the tomb of an army, we carried on:

'After all, what is it that makes the greatness and horror of war?'

'The greatness of people.'

'But we're the people!'

The man who had spoken looked at me questioningly.

'Yes,' I told him. 'Yes, my good friend, it's true! It's only with us that they can make battles: we are the raw material of war. War is made up only of the flesh and souls of ordinary soldiers. We are the ones who form the plains of dead and rivers of blood, all of us – each one silent and invisible because of the immensity of our numbers. The empty towns, the ruined villages, are the desert of us. Yes, it's all of us, and us entirely.'

'That's true, it's the people who are war; without them there would be nothing, just a few whines in the distance. But they're not the ones who decide about it. That's the masters who are in charge.'

'People today are struggling to have no more masters leading them. This war is like the French Revolution, still going on.'

'So that way we're working for the Prussians as well, are we?'

'Well, that's what we've got to hope,' said one of the wretches on the field.

'Bleedin' hell!' said the *chasseur*.

But he shook his head and added nothing to this.

'Let's look after ourselves! We oughtn't to be meddling with the affairs of others,' chomped the stubborn grouch.

'Yes, we should . . . because what you call others isn't others at all, it's the same!'

'Why do we always have to march on everybody's behalf?'

'That's how it is,' said one man; and he repeated the words he had used a moment earlier: 'Too bad or so much the better!'

Then the man who had questioned me said: 'The people are nothing and should be everything' – repeating an historic phrase, more than a century old, without realizing it, but bringing out its great universal meaning.

And the survivor of torment, on all fours on the greasy soil, raised his leper's face and looked in front of him eagerly, into infinity.

He looked and looked. He was trying to open the doors of heaven.

'The nations should understand one another, through the hides and on the bellies of those who exploit them in one way or another. All the peoples of the world should understand one another.'

'In short, all men should be equal.'

The word seems to come to our help.

'Yes, equal . . . Yes, yes . . . There are great ideas of justice and truth. There are things you believe in, towards which we always turn as though towards the light, to hold on to them, most of all equality.'

'There's liberty and fraternity too.'

'But most of all there's equality!'

I tell them that fraternity is a dream, a vague, muddled feeling, and that while it is contrary to man's nature to hate an unknown person, so it is equally contrary to it to love him. Nothing can be based on fraternity. Nor on liberty: it is too relative in a society where inevitably all elements divide one another.

But equality is always the same. Liberty and fraternity are words, equality is a thing. We're talking of social equality, because every individual has more or less value but each should participate in society to the same degree, and this is just, because the life of one human being is as great as that of another: equality is the great formula of mankind. Its importance is immense. The principle of the equality of rights of every creature and the holy will of the majority is infallible and must be invincible: it will bring every kind of progress with a truly divine power. First of all it will bring about the great bedrock of all progress, the resolution of conflicts through justice, which is precisely the same thing as the general interest.

These men of the people, dimly seeing they know not what Revolution – a Revolution greater than the other, with themselves as its source – rising already, rising in their throats, repeat: 'Equality!'

It is as though they are spelling out the word, then they can read it clearly everywhere and there is no prejudice, privilege or injustice on earth that does not crumble before it. It is a reply to everything, a sublime word. They turn the idea around this way and that and see in it a kind of perfection. And they see injustice burning with a blazing light.

'It would be beautiful!' one of them says.

'Too beautiful to be true!' says another.

But the third one says:

'It's because it's true that it is beautiful. It has no other beauty. But it's not because it's beautiful that it will happen. Beauty's out of fashion now, like love. It's because it's true that it's inevitable.'

'So if justice is what people want, and the people are strength, let them have it.'

'We've started already,' says an obscure voice.

'When all men have become equal we'll be forced to unite.'

'And there will no longer be frightful things under the sun done by thirty million men who don't want to do them.'

It's true. There's no answer to that. What kind of argument, what ghost of a reply can anyone – dare anyone – proffer to that: 'There will no longer be frightful things under the sun done by thirty million men who don't want to do them'? I listen and follow the logic of the words spoken by these poor folk cast on the field of pain, the words that arise from their wounds and their hurt, words that are bleeding from them.

And now the sky covers over. Near the horizon large clouds like a breastplate tint it blue. Up above it is crossed by vast sweepings of damp dust – a feeble luminous silvering. The weather is overcast: there will be more rain. We are not done with the storm and the length of suffering.

'We'll be asking ourselves,' someone says, 'why do we make war after all? Why? We don't know. But for who – that we can say. We'll be forced to realize that if every country brings the raw flesh of fifteen hundred young people for the idol of war to devour every day, it's for the pleasure of a definite number of ringleaders; that whole nations go to the slaughter, lined up in troops of armies, so that a caste decked in gold braid can write its princely names into history; and so that gilded people of the same order can do more business – a matter of people and shops. And when our eyes are open we'll see that the divisions between men are not the ones we think, and that the ones we think aren't the real ones.'

'Listen!' someone said, interrupting.

We fall silent. In the distance we can hear gunfire. Far away the rumbling shakes the air and this distant force makes waves that break weakly against our muddied ears, while around us the flood continues to impregnate the ground and slowly undermine the hills.

'It's started again . . .'

And one of us adds:

'Ah, what a weight we have against us!'

Already there is a sense of uneasiness, a hesitation in the tragedy of this emerging debate between these abandoned men, like an immense masterpiece of fate. It is not only pain and danger or the misery of the time that they see beginning again and again. It is also the hostility of things and people to truth, the accumulation of privilege, ignorance, wilful deafness, bad faith and prejudices; and savage situations accepted, immovable masses, inextricably tangled lines . . .

And the groping dream of ideas is carried forward by another vision in which the eternal adversaries emerge from the shadows of the past and stand forth in the stormy shadows of the present.

Here they come . . . It seems that one can see silhouetted against the sky, on the crests of the storm that is casting its tragic shadow over the world, the cavalcade of warriors, prancing and shining, their chargers bearing armour, plumes, gold braid, crowns and swords . . . They roll on, clear, magnificent, throwing out flashes of light, laden with arms. This warlike column rides past with its antiquated gestures, cutting through the clouds that span the sky like a savage theatrical decor.

Far above the feverish gaze of those on the ground, the bodies buried under the mud of the earthly lower depths and the wasted fields, this whole procession advances from the four corners of the horizon, driving back the infinity of the sky and hiding its blue depths.

And they are legion. There is not only the warrior class, which cries out for war and loves it; there is not only the class of those whom universal slavery endows with magical powers – hereditary powers – standing upright here and there above the prostration of the human race, which suddenly lean on the balance of justice because they see much profit to be made. There is also a whole crowd of those who, knowingly or otherwise, serve their fearful privilege.

At that moment one of the dark and dramatic speakers reaches out his hand as though he could see them and says: 'There are some who say: "How beautiful they are!"'

'And those who say: "Races hate one another!"'

'And those who say: "I fatten war and my paunch grows!"'

'And those who say: "There has always been war so there always will!"'

'There are those who say: "I can't see any further than the end of my nose and I won't allow anyone else to do so!"'

'There are those who say: "Children come into the world with red or blue knickers on their bottoms!"'

'There are those,' growls a hoarse voice, 'who say: "Bow your head and believe in God!"'

Oh, how right you are, you poor numberless workers in battle, you who will make the Great War with your own hands, an all-powerful mass not yet serving to do good, an earthly crowd in which every face is a world of suffering – you who, beneath a sky in which long black clouds are tossed or spread like the hair of dark angels, dream bowed beneath the yoke of a thought! Yes, you are right. All this is ranged against you. Against you and against your great general interest – which, as you have started to realize, is identical with justice – there are only the sabre-rattlers, profiteers and crooks.

Only the monstrous interested parties, the financiers, the great and small wheeler-dealers, encased in their banks and their houses, live by war and live in peace during war with their brows stubbornly fixed on some dark doctrine and their faces closed like a money box.

There are those who admire the flashing exchange of blows, who dream and exclaim like women at the sight of the vivid colours of uniforms; those who are intoxicated by military music or the songs doled out to the people like tots of rum – the dazzled, the feeble-minded, the fetishists, the savages.

There are those who are mired in the past and have only the word 'formerly' on their lips, traditionalists for whom an injustice has the force of law because it has been repeated so often, and who long to be guided by the dead, and who strive to subject the future and progress – living, passionate progress – to the empire of ghosts and fairy tales.

And with them are all the priests, who try to excite you and put you to sleep with the morphine of their paradise so that nothing will change. There are lawyers, economists, historians (and who else besides?), who tie you up in theoretical statements, who proclaim the antagonism between races, when in fact every modern nation is just an arbitrary geographical unit within the lines of its frontiers peopled by an artificial amalgam of races. They are the same spurious genealogists who fabricate false philosophical certificates and imaginary titles of nobility to serve their ambitions of conquest. Short-sightedness is the sickness of the human spirit. In many cases scholars are a breed of ignorant men who lose sight of the simplicity of things, extinguishing it and blackening it with rounded phrases and petty details. What you learn in books are the small things, not the great ones.

And even when they say that they do not want war these people do all they can to perpetuate it. They feed national pride and love of supremacy through force. 'We alone,' they say, each behind their barrier, 'we alone possess courage, loyalty, talent and good taste!' They make something like a consuming sickness out of the greatness and richness of a country. Out of patriotism – which is respectable as long as it remains in the realm of feelings and the arts, just like the love of family or one's province, which are equally sacred – they make a utopian, non-viable concept, out of balance with the world, a sort of cancer that absorbs all living forces, takes over everything and crushes life, a contagion that either ends with the crises of war or the exhaustion and asphyxia of armed peace.

Morality is delightful – and they pervert it. How many crimes have they made into virtues, with a single word, by calling them 'national'? They deform even truth, putting their individual national truths in place of the eternal one. They make as many truths as there are peoples, distorting and twisting Truth itself.

These people carry on their childish debates, ridiculously vile, which you hear growling above you: 'I didn't start it, you did!' 'No, it wasn't me, it was you!' 'You begin!' 'No, you!' These puerilities perpetuate the vast wound of the world because it is not those really involved who debate them, far from it, and the will to end it is not there. All these people who cannot or will not make peace on earth, all those who, for one cause or another, cling to the old order of things, find or invent justifications for it, these are your enemies!

They are your enemies as much as today the German soldiers who are lying here among you and who are nothing but poor dupes, domestic animals, horribly deceived and brutalized . . . They are your enemies, wherever they were born, however they pronounce their names and whatever language they use for their lies. Look at them, in the sky and on earth. Look at them all around. Recognize them once and for all, and never forget!

'They'll tell you: "My friend, you were a great hero!" ' growled a man on his knees, leaning forward, both hands in the ground, shaking his shoulders like a bulldog. 'I don't want them to tell me that!

'Heroes? Some kind of extraordinary people? Idols? Come off it! We were executioners. We did our job as honest killers. We'd do it again, with all our strength, because it's a great and important thing to do the hangman's job, to punish war and choke it to death. The act of killing is always ignoble – necessary sometimes, but always ignoble. Yes, hard and tireless executioners, that's what we were. But don't talk to me about military virtues because I killed some Germans.'

'Nor me!' yelled another voice, so loudly that no one could have challenged it, even if we had dared. 'Nor me, because I saved the lives of Frenchmen! So what, are we going to worship fires because of the beauty of firefighting!'

'It'd be a crime to show the finer side of war,' muttered one of the dark soldiers. 'Even if there was a finer side.'

'They'll tell you that,' the first man went on, 'so as to pay you in glory – and to pay themselves too, for what they didn't do. But military glory is not even true for us ordinary soldiers. It is for some, but apart from those chosen few a soldier's glory is a lie like everything in war that seems to be beautiful. In reality the sacrifice of soldiers is a dark repression. The multitude of those who make up a wave of attack have no reward. They run forward and throw themselves into a frightful oblivion of glory. They won't ever be able to gather up all their names, their poor little nothings of names.'

'We don't give a damn,' one man replied. 'We've got other things to think about.'

'But can you even say all that?' stammered a face spattered with mud which stuck to it like a hideous hand. 'You'll be cursed and tied to the stake. They've built up a religion around the flag of honour which is as wicked and stupid and malevolent as the other kind.'

The man got up, fell back, then got up again. He was wounded beneath his foul armour of mud and was bleeding on to the ground. When he had finished speaking he stared wide-eyed at the ground and all the blood he had given to heal the world.

One by one the others rise. The storm thickens and closes in on the expanse of despoiled and martyred fields. The day is full of night. It seems as though hostile new shapes of men and bands of men are constantly being conjured up at the summit of the mountain ranges of the clouds, around barbarous outlines of crosses and eagles, churches, sovereign palaces and the temples of the Army, multiplying, hiding the stars which are less numerous than mankind – and even that these ghosts are moving everywhere in the broken ground, here, there, among the real beings who have been scattered about, half sunk into the ground like grains of wheat.

Those of my companions who are still alive have finally got up. They have difficulty staying upright on the decomposing soil, shut up inside their mud-caked clothes, fitted into these strange coffins of mire; rising in their monstrous simplicity like ignorance from the depths of the earth, they move around, and shout, their eyes, arms and fists raised against the sky from which daylight and the storm are falling. They flail around like victorious ghosts, like the Cyranos or Don Quixotes that they still are.

You can see their shadows moving across the great melancholy mirror of the ground and reflected in the pale stagnant surface of the old trenches, which alone whitens and inhabits the infinite void of space in the midst of this polar desert with its misty horizons.

But their eyes are open. They are starting to realize the endless simplicity of things. And truth not only lights a dawn of hope in them but also builds a renewal of strength and courage.

'Enough talking about others!' one of them orders. 'Too bad for others! Us! All of us!'

An understanding between democracies, between immense powers, a rising of the peoples of the world, a brutally simple faith . . . All the rest, all of it, in the past, the present and the future, is entirely unimportant.

And one soldier dares to add this remark, though he begins in almost a hushed voice:

'If this present war had advanced progress by a single step, its miseries and its massacres will count for little.'

While we wait to join the others and resume the war, the black sky, clogged with storm clouds gently opens above our heads. Between two masses of mirky clouds a tranquil ray shines out and this line of light, so tightly enclosed, so edged with black, so meagre that it seems to be merely a thought, brings proof none the less that the sun exists.

December 1915

PENGUIN MODERN CLASSICS

THINGS FALL APART
CHINUA ACHEBE

With an Introduction by Biyi Bandele

'A great book, that bespeaks a great, brave, kind, human spirit' John Updike

Okonkwo is the greatest wrestler and warrior alive, and his fame spreads throughout West Africa like a bush-fire in the harmattan. But when he accidentally kills a clansman, things begin to fall apart. Then Okonkwo returns from exile to find missionaries and colonial governors have arrived in the village. With his world thrown radically off-balance he can only hurtle towards tragedy.

First published in 1958, Chinua Achebe's stark, coolly ironic novel reshaped both African and world literature, and has sold over ten million copies in forty-five languages. This arresting parable of a proud but powerless man witnessing the ruin of his people begins Achebe's landmark trilogy of works chronicling the fate of one African community, continued in *Arrow of God* and *No Longer at Ease*.

PENGUIN MODERN CLASSICS

I, CLAUDIUS
ROBERT GRAVES

'One of the really remarkable books of our day, a novel of learning and imagination, fortunately conceived and brilliantly executed' *New York Times*

Despised for his weakness and regarded by his family as little more than a stammering fool, the nobleman Claudius quietly survives the intrigues, bloody purges and mounting cruelty of the imperial Roman dynasties. In *I, Claudius* he watches from the sidelines to record the reigns of its emperors: from the wise Augustus and his villainous wife Livia to the sadistic Tiberius and the insane excesses of Caligula. Written in the form of Claudius' autobiography, this is the first part of Robert Graves's brilliant account of the madness and debauchery of ancient Rome, and stands as one of the most celebrated, gripping historical novels ever written.

With a new Introduction by Barry Unsworth

PENGUIN MODERN CLASSICS

THE PLAGUE
ALBERT CAMUS

'A matchless fable of fear, courage and cowardice' *Independent*

'On the morning of April 16, Dr Rieux emerged from his consulting-room and came across a dead rat in the middle of the landing.'

It starts with the rats. Vomiting blood, they die in their hundreds, then in their thousands. When the rats are all gone, the citizens begin to fall sick. Like the rats, they too die in ever greater numbers.

The authorities quarantine the town. Cut off, the terrified townspeople must face this horror alone. Some resign themselves to death or the whims of fate. Others seek someone to blame or dream of revenge. One is determined to escape. But a few, like stoic Dr Rieux, stand together to fight the terror. A monstrous evil has entered their lives but they will never surrender to it.

They will resist the plague.

Translated by Robin Buss with an Afterword by Tony Judt

OTHER TITLES IN THE SERIES

THE CARTER OF *LA PROVIDENCE*
GEORGES SIMENON

What was the woman doing here?

In a stable, wearing pearl earrings, her stylish bracelet and white buckskin shoes!

She must have been alive when she got there because the crime had been committed after ten in the evening.

But how? And why? And no one had heard a thing! She had not screamed. The two carters had not woken up.

Maigret is standing in the pouring rain by a canal. A well-dressed woman, Mary Lampson, has been found strangled in a stable nearby. Why did her glamorous, hedonistic life come to such a brutal end here? Surely her taciturn husband, Sir Walter, knows – or maybe the answers lie with the crew of the barge La Providence.

Translated by David Coward

PENGUIN MODERN CLASSICS

THE SPY WHO CAME IN FROM THE COLD
JOHN LE CARRÉ

With a new Introduction by John le Carré

Alex Leamas is tired. It's the 1960s, he's been out in the cold for years, spying in Berlin for his British masters, and has seen too many good agents murdered for their troubles. Now Control wants to bring him in at last – but only after one final assignment.

He must travel deep into the heart of Communist Germany and betray his country, a job that he will do with his usual cynical professionalism. But when George Smiley tries to help a young woman Leamas has befriended, Leamas's mission may prove to be the worst thing he could ever have done.

In le Carré's breakthrough work of 1963, the spy story is reborn as a gritty and terrible tale of men who are caught up in politics beyond their imagining.

'He can communicate emotion, from sweating fear to despairing love, with terse and compassionate conviction. Above all, he can tell a tale' *Sunday Times*

'A portrait of a man who has lived by lies and subterfuge for so long, he's forgotten how to tell the truth' *Time Magazine*

PENGUIN MODERN CLASSICS

NINETEEN EIGHTY-FOUR
GEORGE ORWELL

'His final masterpiece ... enthralling and indispensable for understanding modern history' Timothy Garton Ash, *New York Review of Books*

Hidden away in the Record Department of the sprawling Ministry of Truth, Winston Smith skilfully rewrites the past to suit the needs of the Party. Yet he inwardly rebels against the totalitarian world he lives in, which demands absolute obedience and controls him through the all-seeing telescreens and the watchful eye of Big Brother, symbolic head of the Party. In his longing for truth and liberty, Smith begins a secret love affair with a fellow-worker Julia, but soon discovers the true price of freedom is betrayal.

'The book of the twentieth century ... haunts us with an ever-darker relevance'
Independent

With an Introduction by Ben Pimlott

THE AUTHORITATIVE TEXT

PENGUIN MODERN CLASSICS

A HANDFUL OF DUST
EVELYN WAUGH

'One of the twentieth century's most chilling and bitter novels; and one of its best'
Nicholas Lezard, *Guardian*

After seven years of marriage, the beautiful Lady Brenda Last is bored with life at
Hetton Abbey, the Gothic mansion that is the pride and joy of her husband, Tony.
She drifts into an affair with the shallow socialite John Beaver and forsakes Tony
for the Belgravia set. Brilliantly combining tragedy, comedy and savage irony, *A
Handful of Dust* captures the irresponsible mood of the 'crazy and sterile generation'
between the wars. The breakdown of the Last marriage is a painful, comic re-
working of Waugh's own divorce, and a symbol of the disintegration of society.

'This is a masterpiece of stylish satire, and is funny too … a marvellous book'
John Banville, *Irish Times*

Edited with an Introduction and Notes by Robert Murray Davis

PENGUIN MODERN CLASSICS

ONE DAY IN THE LIFE OF IVAN DENISOVICH
ALEKSANDR SOLZHENITSYN

'It is a blow struck for human freedom all over the world ... and it is gloriously readable' *Sunday Times*

This brutal, shattering glimpse of the fate of millions of Russians under Stalin shook Russia and shocked the world when it first appeared.

Discover the importance of a piece of bread or an extra bowl of soup, the incredible luxury of a book, the ingenious possibilities of a nail, a piece of string or a single match in a world where survival is all. Here safety, warmth and food are the first objectives. Reading this book, you enter a world of incarceration, brutality, hard manual labour and freezing cold – and participate in the struggle of men to survive both the terrible rigours of nature and the inhumanity of the system that defines their conditions of life.

Translated by Ralph Parker

WINNER OF THE NOBEL PRIZE FOR LITERATURE

PENGUIN MODERN CLASSICS

OF MICE AND MEN
JOHN STEINBECK

'A thriller, a gripping tale that you will not set down until it is finished. Steinbeck has touched the quick' *The New York Times*

The compelling story of two outsiders striving to find their place in an unforgiving world.

Drifters in search of work, George and his simple-minded friend Lennie, have nothing in the world except each other and a dream – a dream that one day they will have some land of their own. Eventually they find some work on a ranch in California's Salinas Valley, but they are doomed as Lennie, struggling against extreme cruelty, misunderstanding and feelings of jealousy, becomes a victim of his own strength. Tackling universal themes, friendship and a shared vision, and giving voice to America's lonely and dispossessed, *Of Mice and Men* has proved one of Steinbeck's most popular works, achieving success as a novel, a Broadway play and three acclaimed films.

With an Introduction by Susan Shillinglaw

WINNER OF THE NOBEL PRIZE FOR LITERATURE

Contemporary ... Provocative ... Outrageous ...
Prophetic ... Groundbreaking ... Funny ... Disturbing ...
Different ... Moving ... Revolutionary ... Inspiring ...
Subversive ... Life-changing ...

What makes a modern classic?

At Penguin Classics our mission has always been to make the best
books ever written available to everyone. And that also means
constantly redefining and refreshing exactly what makes a 'classic'.
That's where Modern Classics come in. Since 1961 they have been an
organic, ever-growing and ever-evolving list of books from the last
hundred (or so) years that we believe will continue to be read over and
over again.

They could be books that have inspired political dissent, such as
Animal Farm. Some, like *Lolita* or *A Clockwork Orange*, may have
caused shock and outrage. Many have led to great films, from *In Cold
Blood* to *One Flew Over the Cuckoo's Nest*. They have broken down
barriers – whether social, sexual, or, in the case of *Ulysses*, the
boundaries of language itself. And they might – like *Goldfinger* or
Scoop – just be pure classic escapism. Whatever the reason, Penguin
Modern Classics continue to inspire, entertain and enlighten millions
of readers everywhere.

'No publisher has had more influence on reading habits than Penguin'
Independent

'Penguins provided a crash course in world literature'
Guardian

The best books ever written

SINCE 1946

Find out more at www.penguinclassics.com